THE
SERPENT
CLUB

a thriller

TOM COFFEY

POCKET BOOKS
New York London Toronto Sydney Singapore

This book is a work of fiction. Names, characters, places and incidents are products of the author's imagination or are used fictitiously. Any resemblance to actual events or locales or persons, living or dead, is entirely coincidental.

 POCKET BOOKS, a division of Simon & Schuster Inc.
1230 Avenue of the Americas, New York, NY 10020

Originally published in hardcover in 1999 by Pocket Books

ISBN: 0-671-02828-6

First Pocket Books paperback printing March 2000

10 9 8 7 6 5 4 3 2 1

POCKET and colophon are registered trademarks of Simon & Schuster Inc.

Front cover photo of woman in water © Sally Gall/Swanstock

Printed in the U.S.A.

To Jill

> Come, seeling night,
> Scarf up the tender eye of pitiful day;
> And with thy bloody and invisible hand
> Cancel and tear to pieces that great bond
> Which keeps me pale! Light thickens; and the crow
> Makes wing to th' rooky wood:
> Good things of day begin to droop and drowse;
> Whiles night's black agents to their preys do rouse.

> —MACBETH

part one

I like the night. It's more honest than the day. Things are hidden but there's much to hear—police sirens, lovemaking, echoes of gunfire. Sometimes I make out music wafting through an open window.

I like the anticipation that strikes me as the sun goes down. I feel energized by the waiting, but wanting is always better than having.

Murders are done in the dark; plots hatched; husbands and wives lied to.

I spend most of my days discovering what happened at night.

one

there's a body at the top of Sepulveda Pass. I want more information but that's all I hear before the scanner moves on to robberies and assaults and domestic disputes.

I could use a story so I drive to the scene. I know the shortcuts.

Two squad cars and an unmarked vehicle are parked beside the road. It's not much really. A uniformed cop stops me at the edge of the roped-off area, but I recognize the detective standing over the body. I call his name.

"Let him through," the detective says. "He's okay."

The cop stands aside. "Fucking vulture," he says.

I walk up a slight slope and shake hands with Frank Gruley. He points at the ground. Below us is a girl who looks to be twelve or thirteen. She's naked except for a pair of white socks. A thin layer of dirt and sand covers her body. Bugs whiz by, settle on her, take off. I notice patches of dried blood on her face and head, part of which has been smashed open.

"Was she killed here?" I ask.

He shakes his head. "Dumped."

"ID?"

"Not yet."

I make the notes and walk back to my car. Gruley goes with me. He says the girl most likely was raped. There are bruises on her genitalia and traces of semen. He says a case like this can bother him. He's a professional but he has two girls himself and he can't stop imagining what might happen. I tell him it sounds awful, having to worry all the time.

He says they think several perps were involved but they'll have a better idea once the tests are done. The hair and fiber guys went over her thoroughly. The girl was beaten over the head with a blunt instrument, probably a baseball bat. They found slivers of wood in her skull. Near the body was a footprint, size ten and made by a shoe nobody recognizes. This could be important. Or maybe it isn't.

They think the girl put up a fight. Some skin from another person was found under her fingernails.

The detective scratches the ground with his shoes. Their leather is dusty and faded, and I wonder how long he intends to keep wearing them.

"That's the first body I've ever seen," I tell Gruley.

"What did you think?"

"Why would somebody do that to someone?"

"Usually it's because they feel like it."

Back at the office I write the story. It's only a few paragraphs long.

• • •

I walk around to the rear of Noreen's place, past the red Volvo with an AAA sticker and the garbage cans and the papers set out for recycling. As I let myself in, I hear a dog barking in a distant yard. He sounds angry about something.

"Is that you?" she asks.

"No," I reply.

Noreen watches the news in the living room. The colors from the set reflect back, turning her normally translucent skin blue and purple. There was a smog alert today in the Valley.

"Where's Kristen?" I ask.

"At her father's. She's at her father's every Thursday. I've told you that."

I kiss her on the cheek. She keeps chewing a piece of gum. I wonder if I've done something wrong and decide I must have. She asks what I'd like for dinner. I say it doesn't matter. She says she doesn't feel like cooking and I say that's all right. We can order takeout we can get a pizza we can go someplace. It doesn't matter.

We eat Mexican. Noreen knows the owner. Raul engages in a bit of a fuss and my ladyfriend smiles at the waitress. When the meal is over Raul insists on joining us for a drink. I'd prefer to leave.

"Things are very bad," Raul says.

I say the place is crowded. Business looks fine.

"That's not what I mean," he says. "I'm talking about the gangs and the drugs and the lack of values. Nobody cares about anything anymore."

"People used to care," I say. "It never accomplished anything."

• • •

The girl's name is Megan Wright. That's the first thing I learn at work. She went to a private school in Sherman Oaks and her teachers say she'd just started, but she seemed to fit in. That's the most important thing at that age. Fitting in.

I call Gruley and ask how he made the ID. He says it's his fucking job to make an ID in cases like these. I say I realize that but I'd like some specifics. He says they matched her against a missing person's report. The mother made the ID at the morgue.

"How'd she react?" I ask.

"All things considered, she was pretty calm."

My editor wants a picture of the girl.

The Wrights live in one of those communities that's surrounded by a high stucco wall and protected by a gate and booth occupied by a minimum-wage security guard. A couple of TV trucks are parked outside, so I continue to drive. On Ventura I pull into a strip mall and take out the reverse directory I keep under the driver's seat. The police scanner reports that an elderly couple has been found bound and gagged in their home in Reseda. The woman has had a heart attack. Emergency units are responding to the scene.

After a few tries on my car phone, I find a house near Megan's that seems unoccupied. I use papers and notebooks to stuff a package from a courier service that I keep for situations like this. Then I drive back. The guard leans out of his cage as I pull up. I display the package and say I have to deliver it to Mr. Roswell's house. I'm from the office and it's important he get the material right away.

The guard rings the house. "There's no answer," he says. "I can take that for him."

"I have to deliver this personally. Can you let me in? It'll take five minutes."

"You know where you're going?"

I assure him I do.

The gate goes up. I enter a world of winding streets and lookalike houses, putty-colored with red roofs. Street signs with large eyes at the top advertise the presence of Neighborhood Watch.

When I find the Wrights' address I park in the driveway and walk to the door as if I belong. The blinds are drawn and I hear no sound except for the bell echoing through uninhabited rooms. As I head back to the car I rehearse what I'll tell my editor.

"What do you want?"

It's a female voice. It demands attention. I haven't heard anything open but she's standing in the doorway, her form bordered by the frame. With the cool dark of the house behind her, nothing about this woman is distinct.

"I wasn't expecting anybody. They didn't call from the gate. What do you want?"

I identify myself and ask if she's Megan's mother. She says she is.

"I'm terribly sorry about what happened," I say.

The words spill out of me. I've said them before. I've said them so often.

"I know this seems rude and intrusive, but I'd like to take a minute of your time and ask you some questions. I want to find out what kind of a girl your daughter was."

The woman says nothing. She stands perfectly still.

"I want to make sense of this tragedy," I say. "For myself and for my readers."

I'm almost at the door. I've approached it slowly.

"Sometimes it's good," I say. "Sometimes it's good to talk."

She tells me to come in.

We stand in the hall a few seconds. Her eyes are clear and she's wearing a touch of makeup. She's dressed in white shorts and a pale pink top. I tell her the house is nice. She thanks me and asks if I need anything. For a second I think about the picture, but it's too soon to mention it. She leads me into the living room and perches on the edge of a leather sofa. I take a high-backed chair. The woman's posture is perfect and her hair is blond and I figure she's about the same age as Noreen. She puts her hands on her knees, looks at me directly and tells me to go ahead.

"When did you first think something was wrong?"

She says she got home quite late that night—it was the night before last, as she recalls—and didn't bother to check on the kids. It wasn't until morning—

"Excuse me," I find myself saying.

I don't have children so I'm unsure how these things are handled, but I know my girlfriend always looks in on Kristen after we've been out. So I ask:

"Why didn't you check on them?"

"It was quite late," she says. "I was very tired. I work hard."

I tell her I understand. I ask her to continue.

She says it was only in the morning that she began to realize what had happened. Jeffrey (that's her youngest) got ready for school and came downstairs for breakfast while she discussed what needed to be done that day with Maria (that's her housekeeper), and all the while she had a terrible headache and it was getting late and there was no sign of Megan so she asked Maria to go upstairs and fetch the girl. A few seconds later Maria came running down saying Megan wasn't there and the bed hadn't been slept in and somebody had better do something. Actually she was carrying on in Spanish so it took a few minutes to figure out, but once they did she called the police. They told her the girl had probably run away. She'd turn up in a couple of days. Most of them do.

"Did they say anything else?" I ask.

"They told me not to worry."

I ask if Megan had seemed upset about anything in the days before she died, if she was anxious or preoccupied about something, if an event out of the usual had occurred that might have some bearing on what happened.

"She stayed out late a few times," Megan's mother says. "We fought about that. And she bought some terrible clothes her last few trips to the mall. I tried to make her take them back, but she wouldn't."

She was discovering boys and staying over at friends' houses and talking on the phone for hours on end. She was keeping a diary. She was starting to have secrets but all girls do, especially from their mothers.

"Have you looked at her diary?" I ask.

"No. And I won't. The diary was hers. I have no right to read it."

"The police might want it."

"They can't have it. I'd burn it before I'd give it to them."

I ask if she has any theories about who could have done it or why. She looks up at the ceiling and down at her hands, then twists her fingers around each other until the veins in her wrists stick out. I notice that she's wearing no rings. She hasn't alluded to a husband or father.

She shakes her head and says this whole thing is puzzling to her. Perhaps it was drug addicts who thought she had money or just did it for the thrill. There seems to be a lot of that these days.

I thank her for her time. As she leads me to the door she says she hopes I got something useful. She's never seen her name in the paper. I tell her she's been more than cooperative and I appreciate what she's done and then I say there's just one more thing . . . one more thing that would help.

She asks what it is.

I say I'd like a picture. My editors want to run it with the story to let our readers know what this wonderful young girl looked like and who knows, maybe somebody saw something.

She says she'll be right back. After she disappears I look around. The front hall has some prints of Impressionist paintings. Off to the side is a den with a large-screen TV. In back is a kitchen that's light, open and airy. Beyond that a swimming pool glitters in the yard.

Megan's mother returns with her arm outstretched.

At the gate the guard says I took more than five minutes. I apologize for getting lost. I tell him I didn't know where I was going after all.

Noreen says she can't believe the woman was so calm. In fact she can't believe Megan's mother even talked to me.

When we go to bed I tell her to let loose. That's what I want. I know she wants it too. She can yell, she can scream, she can let me know exactly what I'm doing to her.

She says she can't. She's afraid of waking Kristen.

When we're through Noreen asks if I've ever considered getting another job. I say I don't know what else I could do. I have a pretty good salary and my work is more interesting than most and I'm not qualified to go into business, if that's what she has in mind.

"You're wrong," she says. "You're limiting yourself. There are other things you can do."

"Like what?"

"Public relations. Advertising. Businesses are always looking for people who can communicate."

I tell her I like what I do.

Megan's hair is dark and teased and falls over the left side of her face. Her eyebrows are quite dark.

They changed the lead.

Noreen tells Kristen to put on her blue dress. It's just been cleaned and today's the class picture. Doesn't she want to look good for the class picture? Kristen says she'd look fine in a sweatshirt.

Megan's face is thin but not pinched. Her eyes are deep-set. I wonder what color they were. I should have looked at the photo more carefully before I gave it away.

"Put on your dress."

"I don't want to."

"Put it on."

"*Moooooommmmmmmmmmmmmmmmmmm!!*"

I pour some coffee that I made myself. I don't trust Noreen. She keeps trying to give me decaf.

The dress hangs limply on Kristen, reminding me of a flag on a windless day. I say hello in as cheerful a tone as I can muster. I once read that children like bright, happy sounds. Kristen takes out a box of cereal and dumps it into a bowl.

Megan's nose is small and straight, and I notice she's wearing an earring. I try to figure out why they changed the lead.

"Mooommmmmmmm!"

"What?"

"I want some juice!"

"Can't you get it yourself?"

"I'm eating my cereal!"

I go to the refrigerator, take out the juice and pour it into a glass. Kristen glares as I put it in front of her.

The corners of Megan's mouth are turned up slightly. For a moment I think of the Mona Lisa.

I'm glad for this chance to see her whole.

I hate the screamers, the ones who weep and wail and wonder aloud at the fate of whoever it is I'm writing about, always saying they never believed this could happen to them although the one great lesson of the modern world is it can happen to anyone, anytime; we are all potential victims.

We look for motivation behind the violence— why did he do it, why did it happen to her? Those questions are pointless of course. Things happen because they do.

I liked Megan's mother.

two

After her name and address become part of the public record, the media camp out just beyond the gate. The news at noon has shots of a car with tinted windows rolling into the street. Cameras and microphones and reporters bang into the vehicle. I hear what sound like shouted questions but they overlap, step on each other, cancel out. The car breaks free of the pack and speeds away. Megan's mother heads into seclusion.

I write a short piece that says police are doing what they can but there are no suspects, no motives, no new clues. They've set up a hotline for people who might have information. The number is toll-free of course.

Fresh deaths await me—a gang shooting in Compton, a bar brawl in El Monte, a robbery victim found at home in Van Nuys. That one is nasty. She was discovered bound and gagged and she'd been raped, and whoever did it extinguished their cigarettes on her flesh. The house was ransacked. Police say they've rarely seen an attack so vicious and only a couple of hundred dollars' worth of jewelry is missing.

My editor says she's pleased with the story and glad I got the picture. She's going to put me in for a prize.

I could get thirty dollars.

Frank Gruley tells me that Megan's father lives near the beach. He gives this to me exclusively. He says he's doing it as a favor. He says I'm a good guy. He says I owe him one.

When I ring the bell a woman answers. She looks about twenty-five, with a permanent tan. I ask if Megan's father is there and she says he's at the surf shop around the corner.

"Does he own the place?" I ask.

"No. He just works there."

She looks at me with a slight frown, as if she thinks she should recognize me. Maybe we met at some long-forgotten party. Perhaps I interviewed her after somebody got killed. Or she could just be shocked by my appearance. It must be years since she's seen a man wearing a tie.

She asks if I'm the guy who called last night. I say I might be.

"He's usually behind the counter," she says. "He's expecting you."

The surf shop is bright and features the canned sound of waves rhythmically swiping the beach. Near the cash register is a guy with the bronzed, well-muscled look of a man engaged in nonstop battle against the onset of middle age. I identify myself and ask if he's Megan's father. He says he is. I say it's a shame what happened. He has my condolences. From everything I've heard she seemed like a nice young girl. He says he wouldn't know. It wasn't like they were close or anything.

I ask when he saw her last.

He says he isn't sure. It might have been Christmas. He remembers he got her something and he thinks it was a bathing suit and a nice big beach towel, but he can't be certain. His ex-wife would probably know. She's good at things like that. I ask if he has any special memories of Megan, anything at all. He says he remembers taking her to Disneyland once when she was small, like four or five or six or seven, and she was all excited and went on every ride and tried to pull the ears off Mickey Mouse.

I ask when he and Megan's mother got divorced.

He says it was just after Jeffrey was born. The two of them were drifting apart. It was nobody's fault.

I ask how he makes a living.

He says the surf shop supports him fine. In fact he's expecting an important customer at any minute.

Feral-looking men toting packs of equipment take up positions outside the church, ready to shoot anything that's news. The minister has barred them from entering. I think it's because they're all wearing T-shirts.

It's nearly full inside. I slide into a pew in back. Up front Megan's mother is shrouded in black. Next to her is a man who is not Megan's father. He wears a dark suit, striped shirt and red tie. His hair is turning to gray.

He sits with his hands on his knees and stares straight ahead, unblinking, jaw set. He must have been taught that this is the way men act.

Megan's casket is covered with lilies.

The minister says she is with God now and we should be happy for her. It's terrible when the life of one so young is taken so brutally, and everyone here extends their sympathy to Megan's loving family. They have suffered a grievous loss. He understands from talking to those who knew her that she was a wonderful girl. He wishes he had been acquainted with her. Nonetheless from reading the Bible we know that God has a plan and, however incomprehensible it may seem, this is part of it. Sometimes the events of this world appear cruel, arbitrary and capricious, but we have to put our faith in Him and His divine wisdom. Just as Jesus said in the Gospel according to Luke—

Two blond boys are in the pew with Megan's mother and the man accompanying her. One of the kids is small. I figure he must be Jeffrey. The other one is taller, thin but not skinny, with the golden brown skin and straw-colored hair that reflect a life spent at ski resorts and the beach. Behind the boys are rows of kids on either side of puberty. Some of the girls are crying. As their soft boohoos float through the church, infiltrating my ears, I ask myself if they're really sad or if this display of emotion just seems like the right thing to do. Can they tell the difference between Megan's killing and the thousands of fake ones they've seen on TV?

I look around the church and try to calculate the number of mourners. I've always been bad at estimating crowds, but the number I give will be treated as fact. I glance at my watch. I'll go to the burial in case something happens. By the time I get to the office I'll be right on deadline. I should have brought a laptop. I could have filed from the graveyard.

One of Megan's classmates steps up to the pulpit. In a high-pitched voice that cracks every so often, she says she knew Megan for only a short time but she seemed nice and she's really going to miss her.

They allow the mourners to leave before wheeling the casket down the aisle. Megan's mother puts on sunglasses as she steps outside.

"There she is."

The camera crews stir behind the barricade.

"Get her."

"Get the mother."

"Make sure you get her."

I call Megan's father at the surf shop.

"I didn't see you at the funeral," I say.

"I don't do funerals," he says. "Besides, I had something going on down here."

I ask if he remembers where Megan went to school before she enrolled at her current one. He says he isn't sure. I ask if his ex-wife and his children had lived in the gated community a long time and he says no, they just moved from West Covina. He doesn't recall the exact address, but they'd been there for years. I say they made a big leap in one step and he says that's true, but his ex-wife's a smart woman and has never lacked ambition.

I tell him to have a nice day.

"You too," he says.

Noreen and I watch the news while Kristen does her homework. The bubbleheads begin the broadcast with footage from the funeral.

"There you are," Noreen says.

I'm coming down the steps of the church, squinting under the sunlight. I seem taller than I imagine.

The newscaster says there are no new leads in the case.

Noreen says she recognizes the man with Megan's mother. At least he looks familiar. I ask what his name is and she says she doesn't remember.

Last year's phone directory lists a West Covina address for Megan's mother. I determine that there are three middle schools Megan could have attended and ask our education reporter which one was most likely. She shrugs. She doesn't know the area well and besides the boundaries are never clear.

There are no records of Megan at the first two places I call. At the third school I hear the shuffling of paper and the clicking of a mouse and then I hear that yes, she did go here, last year she was enrolled in seventh grade. I ask for the names of her teachers, which I am given grudgingly, and then I request to be put through to the principal's office.

"Certainly," I'm told.

I hear some buzzes and beeps and the line goes dead. I look in the phone book and call the principal's number directly. A secretary answers. She asks who I am and what this is about. When I tell her, she says I'll have to hold on for a moment.

Several minutes pass. Every once in a while somebody picks up the phone and asks why I'm on the line. Finally I hear: "This is Consuelo Rivera."

I identify myself and hear a yelp of surprise. "You're not the man from the retirement fund."

I say I have just a few questions. As she may already know, a girl who attended her school last year was found murdered a couple of days ago. Rivera says she wasn't aware of that and asks for the name of the girl. When I tell her, she says she doesn't recognize it. Then I hear a click followed by a hum and static.

I call the school office and ask if I can leave a message for Megan's homeroom teacher from last year. The voice on the other end sighs deeply and says oh, all right, go ahead. I leave my name and number and explain why I want to talk to her. I give the best times for calling. The voice says she'll put this message in the teacher's mailbox. She can't guarantee that the woman will get it.

I get a hamburger at a drive-through place and watch CNN at home. When I get bored with that, I turn on the stereo. Then I flip through a magazine.

I'm familiar with all the space in my apartment. I know where the rug is wearing thin and where the furniture is scratched and where the cracks are forming in the walls. I know which stains on the stove are impossible to remove.

I hear there are coffeehouses now in Hollywood. I hear they're the hot new thing.

three

I call our morgue and ask the researcher to find a fact for me. She tells me to go ahead. I say the man in the picture on today's front page is causing a stir. Everyone claims he looks familiar, but no one knows his name.

She gets back to me a half-hour later. After pointing out that the man's face is partially hidden and he's wearing sunglasses and is a little bit out of focus, she says she's nevertheless about ninety-five percent certain it's Jeremiah Devlin.

"Who's Jeremiah Devlin?" I ask.

She laughs and says I've asked some stupid questions over the years, but that's just about the stupidest. She tells me to check the clips.

A trip through our electronic library reveals that Jeremiah Devlin is the CEO of an electronics firm that has billions of dollars in contracts with the Pentagon. He also owns office buildings downtown and subdivisions in the Valley and large tracts in the desert that are being turned into the exurbs of Los Angeles. The stories mention his beach house in Malibu and his ski chalet in

Idaho and his yacht and his jet and of course his private zoo. His home in the Valley has an Olympic-sized pool. He's on the *Forbes* list. He spends a lot of time in Vegas and Tahoe. He's leveraged. From the stories I learn that his wife died several years ago and he hasn't remarried. He has one child, a boy named Brad.

Most of the accounts note that Jeremiah Devlin hates publicity.

My editor says she likes this story. So far the murder is ours. We've been way ahead of the competition. In fact some guys on the copy desk have started a pool on who the killer is.

I drape my arm around Noreen's shoulder and slip my hand under her shirt. She rises a few inches off the couch. Her skin is goosebumpy and I turn her head toward mine and stick my tongue in her mouth. She breaks away and tells me to stop. What if Kristen walked in?

We go to the bedroom and lock the door. Soon our clothes are off and I want this woman to talk, I want her to shout, I want her to scream, I want to know what she's thinking, I want to know how she feels, I want to know what I'm doing to her, I want—

She tells me to put on a condom.

I do.

We finish.

I lie in her arms, my breathing hard but shallow. Her hands rest on my back. I tell myself I should be satisfied. Sex is great, it ends our worries, it fulfills our needs—but I've not had an epiphany, only a bit of a release. Nothing has changed and I'm left with myself, and with her, and with all the problems of our lives.

Everything I've ever seen or read tells me it's supposed to be different in bed.

Noreen says I'm heavy.

The voice on the other end of the phone belongs to an African-American woman who sounds like she tolerates no nonsense from anyone. I tell myself this is a good quality in a teacher of twelve-year-olds.

She says she got my message, but the handwriting was so bad she couldn't tell what I wanted to talk about. In fact she could barely make out the number.

I ask if she remembers Megan Wright.

"I do," she says. "I saw her picture in the paper and wondered if it was the same girl. If you don't mind my saying so, I don't have many Caucasians in my class."

I ask if there was anything special about Megan that she can tell me. She says the girl liked animals. I ask if that was the most distinctive thing about her and the teacher says it's what sticks in her mind. Of course it's funny what you remember. Sometimes you recall the most trivial things and forget what's important.

I ask if she can think of anything that might have a bearing on Megan's death.

"She seemed . . . preoccupied."

"What do you mean?"

"Like there was something going on that was dominating her thoughts. Something that was unrelated to anything in school."

"Did you ever ask her about that?"

"Once I said to her, 'Child, you're walking around like the weight of the world is on your shoulders.' And she looked at me and gave me that little smile like she had in that picture. And she said, 'Sometimes it is.' "

"Do you have any idea what she meant by that?"

"Teaching is a hard profession, sir. I see the children now—they're old beyond their years. They're growing up too quickly. And we're expected to do the jobs the parents once did, because they're divorced, or working too hard, or just not interested.

"So to answer your question, I would have to say no, I did not know what she meant. I could guess, but I do not know."

I ask Frank Gruley if he has any plans to talk to Jeremiah Devlin. I hear silence and gulping on the other end of the phone and finally he says he can't comment. I ask if the hair and fiber analysis is complete and he says it isn't so I ask what he's working on at the moment. He says they're trying to reconstruct Megan's last night. I ask how it's going. He tells me he can't say anything.

"Even to me?"

"Especially to you."

When I inform my editor about this she says the cop's being an asshole but what do you expect, they all are. I say the link between Megan's mother and Jeremiah Devlin is interesting and my editor says it's worth mentioning but she's more intrigued by the idea of re-creating Megan's last night. She tells me to work the story even if the cops won't cooperate.

I have other things going—gangs in Carson, a chop shop in Northridge, rumors of a big drug bust in the South Bay. Then there are the everyday crimes that go into the roundup. My editor tells me not to worry. She's been thinking about this. She wants me to handle Megan full-time.

"Where should I start?" I ask.

"Her friends. And talk to her mother again. Is she back at the house?"

"Maybe."

I say nothing more. My editor hovers over me, ready to lap up words of gratitude for my new assignment. As I reach for my Rolodex, she asks if anything's wrong.

"Nothing's wrong," I say.

"Good," she says. "Because this is what you want, isn't it?"

The girl at the door is tall and thin and as soon as she speaks I see the braces on her teeth. She may be pretty but a baseball cap covers much of her head. I identify myself and tell her I want to ask a few questions about Megan. After all they were friends and I was moved by what she said at the funeral. The girl says okay but she wants me to hurry. She's, like, busy. She keeps the storm door closed. Her eyes are bloodshot.

I ask if she saw Megan at all the day she was killed. She says she did. At least she thinks it was the same day. She went over to Megan's house after school. It was her first time there and they used the pool and stuff and then some boys came over. I ask what they did. She says she doesn't remember. They just did stuff. I ask who the boys were and she says she thinks it was Brad and some of his friends.

"Brad?" I say. "Brad Devlin?"

She shrugs.

"I don't know his last name. He's just 'Brad.' He drives a Lexus."

"How did he and Megan get along?"

"I dunno."

"Did Megan seem upset or worried about anything?"

She shrugs. She says it wasn't like she and Megan were close or anything. As she said, it was only her first time at the house. Megan talked about it like it was a palace but actually it was nothing special. She'd seen bigger pools.

From inside I hear a voice with the crack and whine of male adolescence: "Whatcha doing, Alexis?"

Without turning around she shouts, "Nothing!" The word reverberates.

A skinny kid with long hair parted in the middle comes up behind the girl. He's shirtless, so it's hard to miss the tattoo of a snake etched on his pale chest. Just under the drawing, in case an observer has missed it, the word "Snake" is tattooed in Gothic lettering. The kid has a ring through each nipple, and he looks at me as if we know each other.

I ask if he ever met Megan.

"Yeah. I saw her here a couple of times."

"Did you do anything with her?" I ask.

"Stuff."

"Like what?"

"What do you think?"

The odor of cannabis wafts from his skin.

"Did you like her?" I ask.

"I guess." He sticks out his hand. The gesture surprises me. "My name's Grant. Grant Fisher. But you knew that. Because we've met before, right?"

I tell him I think he's mistaken.

He laughs. "You're trying to find out who killed her, right? Maybe we all did. Maybe it's a gigantic conspiracy, like the way they killed that president. What was his name?"

"Kennedy."

He laughs again.

"Did you kill her?" I ask.

"What do you think?"

"I don't know if you're the type."

He tells me that he likes me.

Alexis asks if we're done.

Radio news leads with a mugging that occurred late last night in Encino. A middle-aged Asian male in a late-model Ford had stopped for a red light when he was set upon by a gang of youths who smashed his windows and slashed his tires and dragged him from the vehicle, beating and kicking him and stealing his watch and wallet. After the authorities were summoned, the man was taken to a nearby hospital, where he is in critical but stable condition.

Police are puzzled by the incident.

• • •

The rest of my projects are farmed out to other reporters while the roundup goes to an intern named Rebecca just out of Loyola Marymount. She says she's looking forward to the beat. It seems intense and exciting and she's sure she'll have lots of questions. I tell her to ask me anything she wants.

There's a different guard at the gate. I flash the envelope and tell him I have to deliver it to Mr. Roswell. I'm from the office. It's terribly important.

A Latina in a white uniform answers the door at the house where Megan once lived. I ask if Mrs. Wright is home. When the Latina asks who I am, I give her my card.

The sun burns the back of my neck. I imagine my skin turning red and searing.

Megan's mother wears a long, flowing dress that reaches almost to the floor. She asks what I want. I say I have a few more questions. She says nothing. She stands with her arms at her side.

I ask if she and Megan talked about anything the night she died.

She says she didn't eat with the kids. As she told me before, she was out all day. By the time she got back their dishes were in the washer but there was a plate left over. So she microwaved it and ate by herself and went to bed.

I don't know if I believe this.

"A number of people have remarked on how calmly you've handled all this. They say it's, well . . . unusual."

"I don't believe in flying to pieces, if that's what you mean. And, if you must know, I've been on medication."

I look up and see pale blue, almost turning to yellow, as if the sky is surrendering to the sun.

"How long have you known Jeremiah Devlin?"

"I should have known," she says. Her voice gains intensity and momentum. "I should have known you were a goddam gossip hound. Just like the rest of them. You're nothing but a vulture. A fucking vulture. I don't know how you got here, mister. I don't know how you got past the gate, but I'm sure as shit gonna call them if you're not out of here in thirty seconds."

I smile at her. "Have a nice day, Mrs. Wright."

Noreen is worried about Kristen. The girl is doing badly in school and she never hangs around with the other kids and she's been awfully quiet lately. All she wants to do is stay inside and watch television. Sometimes she plays with her dolls.

"Have you ever thought of having children?" Noreen asks. I have no reply.

Rebecca smiles and says she hates to bother me because she knows I'm really busy, but she's trying to reach a sergeant in Boyle Heights and he won't take her calls.

I get through immediately. I have his number speed-dialed.

"Why are you giving our new girl a hard time?" I ask. I wink at Rebecca. She rolls her eyes.

The sergeant says there are nuts and flakes and bad

guys who call up pretending to be reporters, so the folks at the switchboard are under orders to put through only the names they recognize. I tell him to add Rebecca's to the list. He asks what I'm doing now. He asks if they've given me a real job.

"I'm on Megan Wright full-time."

"Christ," he says. "I'm glad they didn't dump her in my division."

I look up at Rebecca and ask her extension. I could swear I catch a whiff of jasmine.

"Who's the new girl?" the sergeant asks.

"Our intern. She's gung ho. She'll get over it."

"She pretty?"

"Yeah. Seems nice enough. She's black."

"You mean African-American. Or whatever the fuck they're calling themselves these days."

I tell him I'm surprised he didn't use the n-word.

"I'm too smart to do that," he says. "You never know when you'll have to testify."

The boy rushes through the gate, gaining speed as he descends the hill, negotiating the curbs with the grace and efficiency of a sprinter gliding over some hurdles. I cruise after him, admiring his technique and careless self-confidence.

He wipes out.

It happens in an instant.

The board rears up and the boy flips with it, keeping his feet on the thing for a second before losing contact and falling to the concrete. He lands on his butt and rolls over a couple of times as the board plops down on a nearby lawn. Its wheels continue to spin.

I stop my car and run to him. The boy gets up and walks over to the board, inspecting its wheels as if they've somehow let him down.

"Are you all right?" I ask. "That was a pretty bad spill."

"It doesn't hurt," he says.

He fingers the wheels, maneuvering them as if he isn't sure they're working properly. He frowns a bit.

"Your name's Jeffrey, isn't it?"

He looks at me for the first time.

"How come you know my name?"

"I was at your sister's funeral."

He looks at the skateboard again, closing one eye and bringing it close to his face, like a jeweler scrutinizing a diamond for flaws.

"My mom says we're not supposed to talk about that."

"Why not?"

"Because. It's a bad thing."

"Why is it bad?"

"I dunno."

I raise my hand to shield my eyes from the sun. Doesn't it ever get cloudy anymore? Doesn't it ever rain?

Jeffrey's a blur now, a lump of something with no features whatsoever. He puts the skateboard on the ground.

"Do you miss your sister?"

"Not really."

"Do you know what happened to her?"

"She got killed."

"What did you have for dinner that night?"

"Chicken enchiladas. Maria made them."

"You and your mom and Megan had dinner together?"

"Just me and my mom. Megan was out."

"I thought your mom was out that evening?"

"She left after dinner."

He gets on the skateboard. I sense I'm at the end of his attention span and I have to resist a desire coming from a strange place within me to grab this boy and yell at him, shake his frail body until he tells me what he knows and then leave him on the street, alone and crying and frightened.

His sister's skull was broken. Her almost naked body was left on a dusty hillside.

"Where was Megan? Who was she with?"

"Brad, I guess."

"Where did they go?"

His back is to me. He has one foot on the ground and the other on the board. I bring my hand close to his shoulder.

He's off.

I've never met Kristen's father; I don't know what he looks like; there are no pictures of him around the house. I've heard his voice on the phone a few times. He's an air traffic controller who speaks in flat and even tones, like a guy who doesn't get too excited about things.

four

rebecca and I get a burger apiece and split a basket of fries. She says she's learning a lot and getting so many stories in the paper she's sick of seeing her byline, although so much of her stuff is rewritten it's hard to tell if she's doing it right. She never gets any feedback. Nobody seems to have the time. I say cop stories are routine. There's a certain way to write them, key elements you always play up. She asks what they are. She says she wants to know.

"Blood, guts, gore."

She dips a fry in the ketchup.

"Is that your secret?"

"It's no secret."

"There has to be a secret. Everyone tells me how good you are."

She leans toward me and puts her hand on my wrist and asks me this:

"Who killed Megan?"

"Some kid named Brad, probably."

"There must be a million kids named Brad in the Valley."

"Yeah, but only one of them is Jeremiah Devlin's son."

She looks around as if hoping somebody she knows will walk by and spare her from pursuing this conversation.

"Who's Jeremiah Devlin?" she asks at last.

I push myself from the table and break the touch of her skin and wipe my hands and mouth with a paper napkin. Then I toss the napkin onto my tray.

"Jesus, didn't they teach you anything in college?"

Noreen stares at the TV. The weather's on. It's supposed to be sunny tomorrow.

"Kristen saw a psychologist today," she says. The appointment was set up by the school district and Noreen left work early to be there. Her boss was upset and said this better not happen again. The company can always find a replacement for a data processing supervisor.

The psychologist asked Kristen her name. The girl answered in a low and nervous voice. Then the psychologist asked where she lived and Kristen gave two addresses, her mother's and her father's. When the psychologist asked Kristen for her phone number, she gave two of those also.

The psychologist asked more questions and ran Kristen through a battery of tests. When they were done he said the results were preliminary of course and he'd have to analyze them further, but from what he can tell it seems obvious Kristen blames herself for the breakup of her parents' marriage and continues to hope they'll get back together. These feelings are common among the children of divorce. Sometimes they never go away.

Noreen looks up at the ceiling and down at the floor, everywhere but at me.

There's one more thing she wants me to know. It's been gnawing at her all day and she wonders if she should even tell me but she's going to because—well, she's just going to. The beer I'm drinking is flat and Noreen says that at one point in the session the psychologist asked Kristen if anything in particular was bothering her and Kristen nodded and said yes very softly and the psychologist asked what it was and Kristen said, "My mommy has a boyfriend."

Noreen shuts her eyes.

Whoever did it did it at night. He brought the body here during the darkness. He was free to do it then. He carried Megan's dead weight up the slope to the top of Sepulveda Pass and laid her out in the open, as if he were proud of what he'd done.

The lights of the Valley stretch out in the distance, and I think of the people in cars, the people in malls, the people in their homes nestled in front of their televisions while murders are done.

I wonder what it's like to feel someone's life ebb away. To be the cause of it.

I go back down the slope but before I reach my car I catch a glint of moonlight reflecting off something on the ground. It's under a bush and some dirt and it looks as if it's been there awhile.

I pull the thing up with a pen and shake off the dirt and bring it close to my face. It's a gold band laced with stones, small but thick and broken in back.

Rebecca informs me that Megan's father has been arrested for setting up a drug ring at the beach. Apparently he organized it from the back of the surf shop. Bail has been set at a million dollars.

When I call Gruley he says there's no way he's going to talk about it.

I ask if Mr. Wright is a suspect in his daughter's death.

Gruley says nothing has been ruled out, although they believe he spent most of that night in a meeting with several Colombians.

I ask if it's possible Megan knew about his activities. Maybe he was afraid she'd expose them.

The detective says that's an interesting theory. Every case has interesting theories.

I ask if he's talked to Brad yet.

"Brad who? There are a million guys named Brad. More than a million."

I tell him what I know: Megan left the house that night with a kid named Brad. Brad's father is Jeremiah Devlin—remember him?—who, it appears, has a relationship, probably romantic, with Megan's mother. "That Brad," I say.

The detective tells me off the record that he's certainly very, uh, *interested* in what Brad was doing that night. And he'd be quite happy to talk with the boy because there are a number of things they'd like to go over but he's been, shall we say, unavailable for comment.

"You mean you can't find him," I say.

"I'm not going to confirm that."

"Maybe they stashed him in Monte Carlo or something."

"Maybe they did. The very rich are different from you and me."

"Yes, they have more money."

"I knew you'd say that."

I hear the sound of papers being shuffled and I sense he has more facts to tell me, so I stay on the line. He says ever so casually that he's been doing some reading this morning.

"What is it?" I ask.

"An autopsy report."

I wait for him to say more.

"Age—thirteen. Sex—female. Race—Caucasian."

"Came from the Caucasus."

"Height—five-foot-three. Weight—one-hundred-two. Cause of death—"

"Head smashed in like a melon."

"Drowning."

"*What?!*"

Heads turn. I wish I had said nothing. I hate it when people stare at me.

"That's what it says. Her lungs were filled with water."

"That doesn't make sense."

"Since when are killings supposed to make sense?"

"But why was she beaten like that?"

"I guess they wanted to make sure she was dead. Or else they just enjoyed doing it."

"Why are you using the plural?" I ask.

"I wasn't aware that I was," Gruley says. "It might have been a 'he.' Or a 'she,' for all I know."

Steam rises from the medical examiner's coffee, smoke from his cigarette, and a half-eaten jelly doughnut lies in front of a picture of his wife. The walls of Dr. Jack Karch's office are covered with framed photos that show him at work on celebrities and presidential candidates.

"I keep expecting to see you down there someday," he says. "On one of my slabs."

He takes a bite from the doughnut. A trickle of jelly oozes out the side. Years of working with chemicals have turned his fingernails a faint shade of green.

I say I find his report a little hard to believe.

"How do you think we feel?"

He tells me they could have said the easy things—blunt head trauma, yes the girl was definitely raped, case closed, let's move on to the next one. There are always so many bodies. But facts are facts. They demand attention. The girl was drowned.

"Drownings can be accidental," I say.

"Getting your head cracked open usually isn't."

"Did the rape occur before or after she was killed?"

"Can't tell. We may be dealing with sick fuckers. Pun intended."

"How long had she been dead before the body was found?"

"Ten, twelve hours. A while. Rigor mortis had set in. You would have noticed that if you were as observant as you think you are."

I ask if he's told anyone else about the results and he says someone called from Jeremiah Devlin's office so he gave her the details. I ask if he's giving out this information to just anybody who wants it and he says it's all part of the public record and he sure as hell isn't going to tell Jeremiah Devlin to get lost. I ask if Megan's mother has called and he says she hasn't. But he hears she has something going with the rich guy, so he assumes he's told her.

I say Megan's mother has made out quite nicely for herself.

"You have a suspicious mind," Karch says. "That's why I like you."

I open the drawer where I keep my special things. A small manila envelope has what I'm looking for. I shake out what's inside and it spills onto the table. I pick it up with a pair of tweezers and hold it against the light.

The stones are diamonds, cut up and sprinkled throughout the necklace. The gold is eighteen karat. I've checked it against a catalog. Engraved inside this object I now regard as precious is the symbol of the store in which it was sold. I recognize it as one of the upper-end shops at the Beverly Center.

The phone rings. I'm so startled I drop the tweezers. The answering machine kicks on and I hear Rebecca's voice saying there's something she wants to talk about and she's sorry to bother me at home but it's important. She leaves her number. She tells me to call anytime.

I pick the necklace off the floor and blow off the dust and dirt before sliding it back in its place.

I wonder if it fell from her body. I wonder if it was even hers. I wonder if there are fingerprints or microscopic bits of blood or anything else the police might find useful.

I should give it to them but I want to keep it. Somehow this object connects me to her. It gives life to the beaten-up thing I saw at the top of Sepulveda Pass.

What did she know? I ask myself. *What can she tell me?*

When I call Rebecca she says she was going over her notes and something struck her, something strange that didn't add up, so she thought she should talk it over with someone who might have an answer or at least an explanation.

I tell her to go ahead. I'm listening.

She says Megan's father posted bail, but he doesn't have that kind of money. Or shouldn't have. She also wonders how he came up with the funds for that drug ring he's supposed to be masterminding. An operation like that requires a lot of cash—which, once again, our aging surfer dude doesn't have. Or shouldn't have.

I say it's like any other business. Having your own capital is unimportant. The key is financing.

"That's my point," Rebecca says. "Who loaned him the money? He's not what I'd call a good credit risk."

I'm about to reply, to give some logical or at least plausible response, when I stop because I realize I don't have one.

• • •

As I punch in the number, I tell myself this is crazy, this is stupid, this will never work, this is—

"Mr. Devlin's office."

"Is Mr. Devlin in?"

"I'm sorry, he's in a meeting. Can I help you?"

As I identify myself I feel the voice on the other end contracting, ready to address me in brusque tones indicating that I am, as a lower life-form, barely tolerated.

"What is this in reference to?"

The voice is used to fielding calls about mergers and acquisitions, contracts and negotiations, deals and debentures. I can tell it's ready to refer me to the PR people.

I say I'm calling about his son. I understand Brad's name has been mentioned in connection with the Megan Wright case. I was at the funeral and I was touched by the concern they showed for the girl and her family. I have a few questions I'd like to ask.

"I'll give him the message, sir."

Noreen kisses me as I walk through the door. Kristen is at her father's tonight. We drink some wine and watch the news on TV. A correspondent stands in front of a used-book store in Burbank that was ransacked by a gang of youths last night. They beat the owner to death and sexually assaulted a female clerk and smashed and ripped a lot of merchandise, but they took no money. Police say they're baffled. Back at the studio the anchor asks the weatherman how long the heat wave will last.

We go to the Mexican place. Raul asks how Kristen is. Noreen says she's fine. Lately she's been seeing a child psychologist and it appears to be helping. Kristen is a quiet girl who keeps things inside, but now she's expressing herself and that's good of course. Now they know what the problems are. Raul says it's amazing what goes on in the minds of children.

When Noreen excuses herself Raul leans close to me and says I'm a lucky man and I ask why and he says it's because of her, she's a good woman but she carries around a lot of sadness. He asks if I am kind to her and I say I do the best I can.

After Noreen returns Raul says he's been reading my stories and the case is getting more complex with each passing day and I nod and say yes, it's a weird one all right. Noreen says she doesn't want to talk about it. Raul says it's a privilege to know someone who does such interesting work, whose job is so very important. Noreen asks if we can talk about something else. Raul says he's mentioned my name to many of his friends and they're all following the case; everyone wants to know who committed the crime. He says it's almost as if I'm orchestrating the stories so everyone will know my name. I tell him I'm not that clever and I'm not sure who did it and I don't think the police are either. Noreen says let's please change the topic of discussion please.

Back at Noreen's there's a message on the machine. Kristen has called to say good night. Her voice says, "I love you, Mommy," and then there's a pause.

"I wish you were home, Mommy. How come you're not home?"

Noreen bites her lower lip. I stare at the floor and notice some cracks in the tile. My ladyfriend sighs and walks into the living room.

"It's not your fault," she says. It's a voice with no body attached to it.

I've been absolved for a sin I was unaware of committing. I try to think of what I've done wrong, words I might have said or failed to say, thoughts I attempt to suppress that she no doubt senses anyway.

"Kristen's problems aren't your fault," Noreen says. "I don't think anyone's at fault."

Things just happen. We search for meaning behind events but there is none. We waste our lives in a futile quest for reasons.

I get my jacket and reach into the pocket. I can feel my car keys.

I once asked Noreen why she got divorced. She said it was because she wasn't happy.

"Are you happy now?" I asked.

"No," she said. "I'm still unhappy. But in a different way."

five

the voice on the other end says this is Mr. Devlin's office calling and at first I think it's a joke. Everyone has told me that Jeremiah Devlin never returns phone calls.

"What can I do for Mr. Devlin?" I ask.

"He'd like to talk to you. Hold on please."

I wait a few seconds and then another voice enters my ear, a voice that's even and strong and obviously in command.

"This is Jeremiah Devlin."

I thank him for returning my call and tell him I'd like to talk about Megan Wright. He says she was a fine girl. What happened was a tragedy. I say I have some questions he may not like but problems have arisen, loose ends that need to be tied together. It's my job to resolve these things.

He tells me to go ahead.

"How well do you know Megan's mother?"

"I don't discuss matters of that nature."

"But you know her. You have some kind of a relationship with her."

"It would not be untrue to say that."

My neck and shoulder hurt from the way I'm holding the phone. The call surprised me. I didn't have time to assemble my headset.

"How did your son get along with Megan?"

"Quite well, I thought. They're both young. They liked the same music, movies, TV shows. I think most of it is trash, personally."

"Did Brad see Megan the night she was killed?"

"No. He was with me in Tahoe."

"That's not what the police tell me."

"The police don't know all the facts. Nor do you."

"Brad's name has been mentioned during the investigation. The police say they want to question him, but he seems to have dropped out of sight."

I wait for the phone to be slammed down.

"I'm late for a meeting," Jeremiah Devlin says. "Come to my office this afternoon. Around four."

I try to think of a way to get there. Traffic is always bad at that time of day.

As I head out the door Rebecca rushes up and says she was down at the surf shop and Megan's father has been fired of course, but on a hunch she brought along a picture of Jeremiah Devlin. She showed it to the girl behind the counter and asked if she'd ever seen this man. The girl squinted at the photo and held it in her hands and finally she said yes, he did look familiar, in fact she remembered seeing him at the store a few times and she was always impressed because he looked so distinguished and stuff. He'd walk into the store and look over the Jams and the wetsuits, and Megan's father would go up to him and ask if he needed help. The two of them would talk in low tones right near the Boogie boards, although a couple of times they used the office in back.

Jeremiah Devlin's office is in an industrial park just off a freeway in the Valley. I expected something better.

His secretary tells me to wait. She asks if I'd like a cup of coffee or glass of water. I decline.

I notice an enlarged framed photo on the wall. It shows a lot of scrubland with mountains rising in the background; California before the sprawl.

"Mr. Lowe?"

I turn around.

"Jeremiah Devlin."

The man before me is tall and slender, with the kind of tight skin that's gained either through physical training or plastic surgery. He looks a few years shy of fifty.

I shake his hand and thank him for inviting me.

"Let's talk in my office," he says.

We enter a room that's wide and deep and dark. I like the dimness of it, the feeling that I'm in shadows. On the wood-paneled walls are eighteenth-century paintings depicting various aspects of the hunt. In one a hound clenches a blood-soaked goose in its jaws.

Devlin asks why I was so intrigued by the picture on the wall in the lobby. I say I'm not sure. I just like old photos. He says it was taken by his father the day he broke ground on this plant. Everyone said he was crazy to build so far out in the Valley but the land was cheap and he had a vision and the operation kept expanding until the firm became the largest of its kind in the world.

I ask if he ever gets concerned about going out of business.

"As long as war is the health of the state, we'll never have any worries. That's off the record."

"Are you diversifying?"

"We have our fingers in many pies."

He stops at his desk and says he wants to introduce a couple of people. The first is Morgan Osborne, his personal attorney. The second is his son, Brad.

Osborne looks pasty, pudgy and confrontational. I remember Brad from the funeral.

"The police maintain they want to talk to my son but can't find him. As you can see, locating Brad is a very difficult task."

I find myself smiling.

Devlin sits behind his desk and leans back in his chair. "Ask us anything," he says.

I take out my tape recorder and say I hope they don't mind but I like to do this for important interviews and I'm sure they can understand. Osborne says he certainly can, takes out his own tape recorder and puts it next to mine.

We all laugh.

"Brad," I ask, "where were you the night Megan was killed?"

"Is Brad a suspect?" Osborne asks.

"As far as I'm concerned, everyone is guilty until proven innocent."

"I wish the police were that straightforward," Jeremiah Devlin says.

"I was in Tahoe with my father," Brad tells me. "Sometimes I go with him on his trips."

"The police say you went over to Megan's house that night. They say the two of you left together."

"I was in Tahoe."

"I talked to the girl who gave the eulogy at Megan's funeral," I say. "I think her name is Alexis?"

Brad nods. I decide to make my next statement more definite than it really is. I want to see how he'll react.

"She says she was at Megan's house the day she died."

"I wouldn't know. I was in Tahoe."

"She says you and some of your friends were there too."

"I was in Tahoe."

"Then why did she say those things, Brad?"

"She's confused," he says. "She's *always* confused."

"What do you mean?"

"I don't want to say anything. I was in Tahoe." He looks down at his feet before turning to Osborne as if he were an actor who's forgotten his lines. "Maybe we can make this . . ."

"Off the record," Osborne says.

I make a motion that could be construed as assent.

"She uses drugs, man. She's in a fucking cloud most of the time."

"Be careful with your language, Brad," Jeremiah Devlin says.

I glance up from my notepad. Father and son never seem to look at each other.

"I told Megan not to hang out with her," Brad says. "She knows some guys . . . I hope Megan never met them. But maybe she did. Maybe that's why . . ."

"What kind of guys, Brad?"

"Bad guys. Bad news."

"Like Grant Fisher?"

"Do you know him?"

"We've met."

"He's the worst. I wouldn't be surprised if he—"

Osborne interjects. "I believe we've entered an area in which it's best for my client to remain silent."

"That may be true," I say, "but it's not best for me."

Jeremiah Devlin smiles, showing bright, wide, even teeth, easily the whitest thing in the room. But his eyes remain narrow and focused. In this light they look gray.

"What did you do in Tahoe, Brad?"

"Waterskiing. It's great. Really on the edge."

"He sat in on some meetings too," Jeremiah Devlin says. "I'm trying to teach him my business. Some exercises are more productive than others."

"I suppose you can verify all this?"

"You can check his academic records. Brad attends the Hilliard School. He wasn't in that day. Or you can talk to any of my managers in Tahoe."

I make some notes and hope they think I'm just catching up. The truth is I've run out of questions. I was unprepared for a solid alibi.

"What does Megan's mother do for a living?" I ask.

I feel like a fisherman casting out a line, hoping despite the horrific odds that this time he'll catch something.

"This isn't about her," Devlin says. "It's about Brad and his whereabouts the night Megan was killed."

Sometimes, I tell myself, *you do land the fish.*

"Megan's mother recently bought an expensive home in a gated community," I say. I'm looking at my notebook, as if I have this written down. I hope no one can see that the page is blank. "She also enrolled her children in private schools. I've met her ex-husband, and he's not the kind of guy who could support them that way."

"She never got a dime from him," Devlin tells me. Megan's mother could not have said it more bitterly.

"So what happened?" I ask.

Devlin leans forward in his chair. I haven't had a staredown like this since sixth grade. I feel my heart racing and my breath getting shallow. I think of what Brad said about waterskiing.

"She threw you out when you asked about me," Jeremiah Devlin says.

"You can throw me out too. It's your office."

Devlin leans back in his chair and looks up at the ceiling.

"She works for me. More accurately, she works for my primary company. She's an outstanding manager. Last year she reduced her division's workforce by ten percent while increasing its production and profitability. I gave her a substantial bonus. I believe she used that money to put a down payment on the house."

"She told me she got home late the night Megan

died," I say. "But she wasn't with you. So where was she?"

"Probably at work. Do you know much about her?"

I have to shake my head.

"Her husband deserted her. She raised her two children by herself, and got an MBA by going to Pomona College at night. She's an admirable woman. A lot of people in this country no longer respect hard work and discipline, but I sure as hell do."

Brad pipes up. I'm surprised to hear his voice. I think we all are. This no longer seems about him. "I have an idea," he says. "I think the police got the days mixed up. I went over to Megan's the night before I went to Tahoe. We hung out together. Alexis was there too. I *know* she got the days mixed up."

"Did you do that a lot?" I ask. "Hang out with Megan?"

Brad looks at the lawyer before answering.

"Sometimes. Not a lot. She was neat. It's a shame what happened."

"Did Megan ever go up to Tahoe?" I ask. I'm fly-fishing now.

Devlin shakes his head. He says Tahoe is a special place for him. He's zealous about his privacy and that's his most private of places. Not even Megan's mother has been there.

"Why are you making a point of that?" I ask.

"I wasn't aware I was making a point about anything."

"You seem to be saying something about your relationship with Mrs. Wright. I'm wondering what it is."

I notice Devlin glancing at Osborne, who nods imperceptibly.

"Let me put it to you this way," Devlin says. "I care about what happens to Megan's mother. I care very deeply."

"How did you get up to Tahoe?" I ask Brad. I hope shifting gears so abruptly will get him to say something I can use, but his father answers instead.

"He flew up with me on a company plane," Devlin says.

"And when did you come back?"

"When we heard about Megan."

"You came back together?"

Devlin and his son look at each other for the first time since the interview began.

"I don't recall," Devlin says. "It's all a blur. Brad may have returned before me. I honestly don't remember. I was quite upset."

I can still see the insects covering her body. I can still hear their whine and buzz.

"We all feel Megan's death," Jeremiah Devlin says. "We're all grieving deeply. But I want to say something—and I want you to print it."

He gets up from behind his desk. I feel like telling him there are no guarantees.

"Brad has been the object of rumor and innuendo. I've heard these things. We've all heard them. But *nobody* has come forward with proof—because there is none. Brad was with *me* that night."

His voice rises as his fist slams into the desk. I want to tell him that I hate scenes.

"I *resent* this gossip. I *resent this shit!*"

Brad crosses his legs and clasps his hands behind his neck. His eyes are fixed on an indeterminate point between the ceiling and the end of his nose.

Osborne doodles on a piece of legal paper.

"Brad is no more responsible for Megan's death than anybody else in this room. The police have to realize that. They're no closer to making an arrest now than they were the day her body was found. And they won't make an arrest until they shift the focus of their investigation. I can guarantee that."

I snap off my tape recorder and thank them for their time. My deadline is approaching. Jeremiah Devlin walks to the door with me.

"You've discussed all this with Megan's mother," I say. This is more of a statement than a question.

He nods. "She understands the situation. It's been difficult for her."

He lowers his voice.

"My son," he tells me. "I have great plans for him. High hopes."

"I can see that."

"It almost seems as if someone is trying to set him up. But I'll crush anyone who harms him."

I put my notepad in my jacket and for the first time look directly at Jeremiah Devlin. There are a few small, faint scars on his face, as if he's cut himself shaving.

I point to my own neck, which has similar marks. "No offense, Mr. Devlin, but can't you afford a better razor than the kind I use?"

He displays his teeth again and says, "It's a perennial condition. I have sensitive skin."

"So you don't go to the beach much?"

He shakes his head.

"That's strange," I say. I tell him that he's been seen in a surf shop talking to Megan's father.

"I haven't been to a place like that since I was twenty," he says. "I used to spend my summers in the South Bay. That was before we learned about melanoma."

My editor says she needs the story fast for the first edition. We can make it better later.

I ask Rebecca to transcribe the tape while I start writing.

Gruley isn't in his office. He's not at home either. I leave holes in the places where I expect him to help me.

My editor says she has to have the story.

Rebecca sends me a message saying the stuff on the tape is fantastic.

I try Gruley's office again. The woman who answers the phone says she's not going to beep him for me and she has no idea where he is. He could be on a case. He could be stuck in traffic. He could be at a bar or a ball-game or—

I ask what his favorite bar is. After she tells me I call Information, then hit pound, zero and get through to that number. I ask if Frank Gruley is there. The guy who answered says he isn't sure. He'll have to look. I promise I'm not calling on behalf of the detective's wife.

I think I hear him laugh.

Gruley asks how I found him. I tell him it's my fucking job to find him when I have to. I recount the interview in Jeremiah Devlin's office as quickly as I can.

"Off the record," Gruley says, "what they're telling you is complete bullshit."

"They say they can prove it."

"If you get enough people to lie, you can prove anything."

I tell him I need something I can print. I work for a family newspaper and the term "complete bullshit," while descriptive, won't get past the desk. Detective Frank Gruley clears his throat. His voice assumes the Official Tone used by public servants at press briefings as he says the investigation is serious and ongoing. The police are pursuing every lead. He's sorry if feathers are being ruffled, but that's the nature of the business.

I ask if Brad Devlin is a suspect.

What follows is a long pause interrupted by deep and rhythmic breathing.

"I shouldn't be telling you this—" Gruley finally says.

Tell me, tell me, oh please God tell me.

"—but yes. Yes, he is."

I type in his comments and ask Rebecca to double-check the quotes from Jeremiah Devlin. She says they're right on the money, so I send the story over.

My editor says she likes it. The piece has guts. It's strong. It's the best thing we've put on page one in a long time.

But it's missing something.

She sits at her screen, moving the cursor around like a sports car weaving through traffic.

She wears wire-frame glasses. Her name is Trish Yamamoto and she was only recently promoted to the metro desk from one of the suburban bureaus.

She stops the cursor near the top of the story.

"It's here."

What's where?

She says I need something from the lawyer. I've just quoted my unnamed police friend but there's no reaction from Brad's attorney. The story is good and everything's supported but we have to be careful. Jeremiah Devlin is a powerful man.

Rebecca finishes transcribing the tape and sends it to my queue and asks if there's anything else she can do.

I tell her to stick around. I might need her for something.

When I call Osborne I say I'm sorry to bother him at home but I've been talking to the police and one well-placed source in the investigation has informed me that Brad is definitely a suspect.

I look at the clock. We're already past deadline.

I ask if he has any comment.

Osborne says he can't believe the police have nothing better to do than smear a fine young man who couldn't possibly have committed the crime. It's enough to shake one's faith in law enforcement.

"For the record," I say, "you're stating that Brad is innocent?"

"Let me phrase it this way," the lawyer says. "Brad played no role in this unfortunate occurrence."

I insert what he says. Trish claims that should do it. She likes what I've done. I say good night and lock my desk. On my way out Rebecca says I look like a guy who could use a beer.

• • •

We have a drink at a place near work and then we eat Chinese. Rebecca loves moo shu. I think about going home but Rebecca says she knows a good bar at the beach where sometimes they have a band.

The group plays Motown covers. We dance a bit. It occurs to me that the originals came out before she was born.

She lives close by and asks if I'd like to stop in for one more. Her apartment is on the second floor and I tell her I would have declined the offer if I'd known stairs were involved. She says I'm a lazy bum and I say no, I'm just getting old. She says she doesn't believe me.

On our way up I can see the ocean and hear the waves and I say it must be nice to live here and she says it is, she grew up in the desert but always dreamed of living near the water because it seemed so peaceful and now here she is and it's really strange how things can work out just the way you hoped.

I was eating an ice cream bar in the kitchen at Noreen's house.

"Do you know how many calories that thing has?" she asked.

I confessed that I didn't.

"Four hundred. And how many grams of fat?"

I shook my head.

"Twenty. And you stay thin."

"I've always been thin."

She sat at the opposite end of the table. Her face was flushed.

"It's so unfair," she said.

six

*i**n the morning I think about what happened. I tell myself I'm not surprised . . .*

As soon as the door was shut, I slid my tongue in her mouth and ran my hands over her arms her breasts her thighs. They felt so smooth; I'd forgotten how skin like that feels. She pressed her body against me and I wanted her right then, right there, on the floor with the lights blazing and the windows open and the sea breeze ruffling the curtains.

I grabbed her hand and led her into the bedroom. She stumbled a bit behind me.

. . . but she did surprise me. . . .

I took off her clothes and unsnapped her bra. I still had my pants on.

She told me to take them off.

I lay on top of her and she wiggled underneath. I slipped my finger inside her.

She pushed me away.

. . . I didn't understand. . . .

"I want you to be aggressive," she said. "I want you to really want it."

. . . If I lose my control, the only thing left is my desire. . . .

"How aggressive should I be?"

"I'll let you know if it's too much."

I put my hand on her neck and pushed her down on the pillow.

"That's okay," she said.

I bit her ears, her shoulders, her nipples.

"I want you to be demanding," she said.

. . . I didn't know. . . .

I crawled up the bed.

"What do you want?" she asked.

I told her and she said she wasn't sure so I yelled in a tone that blended authority with urgency and desperation. She batted her eyes and smiled before opening her mouth. I let her do that awhile. Then I went back between her legs and soon we were in a rhythm and she was starting to groan.

And then I took it out of her.

"Why did you do that?"

She sounded upset and afraid. I liked that.

I found my belt and pinned her hands against the headboard. I looped the leather strap around her forearms and through the bedspread.

"That hurts," she said.

"Good."

I plunged back into her and she gasped and moaned and then said yes oh yes that's it, that's good white boy, do it harder, and soon she was screaming and I was too. . . .

I sense the sun shining outside and hear the soft

sounds of the waves and the gulls, and I imagine foamy white surf rushing up the beach. It's blinding if you look too quickly.

Rebecca's head rests on my chest. The sheets are strewn at the foot of the bed. I see faint welts on my lover's wrists.

As I drive back to my place the radio reports on a robbery and assault late last night in Woodland Hills. The husband and wife were asleep when some youths broke in and smashed the china, ripped the furniture and trashed the TV and stereo system. They beat the husband and raped the wife and took small amounts of cash and jewelry. Police say they can't explain why the attack was so vicious.

"Megan kept a diary," Trish says as soon as I get to work.

I remember this fact. I think others are more important.

"What happened to it?"

"I have no idea."

"Get one."

When I call Frank Gruley he says they asked Megan's mother to give it to them but she said she'd burned it, just as she'd threatened. I say I don't believe her and he says he doesn't either, but what are you going to do. They could get a warrant but they'd look ridiculous.

There's no answer when I phone the house where Megan once lived. The machine isn't even on.

I work on my cover story as I drive into the Valley. Sitting in the shack is a small young man with the frightened look of a guy who's in this country illegally. I flash my ID but most of it is covered by a business card from someone I once met who works for a cable company.

"We've had complaints from this area," I say. "We think the cable's been cut. I want to check things out."

"Nobody said anything to me," the guard says. His accent is heavy with echoes of poverty and death squads.

"I don't have time for this," I say. "What's your supervisor's name?"

He steps back into the shack and opens the gate. I drive to the Wrights' house and stand at the door for at least five minutes but the only sound I hear is a bell ringing through empty rooms. When I look up I see closed windows and drawn blinds.

Back in my car I take some papers concerning my paper's health insurance policy and stuff them in the envelope from the courier service. When the envelope seems properly bulging, I shove it under my arm and walk up to the front door of the house next to Megan's.

Nobody's there.

I cross the street. This time the bell produces a stirring, and I hear lightly borne feet coming toward me. As the door opens I straighten my back and think about what to say. I've exhausted the cable angle.

Before me is a girl who looks ten or eleven. She's blond and barefoot and chewing gum. She takes off the headphones that had been plugged into her ears and drapes them around her neck. I hear the tinny sounds of the latest Madonna.

I smile and ask if her mother's at home. She says no. Mom's at work.

"How about your father?"

"You mean my stepdad. He's working too. My father lives in Seattle. Or maybe Denver."

"You're home alone?"

"Yeah. My brother usually gets back late. He has football practice after school and then he goes over to his girlfriend's. I think they have sex."

"Maybe you can help me. I'm from the office and I have a package for Mrs. Wright." Here I pat the envelope, as if offering proof that I'm legitimate. "It's important that she get it, but she's not home. Do you know if she'll be returning later?"

"I doubt it," the girl says. "She hasn't been there for a while."

"Do you know where she is?"

"She's living with her boyfriend."

"Jeremiah Devlin?"

The girl shrugs. I can tell the name means nothing. "I can take that package," she says. "I'll give it to her if she ever comes back."

"That's all right. I have to hand it to her personally. But thanks for offering."

The girl works her gum energetically, cracking it every few seconds so it makes a sound that reminds me of chalk breaking. She makes no move to close the door. I have the impression that she enjoys this chance to talk. I wonder when she last had a conversation with her parents or stepparents or whatever adults are involved with her living arrangements.

"I've seen Mrs. Wright's name in the papers," I say. "Isn't her daughter the one who got killed?"

The girl says yeah and it's kind of scary when you think about it because it means there's a murderer running around loose. Of course it's kind of exciting too. The whole thing is random.

"It doesn't look random in the newspapers," I say.

She says she doesn't mean it that way. She says it's strange and weird. Events like that are called random these days.

I tell her I'm sure the police will find whoever did it. She says she isn't so certain. People get away with things all the time.

I ask if she knew Megan.

"A little. She just moved in. She was older. And she hung out with boys."

She makes a face indicating a belief that all males are icky.

"Did she have a boyfriend?"

"There was this one guy she saw a lot. At least she got in his car all the time."

"Do you know his name?"

She shakes her head.

"What did he look like?"

"Blond, tall, good-looking. He was definitely older. Maybe even a senior. I think they had sex too."

I look away from her, down the block, at the stucco colonials trimmed with red that line the street. They all shimmer in the sun.

I find myself squinting. I think I'm getting a headache.

"Where did Megan go that night? All the stories I've read say that nobody can figure it out."

"Maybe she got in his car. She rode in it all the time. He's got a Lexus. It's really nice."

She cracks the gum again. She seems to be thinking about something.

"Y'know," she says, "I think I'm gonna have sex one of these days. Just to get it over with."

The jewelry store I'm looking for is sandwiched between a taco shop and a place that sells sweaters. The salesgirl is behind the counter and on the phone. I browse a bit, examining the gold and silver and diamonds locked behind glass.

"We went to the movies, but the line was too long," the salesgirl says. A pause. "Didn't you just *love* that dress? I'd *kill* for something like that." Another pause. "He did *that* to her?"

I stop at the counter and smile.

"Hold on," the salesgirl says into the phone. She covers the mouthpiece. Her nametag identifies her as Rochelle. "Can I help you?"

I identify myself and tell her I'm working on a story about Megan Wright. Rochelle nods and says yes, she's heard about this case on television. She asks if I'm doing a survey or something.

I reach into my pocket and take out a small manila envelope and shake the contents onto the glass counter. I pick up the necklace with my pen and hold it in front of her.

"Do you remember selling this?" I ask.

"I've gotta go," Rochelle says into the mouthpiece. She brings her face close to what I'm holding. She says she's a little nearsighted.

"Tell me about it," I say.

Rochelle says she sold it a couple of weeks ago to a guy who came in eating a taco. The store has a strict policy about no food allowed, but she's not into rules. The guy said he wanted it for a friend. He motioned to a girl who was standing near the door.

"What did the guy look like?"

"A kid. Sixteen or seventeen."

"Blond? Tall? Good-looking?"

"Yeah. How did you know?"

"Describe his friend."

"She stayed near the door most of the time. She was eating ice cream. I didn't get a good look at her."

"Can you tell me anything about her? Did she seem happy or sad or upset or——"

"Happy, I guess. He was buying something for her."

Rochelle says what she remembers most is how the guy paid for it. That's why the whole thing sticks in her mind. She told him the necklace was really expensive and he gave her this goofy smile and said he thought he could handle it. He took out a gold card. She was surprised. She'd never seen a guy that young with a card that good.

"He drives a Lexus too," I say.

"Wow. I'm glad I was nice to him."

She giggles and tells me she ran the card through and it all checked out, so of course she finished the sale. There was a nice commission and everything. She asked if he wanted it wrapped and he said no, it wouldn't be necessary. He gave it to the girl standing near the door. She smiled as he put it around her neck.

I ask her what day this happened. It's very important that I know.

She says she doesn't remember.

I tell her I think it occurred on September fourteenth or fifteenth, a Tuesday or a Wednesday.

She says she'd like to give me an answer but she can't. She works here five nights a week and after a while they all run into each other.

I ask if they still have the sales slip on record. She says they should, but that kind of stuff is confidential. I take out my wallet and let a twenty fall from it and tell her that if it wouldn't be too much trouble, I'd really appreciate it if she could check on this for me.

She says they keep their files in back. It might take a couple of minutes.

I tell her I'll wait. I walk around the store and try to look as if I'm interested in the merchandise.

I've never paid for information before.

"Is this what you're looking for?" Rochelle asks when she returns.

She puts a piece of paper on the counter. I bend over to examine it. I don't want to touch.

The amount is three thousand dollars and the purchased item is listed as a gold necklace with diamonds and the whole thing is signed, in a jagged adolescent hand, by Brad Devlin.

The date is the fifteenth.

The day Megan was killed.

• • •

The beach is different at night. The water is darker than the sky and glints of moonlight reflect off the surf. In the absence of people the sound of the waves is louder, insistent, repetitive, numbing.

I open a bottle of beer. Rebecca stretches out on the blanket, placing her feet in the sand and resting her head in my lap. She asks for a swig and I give it to her. While she's drinking I run my hands around her shoulders and down her arms.

She starts talking in a low voice that mimics the rhythms of the ocean. One night at school she was walking across campus when this guy leaped out of the bushes and pointed a knife at her; it was this big fucking thing that could have killed a cow and he said she was gonna follow him and do exactly what he said and he didn't want her shouting for help or running away or anything foolish like that because then he'd have to slash her pretty face and we didn't want that to happen, did we? So they began walking down an empty path. She could sense the knife at her back although she couldn't feel it and she knew she should have been terrified but instead she was calm, almost serene, because for some reason it seemed as if this whole thing was occurring to somebody else and she was observing the incident instead of experiencing it.

She stops. She says she knows this sounds strange. I tell her it's random but that describes everything these days and she should go on.

She says they entered an alley. It kept getting darker and darker until finally she could see nothing at all;

she'd never been in pitch blackness before and she thought it must be what death was like, and still they kept walking until finally she heard a noise; it sounded like the guy behind her was falling and then she heard a scream; it was loud and awful and primal, the scream of something in total agony. It didn't sound like a noise that could come from a human.

She ran of course; she ran all the way back to her place and locked the door and rushed to her bedroom and dove under the covers and pulled the sheets up around her head. The next day she went to class just as she always did and after a while she started to wonder if she had imagined the guy and the knife and her own feelings of not being a part of it.

I run my hand through her hair. I enjoy its kinky feel. She rolls over and rises to her knees. We kiss. I like the faint taste of alcohol on her tongue. I wrap my arms around her and we sink down on the blanket, my hands under her shirt and her bra, inside her jeans and her panties.

"Somebody might see us," she says.

"Good," I say.

As she unbuttons my pants she asks if I like what she's doing. I push her jeans down until they bunch around her ankles. She kicks them off and I hear them hit the sand a few feet away. I lie on my back and she says that's it, I'm a good boy, that's exactly what she was hoping for. She lowers herself a little bit at a time until with a final push she grinds down all the way.

We stay like that for a minute. There's no motion at all. Then she lifts herself up and pushes back down and starts going faster and faster, shutting her eyes and snapping back her head.

I enjoy watching her. I enjoy what I'm doing to her but I'm unsure about what she does to me, the way she strips away my layers and leaves me with no thought or intelligence or control, just passion and need and lust. Her skin is the color of the night and as I watch myself disappear into it I imagine that I'm vanishing into a place where there's nothing except the sensation of feeling, and as I climax I look out beyond her and see a full moon hovering over the horizon; I can even see a few stars, and the sounds I hear are the soft lappings of the waves mingled with her screams.

At the checkout line in the supermarket I always flip through the pages of the Grocery Press. I have a special fondness for Elvis sightings.

"I saw him right there," the heavyset woman tells a reporter. She lives in a trailer park. "I came in to play the Pick Six and saw him by the frozen pizzas and I couldn't believe my eyes, but I walked up to him anyway, just as plain as could be, and told him that Viva Las Vegas is my favorite movie of all time, and he smiled at me in the way only he can and said, 'Thank you, ma'am; you're very kind,' and then he paid for his food and walked away.

"I'd recognize that voice anywhere."

seven

We're in bed together, a tangle of arms and legs and sweat. I'm spent but still inside her. Rebecca says this is when she feels closest to me; it's like we've shared something that's just between us and now we're enjoying the memory as a couple.

I rub my mouth against hers and she wraps her legs tighter around me. I start to stretch out but she tells me to stop. She wants me to stay still. She likes how it feels.

Her hands are strong. I haven't noticed that before.

"You seemed tense," she says.

"I was."

"What happened?"

"Everything."

"I've always heard how calm you are. That nothing ever bothers you."

"Sometimes that's a facade."

"Tell me," she says. "Tell me what's bothering you."

"Do you really want to know?"

She sinks her head so deep into the pillow I'm afraid I'll lose her.

"Tell me."

I talk about the diary and the gold necklace and Brad's car, the stunt I pulled to get Megan's neighbor to talk, the twenty I paid to look at the receipt in the jewelry shop. I tell her I know I should give the necklace to the police, but I'm developing a strange feeling about this case.

"You mean this story," Rebecca says. "You're talking like a cop."

"I mean the case. I'm finding out information nobody else is. I'm talking to people the authorities haven't spoken to."

"Maybe you're better than they are."

"Maybe nobody wants to solve the crime."

Rebecca looks past me. Her grip gets looser.

"I'd love to see that diary," she says.

"Her mother said she burned it."

Rebecca shakes her head. "No mother in the world would do that. They're far too nosy."

"Maybe she read it and then burned it."

Rebecca doubts it. She thinks Megan's mother would want a remembrance of the girl, physical proof that she'd once lived and breathed and thought.

In that case, I say, she probably has it with her and the thing is stashed away in one of Jeremiah Devlin's many homes.

"Maybe," Rebecca says. "Maybe not. Maybe she feels it belongs in the house."

It could still be there, a ghost haunting the rooms and those of us who are now involved.

"You said the house was empty."

Rebecca's eyes lock with mine and I know exactly what she's about to propose and I get scared—not because of what she's suggesting, but because our thoughts are moving in the same direction and it's as if we're sharing one mind and now I'm only part of a whole and a piece of me has died.

"What you're contemplating," I say, "is highly illegal." I tell her I've never done any breaking and entering. It seems dangerous and I'm not sure I'd be any good at it.

"Committing a crime is easy," she says. "What's hard is making up your mind to do it."

She moves her right hand off my back. I can't see where she's taking it.

"Besides," she says, "I know you've got balls."

And then she grabs them. I let out a yell and she laughs and I'm so startled and pissed off I slap her across the face.

Her eyes go big and she reaches up and draws my head down toward hers. I smell her breath and her body; it's the smell of sex, the scent of both desire and satisfaction, and she tells me that she likes it, she likes it when I'm angry and make demands, she likes it when I lose control, and I feel myself getting stiff inside her and her grip on me is strong again, and she says she can't believe it, and I tell her it's her fault, she's done this to me, and she rises up and bites my earlobe and whispers fiercely that she's glad, she's glad for what she's done, and as we start rocking back and forth she wraps her legs around my hips and her nails dig deep into my back.

• • •

Noreen calls me at work. She says I'm never at home. I tell her I've been busy.

"It's over, isn't it?" she asks.

"I guess," I say.

"We tried," she says. "We tried to make it work. But we couldn't. I know I tried. I did the best I could."

I tell her it's nobody's fault. I hear a gulp that I believe is a prelude to weeping. She says I've left some of my stuff at her place.

"I guess I should pick it up."

"I guess you should."

"What's a good time for you?"

"Tonight. Tonight is good."

"I'll be there around seven."

"Okay."

Howard Fussman's office is a glass cage about the size of a rabbit hutch, with a view of the watercooler and coffee machine.

"Hi howareyou," he says as Trish and I enter.

We tell him we're fine.

He says he's uncomfortable with the story. It's not the kind of thing we usually do. As the city editor he feels he's one of the stewards of a responsible paper with a national reputation. Covering a tawdry murder is something for a New York tabloid.

I tell him the case is fascinating. Everybody's talking about it.

"That's part of the problem," he says. "It strikes me as pandering."

"The readers help pay our salaries," I say. "It's all right to pander to them once in a while."

I smile but there's no response. He's a slight man with little hair and no sense of humor.

Trish asks where the story is going. I say it'll go wherever the facts take it. I know that's clichéd but—

"Is Jeremiah Devlin involved in this girl's death?" Fussman asks.

"Megan," I say. "The girl's name was Megan Wright."

"Is he?"

"I'm not sure. His son has a lot of explaining to do. The old man is probably trying to cover up for him."

Fussman jots a note on an office memo pad that has his name embossed at the top. He says he doesn't know how much longer he can keep me on the story. With all the cost-cutting in the newsroom it's difficult to justify allocating one reporter to one crime, and besides I haven't produced anything in a few days. He's putting together a team to examine the long-term effects of the drought and he wants the intern to join it as a researcher, but that's impractical right now because she's doing the cop roundup.

"Rebecca," I say. "The intern's name is Rebecca. She's quite good."

"That's what I've heard."

As soon as we're out of the office Trish asks if I've found out anything about the diary. I shake my head. She says she needs something from me. She really likes this story and we have to publish something, even a small item, just to regain our momentum.

I ask if we can talk in private. She suggests the cafeteria. As we walk down the hall I listen to the sharp sound of her heels striking the floor.

I steer her to an empty table surrounded by others in a sea of vacancy. The light is harsh and glaring and casts no shadows. The vending machines are aglow, offering us stuff in cans and stuff in bags and stuff on sticks if only we'll insert our change. None of it is good for us, but that's part of the attraction.

I ask if she wants anything. She says she doesn't. I buy myself a soda.

"What is it?" she asks as I take my place opposite her.

I drum my fingers on the plastic tabletop and lean forward in the plastic chair and finally I tell her the facts that I'm sure of, but I withhold the tactics I employed. She's a purist and I'm sure she'd disapprove.

"Why are you sitting on this?" she asks.

"You wanted me to re-create Megan's last night. I haven't finished."

"I was too ambitious. We're journalists, not historians. We can't wait."

I tell her I'm afraid my sources will dry up and I'll be unable to prove what I believe happened. Trish says she appreciates my concerns, but that's a risk we'll have to take.

The cafeteria has no windows. I pick up the faint odor of stale sauerkraut. For a moment I wonder what it's like outside and then I remind myself that it's sunny, nowadays it's always sunny, the land has been cursed by eternal sunshine.

Just once more I'd like to feel the rain in my face.

"When can I see the story?" Trish asks.

"You'll have it by four."

With the imperious tone usually associated with papal pronouncements, a secretary informs me that Morgan Osborne is in conference and may well be tied up all afternoon. I tell her it's important that we talk. I've discovered some things about Brad Devlin's whereabouts the night Megan Wright was murdered.

"He usually doesn't speak to members of the press," the secretary tells me.

"Give him the message."

I call Gruley and ask if the hair and fiber reports have come back yet. He says they have and I ask if they indicate anything interesting. He says they always do.

"Would you care to share with the class?" I ask.

"There were fibers on her body. Since she was almost totally naked, we're wondering where they came from. And there's hair on her torso that doesn't match hers."

"How about the skin under her fingernails?"

"We've analyzed that too. It wasn't hers. Obviously."

"Whose was it?"

"We don't know yet."

"Are you going to try to match the hair and the fibers and the skin with Brad Devlin?"

Gruley says nothing. I hear the soft wheeze of a man who's been drinking too much alcohol lately.

"What's the matter?" I ask.

"I can't talk about it over the phone."

"When can you talk?"

"Sometime in the future. Not now."

I ask how thorough a search he conducted of the scene where the body was found.

"What kind of bullshit question is that?" he asks.

"Are you sure you found everything?"

"Everything important."

"I don't think so. Read the paper tomorrow."

I hang up and start writing. The lead says new questions have been raised about Brad Devlin's activities the night Megan Wright was murdered. I cite witnesses overlooked during the police investigation.

The second paragraph details Brad's alibi and notes that he's the son of Jeremiah Devlin.

I continue typing. The words are neutral and I use only facts, but their effect is damning. By the time my readers have finished this over their bran flakes and juice, they'll wonder why Brad Devlin hasn't been indicted and convicted and strapped into a gurney to await lethal injection.

Morgan Osborne calls back. He tells me he's a busy man. I start reading the story to him. After the first paragraph there's no response so I move on to the second. I pause but there's no reaction so I go on to the third, then the fourth and the fifth. The story points out that Brad Devlin apparently purchased a three-thousand-dollar necklace at the Beverly Center on September fifteenth, the day Megan Wright was killed. The story notes that Brad and his father have claimed he was in Tahoe that day.

I want Osborne to say something. I expect him to cut through but there are no words, just the sound of his breath growing tighter and more constricted. He's facing the inquisition of the media in the spotlight of the public eye and I'm sure he's unprepared for this after years spent in shadowy offices putting a legal veneer on Jeremiah Devlin's business affairs.

I read on, through the ninth and tenth paragraphs, the details accumulating until the pattern is clear, the case is made, one thing leads into another in a way that leaves no room for doubt, reasonable or otherwise. Finally I stop and tell him, "That's as far as I've written."

"All that," he says at last, "all that *shit*"—he spews out the word as if it shows his utter contempt for me and what I'm doing and how I've spent my life—"you plan to put that in the newspaper?"

"Yes," I say. "If my editors let me."

"Who gave this to you? The police?"

"I can't tell you my sources. You know that."

"Brad was not involved in this young girl's death," Osborne says.

"Megan," I say. "Her name was Megan Wright. It seems to me there are some inconsistencies in Brad's story."

"You're not on the police force."

"Have they asked you about this?"

The attorney waits. He wants me to seize onto every word he's about to say as if they're somehow necessary for my survival. Silence makes people pay attention.

"For the record, I'm not going to add anything beyond what I've already said. But I will tell you something. Off the record."

"What is it?"

"If I were you, I'd be very careful from now on."

It's Thursday night, so Kristen won't be in. Kristen is never here on Thursdays. She spends the night at her father's.

I park on the street and approach the front door. It feels strange after so many months of going around to the back. I'm used to letting myself in but that was when I was an admitted presence, as much a part of the ambience as the television.

I ring the bell. It's as if I were coming here for the first time.

I brought her a rose. She smiled and said she wasn't expecting this. It was awfully sweet of me. She asked the babysitter to put the flower in a vase and told her we'd be back around eleven.

Noreen answers the door and tells me to come in. The living room is the same. I recognize the sofa and the lights and the chairs and the plants that always seem to need just a little more water. At first I wonder what's different and then I see it in her rigid stance and unblinking eyes and the way she stands a few feet farther away than she used to.

The house hasn't changed of course. What has changed is us.

She asks how I've been and I say all right, but busy. She asks if I'm still working on that murder story and I say yes, I'm still at it. Then I ask how Kristen's doing and she says fine, her grades are much better.

Noreen asks if I'd like a beer or a cup of tea or anything and I decline. I say I'd just like to get my stuff and leave. I'm kind of tired.

She says everything is in the bedroom.

My socks and underwear are stacked neatly on the bed. In the closet my shirts and pants are still on hangers but there's a gap of several feet between them and her clothes, as if she's afraid my apparel might contaminate hers.

I put a battered canvas bag on the bed.

"Your stuff will get wrinkled in there," she says.

"That's okay. I have to go to the cleaners anyway."

She watches me, her back leaning against the wall, as I zip the bag closed. It's a tight fit. I didn't realize I had so much here.

I sling the bag over my shoulder and start walking out.

"Will I still see you?" she asks. "Will we stay in touch?"

I mumble a few words.

"I hope we do," she says. "I'd like to be friends."

Women say this and it's always struck me as odd, this belief that it's easy or even possible to downgrade a relationship from the intimate to the merely friendly. A friend is someone who makes you laugh or takes your mind off things, but she has problems that she demands I become involved in and their weight makes me claustrophobic; around her I confront a joyless life with limited options.

She dislikes my work. She doesn't understand that I want to be free from her disapproval. She has never made me laugh.

I have my hand on the doorknob.

"Is there somebody else?" she asks.

I stop my hand but I don't turn around.

"Why do you say that?"

"Because I'm curious. I want to know. I'm sure you can sympathize."

I tell her there is.

"What's she like?"

"She's nice."

"That doesn't tell me anything."

"What do you want to know?"

"Is she young? Is she pretty? Is it serious? How did you meet her? Stuff like that."

"She is young. She is pretty. I don't know if it's serious. I met her at work."

"You don't want to talk about it, do you? You don't want to share what you're thinking. You never did."

"That's the way I am."

"How can we be friends if you don't let me know what's going on in your life? What do you do with this woman? Where do you go together? What do you have in common?"

She keeps clinging to me. She can't let go.

I open the door.

"How's the sex?" she asks.

I turn my head and look at her.

"Great," I say. "Absolutely great."

"Get out of here."

As I walk toward my car I feel myself being pulled into the night. I enjoy the anonymity and cover only darkness can bring. The strap from my bag digs into my shoulder but I don't mind the pain; I know I deserve it; I want the weight to hurt some more. The bag contains all my sins. It represents everything I've done wrong. It's my burden and it would only be right if I had to carry it forever.

eight

my story is huge, which is what I expected. The electronic media float the words "questions" and "allegations" over the airwaves until they seep into the consciousness of Southern California, like tough desert grass soaking up and storing the last winter rain.

Police decline any comment except to say the investigation is serious and ongoing. They have a lot of leads. Checking them out is a painstaking process. They're asking the public to exercise a little patience.

During a news conference on the courthouse steps Murray Cain, the underfinanced challenger in the district attorney's race, brandishes the front page of our Metro section and says the failure to bring anyone to justice for this horrific crime is an affront to the community. If he were in office he'd have his best investigators working round-the-clock and they'd be under orders to go wherever the facts led, even if that might frighten and offend certain rich and powerful segments. Yes, Cain says with the mixture of disgust and resignation that identifies him as an outsider desperately trying to get in, the scent of cover-up is in the air.

A little later District Attorney Robinson Shields responds by reading a statement from the recesses of his book-bound office. Grandstanding ploys won't solve this case, he intones, but hard work will. He understands the public's desire to see the perpetrators punished (I note the use of the plural, even if no one else does) and while his office is working diligently to ensure that result, it won't be rushed by opportunistic political stunts or sensationalistic accounts in the media.

I've been in Shields's office a few times and what I remember most clearly is the track lighting, which was installed by the chief electrician at one of the movie studios. It's strong but subtle, so photographers and camera crews don't need their own lights. A deputy prosecutor once told me that Shields has forbidden anyone to touch his books, for fear a misplaced one will show up on television.

Morgan Osborne issues a press release that says my story is baseless, full of innuendo and totally without corroboration.

Trish says we have to talk. She leads me to a back stairwell, smooths her skirt and eases herself down, comfortably and confidently, on one of the steps. Her feet reach the landing and I notice that she's wearing pumps.

"We have to keep this story moving," she says. "We've regained the momentum and we can't lose it."

"I can go to Tahoe. Maybe I'll find something up there."

"Sending you would come out of our budget. We'd

need approval all the way up the chain of command. I don't see that happening. Not with all these rumors about layoffs."

I scuff at the landing with the heel of my shoe. I guess I can call around and shake out my sources, see if they drop a piece of information that I can turn into a story.

The truth is, I'm out of ideas.

Trish pushes her glasses back on the bridge of her nose.

"What happened to her father?" she asks.

"I don't know. Rebecca's supposed to keep tabs on his case. If something had happened, I'm sure she would've told me."

"Look into it anyway. At least I can say you're working on something."

"I'm always working. I work hard. You know that."

She sighs and looks at her nails.

"A lot of people around here don't like this story," she says. "We always have to look like we're making progress. The minute we hit a dead end, they're liable to pull the plug."

She gets up and smooths her skirt again. As we walk up the stairs she tells me that at yesterday's news meeting the national editor asked her where the story was going. He said he knew it was outside his department but he was curious. Anyway some of the people at his health club were asking and he couldn't give them any answers.

So Trish said this: "Tell them they'll find out if they keep buying the paper."

A couple of editors chuckled but many of them groaned and one guy on the layout desk said statements like that didn't exactly fill him with confidence. Trish acted as if she didn't hear them and kept presenting the items on her budget, but privately she resented these comfortable men leading comfortable lives running a comfortable paper for the benefit of people just like themselves.

She opens the door to the stairwell and I hear the sounds of the newsroom, snippets of conversation and occasional muffled laughter, but mostly what I hear is the soft *plup-plup-plup* of fingers striking computer keyboards.

"We're scared of this story," she says. "We don't want to admit it, but we are. We've never taken on anybody like Jeremiah Devlin, and it's making us all very nervous."

A trip to the beach reveals that Megan's father has moved and left no forwarding address. None of his neighbors know where he is or if the blond went with him. Most of them don't even know who I'm talking about.

A visit to the surf shop produces nothing but blank stares.

I sit in the car and watch the waves sparkle and dance. Megan's father doesn't strike me as the kind of guy who'd enjoy going on the lam, but he's engaged in unusual behavior for a man out on bail.

There's one other alternative. I drive to the courthouse and park in the garage below the building. After riding the elevator up to the ground floor, I grab the first phone I see and call Rebecca.

"What's going on?" she asks.

Her voice is thrilling but I'm in no mood for seduction. I tell her I need the case number for Megan's father. She finds it in her notes and asks why I want it. I tell her I don't have time right now.

In the records office I smile at the middle-aged black woman behind the desk. Shirley says she hasn't seen me for a while. I tell her I've been busy. She says she thought of me at church Sunday during the preacher's sermon about the prodigal son. I tell her I don't know how to react to that and she says I shouldn't attach too much significance. Sometimes things remind her of other things. She can't explain why.

I tell her I'm updating my files and want to check the progress of a case. When I give her the number she says it'll take a few minutes. I can wait or come back. It makes no difference to her. I tell her I'll be looking for a drink of water.

A sign over the fountain asks that you be considerate in your usage because of the drought. I wet my lips and look around. A prosecutor I know is sitting on a bench in the lobby. It looks like she's going over some briefs. I walk over and say hello. When she registers that it's me, she jumps an inch or two before settling down.

"I can't believe you came here today," she says. "Charles Manson is more popular in our office than you are."

"I'm not surprised. When he makes the news, you get good publicity."

She snaps her briefcase shut and says she's running late. When she stands I get up with her.

"I never thought you were the crusading type," she says before striding across the lobby. The late morning sun casts patterns of parallel lines on her back.

When I return to the records office Shirley glances at me but says nothing until I start drumming my fingers on the countertop.

"You're late," she says.

I tell her I was gone for only a few minutes.

"Late on the case. It was dismissed last week."

"On what grounds?"

"Insufficient evidence."

"Since when does the county require evidence to prosecute people?"

Shirley says I have an attitude and I tell her it's true, my attitude is sunny and pleasant and I find life a sheer joy. Then I ask her who filed the motion to dismiss and she names the prosecutor I just saw in the lobby. I thank Shirley for being so helpful and she says I can save the flattery. She knows I don't mean it.

"Fuck," Rebecca says at lunch. "Fuck fuck fuck fuck fuck fuck fuck."

I'd like to tell her to take it easy, this isn't a crisis, there's no reason to be so hard on herself. But I can't. The truth is, she's screwed up big time.

"I was working on other stuff. Nothing was happening here and I let it slide. Oh fuck. Fuck. Fuck fuck fuck fuck fuck fuck fuck."

I tell her about a story I did way back when. It concerned the husband of a young woman whose body had been found in a trash bag out in the desert. He was an auto mechanic and she was a hairdresser and they were both a year or two out of high school. The cops wouldn't say anything about the investigation but I needed something for the paper so I met the guy at a diner and he talked about how much he loved her even though their money was tight and they lived in a trailer and fought all the time. He told me love was funny that way and he still couldn't believe she was dead. As he answered my questions he kept taking off his wedding ring and twisting it back on. At the end of the interview we shook hands. I wished him good luck, returned to the newsroom and wrote up what he said. Two days later he was arrested and confessed everything. The authorities said it was like he wanted to talk. They sent him to San Quentin. The last time I heard of him, he'd become the top guy in the motor pool. Everybody always said he was a good mechanic.

"What's the point?" Rebecca says.

"I made a big mistake."

"What was it?"

"I never asked him if he did it."

"Twice in one day," the prosecutor says over the phone. "My horoscope warned me stuff like this would happen. Of course I'm a Virgo, so I don't believe in that shit."

I ask why she dropped the charges against Megan's father.

"I don't have the power to drop charges," she

reminds me. "Only the judge does. You can ask him why he did it, but judges hate to justify themselves."

I dislike Monica Rosen when she talks like this, but her ability to split hairs and resplit them, then assemble them in a design you never thought possible, explains why she graduated at the top of her class from Boalt Hall.

"Why did you file the motion to dismiss?" I ask.

"This office felt there wasn't enough evidence to obtain a conviction," she says. "Or sustain one, should an appeal be filed."

I tell her the procedure doesn't make sense. After a high-profile arrest, followed by allegations that the man is the head of a major drug ring, the whole matter is dropped so quietly nobody finds out about it until a week after it happened.

"Your paper fell asleep on the story," she says. "That's not my problem."

I ask if she knows where Megan's father went.

"We only keep track of people in the system. Right now he's as innocent as anybody."

I ask if she ever followed up on the report that Jeremiah Devlin had talked to Megan's father at the surf shop.

"No," she says. "It's an interesting piece of information. But in and of itself, it's insignificant."

In a half-joking manner I say she must be at loose ends and suggest she take the Brad Devlin case to a grand jury.

"If I was going to do that," she replies, "the last person I'd tell is you."

This makes me suspicious, but I have to call Shirley. She asks what I forgot. She says I talk to her only when I want something. I'm as bad as her kids.

I tell her I need the name of the lawyer who represented Megan's father. I should have written it down while I was there and I don't know why I didn't. With a sigh that's too dramatic to be weary, she says she'll look it up.

While I'm on hold a clerk from the city desk leans into my cubicle and says Rebecca's on line two. She's at a pay phone. I tell him to get the number. I'll call her right back.

Shirley informs me that the name I'm looking for is Daniel Yang, an associate in the firm Smith Pierce Fenner & Wilson.

I call Rebecca and ask where she is.

"The beach," she says. "I tried the cops but they wouldn't tell me anything."

She found a bartender who remembers seeing Megan's father about a week ago. He was with a blond. The bartender tried not to eavesdrop but they were the only people in the place. It was the middle of the afternoon. The blond said she wasn't sure about Australia and the guy said they had no choice and besides it was beautiful— great climate, terrific beaches and they sort of spoke English. The blond said she didn't want to leave L.A. The guy said it was too late to feel that way. Everything was taken care of.

A call to Daniel Yang is intercepted at the secretarial level. I leave a message and access our electronic library, where I start connecting names with other names, wondering if there are relationships the computer sees that I do not. And as I wait for a phone call I don't expect, I discover an interesting piece of information—although in and of itself, it could be insignificant.

Morgan Osborne was once the managing partner of Smith Pierce Fenner & Wilson.

When I stop at a light the radio says police are still investigating an early morning robbery in Van Nuys. A gang of youths broke into a house and ransacked it, then raped a teenage girl who'd been asleep in her bedroom. They forced her mother to watch before she was in turn assaulted by one of the youths who was apparently the ringleader. The others cheered him on. Police say they took nothing of value from the house and can't explain why the attack was so vicious.

As night crawls down to the horizon, darkness crowding out the day, I think of the womanchild waiting for me. My breath gets quick and shallow and my palms grow wet. I lean over and open the glove compartment. Inside is a souvenir from one of my earliest stories, long-forgotten words about a guy who died in police custody. I don't even remember his name. The cops said that after they brought him in for questioning he went into a cocaine-induced seizure, repeatedly bashing his head against the wall of the holding cell. There was nothing they could do.

The incident caused an outcry. There were allegations of brutality from the guy's family and the civil rights groups, but the internal investigation cleared everyone and the grand jury refused to indict.

When the whole thing was over, the sergeant who was on duty that night gave me the handcuffs the prisoner had been wearing. They rest comfortably atop the maps and papers I always keep within reach.

When I was three or four I was standing in the middle of the street, several houses down from mine, while a few feet away a big white dog with black spots and a bad temper snapped and snarled, and I couldn't recall how I'd gotten there and I was afraid to run and I was afraid the dog would kill me and above all else I didn't know why this animal was tormenting me because I hadn't done anything.

Sometimes I have nightmares about a hound or Doberman or mastiff lunging at me with no warning, knocking me to the ground as it growls and drools and bares its carnivore teeth, tearing at my throat as it pins me down. In the nightmare, I don't have time to scream.

nine

as soon as I'm awake I turn on the news. The DA's office says the drug case was routine, the dismissal perfectly in order. Despite the suspicions of the so-called civil liberties lobby, The People do not prosecute anyone unless the evidence is sufficient. In fact they're pleased when justice is served and innocent persons go free.

Police say the matter is closed. They have no further comment.

Rebecca stirs as I emerge from the bathroom. Above her on the headboard, the morning sun glints off the handcuffs.

At work I check my voicemail. There's a call from Connie Battaglia. I recognize her name from the trades. She used to work at one of the agencies but now she's gone solo. She asks if I've ever thought of writing a book.

I pour myself a cup of coffee and put on my headset. A call comes in, but I let it go for a couple of rings while I sip my drink.

"Metro. Ted Lowe."

"This is Daniel Yang. I read your story in the paper." His voice resonates with temporary aggravation, as if I've ruined his lunch plans.

Daniel Yang starts talking. After a while I discern that his displeasure stems from my mention, deep down in the article, that Morgan Osborne was once managing partner of the firm in which he, Daniel Yang, now labors as an associate.

"That has no relevance to the matter at hand," he says. "I can't understand why you included it."

"It's a fact, isn't it?"

"But facts form a pattern. At least they should. Otherwise they're just random bits of information."

He goes on to say that anyone who read my story probably believes that he or his firm or Morgan Osborne pulled strings to get the charges dismissed. He assures me it didn't happen that way.

"Then how did it happen?"

He says the DA's office had based most of its case on wiretaps, so he filed a discovery motion and listened to the conversations. Almost all of them were garbled.

"They must have known that going in," I say. "Why did they arrest him?"

"In the war on drugs, as in any war, propaganda is more important than victory."

I imagine a modern-day Goebbels laboring in a windowless lair in Washington, churning out releases and videos that say we are *winning* this struggle, triumph is in our grasp if only we persevere, the statistics support us despite the evidence of your eyes so if we lose, if the forces of darkness overwhelm us and unleash their barbarity upon our beloved land, the fault does not lie with those who made the policy (it never does); the fault lies with the Others, those who do not believe: the liberals (their influence is pernicious), the people of color who live only for the moment (they're not like us, you know), the media, the courts and let's not forget the Jews (their money must be behind the traffic).

I ask Daniel Yang if he has any idea where Megan's father is. He says he doesn't. And if he did, he wouldn't tell me. I ask if Megan's father could be in Australia by now with his companion. Daniel Yang says he has no idea. He does know that Australia has strict rules about immigrating.

"That's another thing you missed," Daniel Yang says. "I must say I find journalism a very sloppy profession."

I park on the street and walk past a liquor store and a florist. The sun bounces off the windows and into my eyes. It's impossible to see what's on the other side of the glass.

I stop at a door next to a dry cleaner and check the address. I got it from the phone book so I figure it's good. I open the door and walk up the narrow stairway, peeling paint on either side and the smell of cleaning chemicals substituting for air. My shoes make a faint squeaking sound on tired linoleum. Bare bulbs burn over all the landings.

When I knock on the door a voice tells me to come

in. The voice is eager and hopeful, the sound of a man wishing for good things, but not expecting them.

The tone of the voice will change as soon as its possessor sees me. I've known Maynard Reynolds a long time, although I haven't talked to him in years.

"Oh fuck," he says as soon as I enter the room. "For one brief, shining moment, Maynard thought he had a client."

He has a rickety desk and a couple of wooden chairs that would command a nice price at an antiques store. He also has a PC from Mattel and a filing cabinet that might reach his waist. Outside the window is a view of the concrete wall that belongs to the building across the alley.

"What do you want?" he asks.

I tell him I need information and advice of a legal nature. It concerns a story I'm working on.

"It's about Jeremiah Devlin and his son and that girl and all that crap you've been putting in the paper. Tell Maynard he's right."

I ask if he ever knew, or worked with, or heard anything about Morgan Osborne. Maynard says the man was a terrific tax lawyer, one of the legends. Even the guys from the IRS hated to go up against him.

"He ever do criminal law?"

"Closest he's ever come to that is watching *Perry Mason*. So when young Bradley is indicted, they'll hire a gun. Probably Richard Alvarez. If they can afford him."

Maynard laughs. He still has a sudden, high-pitched cackle that he lets out, almost involuntarily, whenever something strikes him as humorous.

I'm glad I made Maynard's day so amusing. His life has fallen on the serious side for more than a few years.

"What makes you so sure young Bradley will be indicted?"

Maynard leans forward in his chair and for a moment I have a vision of him leaping up and grabbing me by the shoulders and pushing me against the wall. I might like the sensation, that rarefied edge only danger can give you.

"Dispense with the act of ignorance, okay? That might work with some people, but Maynard knows what a calculating sonuvabitch you really are."

I think about leaving.

"Maynard knows why you're here."

It's been a long time since he argued in front of a jury. I guess I'll have to do.

"You need someone who knows how the DA's office works, but the folks downtown would suck on an exhaust pipe before they'd talk to you. So you decided to see your old friend Maynard. You knew he'd be too nice to kick you out."

He laughs again. It's a near-total contrast to his deep and sonorous voice, and I remember that whenever he addressed the courtroom I felt like I was listening to a pastor instead of a prosecutor. Of course his father was once the minister of the largest church in South-Central.

"I'm not convinced they'll indict Brad. As far as I know, they haven't presented anything to a grand jury yet."

"They have to indict him. Your stories guarantee

it. Maynard's former employer is running for re-election and it's all going smoothly, thank you very much, until this thing explodes in his face. Everybody who reads your newspaper thinks Jeremiah Devlin's son is getting away with murder."

I wonder if I'll get to cover the trial.

"If there's one thing on which Maynard would wager his meager annual income, it's this—his former employer does not want to indict young Brad Devlin. If you check the records, you'll discover that through the years Mr. Devlin has been a, shall we say, *generous* supporter of the county's top law enforcement official."

I should've thought to check on this myself.

"This does not mean young Bradley will be convicted," Maynard continues. "They'll put Monica on it—she's their ace—but it'll be a tough case to make. Even you can appreciate that."

"He did it," I say. "I'm certain of it. He killed Megan Wright."

"Whatever happened to the presumption of innocence?"

"C'mon, Maynard. Nobody believes in that anymore."

At first the clerk at the elections commission is reluctant to provide the lists I've asked for. It's only after I point out that the information is part of the public record, and threaten to have my newspaper's attorney call her superiors, that she prints out the names and figures I want.

She should have called my bluff on the attorney. He

charges three hundred an hour. All attempts to use him must be approved in advance by Howard Fussman.

At the office I go over sheaves of paper with names, numbers and dates, row upon row that, when looked at together, spell out the costs of democracy in mind-numbing detail. But I'm interested in only one name, and a half-hour of searching reveals that Jeremiah Devlin has donated money in ever-escalating amounts to all of the district attorney's campaigns.

I also requested a copy of Murray Cain's financial report. An examination of that list also turns up Jeremiah Devlin's name, although the contribution is significantly lower.

I call the flacks for both men. Messages are taken. When I call Morgan Osborne, I'm informed he's not in.

Trish's brows knit together as I tell her what I'm working on. She pushes her glasses back up her nose and says this is off the path a little but it's good stuff, so she'll push it at the news meeting.

"By the way," she says, "I have a request. It's from Fussman."

I restrain the urge to roll my eyes. "What is it?" I ask.

"He wants to know if you ever looked into those allegations Brad made about that other kid . . . What was his name?"

"Grant. Grant Fisher. I haven't looked into them. Because there's nothing there."

"How can you be sure if you haven't looked?"

It's a good question. I say nothing.

"Do you know where he was the night she was killed?" Trish asks.

"Do you?" I say.

"Can I at least tell Fussman you're trying to find out?"

I nod.

"And what about that stuff Brad's father said about being set up?"

"What about it?"

"Is there anything to it?"

I shake my head. "He's blowing smoke."

"Are you sure?"

"Absolutely."

"Can you write a story to that effect?"

"I'm not sure. I don't know if I can prove it."

"Try to. That way you'll get Fussman off my back."

When she walks away I start writing. Everything is on paper before me, so the facts are easy to lay out. I hope my readers can tell that the figures represent more than money.

My phone rings. I keep typing with one hand while I put on my headset with the other. The voice on the other end identifies himself as Murray Cain. His tone is nervous and quavering, like that of a pubescent boy who's been caught masturbating.

"I want to thank you," he says. "I want to thank you with all my heart. I'm glad you brought this matter to our attention."

He says his fundraisers have spent the last hour double-checking their records and they've confirmed that, yes, Jeremiah Devlin did make a donation to the campaign. I feel like saying that I don't need confirmation because I have a goddam piece of paper in my hands that tells me who made the contribution, when it was given and how much the amount was.

I mumble my uh-huhs. I want him to keep talking.

"You know how it is," he says. "Whenever we get money, if the check doesn't bounce, we assume it's okay."

He chuckles a bit and I can tell he wants me to join him. I don't respond. This will force him to use more words as he explains or justifies or evades.

He breathes deeply with a sound that comes close to a gasp, and when he resumes talking his voice slows, gets deeper; he wants every word he utters printed verbatim in the newspaper.

"In light of the investigation into that poor girl's death—"

"Megan," I say. "Her name was Megan Wright."

"Since that inquiry now involves Jeremiah Devlin's son, we feel we must return the contribution Mr. Devlin has made to our campaign. We are in no way judging or prejudging this case—the constitutional safeguards must always apply—but we believe quite strongly that it's best at all times to avoid even the appearance of a conflict of interest. These are the kinds of standards we intend to bring to the district attorney's office—standards, I regret to say, that have been sadly lacking in recent years."

I ask if he has a system that monitors the money coming into his campaign. He says he doesn't want it to sound as if he's pointing fingers because he's the candidate, so he guesses that ultimately he's responsible for what goes on, but in this area he's been relying totally on his finance people.

I thank him for his time. He tells me to have a nice day.

My phone rings again. The district attorney's campaign manager says he understands I've been making inquiries about some donations in this year's election cycle. I say only one contribution interests me. It was made by Jeremiah Devlin. The campaign manager says Mr. Devlin has been a supporter of the district attorney for a number of years. There's nothing illegal or improper about the money he's given.

His voice has the impatient tone that often belongs to Men Who Get Things Done.

"The donation was made before Megan Wright was killed," I say.

"You mean that girl you're trying to sell papers with? You don't care about whose name you drag through the mud, do you? I've known Jeremiah Devlin for years. His son is a fine young man. Mr. Devlin is one of the most outstanding citizens I've ever met. What have you ever done in your life to compare with what he's accomplished?"

I say Jeremiah Devlin's son has been named as a suspect in a murder investigation. Doesn't he think this situation might create a conflict of interest?

"Not at all. The only ones who think something underhanded is going on are people like you."

"Your opponent also received a donation from Jeremiah Devlin. Were you aware of that?"

There's a long pause, a pause from a man who's not used to information he finds disagreeable or upsetting, and finally he says no, he had no knowledge of that.

"He's gonna give the money back," I say. "Do you have any comment?"

"I never say anything about the opposition."

It's late at night, after primetime. I'm propped up in bed with the remote in my hand.

My lover is in the shower. I hear the water squirting onto her.

I flip past the sports channels and the music videos, the stand-up comics and the Home Shopping Network. I stop at the news. There was a killing in Pacific Palisades earlier this evening. A gang of youths encountered a homeless woman in a park overlooking the ocean. They took her belongings from a shopping cart and hurled them over the cliff. Then they tore off her clothes and, one by one, raped her. Police say the woman screamed but no one helped. When the youths were through they slashed her neck and wrists with shards of a broken bottle. Naked and bleeding, they threw her over the cliff and tossed the shopping cart after her. It landed on top of her body.

Police say the woman had nothing worth stealing. They say it was senseless. They can't figure out the motive for the attack.

Sometimes when I sit at my tube and stare at the words I've typed I wonder about the machine and the weird rays it emits while it does what it was designed to do. I wonder if I'm being bombarded with radiation and if I'm going to get cancer and if They know about it but haven't told anyone.

Some of my pregnant colleagues wear lead-lined aprons at their workstations.

ten

On my way out I stop by the city desk and persuade the clerks to switch the TV from the Dodger game to the six o'clock news. This prompts a few dirty looks from the men and one grumbles that it's a *playoff* game, goddammit, but I always like to check what the bubble-heads are leading with before I go home.

A dyed blond with a chirpy voice says the Valley break-ins have grown more brazen and brutal. She promises more details later in the broadcast. The camera shifts to her counterweight, a gray-haired man with a square jaw and lines in all the right places.

"Leading tonight's news—" he intones.

He was doing this before I was born. I wonder if he can connect these events to reality anymore, or if the stuff he's reading is just words on paper with no bearing on anything except his paycheck.

"—District Attorney Robinson Shields has announced he is returning a controversial campaign contribution from Jeremiah Devlin, the wealthy businessman and entrepreneur whose son has been linked to a murder investigation."

Around me people stop talking, stop typing, stop looking at the clock or looking through the wires, stop drinking coffee or eating greasy food from the cafeteria. I keep my eyes focused on the TV. I know everyone is staring at me.

The camera cuts to a reporter standing on the steps of the courthouse. It makes an impressive backdrop although the building has nothing to do with the story. I can't believe this guy has beaten me. They must have spoon-fed the information to him, knowing he'd scarf it up like a baby.

The reporter says the district attorney feels strongly that he has done nothing wrong, and he's afraid that sending the money back will be seen as an admission that something untoward was going on. But in the end he and his advisers feel it is more important to assure the public that the investigation into the death of that poor girl remains totally honest and aboveboard.

The camera cuts to the DA's campaign manager. He essentially repeats everything the reporter just said.

"Fuck," I say. I use the word quietly. Only those closest can hear. "Fuck fuck fuck fuck fuck fuck fuck." I head for my desk.

"How many words?" Trish asks.

"Six hundred," I say.

I put on my headset and start calling. The DA is unavailable of course and so is his campaign manager. I finally get hold of a flack who says the broadcast story was accurate as far as they're concerned and I can just use their quotes.

"I don't do things that way. Why are you returning the money?"

"It's the right thing to do. Am I on the record?"

"I was told last week that you weren't going to give it back."

"We reviewed the situation further. This was the action we wanted to take."

"And it has nothing to do with the fact that you've lost five points in the polls over the last week?"

"Everybody's right. You *are* a cynical sonuvabitch."

Trish tells me she needs the story. We're already a half-hour past deadline.

"One more call," I say.

Murray Cain answers the phone in the glum monotone of a candidate who knows his best issue has been taken away. But I already know how I should write the story. I need the right quotes from him to let me do it.

I ask about what the DA has done. He says it's the right thing but it sure took them a long time.

"The DA's people," I say, "deny that their decision to return the money is related to the fact that you've gained five points in the polls since the story broke."

I can almost hear him smiling. At times I think I should become a consultant.

"I'm sure the voters won't be fooled by this smoke-screen," he says, his voice rallying. "They'll remember who responded in an ethical manner, and who went through contortions in an effort to retain a tainted contribution."

I wish he'd called it blood money.

• • •

Trish summons me to her stairwell. As soon as she sits on her favorite step I tell her I've been kicking myself for not getting that story first. I figure the DA's people gave it to the bubbleheads as a way of getting even.

She waves away my words. That's not what worries her. She would have liked the story exclusively but she says I recovered nicely. The stuff from the DA's challenger was good and TV didn't have it. I say it never occurs to the bubbleheads that there are usually two sides to a story.

"More than two sides," Trish says.

I ask what's bothering her.

She says this was the first story I've had in the paper all week. I tell her I've been trying but nothing's come up. Usually when you drill a well you hit only rocks and dirt.

Trish says the first round of layoffs was announced today. Two-thirds of the people in circulation were let go. The new CEO believes it's more efficient to farm out those jobs to independent contractors who'll work for less, with no benefits.

"That doesn't affect us," I say.

"Everything affects us," she says.

She goes on. At the news meeting Fussman asked if there were any developments in that young girl's death.

"Megan," I say. "Her name was Megan Wright."

"I know her name," Trish says.

She told him there was nothing new and he said it's been a few days since anything happened. Trish asked if he expected a blockbuster every day and he said he did. That got some chuckles from the men around the table. Fussman said the story might have reached a dead end. All stories do after a while. He's also concerned about the allocation of resources. Having a staffer on this full-time makes no sense if we're getting nowhere. Trish said we can't be under pressure to file every day. Besides, if it weren't for us the authorities would have forgotten Megan's death by now.

Fussman asked if we were pursuing the right people. He wanted to know about that other boy Brad Devlin talked about. The girl, too. Did we ever find out anything about them?

Trish told him I was working on it.

She stops and looks at me directly.

"Are you?" she asks.

"I haven't had time," I say. I scratch at the floor with my shoes. I should shine them one of these days.

"Christ," she says. I have the feeling she wants me to look at her.

"Fussman thinks there's something there," she says. "I don't know why. You might think he's a jerk. I might even agree with you. But he's the city editor and he's made a request and you should look into it."

"That would just waste my time," I tell her. "There's nothing there."

Trish asks if I've developed anything that's even close to going into the paper.

"No," I tell her. "I don't think I'll have anything ready for the next couple of days."

She says she's afraid they'll take me off the story. In

fact she's sure the decision has been made. They're just looking for a way to justify it.

I tell her I'd like a few days off. She asks if I'm kidding. I say I have some comp time coming and this seems like a good occasion to use it. She reminds me that vacations and long weekends are a favorite time for reassigning people. I say I'd just like to get away and recharge my batteries. She asks where I plan to do this.

"Tahoe," I say.

"The company won't pay for your trip."

"That's okay. I hear it's nice up there."

She stands and smooths out her slacks. She looks better in a dress but I'm not the person to tell her. As we walk up the stairs she asks if I ever found out anything about Megan's diary.

I lock Rebecca's hands into the cuffs and push her down until she's on all fours in the tub. I use a thick piece of rope to tie the cuffs around the faucet and then I turn on the water and slide my fingers inside her until she tells me she can't stand it anymore and then I get in the tub behind her and sink to my knees and push myself in. She tells me not to stop. She tells me to go harder. She tells me to come inside her. I obey all her commands.

When I'm done I sink back into the water. I like how it rolls over my body, taking away the grit I've accumulated, cleansing me, purifying. When we get out we pat each other dry with big white towels and go into the bedroom. Rebecca turns on MTV.

"I heard something at the office," she says. "It's been bothering me all day."

She says they're talking about moving her off the cop beat. They want to make her a researcher on a twelve-part series about the drought. I say it could be an important project. She says it sounds boring. Everyone knows there's a drought and it won't be over until it rains. End of story.

"I bet they give my beat to that guy from Stanford," she says. "They've always liked him more than me."

I shake my head. "They'll have me do the cop roundup. And the spinoff stories. Two people are doing my old job and we can't have that. What would the stockholders say?"

"What about the murder?"

I tell her I've hit a dead end. Management has no patience with workers who don't produce. "So I've decided to take a few days off," I say. "I'm thinking of going to Tahoe. Wanna come?"

Her eyes flash with understanding as she smiles, then laughs. She says she'd love to go and I tell her we can stay at an inn I've heard about that has a waterfall in the courtyard. The owners serve fresh fruit every morning.

"Helluva story you're working on," one of the old-timers said to me at the watercooler.

I mumbled something that I hoped he interpreted as appreciation. The guy has always made me nervous. He owns a lot of guns.

"Why are you so obsessed with it?" he asked.

"I'm not obsessed," I said.

eleven

a s streaks of light slither through the blinds my eyes pop open and I wonder if I've slept at all. Rebecca is a dark thing huddled next to me, the sheets pulled up over her chin. I get up—I hope silently—use the bathroom, gather the clothes I discarded last night in my frenzy to get at her. As I button my shirt I lean over and lick her ear. She giggles and smiles sleepily.

"Will you call me?" she asks.

"Of course."

"About Tahoe?"

"I wouldn't think of going without you."

I believe I know what I am going to do even though I've said nothing to myself. Some deep part of me is aware of how the day and night will unfold and it is this portion of my being that I obey.

I was taught we have free will. I was taught we are responsible for our actions.

After my first coffee of the day I call Frank Gruley. I figure he too has had time for morning caffeine and a chance to check the box scores and body count. He answers before the first ring is over.

"Christ, did you see this?" he asks. "Dodgers gave up four unearned runs in a playoff game. A playoff game. Christ. Don't they teach anybody how to field the fucking ball?"

"It's a lost art," I say. "Like all the other old-fashioned skills."

"Why did you call?" he says. "I know you hate sports."

"I don't hate them. I even watch them sometimes. I just don't care about them."

I go on to tell him that I'm curious about Grant Fisher. More accurately, my boss is.

"I'm not going to say anything about Grant Fisher," the detective says.

"Why not?"

"Maybe I just don't feel like it."

"Jeremiah Devlin is trying to set him up for Megan's death, isn't he?"

"Could be. Could be he isn't wrong, either."

"Come on. We both know who killed Megan."

"You've met the kid," Gruley says. "What do you think?"

"I've met both kids."

"So you're an expert."

I rent a car from a place I find in the Yellow Pages but wait until dark to drive it. On the radio the forecast calls for sunshine all week. I park at a twenty-four-hour lot and catch a bus that lets me off at the base of the hill on which Megan's community is located. A diner on the corner is open till two. I sit at the counter and drink several more cups of regular.

Sometimes I try to make sense of all the things that pass before me, undertake an effort to create a cosmic whole out of the chaos dominating my life. Although I don't mind the chaos. It's a natural part of the way things are.

I swirl the dregs at the bottom of my cup and consider how it came to be that I am drinking just this substance at just this time in just this place. The truth, of course, is that I don't know. I never really know why I do anything.

I suppose this stuff came from Colombia or perhaps Brazil. I imagine a peasant, his fingers stained the color of indigo, walking through the fields and picking the beans only a few at a time. It's backbreaking labor and when his sack is full he brings it to the foreman, who short-weights it and pays him a few cents for every pound. The stuff is taken by truck or riverboat to a plant where it's roasted, then put on a freighter and shipped to a port in a container, where a huge crane plucks it from the deck and puts it on another truck, ready to fill the grocery shelves the next day.

I imagine the beans going into a grinder and mixing with water that has traveled hundreds of miles across, over and under the desert. The waitress draws it out of a huge metal urn and puts it in front of me and I suppose all she thinks about is whether she has to make another batch. When I drink it the taste is acrid and bitter but for some reason I like it, even the smell makes me more awake as I consider what I'm about to do.

I still haven't acknowledged it to myself. It's as if this is happening to someone else.

I can hear Noreen saying all this caffeine is bad for me, especially so late at night.

Just before midnight I leave some money on the counter and begin to walk. The hill seemed steeper when I drove it. I wear black jeans and a dark jacket.

I stop near the gate just beyond the sightline of the guardhouse. I reach into my pocket and take out a batch of firecrackers I bought the last time I was in San Francisco. The vendor claimed they'd bring me good luck. I light the fuse and toss the pack into the street. *Pop-pop-popping* fills the night air as I press myself against the wall of Megan's community.

I edge toward the guardhouse. It's brightly lit but looks vacant. After a second I observe a hat poking up, followed by a head, and then an upper torso. The guard looks in every direction and slowly leaves the shack. She's armed with a flashlight.

"Who's there?" she asks as she approaches the street. She beams her flashlight up and down, to the left and right, then notices the firecrackers and moves toward them. She squats down and picks them up, shaking her head.

I walk quickly through the gate and make a fast right. By now I know where the house is. When I reach it I turn smartly and go up the driveway and past the garage, sticking close to the concrete barrier topped with wood that separates this place from the one next door. After a few seconds I emerge in the backyard. The outdoor furniture is arranged neatly around the pool, but the grass seems long, the shrubs overgrown.

Megan might have died here. I know I should search for something that might tell me but I'm afraid someone will see me and report a prowler.

I put a deck chair under a window, climb onto the seat and remove the screen. When I press my fingers against the glass it glides up easily, an open portal beckoning me. I ease myself through, land on my feet and close the window behind me.

I hear no sounds. I wait for a dog or an alarm, the ticking of a clock or even my own breathing. In a few moments my eyes get used to the blackness of this space. It differs from the dark outside, where at least I had streetlamps and stars and moonlight. In this house there's no brightness at all. The air is stale and still, everything suffused with gloom.

I remember to crouch. I don't want anyone to see a shadow through the window. As I scurry past the dining room table I run my fingers over it and pick up a layer of dust. The table feels made of real wood, probably oak, and I imagine that their plates and bowls and cups are authentic china carefully ordered from the proper stores.

I recall standing in the hall talking to Megan's mother in what seems like the distant past. I can see her with her arm outstretched, holding her daughter's picture as if it were an offering to the gods of the media. The woman had her secrets that day, but she talked anyway, and I suppose she was as candid as her situation allowed.

I wonder why she opened the door.

I wonder why people talk.

At the foot of the stairs I turn into the audiovisual room off to the left. There's a large-screen TV, so it's likely this is where any family interaction took place. The timer on the VCR is still on. I kneel before the machines and flip through the tapes stacked neatly beneath them. Most are of movies I haven't seen. The Wrights were especially fond of animated features.

As I climb the stairs my hiking shoes sink into the carpeted steps so there's no telltale sound of soles striking wood, no noise indicating human presence.

On the second-floor landing I notice an open doorway immediately to my right and a hall to my left that stretches into the darkness. I turn right. As I enter the room my first instinct is to turn on the lights, but I stop my hand as it reaches for the switch.

The bed is small and the curtains are drawn. After a few seconds I make out posters on the walls and objects on the floor. I move close to one of the posters and run my hand over it, as if that will make me see better, and then I squint and finally I can tell that it's a picture of one of the guys on the Lakers. In the corner of the room is a basketball and a jersey, and scattered all around are player cards that could be worth a lot of money someday.

There's something comforting about the boyishness of this space. It could be my room when I was growing up.

I walk down the hall. An open door on my right reveals a narrow bathroom that ends with a shower. If I were doing this thoroughly I'd root around in there, find out what brand of shampoo they use and whether Megan's mother flosses.

Ahead of me, now clear despite the darkness, is another open door. At first I'm inclined to go in but as I get closer I see a mountainous vanity, a queen-size bed and adult decor.

I stop. To my right is a door that's closed tight and I have to wonder why. It's the only entranceway in the house that's blocked. I put my hand on the knob and start to turn.

It sticks. I turn it the other way but the same thing happens. I yank and pull but I only fill the hall, and possibly the house, with the sound of a locked door denying a desperate bid for entry.

I reach into my back pocket and take out a pick. Rebecca gave it to me. She showed me how to use it. She made it seem easy. I slide it into the lock and twist gently a few times. When I hear something snap, I try the door again.

This time it opens.

I'm told that the explorers of the pharaohs' tombs beheld priceless relics that the ancients buried beside their rulers, items selected with great thought and care because their leader, although human, was also divine.

The riches before me consist of a brass bed, several posters and a menagerie of stuffed animals. As I enter my feet press against the floorboards, which moan softly, unused to the weight I bear.

Her bedcovers are pulled tight over a fluffed-up pillow. The animals are bunched together. I paw through the collection, lifting one toy after another. These things could be witnesses. If only they could talk. I toss them aside in my search but there's nothing between them, nothing underneath except bedspread.

I open all the drawers of her dresser but they contain only clothes. Megan favored tie-dyed shirts and baggy shorts, at least for casual wear. She also had numerous pairs of jeans and caps. In her closet I find some skirts and dresses, as well as tops and accessories that could be worn on occasions more formal than school or hanging out. On the floor are several sets of sneakers. She liked the ones you have to pump up.

All of her belongings have the feel of stuff that's new. They all bear the logos of top-of-the-line makers.

I haven't found what I'm looking for, but there's still one place to search. I should have gone there first. I don't know why I didn't. Perhaps I just wanted to look at all of her things.

I sit at her desk. I imagine Megan hunched over her lessons, brushing her hair out of her eyes as she studied the things schoolchildren must learn—the westward migration of the United States, the hypotenuse of a right triangle, the conjugation in Spanish of the verb "to be." But after a while she'd put away her books or at least push them off to the side and take out what mattered most to her and in it she'd set down what happened that day, as well as her thoughts and hopes and fears.

Most important, I hope, she wrote down her secrets.

I thought no one kept a diary anymore. It sounded like something out of *Little Women*.

I have to see this thing. I have to take it away from here and put it in my possession.

Neatly arranged on the surface of her desk are textbooks on English and history, a ruler and a big long pen with something fuzzy on top. I put my hand on the top drawer and slide it open. The drawer is large and deep and I have to move the chair back to look in all the way. In front are term papers, a stapler and a pair of scissors. In back, shoved against a rear corner, is a dark rectangular object. As I draw it closer to me I discern that it's a videotape. There are no markings on it—no indication at all as to what it can be—and I have to wonder why it's here instead of downstairs in the TV room. For a moment I think of going there and putting the tape in the machine, but I'm afraid the glow from the TV would attract attention. I open my jacket and put the tape in an inside pocket, then zip up tightly.

I put my hand on the bottom drawer and pull it out. The space inside is deep, with books and pads piled atop one another in an orgy of randomness. Apparently Megan didn't mind disorder as long as no one could see it. I get on my knees and sift through the items, pushing them around and aside and burrowing deeper until finally I see a small square book with a white vinyl cover with the words "My Diary" embossed on it. As I bring it toward my eyes I notice a metal lock covering the pages. I tell myself I can break it easily.

What did she write I can't wait to look her secrets are within my reach I can't wait to look everything I want to know is inside I can't wait to look I have to know what's inside I can't wait to look—

The light on the ceiling explodes into brightness and suddenly I'm blind; I cover my eyes with my free hand as if that will restore my sight; my head sinks toward the floor.

"Did you find it?"

The voice sounds young and male. I don't believe I know it.

"We've been waiting for you. We knew you'd come here."

The drawer is only a few inches from me and the small white book shines like a diamond at noon. Rebecca was right. The diary belonged here.

I could push away the boy at the door, bolt from the house and into the darkness that has always protected me.

I raise my head slowly and look at him. He's pointing a gun at my face.

The boy is squat and chunky. He looks sixteen or seventeen. Long greasy hair sprouts from underneath a baseball cap he wears backward. His T-shirt bears the name of a heavy metal band and his shorts reach to his knees.

He waves the gun a bit, pointing to the open drawer. The gesture makes me nervous. If he blasts me away, I want him to mean it.

"Close it," he says.

I push the drawer shut with fingers so dry they slip off. I still have her diary in my left hand. I'm ready to smash the lock, open the book and read.

"Give it to me," he says.

For the first time since this began, he smiles.

"It's mine," I say.

"I'll shoot you."

"I need to have this."

The boy brings the gun closer to my face. I can see into the barrel. I imagine the sound of a trigger being pulled and then, before I've even had time to register what I've just heard, explosive metal smashing into my face.

I wonder if my life would flash before me. I wonder what I would regard as important.

"Have you ever killed anyone?" the boy asks.

I shake my head.

"It's the easiest thing in the world."

As I extend my arm I feel I'm surrendering a piece of her and for a moment I consider yanking it back, clutching the diary to my chest in a melodramatic gesture and saying he can't have it, this was hers but now it's mine, we've bonded in a way he'll never understand.

He takes the diary and tells me to get up.

"They're right," he says. "You're a vulture. Nothing but a fucking vulture."

He backs up a couple of steps. This gives me enough space to walk out. In the hall he tells me to keep going. As I do, he turns out the light in Megan's room.

We go down the stairs. I hear him behind me. I wonder where he's aiming the gun.

"Open the door," he says.

We head into the night and I welcome it the way I'd greet the grasp of my lover. A BMW is parked at the curb. I see two heads in the backseat.

"Get in," he says.

I ease into the front seat on the passenger side. The streetlights cast pale shadows. Lamps glow in the windows of a few of the homes. Perhaps someone is watching us. Most likely no one is interested.

The car's audio system is turned as high as it will go, bombastic drums and screeching guitars backing vocals that remind me of the honking and yelling of rush-hour traffic. The boy hands his gun to one of the kids in back before getting into the driver's seat.

The car glides forward, leaving the house dark and empty behind us.

The heads in back nod in sync, keeping time to this stuff on the stereo. When we stop at the shack, the guard lets up the gate and waves to us. We turn right when we're through. Along the boulevard the shops are closed and shuttered.

We merge onto the freeway and go west for a while. At the interchange we veer south and begin climbing a steep hill. At the crest we get off and cruise for a few minutes on a blackened surface street. Every so often I glimpse the lights in the Valley stretching farther than I can see. As the car slows and halts, I realize it's been a while since I've gone to the top of Sepulveda Pass.

Another car is already there. I'm bad with make-and-model stuff but I believe it's a Lexus. The chunky kid tells me to get out, but the other ones stay in the car. My shoes crunch into the hard sand and I imagine she heard a similar sound that night as he carried her here, heavy footsteps the last signal to enter her consciousness.

But she was drowned. She was already dead. The medical examiner was emphatic about that.

Did she know she was about to die? Or was the whole enterprise a surprise to her? At this moment I feel connected to the girl whose death has drawn me here, to this place at this time, because she must have realized her death was imminent and known they were going to snuff out her life and there was nothing she could do.

I wonder if she asked anyone for help.

I wonder what it was like to do it.

Three guys are standing by the trunk of the other car. Two of them have shorn hair and ripped T-shirts but their faces are dark, lost in the night. The other one's back is to me.

"We've been waiting for you."

I recognize Brad's voice right away.

"Is this the guy?" one of the kids with shorn hair asks. "The shithead?"

"Yeah," Brad says.

"What do you want us to do with him?"

"Nothing yet," Brad says.

The chunky kid gives the gun to Brad.

"We should go to that place in Glendale," one of the group says. "It's ready."

"I hate Glendale," another kid says. "It's a fucking pit."

"If you don't wanna go to Glendale, where do you wanna go?"

"I don't know. I just hate fucking Glendale."

"Let's fucking do it," Brad says. "I'm not gonna stand around here all fucking night."

The chunky kid leads me back to the BMW. He tells the guys in back that we're going to Glendale. In the rearview mirror I see their heads nodding a bit.

"What's in Glendale?" I ask.

"A house."

One of the guys behind me snickers. Soon we're on the freeway, descending in the fast lane, accelerating into the depths of the Valley.

"Why did we go there?" I ask.

"It's what Brad wanted," the chunky kid says.

"Why did he dump her there?"

My head snaps back and I feel a rope pulled taut against my neck; the rough edge of twine burns my skin and suddenly there's no oxygen in the world; I start to gasp; my eyes bulge in their sockets and I raise my arms, extending them as far as they will go; maybe they'll reach some air—

The kid behind me shouts in my ear and at first it's just noise, the sounds rush together and his rage is the only thing that registers, but as my breath escapes his words become distinct and as I hear them I wonder if they're the last words of all—

"—your fucking questions! That shit you put in the newspaper! We're tired of it. That shit just happened, okay? There's no fucking reason or anything! So just stop asking these fucking questions!"

He releases the rope and the air rushes into me; it feels like life; I suck it all down until I start coughing— deep, violent, shaking coughs that force my head to buckle down until it's between my knees and for a moment I think I'm going to puke.

"Christ," the voice behind me says, "if there's one thing I can't stand, it's fucking questions."

The car slows, then stops, then starts again. I believe

we're off the freeway. Behind me the guys talk about a concert they saw last week.

We turn onto a side street, heading deeper into darkness. Outside the window I can see the forms of the houses we're passing, small one-story things spewed out and stamped down here in what was once America's Promised Land.

The BMW turns again and the engine cuts off. We coast for a bit before stopping. When my feet reach the ground I stumble and grab onto the door and pull myself up. Shaking my head, I look around for a reference point, perhaps a shaft of light that could tell me where I am, but even the lamps overhead are out. There are certain things cities can't afford anymore, and lighting the dark is one of them.

The other car stops silently and we walk up the driveway of the house closest to us. The guy who was sitting behind me carries a coil of rope. Several of the others wield baseball bats. I assume Brad still has the gun.

We walk around to the rear of the place, past the garbage cans and the papers set out for recycling. At the back door one of the kids hunches over the lock for a few seconds. The lock pops, the door opens and we walk through.

The kitchen is small. We fill the space. A couple of wiry chairs are thrust deep under a tiny table. The kids reach into their pockets and pull masks over their heads and for a moment I feel exposed, but then the guy standing next to me places a ski mask in my hand.

We creep down a narrow hall that ends with an open door. I see a sleeping form with a blanket drawn lightly over it. A ceiling fan whirs inside the room. Three of my companions walk in and shake whoever it is by the shoulder. The form stirs and when its head rises from the pillow, I can tell it's a woman. She opens her eyes with the tired disgust of a person who doesn't get enough sleep.

Her eyes flash wider. Her mouth opens. She's been awakened in the dead of night and the first thing she observes are three guys in ski masks and immediately she realizes what's going on: the soldiers of darkness have invaded her home; her defenses have proved useless; even here she is not safe.

One of the guys swings a baseball bat toward her face. It smashes into her with a soft crack. I can't tell if the noise is from the bat or her skull. Her head snaps against the wall and her body flops onto the bed. Even in the dark I can see blood running from her nose and mouth. It stains the sheets and her nightgown.

"You hit her too hard," one of the kids says.

"She was gonna scream. If there's one thing I can't stand, it's fucking screaming."

Two of the guys carry her from the room. I step aside as they pass.

"I hope she's conscious."

It's Brad's voice.

"I want her to watch this."

I follow my companions into the living room. One of them makes sure the blinds are drawn. Another turns on the lights. I blink and squint. It's almost like being in the sun.

By now the woman has been tied into a chair, her

hands knotted behind her back and her ankles strapped against the wood. Blood trickles out of her, falling in drops to the floor as her head bobs from side to side. I hear gurgling noises coming from her throat.

She's Asian, about the same age as Megan's mother and Noreen. Her hair is dark and falls in clumps over her face. Her nightgown hangs loosely but I can tell from the contours of her flesh that her skin has grown flabby from childbirth and junk food.

I hear feet slamming against a hardwood floor. It sounds like someone trying to run but being stopped after a couple of steps. The noise of silent struggle follows as several people push and grab and kick each other. I turn in time to see three of the guys dragging a girl into the room. She too is wearing a nightgown, a soft pink garment with a floral design. She flails and wriggles but my companions have too strong a grip.

They fling her onto the couch. She lands on her back. She's already been gagged.

The woman sits up straight and shakes her head, like someone trying to jolt herself awake. She opens her mouth but before she can emit any sounds Brad shoves the gun between her teeth and says she better not do it, if she doesn't stay quiet her fucking head is gonna get blown wide fucking open.

The girl looks like she's Megan's age. The guys tear off her nightgown and throw it to the side, then push her onto the floor. She tries to hit them but my companions only laugh. They pin her arms over her head and one of the guys takes out a pair of handcuffs and snaps them on her wrists.

Brad moves the gun around in the woman's mouth.

"Do you like this?" he asks. "Do you like what we're doing?"

She tries to draw back. Her eyes are so wide they seem like globs of white with little brown beads in the middle.

"You better nod your head," he says. "You better nod your fucking head, bitch. Can you even understand what the fuck I'm saying?"

The girl thrashes on the floor. Two of my companions crouch on either side of her and press her ankles to the hardwood.

"She's giving us a hard time."

"Fucking bitches. They never fucking learn."

One of the guys rapes her. The gag muffles her screams. When he's done he pulls up his pants and calls out "Next!" like a deli manager taking orders at lunch.

I lean forward on the couch to observe more closely. This is like watching my work come to life. Now I know exactly what happens at night.

Brad is the last to go. He gives the gun to one of his friends before heading to the girl. By this point she has stopped resisting and just lies flat and still on the floor of her home. When Brad is through with her, he walks back to the guy now holding the weapon in the woman's mouth. Brad murmurs something and both of them laugh. Then Brad crouches beside her and says something I can't hear. The gun is removed from her mouth and the other guy lowers his pants and positions himself in front of her face.

She could scream now, let out the fear inside and

hope the sound will wake someone who'll call some-body who'll do something.

I cannot act. Perhaps I don't want to.

Instead she does what he wants. There's no fear left inside her. There's probably nothing left at all.

The other guys take their turns. One of them rips off the woman's nightgown and goes between her legs. A few return to the girl on the floor.

One of my companions asks Brad if they should get rid of these bitches. He doesn't respond right away.

"Don't kill us."

The words are soft but startling, muttered in a monotone by a voice that's otherworldly. The woman stirs in her chair, trying to lift her head so she can better plead with these creatures in her house.

"We've done what you wanted. Please don't kill us."

Brad walks toward me and looks down at the floor. The baseball bat has rolled against my feet. I bend over and pick it up with both my hands. I think of what I could do—*rise up, smash him, take them on, avenge the atrocity . . .*

I look in his eyes and I think I see them smiling.

"Isn't this fun?" he asks quietly.

I hand him the bat. He takes a few steps and swings with a smooth, fluid motion, smashing the woman's face. Her body jerks back. She and the chair tumble to the floor. Brad kicks her in the stomach and she absorbs it as if she were a pillow.

Brad stalks to the television, raises the bat and uses his sweet swing to crash through the screen. It shatters with a crinkling sound. I see specks swirling through the air. The light dances off them as if they were crystals.

Some of my companions overturn the furniture, smashing the lamps and ripping the legs off tables. The others run back toward the bedrooms. I hear drawers opened and thrown to the floor, doors torn from their hinges, mirrors cracked and broken.

The sound of breaking glass thrills me. It's a true noise of the night. The people who live here have spent years, perhaps a lifetime, assembling the stuff that lines the shelves and fills the rooms. Now all of it has been destroyed in a few unthinking ticks of the clock.

We leave through the kitchen, saying nothing as we walk toward the cars. I wonder if any of the neighbors saw us and thought there was anything unusual. I imagine the backyard conversations a few hours from now among persons who haven't talked to each other in years, registering disbelief over their fences that such an awful event occurred here. It must be the work of those gangs we keep hearing about. I tell you, we have to do something about Those People.

When we get in the BMW we take off our masks. The chunky kid turns on the radio. I hear screech guitar, thunderous bass, megadrums.

"Good song," one of the guys in the backseat says.

We go slowly, coming to a full halt at all the stop signs, never going faster than the posted speed limit. The streetlights get stronger as we near the freeway. When we exit the road we cruise down a boulevard, then turn left on a residential street lined with two-story houses. We stop before one of them and the kid directly behind me opens his door, says good night and gets out. His two friends say they'll see him tomorrow. He walks up the driveway with his hands in his pockets.

A few blocks over we end up in front of a place with a well-manicured lawn that looks as if it's tended by professionals. The other kid in back gets out. As he closes the door he says he was glad to meet me.

The chunky kid asks where I want to go. I think of the car I rented in that all-night lot, the toll rising with each minute it stays there. But then I realize there are still some things I want to find out. I am good at what I do. I have been trained for this.

"I want to see Brad," I say.

"You're out of your fucking mind," he says.

"You know where he is, don't you?"

"I'm not gonna do a fucking thing for you."

Suddenly I find myself grabbing at his shirt and pulling his flabby round face close to mine and telling him he's going to do what I fucking say and I'm tired of him and his fuckhead buddies fucking around with me and I have half a mind to drive his fucking head through the fucking windshield just because I fucking feel like it.

He pushes himself away from me. I think he'd like to get out of the car, but it's probably his father's.

"Okay okay okay," he says. "There's no reason to act like that. Christ."

He drives me to the top of Sepulveda Pass. A car is parked there. Sitting on the trunk is a solitary figure smoking a cigarette and staring at the lights of the Valley. I wonder if he has Megan's house pinpointed and looks at it for hours, hoping that she'll return if only he keeps vigil long enough. Perhaps he holds imaginary conversations with her as he sits there. Perhaps he tells her he's sorry.

I remind myself that her house is dark. There is no trace of life within it.

Brad doesn't turn as we approach. I stop a few feet from him and watch as he sucks smoke.

"He made me do it, Brad," the chunky kid says. "He made me take him here."

Brad says nothing for a few seconds before asking, "What do you want?" in the bored tones of a convenience store clerk at the end of his shift.

"What are you gonna do with the diary?" I ask.

"I dunno. Read it. Burn it. It doesn't matter."

"You liked Megan, didn't you?"

"Yeah."

"So why did you kill her?"

"Who says I did?"

"Come on, Brad. If you didn't do it, who the fuck did?"

"I could've killed you," he says. "I could've left you in that house. But I wanted to take you with us. I thought that would be better."

"Why?"

"I wanted you to see what we do. I wanted you to see what it was like. You sit on your ass all day and write these stories about what goes on—but you don't know. You don't know anything." He pauses before asking, "What did you think?"

My mouth is dry and my lips are cracking. I've never wanted a glass of water so badly.

"You liked it, didn't you? You liked what you saw."

He pauses, then says this: "Just wait till you see what we do to you."

He throws the cigarette to the ground, gets in his car and drives off. I see the ember of the stub glowing on the tinder-dry ground and grind it out with my heel.

"Why'd you do that?" the chunky kid asks.

"It could start a fire."

"So?"

We get in the BMW and drive back to the Valley. As we swing onto the boulevard where I've left my car, the chunky kid looks at the gauge and says he thinks we need gas. We pull up to a pump. He asks if I have money. I give him a ten and he walks to the booth. As he starts pumping I get out of the car. I've always liked the smell of gasoline.

The attendant's booth is a brightly lit cage that's locked of course, filled with a cash register and cartons of junk food and stacks of gum. Inside it is a form that has its head turned down, as if it's reading something—and then I recognize who it is and it seems shocking that he's here. I don't know if I should walk over and say hello and ask if he remembers me, or if that would add to the humiliation he undoubtedly feels every second he spends here.

I go to the booth anyway. He looks up just as I'm ready to rap on the glass.

"Hello, Raul," I say.

He puts the book aside. It's one of those motivational self-help tomes.

"It's good to see you again," he says. "Are you with the lady?"

I shake my head and tell him we broke up. He says that's too bad. He liked and admired her and thought we looked good together. I say it didn't work out. It's nobody's fault. He nods and says yes, he supposes that's the way it is. He's almost forgotten. It's been a long time since he was concerned with such things.

I say I don't mean to pry, but I'm surprised to see him here. I was wondering what happened to his restaurant. If he doesn't mind telling me.

Raul says he had to close it. He did the best he could but when the economy turns bad you can't force people to go out to eat. I say I'm sorry. I always thought he ran a nice place, with good value for the money. He thanks me and says he'll be back. He plans to go into business again. It's a matter of waiting for things to turn around and then the banks will be more generous and he'll be able to arrange the financing. But it won't be a restaurant next time. That's too hard. He says he's thinking of starting a limousine service but in the meantime he works here. It's not what he wants, but sometimes there are things a man must do.

Raul leans close to the glass and says he wants to discuss something. He's glad the fates have done this and we have this opportunity to talk. I tell him to go ahead. I'm listening. In a low voice that reeks of secrets and conspiracies he says he's been reading my stories, he still follows the case and the evidence seems to point in one direction, doesn't it? I say that it does.

I hear a loud honk, sharp and insistent, and when I turn to look I see the chunky kid drumming his fingers on the steering wheel. I smile at Raul (I imagine apologetically) and say it seems my ride is getting a little impatient. Raul says he understands. It was good to see me again. He'd like to shake my hand but he's not allowed to leave the booth. It's dangerous outside.

I get in the car and we pull away quickly. After a few minutes the kid stops across the street from the lot where I've left my rental. In the trailer that guards the place, light from a bare bulb glares down on a man who has his chair propped against the wall, eyes closed and head back in the classic posture of a veteran of the graveyard shift.

I step onto the sidewalk as the BMW drives away. I stand on the curb and wait for the WALK sign. When it turns I cross the street, enter the lot and stop at the trailer. Its door is locked and low snoring comes from within. I rap on the door. The man's eyes open. His chair surges forward. He's black, about fifty, with the scared but weary look of a man who's been fired from a lot of jobs.

"I was resting my eyes," he says. "That's all I was doing. Just resting my eyes. What can I do for you?"

After I describe the car, he finds my ticket and tells me the cost. I give him the exact amount. He hands me the keys and tells me to have a nice day.

The car is unfamiliar, so I have trouble finding it. I walk slowly and in circles, jangling the keys in my right hand. Off to the east, a sliver of brightness at the horizon foreshadows the arrival of dawn.

By the time I reach my apartment the sun is peeking over the hills that separate paradise from the desert.

The sky is light blue, the air damp but crisp with the aftermath of a fine dew.

I hurry up the stairs and thrust my key into the lock, push open the door and stumble inside. The light on my answering machine is blinking. Inside the lining of my jacket I feel the weight of the video I took from Megan's house.

I could listen to my messages. Perhaps one of them is urgent. I could watch the tape. Plunk it into my VCR. Hit Rewind. Then Play.

None of it interests me right now. I suppose I should be disgusted by what I've seen, maybe outraged, and part of me feels that way, but Brad was right— another part (perhaps even a larger one) found the night thrilling and captivating.

I take off my shoes and belt, shirt and socks, lie on my back and ease my head onto the pillow.

I wake up after noon, make myself a cup of coffee and finally go through my messages. There's one from Connie Battaglia, whom I guess I should start calling "my agent." She says she's sorry to bother me at home, but she feels we really need to talk. I also have a message from Trish asking if I've left town yet.

Rebecca called too. She wants to know what I've found. She says she's really looking forward to Tahoe.

I sit on the couch and turn on the TV, flip through the channels and stop at the news. Hopes have been raised for the release of civilian hostages in the latest ethnic conflict to wrack the former Soviet Union. Officials however are cautioning against too much optimism. Meanwhile the latest economic report indicates that the decline in last quarter's gross domestic product was greater than expected. Stock prices have rallied in anticipation of lower interest rates.

Closer to home, police say a vicious attack took place after midnight at a home in Glendale when a gang of youths ransacked a quiet little house shared by a single mother and her thirteen-year-old daughter. The youths raped and sodomized the females and repeatedly hit the older one with a baseball bat. Both victims are in guarded condition at local hospitals. The youths were accompanied by someone who didn't participate directly in the assaults, a person who watched what was occurring but did and said nothing. The victims say he seemed like an older man.

Police say they are puzzled by the viciousness of the attack.

I could call and let them know exactly what happened and who was responsible. I could contact my newspaper and file a story. I could describe what happened in the kind of detail only a trained observer can provide.

The anchor says the woman was a Cambodian refugee. She came to this country years ago after fleeing the Khmer Rouge.

There is nothing beyond our life. There is nothing beyond what we know. In times that were less knowledgeable—some might call them less civilized—the ancients invented God to explain why things happen. They were afraid to accept the arbitrariness of life, too ignorant to understand the great cosmic joke that the universe itself is just a gigantic accident.

Today we know better. I see lots of bumper stickers that say "SHIT HAPPENS."

twelve

i should say nothing to anyone and go away, perhaps permanently, just race to the airport and catch a flight to the most far-flung place on the departure board. I could abandon my car in the longterm lot with a note detailing but not justifying my actions and after days or weeks or months they'd finally open my vehicle but by then it would have rusted with exposure to the fog and salt and relentless grime of urban air. The police would say the note was disjointed.

I've heard good things about Bali.

I wait a few minutes for the shuttle bus and glance at the other travelers, men and women in dark tailored suits looking at their watches and patting their luggage, ready to go forth to do the business of America.

Of course I know where I'm going. I should let Rebecca know. But I must do this by myself. I can't be with anyone right now.

I book a flight to Reno from a pretty girl who asks if I'd prefer window or aisle. I say I don't care. She asks if I've ever flown into Reno before and I say no and she urges me to take the window. The view is spectacular as you go over the lake and the mountains.

Clouds cover the Sierras. As the plane taxis to its gate we are wished a good day on behalf of everyone in the flight crew. It was their pleasure to serve us. I don't have to wait for luggage because I'm carrying only an overnight bag. I walk directly to the counter of the rental car company our new CEO has told us to use. I figure I can get a corporate rate.

"You don't have a reservation?" the clerk asks me.

"No," I say. "But I need a car."

"But you don't have a reservation? When did you know you were coming here?"

"When I got on the plane."

With a sigh he takes my credit card and prepares all the forms. A line gathers behind me. One of the business travelers says she can't understand what's taking so long. A man says he thinks the computers are down.

The car I get is a new four-door with a sunroof. As I drive south toward the lake, the clouds cling to the tops of the trees.

I stop at a library and ask the middle-aged woman behind the desk where I can find back copies of the local newspaper. I ask if they're online and she says no, they still use fiche. She points them out and asks what I'm looking for. I tell her I'm a reporter. I'm working on a travel story.

I settle into a carrel and start looking up items about Jeremiah Devlin but there are few stories and fewer pictures. I take notes anyway. Once a year he speaks to the Chamber of Commerce.

"That must be interesting work."

I look up at the librarian. Her hair is streaked with gray. There's no one else in the building.

"Sometimes it is."

"What's the best place you've ever been? I like to travel myself. I don't do it enough."

I tell her that I like to think I haven't been there yet. She says that's a wonderful answer. I tell her I need a place to stay. This trip was sudden and I haven't made arrangements, although I've heard about a bed and breakfast with a waterfall in the courtyard. She says she's heard of it too, but she's never been there herself.

"There's one thing you can help me with," I say.

"Tell me."

"I'm from Los Angeles and we have a man; he's quite wealthy; his name is Jeremiah Devlin. He has a home around here. I've heard it's spectacular. Do you know where it is?"

She shakes her head and says she's sorry, she has no personal knowledge, she moves in different circles if I know what she means. She glances over her shoulder and sees someone at the desk returning a pile of books. As she leaves she tells me the paper had a big story about Jeremiah Devlin a couple of months ago. He hosted a benefit of some sort. It was all over the society section.

It would never have occurred to me to look there.

I find a page crowded with pictures and only a few lines of type, photos of local movers and shakers, politicians from California and Nevada, celebrities I recognize from movies and TV. There's one photograph of Jeremiah Devlin. On his arm is a woman I know, although the caption calls her "his unidentified companion." She wears a black gown and a strand of pearls I assume are real as well as gold earrings with diamond studs that glint from the flash of the photographer's bulb. Her hair is swept up and teased in a style I've never seen on her. She smiles brilliantly, her teeth are white and straight and even; they overpower her eyes and that's fortunate because they're dull, and dark, with no hint of mirth or intelligence or even life.

Still, Megan's mother has never looked more beautiful.

I examine the photo for a minute and notice something in the background. I magnify the page as much as possible and bring my face close to the machine, squinting at the image.

I cannot swear to what I think I see. There is room for doubt. I have to qualify my answer, Your Honor.

In the corner, off to the side, a blond adolescent male has his mouth pressed close to the ear of a young girl. Their arms are around each other.

The boy looks like Brad, the girl like Megan. They seem to be enjoying their glimpse of the adult world.

I return the page to its normal size. A couple of the photos showcase the place. The motif is woody—wood floors and furniture, a wooden deck overlooking a wooden pier that juts into the lake. This rustic vacation home is down a dirt road a couple of miles from the highway, although many of the guests arrived by boat or seaplane of course. The text notes that Jeremiah Devlin rarely opens this place to the public, and the indoor inground pool was off-limits to everyone because of the ongoing renovations.

• • •

A large fruit basket sits on the dresser even though I told my hosts there was no need to bother. They said they do it for everyone. It's a policy. I can also order a bottle of champagne.

I hear the waterfall from my room. The sound is supposed to be soothing.

I park my rental in the village lot and walk along the main street. The sidewalks are swept clean and the people I pass by all have the clear, unlined faces of easy affluence. The shops are accessorized with lace-curtained windows and signs lettered in the old English style.

I could go into all of the stores and show the picture but if the people who work here talk to each other they might begin to ask questions.

. . . he was asking about a girl; what did he say to you? what did you say to him? why is he interested in her? what do you think he's looking for . . . ?

I remember that Megan liked ice cream.

I walk into the store on the corner. Inside is a long gleaming glass counter. Under it sit five-gallon containers of rocky crunch and strawberry surprise and a host of other flavors dreamed up by the folks in marketing.

"Can I help you?" the girl behind the counter asks.

She wears a white uniform fringed with black. Her glasses are round and she's a bit overweight. I'm sure that during the slow periods, when she's alone amid all this temptation, she sneaks a bite or two or three because what harm is there?

"What can I get you?" she asks.

I imagine that she lives a few miles out of town with her mom in a small house beaten by the weather and furnished with stuff taken from the municipal dump or purchased at thrift stores, the kind of house in the kind of location inhabited by our ever-increasing servant class. She doesn't know where her father is.

I take out my wallet.

"Actually, I'm looking for somebody."

I slide the picture of Megan across the top of the counter. I cut it out of the paper when it ran with one of my stories.

"Have you ever seen this girl?"

She pushes her glasses back and brings the picture close to her eyes. I notice that the paper is curling at the edges.

"Why are you looking for her? Is she a runaway?"

"Perhaps."

She squints and puts the picture back on the counter and tells me the girl seems familiar. Of course the store gets lots of customers. It's usually not quiet like it is now.

I tell her to take her time.

She picks up the photo again and says she's thinking harder now. She's trying to remember. She recalls a girl a lot like this—she can't be absolutely sure, she wouldn't swear to it or anything, but gosh she does look familiar—coming into the store every so often and ordering the super chocolate fudge swirl. That was her favorite. She seemed like a normal girl, somebody you could go to school with, not like a lot of the other ones around here who, just between us, are really stuck-up.

As I put Megan's picture back in my wallet she says she's quite certain now that it was the same girl. But there's one other thing. As she was saying, the girl seemed quite ordinary, but one day she happened to follow her as she left the store.

"I never do that," she says. "But it was slow, like it is now."

I tell her I understand.

She went to the window and watched her customer skip onto the sidewalk. The counter girl drew back from the glass. She wanted to be in the shadows. She was sampling some ice cream at the end of a tongue depressor. Caramel crunch. It was a new flavor and she felt she should taste it so she could tell the customers what she thought.

Anyway a limousine pulled up in front of the store. It was long and low and black and it stopped right at the No Parking sign. She didn't think too much of this because you see a lot of limos in town and they look really nice with their tinted glass and after a while you get used to them. But what surprised her was when the back door of the limousine opened and the girl got right in, like she was expecting it to be there.

"Was anybody else in the car?" I ask.

"I might have seen somebody."

"Who? Can you describe this person?"

Her mouth crumples and she furrows her brow.

"A guy."

"Tall? Blond hair? Good-looking? A teenager?"

She says she caught only a glimpse of him, but that sounds about right.

"When did this happen?"

She says she thinks it was a few weeks ago. She hasn't seen the girl since. "You think she ran away?"

I say it's possible.

"I hope she's all right. We didn't talk much, but she seemed nice and stuff."

I thank her for her time and her candor. She's been a big help. She says it was no problem and asks if I'd like any ice cream. I decline and tell her I'm not hungry. As I leave the shop she bends over a container of banana nut chip.

I retrieve the rental and join the slow traffic along the shop-lined street. The weather report says cool and cloudy conditions will continue for the next few days. Most of the pedestrians tote shopping bags. I wonder why so many are wearing sunglasses.

Something catches my eye on the other side of the street. It's a figure that seems somehow familiar; I've seen it before; there's something in its movements that I recognize. Coming out of a sporting goods store, toting a new pair of Rollerblades, is a boy of eight or nine with a blank but worried expression.

Jeffrey gets into a limousine that's parked illegally. A man in a navy blue jacket and white shirt closes the door and walks around to the driver's side.

I want to turn; they're about to leave; I have to follow them; there's no way to do it.

In the rearview mirror I see the limo pull out. I look

in every direction and see no cops so I back up a couple of feet before putting the rental in drive and executing a highly questionable U-turn. I almost brush against a car parked at a meter before I'm able to accelerate. The pedestrians who notice me shake their heads.

The limo heads out of town. When we pass the last stoplight it revs up to the speed limit. I try to keep a good distance between us. The road narrows and the trees crowd in even as their tops disappear into the mist. I turn on the radio again and hear a report from the station's Los Angeles correspondent. She says there's an unconfirmed report that hairs and fibers found on Megan Wright's body have been linked to Brad Devlin, and this evidence has been presented to a grand jury. Police and prosecutors lambaste the media for engaging in unfounded speculation.

The limo travels at a steady pace several hundred feet in front of me. There's nothing on the road between us. I wonder if the driver knows that I'm following, if he's looking in the rearview mirror and wondering about the downscale rental that doesn't seem interested in passing him or getting too far behind. Perhaps he thinks I'm a kidnapper. Perhaps I am.

If I rolled down the window, I could catch the scent of birch and pine.

The limo slows and its turn light blinks on. The vehicle executes a clumsy right and is swallowed by the woods. As I pass the spot I brake and pull onto the shoulder. I turn off the radio, make sure nothing is coming and get out of the car. As I walk back I hear the pine needles crunch underneath my shoes.

A dirt road has been hacked out through the woods. Two rutted tracks with a strip of grass between them disappear into the trees. I take a few steps down the path before I see the sign. It's dark brown so it's hard to see and its black letters are hand-painted.

The sign says, "PRIVATE ROAD. KEEP OUT."

I imagine the road is lined with surveillance cameras and microphones. The secrets that are in here will be defended.

When I return to the library I nod and smile at the woman behind the counter. From the shelves I remove some books and magazines on local topics. I spread them out on a desk and begin reading and taking notes. On a map provided by the rental agency I mark what I believe is the location of Jeremiah Devlin's country retreat.

"How's the inn?"

The librarian stands over me. Her lips are curled in an attempt at a smile but she's not showing her teeth. Her glasses reflect the fluorescent lights overhead.

"It's lovely. Everything I wanted."

She motions to the stuff scattered around me.

"Can I help you with anything?"

"I need a guide," I say. "I'd like to go out on the lake."

She sits next to me and says it depends on where I want to go. I point on the map in the general direction of Jeremiah Devlin's place. She scrunches her face and says it's rugged there, she knows of only one or two people who work that area. I say I need names and phone numbers and she reaches across me, her arm brushing against my chest as she pulls a local magazine toward her.

"Here," she says. "This man can help you."

His name is Peter Rourke and his ad says he's an experienced guide who charges reasonable rates. I thank the librarian and write down the information. She looks at her watch and says it's past closing. The town will kill her if she stays open afterhours, what with the budget cuts and everything. I tell her I'll put away the books and magazines I've taken out while she locks up. She says I'm quite thoughtful.

The waterfall glimmers like an apparition as it basks in a spotlight attached to one of the rocks that cascade into the courtyard. The water seems blue and green and white and red and yellow as it runs and glides and bounces down, smoothing the stones before it collects in a pool and eddies away.

"We could stay here awhile," I hear myself say.

"I shouldn't," she says. "I've taken up too much of your time. You must be awfully busy."

I tell her I have a fruit basket and a bottle of champagne in my room. I'd never get to them on my own. I could bring them out. We'll sit at one of the tables.

"I don't want to impose," the librarian says.

I carry the fruit and champagne and a couple of glasses from my room. She sits as far from the waterfall as she can. I suppose she doesn't want to get wet. When I put the things on the table she smiles at me in her toothless way. I peel off the foil, loosen the cap and pop open the bottle. She bites into a strawberry. I fill the glasses and hand her one. I tell her I'm glad she's here. I'm glad to have someone to share this with. We clink our glasses together.

"It's been a long time," she says. "It's been a long time since I've done something like this."

I lean back and look at the sky. Ignoring the weather report, the clouds have disappeared. I believe I can see the Big Dipper. Or maybe it's the Little Dipper. I can never keep them straight. I tell her I've forgotten what the night sky looks like. When you live in Los Angeles, you never see the stars.

"I've spent very little time in cities," she says. "I go to San Francisco once a year. That's about it."

I tell her I like San Francisco. I like the way the fog rolls in. She asks what other cities I've been to and I mention a few and she asks which would be the best for a single woman like herself and I say I'm not sure, never having been a single woman.

She laughs as she pours herself another glass of champagne. She says she's never been anywhere except Hawaii once and Mexico a couple of times and lately she's started to regret it. She's spent most of her life around here but there's so much else to see.

"It's nice around here," I say.

She says that's true but it can be a trap, you can be lulled by a place and then find it impossible to leave even though you should and by the time you realize what's what, it's too late. You're stuck. She supposes that's been the story of her life but then she catches herself and giggles as she swallows and says she shouldn't go on like this, she's sure I don't want to hear it. I tell her I don't mind. She should say whatever she wants to.

There was a man in her life and he was really nice at first. This was years ago. To make a long story short they wound up getting married. He took her out—they went dancing and to the movies and they had picnics on the lake. Imagine her dancing.

I look past her and focus on the waterfall, white foam running endlessly from an unknown source and trickling out beside a path that heads into the trees. I wonder if it's manmade or if it's always been like this, with the owners discovering this spot one day during a hike through the woods and deciding they would build their inn here, this is the location they'd always talked and dreamed about.

"Anyway, that's how it went," she says. "I didn't mean to go on so long."

"It's all right," I say.

She finishes her champagne and reaches for the bottle. Only a mouthful is left.

"Oh my," she says. "I didn't realize." She giggles. "Did you have enough?"

"Finish it."

She does and asks me what the rooms here are like. I say they're Victorian, which means they're a bit on the small side. She asks if she can see my room. She wants new wallpaper and she's been looking at patterns.

From the road I can read the sign. It says, quite simply, "BOATS." I leave the rental idling and walk down a narrow lane toward the shed. I could drive all the way but it would be hard to get out if I ran into trouble. In the morning air I can see my breath before me.

The color of the water is as crystal blue as the sky. All the brochures say the pristine nature of the lake is one of this area's primary attractions.

I walk up the wood steps of the wood shed and open the wood door. Inside the walls are made of wood, as is the counter and several benches where customers must wait during more popular seasons. Fishing and hunting gear are tacked to the walls.

"Can I help you?"

The voice belongs to a man who has just emerged from the room behind the counter. I didn't hear him enter. A life in the woods makes a man quiet when he's entering a situation.

"I'm looking for Peter Rourke. I'd like someone to take me on the lake."

His hair is sandy and his face is red, with deep lines, from years spent mixing with sun and wind and water. I imagine his handshake is firm if not bone-crushing.

He tells me that he's Peter Rourke and it's cold on the water this time of year. I tell him I don't mind. He says he'll do it and asks when I want to leave.

"Nightfall," I say.

He says that's an awfully strange request. He's gone out at night in the warmer months but he's never, as long as he's done this, taken somebody on the lake after dark when the weather's this cold. I take out two hundred-dollar bills and put them on the counter. He asks what those are for and I say they're a deposit. I'll give him three more tonight. He says he was going to ask me where I wanted to go and how I got his name, but for the kind of money I'm paying he'll just shut up and do what I tell him.

The phone rings as I'm preparing to leave my room.

"It's me."

"How are you?" I ask.

"I'm thinking about last night."

I stuff my black gym bag with a flashlight, a tape recorder, a map, a notepad and a pen.

"You were rough," she says.

I put in extra pairs of batteries for the flashlight and tape recorder. Now that I'm thinking of it, I decide to bring along a can of Mace.

"It was all right once I got used to it. I wasn't expecting it, that's all."

I check my watch. I have to leave.

"Will I see you tonight?" she asks.

I don't know what to say. So I say nothing.

"I know you're busy and you'll be leaving soon," she says. "I don't want to seem needy. I'd just like to see you, that's all."

The last bits of orange recede from the sky as I walk down the path to the shed. My back straightens, my step lightens, my arms swing back and I whistle a show tune I didn't even know I recalled.

There's a light on inside. When I push the door open it creaks so loudly I swear I can hear the fish scattering.

Rourke is waiting. I put two hundred-dollar bills on the counter.

"I thought you said three."

"I'll give you the last one when we get back."

"Fair enough."

He puts the money in a strongbox that he locks and puts under the counter. He drapes the box with a piece of bearskin.

The dock is right outside the shed. My hiking shoes clump as they strike the wood. I wish they were quieter. Four small boats are tied to the posts. Rourke tells me he employs several people during the warmer months but the rest of the year he does everything himself. He hasn't brought in the boats yet for the winter.

"What do they do?"

"Who?"

"Your people. When they're not working."

He says he doesn't really know. He's never asked. He figures it's none of his business. They get by— maybe they work someplace else or maybe they collect unemployment, but after the snows melt they come back to him. Sometimes a person moves away and has to be replaced. He doesn't know where they go. Doesn't much care, to tell the truth.

He gets in the boat and extends his hand toward me. I toss my gym bag onto a seat and lower myself. The boat bobs and rocks and I hear the soft *splush, splush* of waves as they brush against the dock.

"Where do you want to go?" he asks.

I open the bag and take out the map and flashlight. I unfold the map and point to the spot I've circled. I used a red magic marker. Rourke says he knows the place I'm looking for. It's about a mile from here. He's been by it many times and he remembers it has a dock on the property. Nice-looking one too.

He brings the rope that had been hooked around the dock into the boat, and we start to drift. I sit down as he fusses with the motor.

"What do you want, anyway?" he asks.

It's a better question than he realizes.

"I'm not stealing anything," I say. "The worst they'll get me for is trespassing."

"But why are you doing this?" he asks as the motor kicks in.

"There's somebody I have to see."

"Oh," he says, and I think I see him smile. "It's like that."

I almost tell him it isn't like that at all but as usual it's best to let people keep their illusions. The boat putters onto the lake and I look at the sky expecting to see stars but the clouds have returned and all that's visible, at least to my eye, is a wispy outline of a sliver of the moon, as if I'm looking at it through a silkscreen. On the shore, lights burn in the few houses scattered in the woods. We pick up speed and the spray starts to sting my face. I'm wearing black jeans with running tights underneath and on top I have a black turtleneck covered with a dark nylon jacket. Over my ears I've stretched a knit cap that's navy blue. Perhaps I should have worn a ski mask.

"There it is," he says. A few hundred yards away is

an empty dock. Tall pines come almost to the water. Somewhere in them I see a light. I believe I can make out the dark and lumpy shape of a large house.

"I'm gonna go past it," he says. "That way they'll think we're going someplace else. Just in case anyone's watching."

I ask him how far he intends to go.

"Till we're beyond their sightline. Then I'll turn it around and cut the engine. We'll row back."

This is more exercise than I was planning on.

When the engine stops I hear nothing at first, but after a while a low howl carries over the water. There are still wolves in the woods. Rourke tells me I have an oar directly beneath my seat and there's no time like the present to start using it. I reach down, pick it up, plunge it into the water. I forgot to bring gloves. Splinters rub into my skin.

As we approach the dock I half expect to see a few guys with Uzis emerge from the trees, casually pointing their weapons and asking us what the hell we think we're doing. I don't have an answer ready in case things go wrong.

As we store our oars I look over the scene. It's a short sprint from the water to the trees.

We warp close to the dock. Rourke stands and the boat pitches to the right but he braces against the dock with his hands. The boat rights itself and there's no telltale sound of wood bumping against wood, just a few big ripples brushing by. They could have been caused by the wind, or a bird swooping down to pluck a fish from the lake.

Rourke takes us under the dock and I feel enclosed, almost trapped, as if the planks overhead were the lid of a coffin. He stops the boat a few feet from land. I can see rocks underneath us. He takes out a piece of rope and ties it against a pile to our left. I do the same with another piece of rope to a pile on our right. The lines are stretched taut.

"Wait here," I say in a murmur. "If all hell breaks loose, get out. Hide my car. I left it on the road."

I give him my car keys.

"How long will you be?"

"This shouldn't take more than an hour."

"You're a fast operator."

"I have to be."

I swing my feet over the edge of the boat. The water pierces through my shoes and heavy socks. I want to cry out.

I motion to the gym bag and he hands it to me. I crouch under the dock and sling the bag under my shoulder. When I reach firm ground I peer out. There's nothing but the burning light and the trees and the night.

I crouch low to the ground and squish the pine needles beneath my feet as I head for my destination. I can see the house now, large and dark and done in a woodsy style.

A glass-enclosed addition juts out from the house. It's a darkened space so I press my face close. A thin film of steam covers the glass and I can see that the room contains a swimming pool, undoubtedly heated, with chairs and lounges and tables scattered around it.

Over the tables are umbrellas emblazoned with the name of an Italian liqueur.

I move a few feet away from the glass and, still crouching, jog parallel to it in the direction of the main building. There's a door close to where the addition abuts the house. I try it but the door is locked. I reach into my pocket and take out the pick that Rebecca gave me, slide the wire into the lock and twist it a few times. When I hear a clicking sound I try the door again, and it opens.

I stand there a few seconds, waiting for a whoop or a siren, some noise to indicate the presence of an intruder. All I hear, far in the distance, is the howling of a wolf.

I step inside and close the door behind me. The stinging smell of chlorine assaults my sinuses while the air's sudden heavy dampness seeps through my clothes. Sweat forms under my cap and over my eyes. I bend down beside the pool and put my hand in the water. A few degrees warmer and it would scald me.

A passageway connects the pool enclosure to the main building. Through the open door I hear the sounds of a television.

I lean against the wall. I'm still in shadow. A light is on in the room with the TV.

I look down and see a binder on a nearby table. I imagine Jeremiah Devlin's houseguests putting their drinks on the table while they do laps.

The binder's covers are heavy. The pages are bound with metal rings. I lift it up and open it slowly. I want to be silent. I turn the pages as noiselessly as I can. Written on them, in hands ranging from elegant to scrawls, are the signatures and comments of just about everyone who has used this pool. The comments are uniformly enthusiastic, with special praise for the renovation. I recognize some of the names. I take it on faith that the others deserve to be included.

The name I'm looking for is written in a girlish hand, with swoops and curves and little curlicues. Megan was here—this house, this room, this pool. Her note says she thinks it's really neat.

I wonder how long you have to hold a girl underwater before she drowns.

Underneath Megan's name is her mother's. She says she and her daughter just love it here.

I edge the paper through the rings, then fold it and put it in the pocket of my jeans. I slip along the wall and crouch low to the floor as I approach the light. At the end of the passageway, off to the right, is the brightly lit room with the television. The passageway blends into the house, becoming a corridor that extends into blackness. To the left, directly across from the entrance to the TV room, is a staircase. The steps resemble wooden planks. You can see the floor beneath you as you rise. I tell myself that if anything of Megan's is still in this house, it's most likely up the stairs.

I turn 180 degrees and start to walk up. My feet sound like a jackhammer on the first couple of stairs but I want to get out of the line of vision from the other room. When I'm halfway up the stairs I stop and turn. Jeffrey is lying on his stomach, his head cradled in his hands and his eyes only inches from the TV. Sitting on the couch behind him is a Latina in a housemaid's uniform. I believe it's the woman who used to work at Megan's house. She appears to be sewing. From the television I hear shouts and laughter.

I carefully place my feet on the stairs as I continue to ascend. Now that I'm out of their sight, I tell myself it's important to be quiet.

It's dark at the top of the stairs. The doors, walls and floor smell vaguely of pine.

I hear a moan that sounds like somebody struggling with a nightmare. I walk on my toes as I follow the noise to an open door.

The room has a four-poster bed with a quilted canopy. There's a large window through which I can see trees and, far in the distance, an inky splotch I assume is the lake. A woman is in the bed. She moves her head from side to side as if hoping it will roll off. When I get closer I see that her hands are tied to the posts, strong rough rope stretched tight and bound around her wrists.

I recognize the woman of course.

My instinct is to turn on the light. I want to describe Megan's mother in case I write a story and I already know the words I can use—"haggard," "worn," "wracked with grief," all the stuff readers expect. But my business is best conducted in darkness.

Her breathing is short and spasmodic and her eyes are closed even as her head snaps from one side to the other. Her cheeks and eyes seem to have shrunk into her face, and her hair is matted and fading to its natural color. She's clad in a silk robe and pajamas and a blanket is pulled up to her shoulders. I push up her left sleeve to look at her arm. Some of the needle marks are fresh.

"No!" she says.

I wonder if she knows I'm here.

"Mrs. Wright," I say as softly as I can. I wonder how they address her here. I wonder if she remembers her name or if she's capable of responding to anything.

It occurs to me that I should shut the door. I walk back, still on my toes, and push the door closed. It creaks slightly and I stop, waiting for the sound of feet rushing toward me. All I hear are more shouts and laughter from the show Jeffrey is watching.

I lock the door and return to Megan's mother. I consider untying her, but the position she's in might make her more inclined to tell me what I want to know.

I push up her eyelids and open my bag. Even in the dark I can tell that her pupils are dilated but darting, incapable of focusing.

"Can you hear me?" I ask as I take out the tape recorder.

Her head rolls to the other side. On the nightstand I notice several syringes and a row of vials. I place the tape recorder amid this stuff and click it on.

Then I slap her. The sound of flesh striking flesh fills the room. It's as loud as an exploding bomb.

I am not enjoying this.

"Don't hit me," she says, her voice low and slurred. She cannot open her eyes.

"How long have you been here?"

"Forever."

"Who brought you here?"

"They did."

She stops. I can't tell if she's lost her energy or is simply unwilling to answer. I slap her again.

"Who brought you here?"

"Don't hit me. Stop hitting me."

"Who brought you?"

"Devlin. His people."

"Why?"

"They said it would be good for me. Will you take me with you?"

"I can't. What about Jeffrey?"

"He doesn't care. They buy him things."

I bring my mouth close to her right ear. Her breathing is more like gasping now, as if the air itself is something foreign to her.

"Do you remember your daughter?" I ask.

She says nothing. I slap her again, this time as hard as I can.

"Stop that," she says.

"Do you remember Megan?"

"Who are you?"

"Do you remember what happened to her?"

"I try to forget. Honestly I do. But I can't."

I'm afraid she's going to sob. I look around for an item I can shove in her mouth but nothing is handy.

"Who killed Megan?" I ask.

She opens her eyes at last. Despite the drugs and the beatings and the various traumas she's experienced, I think she recognizes me.

She screams.

It's loud and terrible and comes from somewhere deep within her; whatever she's seen and whatever's been done to her are coming out, and in her howl I hear terror and deprivation and maybe, just maybe, pleading.

Whoever is in the house will come running and will probably be armed, so leaving the way I entered is no longer an option. I try to open the window but it's locked and I'm sure a close examination would reveal it's been nailed shut but I don't have time for that.

The screams continue, mostly horrific sounds that must be what the laments of the damned are like. The nuns used to warn us about the descent into hell, but I never paid much attention.

The doorknob twists and turns and the door shakes but does not open.

"Shit!" says a gruff voice from the hallway.

I pick up a chair and raise it over my head. I wish she would stop screaming.

Out in the hallway they shoot at the lock. Frank Gruley once told me you should never do that. The bullet could ricochet.

I hurl the chair at the window and the glass bursts in every direction, falling inside the room and shattering out on the roof. I put the tape recorder in my bag and zip it shut and strap the bag over my shoulder.

Her screams get louder and finally a word is discernible.

"Murder!" she says. "Murder! They killed her!"

It's a primal cry from somewhere deep inside. I'd like to find its source.

"Who?" I ask as urgently as I've ever asked anything. "Who are they?"

"Murder!!"

I hear dogs barking within the house.

I run to the window and behind me I hear the door burst open. The same gruff voice yells "Jesus!" as I climb through. Somebody shoots at me but it's nighttime and my clothes are dark so the gunfire is wild.

The roof slopes steeply for a few feet and there's glass all over it. As I near the eaves I slip. Shards tear into my hands and suddenly my palms and fingers are slick with blood mingled with sweat and I can't grip anything and I roll down the shingles, sharp edges cutting my face, until there's nothing beneath me and I feel myself falling through the air; I should be terrified but it's a relief to be free of the pain even for a moment.

I land in a bed of pine needles. I raise myself to my hands and knees. Nothing seems broken. I'm still bleeding but I can stand.

The barking of the dogs gets louder.

I look around for my bag, trying to locate a blob the color of darkness, and even though my eyesight is perfect, I see everything, I cannot find it on the ground. So I look up.

From the gutter, at the edge of the eaves, something that looks very much like a gym bag is hanging precariously.

I stumble to the edge of the house.

"Fuck!" I hear the gruff voice again. "Fuck where is he? Fuck will you look at this. Fuck."

The dogs are baying now.

I put my hands around a drainpipe but as soon as I do it becomes so slippery with blood I lose my grip. I rub my hands against my pants and wipe off the blood on the pipe with my sleeve.

I hear footsteps on the roof.

I grab the pipe and shake it hard. Blood spurts from my hands and again my grip gets looser; I feel my palms sliding off the thing and as they do I ram the pipe with my shoulder, trying for one last good jolt.

The bag plops on my head, then hits the ground. I almost feel like laughing. I pick it up and take off.

"You fucker," the gruff voice says. It's out on the ledge now. "What the fuck do you want?"

My hiking shoes slow me down. I want to sprint but I have weights on my ankles. I hear another gunshot behind me and for a second I brace; I wonder what it's like to feel a bullet enter your body, whether the pain is searing and immediate or if it takes time before you realize what's happened and then, only then, do you break down, gasp for air, cling to life.

Nothing happens.

Blood and sweat trickle into my eyes. I try to blink them clear but that only makes them water more; everything becomes blurry and I wind up brushing against trees, the hard unyielding bark throwing my shoulders back; I feel myself getting even slower; the water is quite far away and I don't even know if the boat is still there.

I hear the dogs behind me. They're outside now. They know I'm wounded.

I stumble on exposed roots and pitch forward; I

almost fall but somehow my legs keep going. The bag slides down my arm. I catch it and bring it back. Low-hanging branches slap and slash my face.

The animals are howling. They've caught the scent of blood.

I see the water ahead of me. It's darker than the night, a vast mass of black that seems lifeless.

I emerge from the trees. I don't have far to go.

Suddenly I stop and turn and look back toward the pine and scrub oak. A pair of cobalt eyes stare at me, unblinking but not uncomprehending. The eyes rest in pools of white.

The wolf howls, although the moon is only a sliver.

I run onto the dock. Bobbing at its edge is the boat, my boat, passage to safety and salvation. My shoes make a heavy *clump-clump* on the wood and I tell myself it's only a few more feet. I reach the edge of the dock and throw my bag into the boat. Rourke starts the motor.

Snarling sounds come from the edge of the woods, growling, guttural noises deep in the animals' throats. These are followed by a roar and then a terrible noise from the dogs—not routine barks at an intruder, but the deep and desperate grunting and yelping of canines fighting for their lives.

The wolf is at their throats.

After we tie the boat I pay Rourke the final hundred dollars. He gives me the key to the bathroom and tells me to take my time if I feel I need it.

When I look at my face in the mirror my first

impression is that it belongs to someone else. It's covered with scratches and scars and blood. So are my hands. Angry red marks travel across every part of my flesh that was exposed to the night, testimony to what I've been through and what I've done.

I take off my knit cap. My hair is matted with sweat. I remove my jacket and turtleneck. Next to my skin is a thermal shirt sopping with perspiration. I unlace my shoes and toss them into a corner, remove my socks and wince at the stench. Finally I take off my jeans and running tights and underpants and pile them in a heap under the sink. I turn sideways and notice a purple bruise on my left hip, which absorbed the heaviest part of my fall.

I go to the stall and turn on the water. It's cold at first and I shiver, but then I get used to it and consider stepping in; a bracing shower would be good for me; I don't need the water to heat up. But soon it turns warm and the room fills with steam and I stop shaking.

The blood and sweat disappear from me as I rub the soap over my body and through my hair. It feels rough and good and I tell myself this could be my first step toward redemption.

I turn off the water and open the metal door. The room is so thick with steam and mist I can't see the walls. In my gym bag is a change of clothes. After I dry myself I put on fresh underwear, blue jeans and a rugby shirt. That's all I need. I take out the tape recorder, then stuff the things I've used in the bag. I'll probably throw them out. The tape recorder fits in the pocket of my jacket.

I use a piece of toilet paper to wipe the mirror. My face is still marked with red lines crisscrossing my cheeks and forehead.

In the main room Rourke brews a cup of decaf. He says he always has one before going to bed and asks if I'd like to join him. I decline. He thanks me for the business and gives me my car keys. He says he'll take me out on the lake anytime. I say I hope further trips will be unnecessary.

I step outside and walk down the wood steps. I like the sound my boots make when they strike the dirt as I head up the narrow path toward the road.

Another car is parked behind the rental.

I dodge into the trees and try to walk as softly as I can but I wasn't raised to tread quietly in the wilderness so every step sounds like an explosion. I make sure the car keys are accessible in my pocket. I locked the door and I'll need to get at it in one swift motion. The sweat begins again and for the first time in my life I wish I had a gun. Nine-millimeter semiautomatics are the weapons of choice these days. Even schoolchildren carry them.

As I get closer I recognize who's waiting for me. She's leaning against the car—a practical midsized American, very good on gas mileage—and looking impatiently every few seconds at her watch, as if she's bored with this party and wants to get on to the next one but can't quite work up the nerve to tell the host that she's leaving.

The librarian opens a roll of Life Savers and pops one in her mouth. I could slide past her. It wouldn't be difficult. I could just ease into the rental and go but doubtless she'd follow me, intent on acting out whatever scene she has it in her mind to play.

I bang my palm on the hood of the car and duck down. She jumps and turns around, then starts coughing. The coughs are violent, deep and hacking.

"What was that?" she asks. She's alone on a dark and deserted road and something unknown is out there and her voice is filled with terror and fear. I admit I like the sound of it. I like the fact that I caused it.

I wish I remembered her name.

"What is it? Who's there?"

I bang on the side of the car and scoot around. I hear her pumps striking the dirt and then the pavement.

"Who are you? What do you want?"

She's calling out, but even so her voice is soft. I doubt it would carry down to the lake.

"I'm not afraid," she says. Her voice quivers. "I've got a gun."

I hear her purse being unclasped and a hand rustling about. I come up behind her. She's wearing a dress that falls just below the knee. Her calves shake so much I'm afraid she'll fall over.

I slap my left hand over her mouth and grab her gun with my right. My palm blocks the force of her scream and I spin her around. Her eyes go wide, and she starts to cough again, hacking so loudly I have to release her. She doubles over, clutching her hands to her stomach.

A Life Saver spits out and lands on the ground. She

gasps a few times. Her breathing slows and she straightens up.

"What are you doing here?" I ask.

She says she went to my room and I wasn't there. She felt she had to see me. She remembered that she gave me Rourke's name and she thought that maybe he knew where I was.

She says she noticed my car and decided to park behind it. She walked down to the cabin and looked around, knocked on the door, then pounded on it, even called out a few times. When she was satisfied no one was there, she came back to her car. She figured she'd wait. She had to see me.

She looks at her pumps, then raises her eyes.

"What happened to you?" she asks.

"I had an accident."

"I don't believe you. I don't believe anything you've told me."

I throw her gun as far into the woods as I can.

"Why did you do that?" she asks.

I should slap her, grab her by the shoulders and drag her toward the rental. I could yank open the back door and throw her in, hoping to hear her yell for help, tear at her clothes as she struggles—

"You had no right to do that," she says.

I hear myself screaming, "Get out of here."

"No," she says. "You have no right—"

"Get away from me!"

She backs away from me as if I were a predatory animal, her eyes wide and frightened. There's plenty of white in them, standing out from the darkness of the night and the dense black of the woods and the deep fury of my rage. She opens the door to her car but always keeps looking at me, even as she gets in and settles behind the wheel.

I could lunge at her. It's not too late to stop her car.

I stand there and hear my own breathing, my lungs filling up almost to bursting and my head full of a noise that sounds like a jet landing.

She slams the door and starts the engine.

"What do you want?" she shouts just before she leaves.

In the morning I have fresh strawberries and melon with my pancakes and coffee. Occasionally I catch some spray from the waterfall. The proprietor asks if I liked my visit and I say I did, for the most part. She asks what happened to my face and I say I fell flat on it while I was hiking, but it's nothing major. She nods and says some of the trails are dangerous.

I read the local paper carefully, but there's no mention of a break-in at Jeremiah Devlin's place or any kind of an incident near a rental car on a country road. When I return to my room I make a long-distance call. Trish Yamamoto answers on the first ring.

"Where are you?" she asks.

I tell her. My things are packed.

"Get back here as soon as you can," she says.

"Don't you want to know—"

"Brad Devlin's been indicted."

part two

In the middle of the night that used to be my friend terrors await me as they do everyone else. Megan's mother comes into my head, every part of her body immobilized except for her mouth which is screaming screaming screaming at me to help her, to free her, to solve the case and above all to DO SOMETHING. I stand rooted to the ground, unable to move, and then her skin flies away revealing her skull but still she continues to scream and then I do too; I'm sitting bolt upright in my bed and my face is flushed and feverish and my breath is short and my heart is trying to pound through the wall of my chest.

Lately I've noticed more gray in my hair. My fingers are dry and cracked. Occasionally they bleed.

one

brad Devlin pleads not guilty and Richard Alvarez asks for an immediate dismissal, which the judge denies. Bail is set at five million dollars. It's posted within an hour.

Outside the courthouse, bodies brush and jostle mine. People jump and yell. In front are the camera crews and photographers. One guy from a TV station knocks over a reporter from the wire service. When she gets up she slaps him and calls him an asshole. He tells her to fuck off.

Behind us a throng of teenage girls, thin gum-chewing things, giggle among themselves.

"Where's Brad?"

"Did you see him?"

"He's so cute."

"He drives a Lexus."

"I think he's adorable."

Richard Alvarez smiles as he enters the embrace of cameras and microphones. Southern California's leading defense attorney buys his clothes on Rodeo Drive and attends the opera regularly. His home is in the hills and he owns a weekend place near La Jolla. I once saw a spread on his lifestyle in an architectural magazine. "I love spectacle," he said. There are rumors he has political ambitions but is unwilling to take the pay cut.

Alvarez says the state's case is flimsy at best, malicious at worst. The evidence is entirely circumstantial. He has no doubt he'll win an acquittal if things ever get that far.

Questions leap at him.

"My client left through the basement," Alvarez says in response to numerous queries about Brad's whereabouts. With a sweeping motion that encompasses cameras, photographers, reporters and teenagers, he adds: "Brad told me he didn't want to face this."

"Does he have an alibi for the night Megan was killed?" I ask.

"He does have an alibi," Alvarez says.

"Is he still claiming he was in Tahoe?"

"He's not claiming anything," Alvarez says. "He *was* in Tahoe."

More questions fly at him.

"Everything will come out at the trial," Alvarez says. "I beg you to be patient, although the canons of your profession seem to prohibit that."

"Why wasn't Brad's father at the arraignment?" I ask.

"He told me he hasn't been to the circus since he was a boy, and has no desire to start now."

"Does he still believe his son is innocent?"

Alvarez smiles. "He hired me, didn't he?"

I'm the only one in the crowd who doesn't laugh. As the attorney steps away, I lob my last grenade.

"Where's Megan's mother?"

Alvarez returns to the microphone. He looks at me as if he's about to cross-examine the only witness who can convict his client.

"Megan?" he asks.

"Megan," I say. "The victim," I say. "Her mother and Jeremiah Devlin have a relationship. I've written about it."

"I have no idea where she is," Alvarez says. "Why should I?" He pauses and looks at me directly. "If you're such a good reporter, perhaps you do."

He and his assistants walk toward the curb as more questions are hurled through the air. I shriek, "WHERE IS SHE?" and feel my face turning red and the veins popping out on my neck and forehead. Close to the street Alvarez talks in Spanish to a bubblehead from Mexican TV before he and his assistants are sucked into a Mercedes with tinted windows.

Monica Rosen strides down the steps, heels clicking briskly, briefcase stationary at the end of her arm. She's changed her hair since I saw her last.

The pack crowds around the microphones.

Monica says The People have a strong and convincing case. Of course she can't provide details right now. That would be unethical.

"Do you have any eyewitnesses?"

"Can you place him at the site where the body was found?"

"Was he in a sexual relationship with the victim?"

"Is political pressure being brought on your office?"

Monica says there are numerous inconsistencies in Brad's statements to police. The People will place him in the company of the victim the night she was killed, contrary to his assertions in various affidavits. The People will also establish that Brad and the victim had a relationship.

"Was that the motive?" somebody asks.

"We don't have to prove motive," Monica says.

As I drive to the office I turn on the news-and-talk station just in time for Farley O'Neill. The station bills him as Southern California's Voice of the Angry White Male. In the latest Arbitron ratings his show was the most popular in the market.

He says in his baritone that he wants to discuss the *media frenzy* that occurred today at the courthouse. It was the most *repugnant* display he'd seen in quite some time by the *jackals* of the press—he himself was tempted to go there in the hyena suit he wore for Halloween. Of course that would be unfair to hyenas and then he'd have the animal rights people on his back.

Debbie from Hermosa is on line two.

"I heard you the other day and I was, like, wondering, do you, like, *rilly* know Brad Devlin?" she asks.

"I certainly do, young lady, and I believe he'd make a fine companion for someone like you." O'Neill goes on to describe Brad in terms that are almost mythic—a fine student, an athlete, an Eagle Scout, a volunteer with senior citizens. None of this, to my knowledge, is true, but it sounds great on the radio.

"Now let me talk about Jeremiah Devlin," O'Neill says. If the son is mythic, the father is a god—a pillar of the community, an astute entrepreneur, a man of upstanding values who raised his boy single-handedly after the tragic death of his wife in an accident aboard his own yacht. His main company provided jobs to tens of thousands of Californians and developed important new technologies before the *liberals* gutted the defense industry just as they've *destroyed* everything else that was *great* about America.

"And who is destroying him?" O'Neill asks. "Who is destroying this fine American I'm proud to call a friend? A newspaper. A newspaper run by *liberals*—"

I'm sure this description deeply offends the publisher and his family.

"—and a *reporter* with his own *ideological ax* to grind."

I can't even remember if I'm registered to vote.

My story recounts the events at the courthouse and quotes a few legal experts I call from the office. They say it will be difficult to find a jury because of all the publicity. A law professor at Loyola says he's available to serve the paper as a consultant during the trial. He'd charge only about a hundred dollars a day. I say I'll pass along his request to my superiors.

Trish asks me to include a line about what Brad was wearing. All trial stories should include a description of the defendant's appearance. I ask her why and she says she's not sure. It's something one of her journalism professors told her. So I inform my readers in the fourth paragraph that during his initial appearance in court, Brad Devlin wore a navy blue suit, white shirt and striped tie.

Trish asks if I found anything in Tahoe. I tell her I'm still developing some information I uncovered up there. She asks if I ever looked into the allegations Brad made about Grant Fisher and his friend Alexis. I tell her I never had the time.

"Fussman isn't going to like that answer," she says.

"It's the truth," I say. "I'm only one guy. I don't have time to explore everything, especially an angle that isn't going to lead anywhere."

"How can you be so sure it won't lead anywhere?"

"Because Brad killed her."

"Can you prove it?"

I can. I can offer evidence that will persuade even the most fervent skeptic. The testimony has no bearing on the night in question, Your Honor, but goes directly to the character of the accused.

"No," I say. "I can't prove anything. I'm still working on it."

"I'm gonna need something," Trish says. "Someday soon."

As I walk out I stop by Rebecca's desk to ask how she's doing. She says okay. Now that I'm covering Brad's trial, they're going to keep her on the cop roundup.

"Isn't that what you wanted?" I ask.

"I suppose it is."

I tell her I'm going home. She says she has work to do.

• • •

When I get back to my apartment I drink a couple of beers while I play my messages. Connie Battaglia says we should have lunch sometime. A producer from Court TV wants to interview me. The last call is from Noreen. She says we need to talk.

I have yet to watch the videotape I took from Megan's house. As I walk around my apartment I tell myself it's a matter of working up the will. It will be all right. I should see whatever it is that Megan wanted hidden. It will be good for the story. For my understanding of it. I tell myself I'll even be able to bear it if her mother appears.

The phone rings while I'm pacing around the kitchen. The sound startles me so badly I drop my mug on the floor, where it shatters and breaks. Glass mingles with slick white foam and I imagine myself slipping and falling, winding up drenched in blood and alcohol.

My tape kicks in.

"You fucker." It's an adolescent male voice, filled with bored anger. "That was you in Tahoe, wasn't it? You fuck." There's a pause. I wonder if he's thinking about broadening his vocabulary. "Brad's father moved her. He moved the bitch. She's in Sun Valley now. Nobody's gonna find her."

I expect him to hang up. But after a few seconds, he has more to say.

"We're going out tonight," he says. "You know where to meet us. It'll be just like the last time." Another pause. "Don't pretend you didn't enjoy it. You fuck."

I fill a plastic bucket with water and soap, then dip in a sponge mop. I run it hard over the floor. I grip it so tightly I'm afraid it will break. I wait for the floor to dry before dumping the contents of the bucket into the sink. I get my vacuum cleaner and run the hose over every millimeter, removing the glass but also the dirt and dust.

I place the mop and bucket and vacuum cleaner in their regular places. I search for the video but as soon as I see it I have to put it back.

I sit in my chair and look at the phone. One call is all I would need to make. I could punch in the number for the police and tell them about a gathering of teenage males at the top of Sepulveda Pass. A squad car could pull by and the officers would ask the kids what they're up to. Better yet an unmarked vehicle can tail them after they leave the spot. I'm sure they'll end up at a house somewhere in the Valley. The results are certain to be worthy of the authorities' attention.

I wouldn't leave my name of course.

Perhaps some good would come of this. All that's required is the will to do it. But I know that many of the police lines flash the number of the incoming call to whoever is receiving it. And in an age where everyone in the world is in contact with everyone else, I believe anonymity and privacy are no longer possible.

I could go outside, into the dark, and call from a pay phone. I imagine a clever operator keeping me on the line long enough to trace the call. A police car would come by; questions would ensue; I see myself being taken into custody.

I could go there and try to stop them myself.

As I sit in indecision I remember a case many years ago in New York. A woman was murdered on the street but it took a long time for the killer to finish his task. It was the middle of the night and she screamed for help and although dozens of people heard her, nobody intervened or called the police or even leaned out a window and told the attacker to stop. In a lot of ways it marked the beginning of the modern era in America.

When I thought the signal was about to turn I eased down on the accelerator and started to roll forward. But the light stayed red. I pounded the brakes and lurched to a stop. A microsecond later something slammed me from behind. I surged forward but the shoulder belt snapped me back. I opened the door and saw a BMW trying to mate with my bumper. A girl with short hair and a lot of rings got out of it. Her nails were bloodred.

"Is my car all right?" she asked.

two

In response to a question from Judge Claire Baden-Howell, both attorneys say they're ready for the case to proceed to trial. The judge sounds pleased as she announces jury selection will begin next week. Monica files a motion asking for some samples of the defendant's skin. The People want to compare his DNA to that of the skin found under the victim's fingernails. Alvarez objects immediately but Brad tugs on his attorney's sleeve and whispers something to him. Alvarez's eyebrows shoot up but Brad nods emphatically, as if he's sure of what he wants to do. In a nonplussed tone Alvarez tells the court that his client has no objection to submitting to the procedure requested by the state.

Monica frowns and squints and purses her lips, as if wondering if she just blundered.

"I watched it this morning on TV. It's fascinating. It must be even more fascinating in person."

Connie Battaglia puts salt on a celery stick and takes a small bite. I barely hear the crunch over the music—tunes from the seventies, which match the decor. Everything in the room clashes, and a disco ball swirls overhead.

"I love this place," she says. "It reminds me of when drugs were cool and sex was fun."

"I still think sex is fun," I reply a few decibels louder than normal.

Connie shakes her head. "It's dangerous these days."

"That just makes it more exciting."

She says she usually tapes Court TV and watches it at night before going to bed. She has milk and cookies and fast forwards through the slow spots. Anyway this morning she couldn't wait. She had to see it while it was happening. She's afraid that now she'll become addicted and won't get any work done.

I tell her I've covered a number of trials. Sitting in a courtroom is tedious. Maybe it's better on the tube.

Connie sips her soda. It has no caffeine or sugar. I wonder what the point is. She says she's impressed with me and my work. I seem to know more about this case than anybody. A waitress with a nose ring and skintight polyester pants puts our food in front of us. Connie says this trial will be huge. It completes the trilogy that began with the Menendez brothers and O.J. It has sex and wealth and a violent murder and will make a terrific movie of the week if she knows anything about the marketplace.

I ask her what she wants me to do.

"I want you to sign a contract," she says. "I'll represent you. We'll put together a proposal. It can be an account of how you broke the story. Or a straightforward look at the case in the third person. It doesn't matter. Every publisher in the country will want your book."

She takes a forkful of chicken salad. I ask her how much money I'll make.

There's no afternoon session so I drive back to the office. On the radio a news announcer says a gang of youths broke into a house last night in Tarzana. They assaulted the homeowner, a single mother who works at Pacific Bell, as well as her twelve-year-old daughter and a friend of hers who was sleeping over for the night. All their belongings were wrecked and the three were raped and sodomized and beaten within an inch of their lives. They're in critical condition at local hospitals. The radio has a soundbite from the mother of the girl who was sleeping over. "I thought she was safe," the sobbing woman keeps saying.

I file early. Trish says she wants to talk to me. We go to the back stairwell and she takes her accustomed step.

"Do you know where Rebecca is?" I ask.

"Why do you want to know?"

"Just curious. I haven't seen her."

"She called in sick."

Trish asks if I ever found out anything about Megan's diary. She says she realizes a lot has happened since she last pushed me about this but still. It would be a good thing to have.

I tell her my sources believe the diary is unattainable, although no one knows exactly where it is anymore.

"What does 'anymore' mean?"

"It was in her house for a while. It's not there now."

"The police don't have it?"

"No."

"Who does?"

"I'm not sure. For all I know it's been destroyed."

I lean back against the wall. I want to put as much distance as possible between Trish and myself, as if she represents a part of society to which I no longer belong. I tell her about my conversations with Connie Battaglia. She says she's not surprised and she's sure it won't be a problem as long as my coverage of the trial for this paper remains my top priority. I assure her it will be.

As we walk up the stairs Trish says writing a book is a good idea. She says I might be able to get out of here.

"What do you mean?"

"Layoffs are coming. It's gonna be ugly."

She says the new CEO ordered a third of the pressmen fired today after the morning run. It's only a matter of time before the newsroom gets hit.

"It won't matter to you, I guess," she says as we enter the newsroom. "You'll be safe no matter what."

I shake my head. "Nobody's safe," I tell her.

The salty air breezes into my face and makes me think of her. I picture us talking and then her taking off her clothes with the lights still on. We won't wait for the bedroom, we can't wait, we'll make love on the floor or the couch or the table and everything will be all right.

Or I could just do what I want. No one will stop me. I know that now.

I ring the bell and feel an eye looking at me through a peephole. The door opens and she stands there in jeans and a tank top, her arms folded across her chest.

"Oh," she says. "It's you."

"Can I come in?"

"It doesn't matter."

She steps away but leaves the door open. I tell her she should close it. You can never tell what might come in.

She says it already has.

"Are you mad at me?" I ask.

Her eyes widen and she's seized by deep, convulsive, mocking laughter. I grab her shoulders and then take her chin in my left hand and force her to look at me.

"Stop it," I say. "Stop it right now. You are not old enough, or smart enough, to treat me this way."

My voice and my anger are rising. Perhaps I'll just let them go.

"You just watch yourself," she says.

She raises her right arm as if she's about to slap me but I shove it down to her side. She tells me it hurts. She tells me to stop.

"I'll stop if I feel like it," I say.

"Do you know where I went today? Do you know why I called in sick?"

I don't answer.

"I had an appointment. At a clinic. They took care of a problem I had."

I put my hand behind her head and try to bring her toward me but she breaks free and backs up toward her room in a crouch. I'm reminded of the way the librarian left me up near Tahoe.

"There's no way in hell I'd bring your baby into the world."

I lunge for her but she sprints into the bedroom and closes and locks the door. I ram my shoulder against it and tell her to come out, to get out here right this minute goddammit and face whatever it is that I am going to do to her.

"You left without me," she says. "You went up to Tahoe, you sonuvabitch, and you didn't even tell me. I've been calling you for days and you never even bothered to call me back."

"*Get out here!*"

"Where have you been? What are you doing at night?"

"*Get out here and face me!*"

"What are you doing? What do you want?"

I stop. Sweat pours down my face and chest and my breathing is hard and heavy and I'm sure my face is flushed. I back up, one foot behind the other as I move unsteadily across the room. Although I have to leave, I can't pull my eyes from her door.

When I get back to my apartment I make myself a cup of coffee. As it brews I get on my hands and knees and reach under my bed. The tape is still there. I think I'm ready now. I take it with me to the kitchen and put it on the counter. As I pour the coffee into a white ceramic mug I play the messages on my machine. Connie says she wants my proposal by the end of the week, if that's possible. Several publishers have already indicated interest. A young woman identifies herself as a production assistant for a cable talk show. She says they're putting together a regular panel to provide commentary on the Brad Devlin case and wonders if I'm interested. The final message is from Noreen. She says it is vitally important that we speak. She's worried about something. She promises she won't make a scene.

I put the tape in the VCR and hit Rewind. I taste the coffee but it's too hot, so I blow lightly across its surface. When the tape finishes rewinding I hit Play. The scene is of a swimming pool. Steam rises from it. The pool is in a glass-enclosed porch that's decorated with red-white-and-blue bunting. In the background I see the bark and needles of massive pine trees.

Megan stands on the other side of the pool. She looks around constantly, as if trying to get used to her surroundings. A voice says, "Over here!" and she smiles and waves at the video camera, which seems to be on a tripod. The camera does not shake or pivot or turn.

Her teeth sparkle and for a moment I see some delight in her eyes; it's the look of a girl who's more than satisfied by her circumstances. She wears a two-piece bathing suit. Her hair falls beneath her shoulders. She's slender and when she dives into the water and begins to swim there's a certain grace to her movements.

Brad appears. His trunks reach almost to his knees. He jumps in and goes to her. She smiles and they kiss. They look like two normal kids and for a moment I wish they were. Then Brad puts his hands on her head and plunges it into the water. She comes up spluttering and gasping. She calls him a bastard. Her voice is soft yet firm, but he laughs at it. She takes a swing but misses. He grabs her arm and twists it. At first she grins but then she yells out in pain and tells him to let go. He twists harder. She tells him to stopit stopit stopit and he says he will if they have sex. She says okay.

They climb out of the pool and take off their bathing suits. Megan lies down and Brad gets on top of her. It's a short encounter. He doesn't use a condom and doesn't pull out. The tape records several similar incidents, most of them in bedrooms.

I sip my coffee. It's just the right temperature now, but I used too much sugar.

Finally there's a scene of Megan alone in a wood-paneled room. She stands at the foot of a king-sized bed. Antlers hang over the headboard. Megan wears torn jeans and a flannel shirt. A voice tells her to disrobe. The voice is deeper than Brad's. It sounds older and somehow familiar. I know I've talked to it.

Megan obeys.

The voice tells her to get into bed.

She does.

I hear heavy footsteps, the sound of a man. When they stop she looks up. I try to tell what's in her eyes but already, despite her age, she's adopted the mask of adulthood.

Jeremiah Devlin stands over her. He's not wearing a shirt. He takes off his belt and tells her to roll over. She complies. He folds his belt in half and whips it against her buttocks. The sound of leather on flesh is like the rough edge of the world tearing away at innocence. He says she's been a bad girl and after a number of slaps she says she's sorry, she's sorry, she's really sorry, she apologizes for everything she's done, she promises to be good.

Devlin takes off his pants and gets into bed with her. As they begin to have intercourse he asks if she likes it, if she appreciates his generosity and is grateful for everything he's done for her. She says she is. He says she knows what to call him. She says she doesn't. He says he wants to hear it and if he doesn't he'll have to smack her. So in a voice that has become deeper and more hollow she says thank you so much Daddy I owe you so much Daddy I'll do anything for you Daddy Daddy Daddy. . . .

A few years after my parents divorced, my father passed through the town I was living in, so we went out to dinner. He asked if I ever heard from "your mother." That's how he referred to her. "Your mother."

I said we sent each other Christmas cards. That was about it. He nodded and finished his soup. Then I asked him a question. I was amazed it came out of me. But he was there and I was curious and so I asked: "Did you ever love her?"

"No," he said quickly. "I don't think I ever did."

three

I call Noreen at home during the workday. As I plot what to say to her machine, she answers. I stumble a bit and say hi. I wasn't expecting her to pick up. She says she has a migraine. She's been in bed most of the day. I ask what's causing it and she says the stress and tension and strain she's under. She's been getting things in the mail.

"What kind of things?" I ask.

"Terrible things. I've talked to the police. But I need to discuss something with you."

"I'm at the office. I can't talk right now."

She says she understands and suggests we get together. It won't be like old times. We'll just be friends.

"That sounds fine," I say, hoping I sound wary.

She says maybe we could go to a coffeehouse. She's been doing that a lot lately and tonight Kristen will be at her father's.

Court convenes after lunch. Morning was spent in private discussions in Judge Baden-Howell's chambers. As the prospective jurors are vetted I look around the room. Most of the seats are occupied by members of the media but sitting a few rows in front of me—his back straight and eyes transfixed and hands planted squarely on his knees—is a man I recognize even though he doesn't belong to my brethren of colleagues and competitors. It doesn't surprise me at all that Raul is in the front.

During a recess I stand and stretch and walk into the hall. Before leaving the room I pat my pocket to make sure I still have my pass. I sit on a plastic bench, unfold my laptop and start filing B-matter. After a moment I hear a familiar voice saying it's good to see me again, he was hoping I would be here and had even prayed for it, but he doesn't want to interrupt me while I'm working.

Without looking up I tell Raul he isn't interrupting me at all. Good reporters can write while carrying on a conversation. He says yes, now that he thinks about it my observation makes sense, but of course he had never considered it before. He tells me he is still fascinated by the case, even more so now that he can witness it in person. I ask if he's ever been in court before and I can feel him shaking his head as he says this is his first time. I say all trials are basically alike. Some just last longer than others. Raul says he admires Richard Alvarez but the prosecutor is appealing also. She has a bearing about her. He likes a woman who knows how to carry herself. He leans close and says she reminds him in some ways of the lady I used to go with. I say I don't see the resemblance and he says he wasn't speaking of physical things, it's more her manner and attitude and the way she goes about her business.

I ask Raul if he's still at the gas station. He says he is. He works all night but now he doesn't mind. It will enable him to come here during the day. I ask what his family thinks and he says they've returned to Mexico. It's much cheaper to live there. He sends them money.

Court ends at five. We all rush outside to hear the spin. When the lawyers are done a young woman comes up to me and asks if I'm Ted Lowe. She's accompanied by a ponytailed guy with a video camera who's wearing army fatigues. I say that I am and she says she's from Court TV. She called me a couple of days ago.

Her hair is short and straight and red. I wonder if the color and texture are real. She shakes my hand vigorously and says she hopes we can work together. I say it sounds good, but I have to talk to my editors. I should get it cleared by them. She says of course. She understands. But she's wondering, since I'm standing here and her cameraman is ready, if I can't say something about the trial for their nightly show. It might get me some good publicity. Anyway it can't do any harm. I tell her to go ahead. The cameraman starts shooting and she asks how it feels to see the subject of so many of my stories answering to the charges that I made. I say I never made any charges. I merely reported what I and other people had found.

Trish stops her cursor near the bottom of my story. It's a short paragraph noting that the judge and attorneys spent the morning in chambers.

"What were they talking about?" she asks.

"I don't know. It was private."

"Can you find out?"

I look at the clock. I'm going to be late for Noreen. I'll apologize. I'll tell her something came up. There was nothing I could do about it. She'll say there's always something you can do about it. Staying late was a choice I made.

"I'll try," I say to Trish.

I call Frank Gruley, who's still at work, and ask what they talked about in chambers this morning.

"I wasn't there."

"That wasn't my question."

He pauses.

"I shouldn't tell you this," he says.

I remain quiet. When a man says something like that, you should just let him keep talking.

"Monica's been looking for Megan's mother," he says. "She wants to call her as a witness. Issue a subpoena if she won't testify voluntarily. She thinks the woman knows a lot about the murder that she hasn't told anyone."

"Has she found her?" I ask. My voice rises about a half-octave higher than normal.

"Not yet," Gruley says. "Monica made an informal request to Alvarez about a week ago. Said she wanted to talk to Megan's mother. Said she understood the woman was living with Jeremiah Devlin. Said she sympathized with her for trying to avoid the media. I hope you're offended."

"I assume Alvarez sat on this request?"

"Monica formally raised the issue this morning in the judge's chambers. And Alvarez said he'd been unable to locate the woman."

One of the cracks in my knuckles had scabbed over, but now it reopens. Blood trickles out and drops onto the keys on my computer.

"So what happened?" I ask.

"Monica went ballistic. Accused Alvarez of hiding the witness. Of deliberately withholding information that should be shared with the prosecution. She said she's shared everything he's asked for in discovery and he's responded by stabbing her in the back. Alvarez feigned being hurt by what she said. Alvarez feigns very well."

"And the judge?"

"Said she wanted to keep all this quiet until she figured out what to do. But she didn't sound too happy with Mr. Alvarez."

"What happens if I print this?" I ask.

"The judge gets angry. Threatens you a little, but you're a sonuvabitch, so you won't tell her anything. Then she'll impose a gag order, but she should've done it already. So it's her own goddam fault."

"So nobody knows where she is?" I ask. My voice sounds faint, as if I'm talking on a phone in a tunnel.

"I don't. Do you?"

"Why do you say that?"

"I was just making conversation. But now I think you know something."

I wonder what I can tell him. I wonder what he'll believe.

"I've heard something," I say. "I can't print it."

"What have you heard?"

I feel a noose tightening around my neck. Breath comes in short, quick spurts. I don't know if the words will get out.

"You might want to check Jeremiah Devlin's place in Sun Valley," I say. I see the trapdoor swinging open under my feet as I begin the plunge to oblivion.

"The DA's office sent somebody up there last week. They didn't find anything."

"Check it out again."

"Why do you say that?"

"I can't tell you."

"It's a good thing for you I'm an understanding guy. Some people I work with would insist you answer that question."

A narrow storefront on Pico is the only place in sight that's lit but I'm so surprised it's there I miss it and have to go around the block. Before I go in I double-check the locks on my car.

People dressed in black lounge on torn and over-stuffed sofas or hard but rickety wooden chairs as they read magazines usually found at the dentist's office. A few have books. Nobody speaks to anyone else.

Noreen sits at a small round table against the wall. She wears sunglasses even though she's inside at night-fall. Her elbow is jammed into the table and her wrist has gone limp. She looks like she should be smoking a cigarette.

I walk up to her and say hi. She jumps a little before

she realizes it's me. She smiles by spreading her lips a bit. She half stands and presses her palms on the table, then leans forward and rubs her nose lightly against my cheek.

After we sit a college-age boy who's attempting a goatee asks what we'd like. Noreen orders an iced decaf cappuccino and a small piece of the mocha java cake with very little icing. I say I'll have the coffee of the day. He asks how I like it. I say I'll take it black.

Noreen informs me that she got the message I left saying I'd be late. She says she appreciates my thoughtfulness and asks if this is a new policy. I think she's smiling or at least trying to. I say I have no policies. It just seemed like the right thing to do.

She asks how I am.

I say I'm doing all right.

The waiter brings our order. The coffee is so strong it almost forces my eyelids off. I might have a second cup. Noreen makes a pleasant humming sound and says the cake is good but they left on too much icing. They always do.

"You were seeing someone," she says to me.

I mumble something.

"What was her name? I don't think you ever told me."

"Rebecca."

"How is she?"

I see my reflection in my drink but it looks as if my eyes and upper lip have been hollowed out. I tell myself they're only in shadow. They're still part of me.

"Why don't you want to talk about her?" Noreen asks.

"Something's come up."

"Can't you tell me what it is?"

"I'd rather not."

"I meant it when I said we could be friends. Why won't you tell me what it is?"

"Are you sure you want to know?"

"Yes."

"She had an abortion."

Noreen swallows a piece of her cake and dabs at the corner of her mouth with a paper napkin. For the first time I notice that her lips are crimson.

"How do you feel about that?" she asks at last.

"She did it without telling me."

"So you must be angry. You do get angry sometimes. You don't like to admit it. So you don't handle it well."

I remind Noreen that she wanted to discuss something with me. That she's been getting things in the mail.

I am a modern man. I form no judgments. I merely absorb and record.

Noreen wipes her mouth. Her napkin looks as if it's been used to stanch a wound. She says she's afraid and I say everyone's afraid. It's a part of the time and place in which we live. But as tears run from underneath her glasses she says she's afraid for Kristen.

I ask her why.

She reaches down and takes a stack of papers from a large carrying bag. The papers are bound with a rubber band. As she puts them on the table she says these are copies. The police have the originals.

Even looking at them upside down, I can see that the notes have all been cut from newspapers and magazines and pasted onto plain pieces of paper.

Noreen hands me one and says, "This was the first."

In huge letters made dark by photocopying the note says, "HOW'S KRISTEN?" She was alarmed but decided not to tell anyone. She thought somebody might be playing games and Kristen was doing so much better academically and socially she didn't want to do anything that might disturb her daughter's new routine. But the notes continued to arrive. They said things like, "KRISTEN IS A CUTE YOUNG GIRL" and "YOU MUST TAKE GOOD CARE OF HER" and finally "WE KNOW SOME BOYS WHO LIKE KRISTEN A LOT." Finally she went to the police and told them she was being harassed. She showed them the notes and they agreed she had cause to worry. None of the letters had a return address of course and there were no fingerprints on any of them. The postmarks were from all over the Valley. The police began to send cruisers by her house several times a night but with all the budget cuts their resources are strained and they don't know how long they'll be able to continue. Meanwhile the post office has helped out by intercepting all suspicious letters to her house but sometimes they still get through. Whoever's doing this is clever. Most of the time the addresses are printed on computerized labels so they almost look like they're part of a mailing. One letter looked like it came from the Hilliard School. Police talked to officials there who said they had no idea who could have sent them.

Virtually anyone who walked into the office might have taken one of those envelopes. We're talking about hundreds or maybe even thousands of people.

Noreen gives me copies of the notes that got through to her. They describe in ever more graphic detail what its senders plan to do to Kristen and they say that, best of all, they're going to strap Noreen into a chair and force her to watch everything they do.

"Whenever I get one of these, I get a migraine," she says. "I got another one a couple of days ago. I keep thinking about it and my head starts pounding. That's why I'm wearing these glasses."

"What did it say?"

As she hands it to me she says she couldn't understand why she and Kristen had been targeted, but maybe this explains it. The note has my byline clipped from the paper. Underneath it, again composed of letters chopped from various periodicals, are the words: "ASK HIM WHY WE'RE DOING THIS."

"Have you shown this to the police?" I ask.

"Not yet. I thought I'd talk to you first. What does this mean? Why are they doing this? Who's doing it?"

Her voice rises, demanding and insistent, and I see what they will do to Kristen and to Noreen and as the scene plays out in my mind I realize that the violence I have recorded and now embraced has washed back on this woman who once meant something to me.

I could tell her I don't know what this means.

I could tell her to show it to the police and I could tell the police everything, but I suspect I will be treated even more harshly than Brad.

Perhaps I deserve to be.

I tell her I think somebody's doing this just to yank my chain. It's a person who's unhappy with some stories I've written. I tell her I'll try to take care of it and ask her to give me a couple of days.

"Do I have a couple of days?" she asks. "Does Kristen?"

"Yes," I say. "Yes, I think you do."

My friend Gary got a job right out of high school putting exhaust pipes on cars at the local Ford plant. He thought I was crazy to go to college, and when I told him I was going to become a reporter he almost spit in his beer. "I hope I'm never in the fucking newspapers," he said. "They'll probably spell my fucking name wrong."

Gary got married and had some kids. I worked at a few papers, always drifting west. We lost touch. But one day I saw a story on the wires. A laid-off autoworker came into his former plant with a high-powered rifle and just started shooting. According to the story, when he was down to his last bullet he turned the gun on himself. After the spree the authorities went to his home and found his wife and kids dead.

Gary's name was in the second paragraph. It was spelled incorrectly.

four

onica's husband drives her to court in a minivan with tinted windows. Sales of this model have skyrocketed since jury selection began. Reporters shout questions about Megan's mother. Monica says in a tight-lipped way that she's saving her remarks for court.

A few minutes pass before the white limousine appears. Long and low, almost cylindrical, it too has tinted windows. Richard Alvarez gets out and the edge of the crowd emits a bit of a gasp. Alvarez wears a dark gray suit, a crisp white shirt from an Italian designer and a tie with a Mayan pattern. A few of the teenage girls say he's cute even though he's kind of old. One wonders aloud what it would be like to fuck him.

But the gasp was not for him because another figure has emerged from the limo. The highschool girls press against the barricade and scream and squeal in a high-pitched roar that reminds me of the time I went to a slaughterhouse and heard the final sounds of the pigs as the conveyor belts took them toward the jagged mechanical knives. I feel bodies surge behind me and I'm carried close to the wedge Alvarez and his assistants have created around their client. I've sensed this kind of aura around rock stars and professional athletes.

I make out some words.

—"Oh Brad I love you, Brad you're so cute, Brad I wanna have your children, Brad you're innocent, Brad you're cute, Brad call me when you get out, Brad"—

The defendant smiles and waves. Reporters hurl questions so quickly none of them can be heard. A camera knocks into the back of my head and I feel a burly guy with a sixteen-millimeter trying to slide around me. I elbow him in the ribs and he doubles over and his camera clatters to the ground. The media surge over it and I hear glass and metal and plastic parts being ground into their original elements.

"We want everyone to know that my client is not in hiding," Richard Alvarez is saying. "He holds his head up high. Because he is innocent. He's not afraid of anything—not even the media."

"Did you know that you're a celebrity, Brad?" one of the bubbleheads asks as she shoves a microphone in his face.

"This is cool," Brad says.

A few girls break through the barricade that separates the media from the people. One of them thrusts a piece of paper at the defendant.

"Sign this Brad please sign this for me."

"What about Megan's mother?" I ask quietly.

Alvarez looks at me. He has heard. He looks ahead. He puts his arm around Brad.

"Oh I wish I could do that," one of the girls says.

"What about her?" I ask, louder.

The defense entourage sweeps up the steps.

"You heard me, Alvarez. What about her?"

I believe I'm shouting. But so is everyone else. We've created nothing but din.

"I'm sure you've all read the paper this morning," Judge Baden-Howell says as soon as she enters the courtroom.

A murmur goes through the room. A few spectators glance at me.

"I'm quite displeased," she says. "It seems we have a leak."

Both Monica and Alvarez swear in open court that they were not the source of the information that appeared on the front page of this morning's newspaper. The judge frowns.

"I understand that the writer of that article is present this morning?" she asks.

I stand. I believe that's what I'm supposed to do. Raul smiles at me from the front row.

"I'm present, Your Honor," I hear myself say.

"I'd like to see you in chambers. Court will stand in recess for a few minutes."

I follow the judge and a stenographer through a door held open by an unsmiling bailiff. I hear my shoes echo on the tile floor. On TV it looks like marble.

Judge Baden-Howell's private room is small and stuffed with casebooks that have overflowed their allotted shelf space, spilling onto chairs and tables in uneven piles. She sits behind her desk without removing her judicial robe and begins as soon as the stenographer is ready.

"You heard me pose a direct question in open court to both counsel," the judge says. "Did either one of them give you the information for your story?"

She blinks rapidly. I assume she's wearing contacts.

"With all due respect, Your Honor," I hear myself say, "I respectfully decline to answer your question."

"Do you know I can hold you in contempt?"

"You've put me in a difficult position, Your Honor. I'd like to assist the court, but I haven't had the opportunity to discuss this matter with my newspaper's attorney, or with my supervisors. I'd like to do so before answering any of the court's questions. And if I'm to be questioned by Your Honor, I'd like to be represented by counsel."

Judge Baden-Howell stares at me as if she's flabbergasted I didn't tell her what she wanted to know.

"I want to see you and your newspaper's attorney in my courtroom right after lunch," she says.

"Very good, Your Honor."

Behind me I hear the bailiff opening the door. I turn and walk out. I leave the courtroom and walk down the hallway toward the elevators. I hope to make it there unscathed but my colleagues flood out of an anteroom that's been set up to handle the media overflow. I'm surrounded by reporters shouting questions I can't hear. I smile and tell them I can't say anything. I have to save the best stuff for my employer.

"Did she threaten to put you in jail?" somebody asks as I step into the elevator.

"I don't intend to go to jail," I say.

As I walk across the newsroom Trish rushes over asking where I've been. Everyone is looking for me. They've located the attorney. He's somewhere in the building. I'd better talk to him. She tells me to stay at my desk.

Rebecca is a few cubicles away, staring at her terminal as if it's the only thing in the world.

Trish leads three men in suits toward us. I recognize Howard Fussman and the managing editor. The other man is unknown to me. I assume he's the attorney. He wears a bow tie and round owlish glasses.

"Hi howareyou," Fussman says to me.

The managing editor suggests we use his office. I haven't been in there since the day I was hired. The walls are lined with framed testaments to our newspaper's excellence from award committees all over the country.

The managing editor sits behind his desk, leans back in his chair, intertwines his fingers behind his neck and asks, "What the fuck do we do now?"

"I never liked this story," Fussman says.

"We have several options," the attorney says.

"What are they?"

"We need to discuss them."

"We're in a precarious position."

"The paper's future is at stake."

"I never liked this story."

Next to me I hear Trish repeatedly saying "Excuse me"—softly at first, then more loudly, until finally she booms out the words in an extremely curt tone that causes the conversation to stop. The men look at her as if she's done something unforgivable.

"This is a no-brainer," she says. "We cite the First Amendment, and if that doesn't work, we invoke the shield law. Judges don't have the power to coerce reporters into revealing their sources. The state of California says so."

The managing editor smiles at her as if she were a bright student who didn't quite understand the complexity of the universe.

"Jeremiah Devlin's attorneys called me this morning," he says. "They informed me that they're contemplating filing libel and defamation suits against this newspaper once the trial is over. They said they can prove we had a vendetta against them."

"I can back up everything I've written," I say.

"That's not important," the attorney says. "What's important is that if we invoke the shield law, in a subsequent action they can say our refusal to cooperate with the court is another sign of the bad faith in which we approached this story."

"I just got off the phone with our new CEO," the managing editor says. "He's quite anxious to avoid a lawsuit by Jeremiah Devlin. For understandable reasons. His pockets are a lot deeper than ours and he could bankrupt this paper if he wants to."

"It seems to me there are several different strategies we can pursue," the attorney says.

"I don't want to go to jail," I say quietly.

"Perhaps if we wargame them out—"

"I don't want to go to jail."

"And reach a consensus, we can move on to—"

"I don't want to go to jail!"

I know I shouldn't be screaming.

"Do you understand that? I don't want to go to jail!"

"There's no need to shout," the managing editor says.

I'm standing now. I don't know how I've risen. I imagine I'm pleading for my life before a tribunal of elders that feels an occasional human sacrifice appeases the gods.

"What's so goddam difficult about invoking the shield law?" I ask. "That's what it's there for."

Trish stares at her shoes. I look around the room, from one person to the next, and notice that no one returns my gaze, although just this once I wish I had the attention of an audience.

"You could tell the judge the name of the person who gave you the information for your story," the attorney says. "We could handle this in chambers and—"

"I won't do that."

"Why not?"

"It's unethical."

He raises his eyebrows.

"Who is your source?" Fussman asks.

"I don't want to tell you," I say.

"Why not?"

"Because I don't trust you."

"Are you going to put it in your book?" he asks.

"Probably not. But if my source says it's all right to use his or her name, I will."

"I don't like the fact that you're working on a book about this story. I think it's distracting."

"Reporters do books all the time. Why single me out?"

"You talked to Court TV the other day."

"They asked me some questions."

"I think you have a conflict."

"I think you're an idiot."

As I head for the door I pass by my newspaper's attorney.

"I expect you to invoke the shield law," I say. "If you don't want to, I'll hire my own lawyer. And I'll be happy to explain to everybody why I did."

When I approach the courthouse a photographer runs toward me and then a cameraman followed by others and I realize that I am, for at least one afternoon, famous. Still and video cameras, microphones, reporters and technicians all crowd around me. I throw my elbows out to create some space but they come closer, touching me, their faces filling my eyes and shouting questions I can't possibly answer. I feel as if I'm about to be swallowed but as I reach the steps I start to run, freeing myself from the pack and gaining, at least for a second, the blessed sense of solitude.

I ride up the elevator alone and step out on the floor where the courtroom is located. As I walk down the hall I see Maynard Reynolds standing with his back against the wall and his arms folded across his chest and his eyes drooping until they're three-quarters closed, as if he's seen this all before and none of it interests him. Everybody walks around him, no doubt remembering his disgrace and regarding any redemption he may have achieved as temporary.

I walk up and shake his hand.

"Why did you call Maynard?" he asks.

I tell him about what happened in the managing editor's office. He rolls his head, as if he's amazed that white people are even more stupid than he imagined.

"You guys have a get-out-of-fucking-jail-free card and you're not gonna use it?" he asks. "What kind of fucked-up-white-man logic is this?"

"They're afraid Devlin's gonna sue them."

"If you're afraid of getting sued, you shouldn't run a newspaper. Are your bosses trying to get rid of you? They don't want you on this story anymore, so they won't mind if you spend a little time with the homeboys?"

"Could be. I never look for reasons. There usually aren't any."

"Bullshit. There's a reason for everything."

"I may need my own lawyer. Can you handle this?"

"Maynard will invoke the shield law. On those rare occasions when Maynard has a client, his top priority is keeping that client's ass out of jail."

I hear my name being called and look down the hall. My newspaper's attorney stands at the door to the courtroom. I believe he's wearing a different tie.

"If he tries to fuck you, Maynard's in the back row. You can always ask for different counsel."

The newspaper's attorney glowers, but I say nothing to him. Raul intercepts me in the doorway to the courtroom. He says he's concerned about me, but he knows I have inner strength, so he's sure I will emerge from this unscathed and perhaps even stronger. Sometimes God tests us. Still, just in case the judge decides to exercise the power of the law, he wants me to know that his cousin Manuel is a guard at the county jail and will look after me. Raul has already telephoned him to that effect.

The attorney leads me to the table Monica has been using, opens his briefcase and takes out several books and notepads. I study the bench, the jury box, the witness stand. I see cracks in the fake wood and shavings that have flaked off and scattered finely over the floor.

"Why did you talk to him?"

These are the first words the attorney has said to me privately.

"Raul is an acquaintance," I say. "I wanted to be polite. He's trying to help."

"Not him. Reynolds. You shouldn't be talking to another attorney. Especially a guy like that."

"I've known Maynard a long time. He doesn't raise his eyebrows when I use a word like 'unethical.' "

Judge Baden-Howell enters promptly at one, pours herself a glass of water and looks at my newspaper's attorney. She asks who he is and whom he is representing. He makes it clear he is representing my newspaper. She asks if he knows why he is here, and he says he does.

"Good," she says. "There's no need to waste time

by going over the background. I'm trying to get a jury seated."

The attorney says he understands Your Honor's displeasure with the leak, but he believes her wrath is directed at the wrong target. The newspaper merely printed information it received, information it believed to be accurate about a matter of considerable interest to the public. He does not need to remind the judge that historically the courts have encouraged a free and unfettered press—

Judge Baden-Howell says she has never uttered words like those nor is she ever likely to. Her primary concern is assuring the Sixth Amendment's guarantee of a fair and speedy trial to each defendant and she certainly cannot provide that guarantee if every conversation she has in chambers appears in the newspaper.

The attorney says he sympathizes with how she feels, but the function of any media outlet is to disseminate accurate information to the public in a timely manner. He does not believe—

Judge Baden-Howell says she has grown weary of self-serving justifications from the news media. She wishes journalists would consider the obligations of citizenship as well as its rewards, which in their case is a nice paycheck and, often, celebrity.

With that, she addresses me by name. I stand. She asks if I'm ready to answer her questions. I ask if it's the same question she posed in chambers this morning. She says it is. I tell her once again, this time in public, that I respectfully decline to reveal the source of my story. Next to me the attorney opens one of the case-books he has brought with him. He tells the judge that, if it please the court, my refusal is amply backed by the state of California. He cites the shield law and reads the statute number. It's quite long.

Judge Baden-Howell sighs. She says she's aware of the shield law. There are doubts about the constitutionality of these ordinances, and it is within her power to send me to jail for contempt, but she has no desire to introduce extraneous legal issues into what promises to be an arduous trial. She was hoping I and my newspaper would not invoke this law. She was appealing to us in a public-spirited way to assist, not hinder, the process of justice.

She goes on for a long time about how irresponsible the press is. I resist the temptation to look at my watch. Eventually she dismisses us and asks the prosecution and defense to come forward. As I squeeze past Monica she murmurs, "This will be good for your book, huh?"

When we reach the hall, the attorney walks away. I look up and down the darkened corridor and tell myself this is what freedom feels like—I can walk around if I want, or get a drink from the water fountain, or go to the cafeteria and buy a can of soda. Or I can do nothing at all.

I have always believed, and have always told others, that none of it really matters. But perhaps, in the end, it all does.

The holding pen for the news media is a few doors from the courtroom. Half-filled plastic cups leak curdled cream and sugary coffee onto tables that have been pushed together. Cans of soda are piled atop one another in aluminum pyramids. Occasionally one tips over, spilling its contents onto a surface where it eventually finds its way to the edge and then, inevitably, the floor. Whatever is in the soda eats away at the varnish and enamel and anything else that was once applied to protect the furniture.

As I enter my colleagues applaud briefly before resuming their vigil around the four closed-circuit TVs that provide this room's *raison d'etre*. Judge Baden-Howell is telling the lawyers that she had hoped to avoid issuing this ruling, but today's events have made it an unfortunate necessity. Therefore as of this moment she is forbidding any attorney to discuss this case outside the courtroom with anyone who is not directly involved with the prosecution or defense.

"Nice going," somebody says to me. "Now nobody can say anything to us."

"They will," I say. "The need to confess is ingrained in the human soul. That's why Catholicism is superior to all other religions."

Monica asks if she can address the court. Judge Baden-Howell tells her to go ahead, if she's brief. The court is extremely anxious to resume jury selection. Monica says she wants to raise the matter of locating the victim's mother. The prosecutor says it's her understanding that there's a chance the woman is residing at Jeremiah Devlin's house in Sun Valley. She asks that the court instruct Mr. Alvarez to pursue this matter with the utmost diligence. The judge turns to Alvarez and says the prosecution's request sounds reasonable. Alvarez says it has always been his pleasure to comply with all of the court's directives. He's sure he can provide a definitive answer by the beginning of tomorrow's session.

On TV all the attorneys look tall and the court itself seems more impressive. The floor gleams. The wood could be real.

Nine jurors have been selected by five o'clock. In the pressroom we agree that one more day ought to round out the panel. With any luck opening arguments will be delivered the day after that. Out of habit, most of my colleagues rush to the foot of the courthouse steps although the gag order means the attorneys will stride past with brusque "no comments."

I'm one of the last to leave. In the hall I see Maynard and we walk together toward the elevator. When we get in I hit the button for the lobby.

"Maynard has one for you," he says as soon as the doors close.

I tell him I'm listening.

"Maynard keeps wondering what happened to the victim's old man. Guy's daughter is killed. Guy's busted for drugs. Guy's released for lack of evidence or bullshit like that. And then?"

"Guy goes to Australia with young blond girlfriend. I think. We were looking into that angle a while ago, but it got overtaken by events."

The elevator stops and we walk across the lobby. Our steps echo, his more loudly than mine. We walk slowly, in deference to his knee.

"In Maynard's opinion, it should be easy for a diligent newspaperman like yourself to find out if he's in Australia."

"I hear they have strict rules about immigrating."

"Sure do. Tourist visa lasts ninety days. After that, you gotta work. And a foreigner who wants to work in Australia needs a sponsor. Who'd help out surfer boy like that?"

I give Maynard a look that is not disbelieving, but genuinely puzzled that he possesses this information.

"Maynard once considered relocating to Australia, back when it seemed like he'd be unable to make a living in the state of California. Or any other state."

"The guy might be dead," I say. "I've considered that too."

Maynard stops and looks around the lobby. The vaulted ceiling soars into darkness, and sculpted into the walls are statues of the state's founders. Most of them were criminals, but they were caught only by history.

"Maynard misses this shit," he says.

I write a main story on the happenings in court and, at Trish's insistence, a first-person sidebar on my close encounter with the legal system. This is, the paper's in-house historians believe, the first story told in the first person ever to appear in the publication's news pages. My e-mail contains congratulatory notes from my colleagues, while my voicemail has recorded a plethora of calls. The most notable is from Connie Battaglia. Interest is soaring in my book proposal. She hopes I'll have it ready by the end of the week. I also hear a few clicks and hums. I suspect Frank Gruley tried to reach me, but was willing to speak only if he got through directly.

As I'm putting my things away and locking my desk for the night, Trish walks over and says Fussman wants to talk to us. I ask if this is going to take long and she says she doesn't know. I ask what he wants and she says she doesn't know that either. She never knows what he wants.

When we reach his office he's on the phone. Trish pokes her head in. I stand behind her. Fussman makes eye contact but says nothing and makes no motion. He turns his back to the door and continues talking.

"I don't believe this," Trish says as she looks at her watch. "I'm supposed to meet my boyfriend in a half hour. We have tickets to the Laker game."

I don't know which surprises me more—her interest in basketball or her possession of a beau.

"Who's your boyfriend?" I ask.

"Nobody you know. He's an architect."

Fussman tells us to come in. Trish puts her hands on her knees as she sits. I see that she is smiling—not showing teeth, but lips upturned, as if she's pleased to be here. I believe I am smiling also, although I don't know why. I consider offering him an apology even if I don't mean it.

"Hi howareyou," Fussman says.

We both say we're fine.

"I'm sorry if I blew off a little steam earlier," I say. "I was under a lot of stress and—"

"I've been on the phone with the managing editor,"

Fussman says. I don't think he listened to me. "He's talked to the publisher several times. We've been in crisis mode all day." He looks at Trish while pointing at me. "We've decided to take him off the story."

Trish stops smiling. I think I do too. If anyone else were saying this, I'd suspect a practical joke.

"Can I ask why?" Trish says in a voice so faint I'd swear she was on a car phone in a tunnel.

"After today's events, we feel his objectivity has been compromised. How can he write about the judge after dealing with her so intimately?"

"Intimately?" I ask.

"Perhaps it was a poor choice of words," he says.

"Perhaps it was."

"But you know what I mean."

"No," I say. "No, I don't know what you mean. I can still cover this story. I have to cover this story. Nobody else knows what I know."

I'm on my feet, looming over his desk and him, his moon glasses looking up at me and his eyes huge but blank, as if they see nothing except what they want. I feel like reaching down and grabbing him, pulling him up, grinding his glasses into the floor, letting my fists dance on his face, wrapping my hands around his neck and squeezing the breath out of him. It would be easy to do. I know how.

"You can't do this to me!"

I'm screaming.

"I've worked too fucking hard on this fucking story for this fucking newspaper for some dipshit like you to take it away from me. You have no fucking idea—"

Suddenly Trish is next to me, resting her soft hand on my elbow as if she knows she has to restrain me.

She looks at Fussman.

"Can we talk about this?" she asks.

"There's nothing to discuss," he says. "We've gone through this all the way to the top and we're in total agreement. Between what happened in court and his behavior in our meeting and this book he's so obsessed with, it wasn't even a close call."

"Who are you gonna give this to?" I ask. "Someone who'll do what Devlin tells him?"

"No," Fussman says, "somebody who'll do what I tell him. Have you ever looked into that girl's friend and the guy she hangs out with? I've talked to Trish about this repeatedly."

"Megan," I say. "Her name was Megan Wright."

"And her friend's name is Alexis," Fussman says. "And *her* friend's name is Grant Fisher and I think there's something there."

"There's nothing there!"

Trish pushes me toward the door with her palm but she's looking at Fussman with an anger that might, in its own quiet way, equal my own.

"Nobody discussed this with me," she says.

"We didn't have to," he says.

I walk into the coffeehouse and pick up a glossy magazine devoted to architecture and interior design. I sink into an overstuffed chair whose innards are slowly oozing out through several holes in the upholstery. A waitress with green hair and a navel ring asks what I'd like.

"What I'd like is illegal," I say. She tells me I'm funny. "What you can get me is a cup of Kona. Black."

I leaf through the magazine. Once I ascertain that Art Deco is popular this year, I flip through the pages with increasing speed. I have to lash out at someone, make my rage known to the world, punish somebody, anybody, it doesn't matter who, as long as I can make someone else suffer.

A picture in the magazine makes me stop.

The woodsy lakeside home nestled among the tall pines has a moosehead over the main entrance. The interior shots display hand-carved furniture mingled with antiques purchased at auction from Sotheby's. The rugs are all made of authentic animal skins. A caption notes that the bearskin covering the living-room floor was from an animal shot by Theodore Roosevelt.

Jeremiah Devlin appears in only one of the pictures. He leans toward the camera, a half smile on his face. His hair is carefully uncombed, as if the photographer's assistant mussed it a little to give it that windblown look. He wears a western shirt with a bolo tie. His jeans are pressed and his leather boots come from an Italian designer. One foot rests on the seat cushion of an oversized chair. The caption notes that this piece of furniture was made by the finest craftsman in Scandinavia. The wood came from a forest near the Arctic Circle.

The accompanying text calls this place Jeremiah Devlin's rural retreat. He has never before allowed it to be photographed this extensively. He tells the magazine that he calls the house and its grounds Eleanor, after his late wife. She used to love it here. She always preferred the mountains to the ocean. The story quotes him as saying he doubts he'll ever marry again. There are too many memories.

The text notes in passing that at press time Mr. Devlin's son had been mentioned in connection with some unpleasantness in Los Angeles, and expresses the hope that the matter will be cleared up soon so Mr. Devlin can get on with enjoying his life.

I notice a detail in one of the pictures. It would be easy to miss. In a shot of his inground pool (the text notes that renovations were recently completed), a small pink bicycle leans against the far glass wall.

"What are you doing here?"

I look up. Noreen gazes at me with genuine astonishment, as if I've just announced that I intend to become a Buddhist monk and pursue enlightenment until I achieve nirvana.

"I could ask you the same thing," I say.

I put the magazine aside, stand up and peck her on the cheek. She says Kristen is doing a sleepover at a friend's house. She's become a lot more sociable at school lately.

"I didn't want to stay home by myself," Noreen says. "I just feel creepy."

I tell her I understand. The waitress returns and I tell her the lady would like an iced decaf cappuccino. I ask Noreen if she'd like any dessert and she says no, the drink will be fine.

"I haven't had a chance to follow up on that matter we discussed," I say.

"The police still come around," she says. "And I know you were busy today. I saw you on TV."

"I'll have more time tomorrow. I've been kicked off the story."

"Why?"

"They think I can't be objective because of what I went through with the judge."

The waitress brings Noreen her drink. As she sips it, my former lover looks puzzled.

"I don't know much about your business," Noreen says, "but that seems like a frivolous reason."

I drink my coffee. I've had it awhile but it still burns my tongue. I tell myself I don't mind.

Noreen leans back in her chair and waves to somebody behind me. I imagine she's signaling the waitress but in a moment a thin young man with frosted blond hair and three rings in his right ear appears over us.

"This is Michael," Noreen says. "He's the manager."

Michael extends a wet palm that I accept gingerly. When Noreen mentions my name, his eyes go wide.

"No!" he says. "Really?"

I show him my ID.

"What a flattering picture. I never photograph that well. What's your secret?"

He squats beside us. His head is at table level.

"I watched Court TV all day. For a few minutes I thought you'd be going to jail."

"We bribed the judge," I say.

He laughs before swiveling his head toward Noreen.

"Do you remember Sonia? She was here two weeks

ago? I introduced you?" Noreen nods. "She's back. She's going to read her Brad Devlin poetry."

"Brad Devlin poetry?" I ask.

Michael throws out his arms. "In *fin de siècle* America, one finds inspiration wherever one can."

He walks to the middle of the room and claps his hands. The already low level of noise gives way to nothing. Michael introduces Sonia and adds that, in an entirely unexpected treat, the person most responsible for Brad Devlin's, shall we say, predicament is here tonight. He points toward me and says, "Ladies and gentlemen, Ted Lowe." Heads turn. I give a little wave. A few people applaud. I hear others asking, "Who's he?"

A small woman with no hips or breasts steps into a single beam of light. Her almost radiant face is framed by jet black hair. She clears her throat and raises her eyes to the ceiling.

> *Young man in the dock*
> *Indicted for our sins*
> *Committing the Holocaust*
> *Of law, murder and media.*
> *Is any among us safe?*
> *Who among you has not committed a crime?*
> *Handsome reckless youth*
> *Scion of wealth and power*
> *Reviled loved adored and feared*
> *He is who we are*
> *And whom we aspire to be*
> *Our country's complete creation.*

Sonia's clothes are also black, as are her fingernails.

The guy next to us was complaining about the media while CNN blared on a barroom TV. They're always tearing down our businesses, he said, and tearing down the military, and making excuses for the black people, and it's enough to sicken a God-fearing American white man like himself. The bartender tried to quiet him. We were regulars. But as the bartender made eye contact with me, the guy suddenly understood.

"You a reporter?" he asked. "You a fucking reporter?"

I nodded. Said nothing. Sipped my draft.

"There's only one thing you fucks are interested in," he said. "Selling newspapers."

"Congratulations," I replied. "You've figured it out."

five

my story is given to Sander Van Arsdale, a Princeton graduate who attended Stanford Law for a year before deciding to "try my hand," as he once put it to me, at journalism. Within a month of his hiring he was covering the Board of Supervisors. That was at the beginning of the year and there are rumors he's grown bored with it. There are also rumors that management will do virtually anything to make him happy.

A notice on the bulletin board says I'll be returning to my previous assignment doing the police roundup and its ancillary stories. Rebecca will become a researcher on the drought project. The note thanks me for my coverage of the trial so far.

I walk over to Van Arsdale, who is throwing as much of a fit as is permitted a man wearing a Ralph Lauren shirt. Fussman nods as Van Arsdale says he'd planned to go to the supervisors' meeting, and while of course he's delighted to be covering the trial, he needs to change gears psychologically and he's concerned the meeting might fall through the cracks and he doesn't want that. There are important items on today's agenda.

The board might even declare the first stage of a drought warning, which would begin the steps necessary to impose an initial level of water restrictions several months from now.

I walk up to them.

"Hi howareyou," Fussman says.

The question is so ridiculous I ignore it.

"Sandy," I say to Van Arsdale, knowing he dislikes the nickname, "if I can be of any help at all, I will."

"Thanks," he says as he continues to shove notepads and binders into his briefcase. He asks Fussman if anyone has been selected to cover the supervisors' meeting and Fussman says no, it hasn't been decided yet. Van Arsdale shakes his head, looks at his watch and says the meeting begins in less than two hours. Fussman shrugs. Van Arsdale snaps his briefcase shut.

"Brad Devlin," I say. "It's a complicated case."

"I know all about it," Van Arsdale says. "They claim he killed that girl."

"Megan," I say. "Her name was Megan Wright."

Van Arsdale leaves.

"Shouldn't he talk to me?" I ask Fussman.

"Not necessarily," he says before entering his office and shutting the door.

I get a cup of coffee and pass by the conference room. The drought project has convened. In the darkened room about a dozen people sit at the head of a table gazing at a blown-up map of the state of California's water system. The map has lines and squiggles and colors that must mean something if you're interested and these people certainly are—their faces display the fervent discipline that biblical scholars bring to examinations of the Dead Sea Scrolls.

Sitting at the rear of the table, away from the others, dare I say self-segregated, is Rebecca. She looks at her nails and lolls her head in a manner that suggests she's thinking about taking a nap.

I return to my desk and start dialing the numbers that were once familiar to me. A few people say "Welcome back." They tell me Rebecca did a good job. She was enthusiastic and asked lots of questions. They'd never tell her that directly, but maybe I can pass it along.

A secretary at a police station in Carson died while I was on assignment, killed in her living room during a drive-by shooting. The perps missed the guy they were after.

My last call is to a cop shop in the Valley. The sergeant on duty says it's all routine—domestic beatings, car robberies and whatnot—except for this one thing he just got. It might make a good story for the newspaper. I tell him to go ahead.

The sergeant says an elderly couple was at home last night watching one of the talk shows when the wife said she heard a noise in the kitchen. The husband said he didn't hear anything and besides he wanted to watch the monologue. The wife reminded him that his hearing was shot so he couldn't understand the goddam monologue unless he'd suddenly learned how to read lips. She insisted he check it out. So the husband went into the kitchen and flipped on the light. Standing there, just inside the guy's back door, was a group of teenage males, all of them dressed in black and wearing latex gloves and ski masks. Several had baseball bats. The guy was so startled he didn't say anything. Of course he'd heard about the Valley break-ins but he never thought anything would happen to him. You never do, you know. One of the kids asked the man why the fuck he turned on the light and he said, "Because I live here," and another kid swung his bat right into the lamp and it exploded into thousands of pieces that seemed to attack the man, tearing into his hands and face and neck.

The lamp was made of Depression glass. The couple had had it for years.

His wife called out from the living room and asked if he had broken something.

"Where's Kristen?" one of the kids said. "Where's Kristen?" another one echoed, and then they all picked it up, repeating, "Kristen, Kristen," as if it were a mantra.

The guy told them there was nobody named Kristen in the house.

The kids called him a fucking liar and pounded him with the baseball bats and their own fists, sending him reeling backward into the living room, where his wife screamed when she looked up from the TV. They beat her too and kept asking where Kristen was. They went into every room and tore everything apart. They dismantled the beds and threw all the clothes from the closets to the floor. They crushed all the knickknacks. They even smashed the television. They kept asking where Kristen was. The couple kept saying they didn't know. They didn't even know anybody with that name. If they did they'd find her.

After the kids left, the husband and wife lay on the floor a long time. They'd lost a lot of blood and most of their bones were broken. Finally the husband pushed and pulled and crawled to their phone and punched in 911. They're in critical condition at a Valley hospital but the husband was able to talk to police, which was good because now they can make their report.

When the sergeant tells me the address of the break-in, my mouth turns as dry as one of the rain-starved reservoirs.

"If my name were Kristen, I'd be pretty nervous," the sergeant says with a chuckle. "I wonder what she's done."

"Nothing," I say quietly.

"What was that?" he asks.

"I'm sure she's done nothing," I say with as much authority as I can generate. "Nobody deserves what happened to those people."

"Sure they do," the sergeant says. "That innocent victim crap is good for the newspapers, but we know it isn't true."

As I hang up I make a few calculations. The house they broke into is less than a mile from Noreen's. The number of the two addresses is identical and the street names are similar, so they must have gotten confused.

I call Noreen's house but no one is there. I leave a message. "It's me. I don't think I can help you after all.

You can talk to the police, but—if it's at all possible—get out of town. Even if it isn't possible."

I call her at work and get a receptionist. I ask to be put through.

"What is the nature of your call?" she asks.

Life and death, I think.

"It's important," I say.

"Is it personal?" she asks.

"Yes. I suppose it is."

"I'm sorry, I can't put through a personal call. We're under strict orders. No personal calls during work hours. They hinder our productivity."

"But this is urgent," I say.

"I'm sure it is."

"Can I at least leave a message?"

I give the receptionist my name and number, my extension and the time I called. I tell her it's vitally important that Noreen get the message. I cannot emphasize that enough.

She takes the information too quickly. I doubt she's writing anything down. So I locate Noreen's fax number on a scrap of paper in my wallet that's wedged in with various business cards I've collected over the years. I get a plain white piece of paper and write on it in letters as big as I can manage: "CALL ME. RE: MATTER WE DISCUSSED. MOST URGENT."

I hope the fax goes through. Sometimes machines can be as unreliable as people.

A bleary-eyed Rebecca leaves the drought meeting and stumbles a bit as she walks toward her desk.

I meet her and discreetly put my hand on her elbow.

"Falling asleep in meetings is a bad idea, even if they are boring," I tell her.

"Why don't you leave me alone?" she says as she halfheartedly pulls her arm away. If she were fully awake she'd put more oomph in it.

"I'm sorry about what happened," I say. "Looks like we both got hosed."

"I guess we did," she says.

I relay the compliments about her work that the people on the beat gave to me. "And if I had my way," I tell her, "I'd have you cover the trial. You know more about the story than anyone on the staff, except me."

Rebecca doesn't respond. I want her to. Usually I don't care when people fall silent, but right now it's desperately important to carry on a conversation with this womanchild.

"Talk to me," I say.

"I've got work to do," she says.

After lunch I get Connie Battaglia's voicemail and tell it that there's a problem. I get a return call within five minutes. She says she's surprised I'm not at court. I tell her that's what the problem is. I'm no longer on the story. I tell her I can still do the book. I have lots of material. The proposal will definitely be ready by the end of the week. In fact I might have more time now. I could probably take a leave of absence to work on the thing.

She says this is a wrinkle she wasn't expecting. She'll have to talk to some people. She asks who's doing the story now and after I tell her she says she'll get back to me.

Noreen does not call.

From a TV a few feet away I hear the judge announce that opening arguments will begin at nine the next morning. The light on my phone flashes on. I pick it up even before it rings. It's a bit past five and perhaps Noreen's workload has eased to the point where she can phone me. In one motion I put on my headset and say, "Metro. Ted Lowe."

"Do you recognize me, fucker?"

It's a voice from behind me attached to a rope screaming in my ear that it doesn't like questions.

"Don't hurt her," I say quietly.

"Don't hurt who?"

"You know."

"I want you to say it."

"Kristen," I say. "Don't hurt Kristen."

He laughs harshly, full of ridicule but no mirth.

"'Don't hurt Kristen.' Why the fuck not? Why shouldn't we do what we want?"

I cannot reply.

"You've never tried to stop us," he says. "You liked watching us. Don't deny it, you fucker."

"I could call the police," I say.

"You won't. You'd spend more time in jail than we would. But the cops won't believe you anyway."

"Why did you call me?" I ask. "What's on your fucking mind, if you have one?"

"We all think it's too bad about your story. But you

were a pain in the ass. Brad's old man leaned on your publisher. They played golf together. He's a pretty cool guy, Brad's old man. You see, we can do whatever we want. And when all of this bullshit is over, after we're done with Kristen, we're gonna take care of you. Maybe that nigger bitch too."

"You've been watching me," I say.

There is no answer.

"How long have you been watching me?"

As I put my key in the lock and notice the play of my long shadow against the wall and the door, I hear footsteps behind me.

I whirl around. I'm ready.

Noreen stands there with her arms wrapped around Kristen. The child falls shy of her shoulders.

"I got your messages," she says. "All of them."

"Why didn't you call back?" I ask.

"I don't trust the phones. Or the fax. I don't trust anything anymore. I don't even trust you."

I hustle them inside and leave the blinds closed. Kristen asks why she's here. She says she doesn't like this place.

"What's going on?" Noreen asks.

"Can you get out of town?"

She nods stiffly. Then she shakes her head. She says she's afraid of losing her job. It's not the money so much as the benefits. When you have a kid, you really need the medical.

I ask if her former husband can carry Kristen for a while.

She says he's involved with somebody. He used to complain about how little time he spent with Kristen but now he acts like it's a burden whenever she stays with him.

I tell her they have to leave Los Angeles.

"What is it?" she asks. "What are we up against?"

"Something bad," I say. "Something evil."

"Are you part of it?" she asks.

I gaze at her and the girl in whom she has invested her life. Noreen looks more weary than angry while Kristen is thin and waiflike, with wide eyes that take in everything although they'd prefer to leave out the cruel and the ugly and the wicked.

"I'm trying to get out," I say.

Noreen closes her eyes and shakes her head and walks away from me.

"I should go to the police," she says. "I should give them that note and—"

"The police can't help you!"

"Why is he yelling at you, Mommy?"

"Nobody can help you! You don't know what they're like! It doesn't matter what the police do—if they want to kill you, they will!"

"What have you done?" Noreen asks. "What have you done to yourself? What have you done to us?"

I sit in a chair and lower my head into my hands.

"He's scaring me, Mommy."

"You have to escape," I tell them.

"Should we leave now?"

"No. They might be waiting. They attack at night."

Noreen stands behind Kristen, tightly gripping the

girl and wearing the faraway but fierce look of a woman who realizes that the wrong decision could kill the people she loves the most.

She releases Kristen, who turns to look at her mother. Noreen opens her pocketbook and takes out an envelope, which she hands to me.

"This is the last note I got," she says. "The one that mentions your name. I want you to give it to the police."

I put the envelope on an end table and tell Noreen to stay here tonight and to use my bed. I won't be sleeping.

Kristen says she wants to go home.

"We can't go home," Noreen says.

I remember ambulances with flashing lights and white-dressed people shouting at one another while they pushed wheelchairs and stretchers. As we walked across the parking lot it got darker and I remember feeling better because we were getting away from a terrible place.

When we reached the car my father strapped me in. As we drove away he told me that my sister had just died of leukemia. The doctors had done their best and he and my mom had prayed a lot, but in the end there was nothing they could do. I asked what leukemia was and he said it was a disease and it was very bad, a cancer that got into people's blood and killed them. I asked what cancer was and he said it was something inside people that just kept growing until finally all the bad cells in the body drove out all the good ones.

six

In the morning I give Noreen my car keys and tell her to take my vehicle. I'll use hers. I ask her to call me at work when she's a good distance from L.A. I promise to send them money if they need it.

On TV, just before opening arguments, Monica approaches the bench and says a matter has come to her attention that could be highly relevant to the course and outcome of the trial. She says they should speak about it privately. Judge Baden-Howell asks if this is absolutely necessary and Monica assures her it is. The judge orders a short recess and proceeds to her chambers, followed by the two lead attorneys.

On TV the commentators have nothing to comment about. They speculate over what this could mean, and whether it's good for the prosecution or the defense. They ask questions of the lawyers on their expert panel, who all say this is highly unusual. The station breaks for a commercial.

• • •

Monica's opening statement is swift and forceful. She acknowledges there are no eyewitnesses to the crime but says a web of physical evidence incriminates only one person—the defendant, Bradley Devlin. As she points at him, I believe he represses a smirk. Monica says the defendant repeatedly struck the victim over the head with a large blunt object, most likely a baseball bat, then stuffed her body into his car and left her lifeless form at the top of Sepulveda Pass.

"We know this," she says, "because there was a footprint found near the body." She describes the shoe that made the print and concludes: "That shoe belonged to the defendant, Bradley Devlin."

This causes a *whoosh* in the courtroom.

"Did you know about the footprint?" Trish asks.

I shake my head. I know a footprint was found near the scene, but I never discovered that a connection had been made between it and Brad Devlin's shoes.

Richard Alvarez tells the jury: "This young man has been falsely accused by a district attorney's office that *knows* he is innocent, but in this election year is interested in placating a sensationalistic press which has spread lies, smears and innuendo."

Monica objects so loudly I'm afraid she's going to scratch her vocal cords. The judge bangs her gavel and tells Alvarez to stop right this minute or she'll hold him in contempt. This is an opening statement, not a closing one. He is to confine himself to the facts.

• • •

Noreen calls shortly before lunch from a phone booth at the edge of the desert. I ask if she thinks she's being followed and she says no, but she's been checking her rearview mirror a lot anyway. In the background I hear Kristen saying she's thirsty. She wants something to drink.

Noreen says she called work this morning and told her supervisor something had come up and she'd have to leave town for a few days. In that case, he said, she shouldn't bother coming to work again.

I ask her where she's going. She says Vegas sounds good.

Detective Frank Gruley is the first witness for The People. He describes what he found at the top of Sepulveda Pass and details the unsuccessful attempts police made to interview Brad Devlin in the days after the murder. Alvarez objects repeatedly. He is repeatedly overruled.

After a half hour on the stand, Monica asks Gruley about the receipt for the necklace. He says he got a subpoena for the receipt after reading an article in the newspaper.

"There's a problem with the receipt, isn't there?" Monica asks.

Gruley says there is.

"Can you tell the court what it is?"

The detective admits that the LAPD's evidence storage facility seems to have misplaced the receipt. This causes another *whoosh* in the courtroom that the judge, who looks astonished, doesn't even attempt to silence. Gruley says he has a description of the receipt, which he filed into his own notes right after he obtained it. He's also trying to get a copy of the receipt from the credit card company, but this process could take a few days. It was only this morning that he discovered the receipt had been misplaced.

As Alvarez approaches the witness stand, he tugs at his jacket as if he's afraid a thread visible to everyone but himself is hanging off it. He begins his cross-examination by asking if it's customary procedure for the police department to follow up on newspaper reports. Gruley scowls and says it's customary police procedure to pursue all relevant leads.

"Even when they appear in the newspapers?" Alvarez asks.

"If it comes to that."

"When this article appeared, what did you do?"

"I obtained a warrant and went to the jewelry store. I examined their records and took the receipt."

"Did you attempt to interview the reporter who wrote that article?"

"NosirIdidnot."

"Why not?"

"I didn't feel it was necessary."

"Perhaps you would have learned where he obtained his information."

The detective shrugs.

"Did he obtain it from you?" Alvarez asks.

For an instant I'm afraid Gruley is going to leap off the stand, grab Alvarez by the lapels, shout a few ethnic slurs and engage in nighttime police tactics. But in moments his gaze fades from pure blind hatred to the merely angry.

"Nosirhedidnot."

"Then where did he obtain the information?"

"I'm not sure. Perhaps you should ask him."

Gruley should stop. But he doesn't.

"Of course he wouldn't tell the judge what she wanted to hear, so I doubt he'll tell you."

Alvarez wheels around to the bench and throws out his arms but before he can say anything Judge Baden-Howell has rapped her gavel as hard as she can without shattering it. Her face is scarlet. She tells Gruley to watch what he says. He is to answer the question. And that's all.

Frank Gruley nods meekly. His age and background make him the type of man who's much happier confronting a guy with a gun than a woman who's angry at him. He slouches in his chair and begins to shrink as Alvarez asks what he did with the receipt. The detective says he gave it to Sergeant Harris Benton, who was then in charge of the storage facility. Alvarez asks what happened next to the receipt. Gruley says he assumed it was placed in the file along with all the other materials in the case.

"'Assumed'?" Alvarez asks with a tinge of mocking irony.

Gruley shrugs. This is not the type of body language a jury will find convincing. He says he's not sure what happened to the receipt. They've been trying to locate Sergeant Benton, but he's put in for retirement and nobody knows where he is.

● ● ●

I send a perfunctory cop roundup to the desk and read in on Van Arsdale's story. He tops it with Gruley's cross-examination, which will resume in the morning, and says it has caused enormous problems for the prosecution. He cites one source close to the defense as saying the detective's answers reveal "shoddy" police work.

I understand why he led the story this way, but he doesn't mention the footprint until the twentieth paragraph. By that time the story will have jumped off the front page and nestled somewhere amid the Nordstrom ads. Brad's avoidance of the authorities in the days after the murder is even lower. Given our space constraints, it will border on the miraculous if that information gets into the paper at all.

I wander toward Van Arsdale's desk. Fussman stands over his shoulder. I hear Van Arsdale say he believes he's developing a rapport with the defense team. They told him they're looking forward to getting a fair shake now.

I stop beside them.

"Hi howareyou," Fussman says.

I crouch beside Van Arsdale.

"How's it coming?" I ask.

"Okay," he says. He turns to Fussman and asks what happened at the supervisors' meeting. Fussman says they delayed action.

"It's a complicated case," I say. "Don't lose sight of the big picture. It's obvious Alvarez is trying to—"

"I think I've got a handle on it," Van Arsdale says.

"We're doing fine over here," Fussman tells me.

I nod, as if to say "of course," get up and walk

away. I hear Van Arsdale say he needs to leave the office soon. He's having drinks with one of the junior members of the defense team. It's just a social thing so it's not a violation of the gag order.

I root around my desk in a pointless search for nothing. From across the room I can see Rebecca glancing at me as if I'm a dangerous animal that needs constant watching.

Behind me I hear Fussman and the managing editor on their way toward the conference room. The managing editor says he's been reluctant to lead the paper with this story so far, but today's developments are different. They raise significant issues. This is no longer just a sensational murder but a story of police incompetence and misconduct. He wouldn't be surprised if this turns out to be a matter of overzealous prosecution. Fussman says he agrees entirely and adds that Van Arsdale is looking into the question of whether the authorities have targeted the wrong person.

I slam my top drawer shut. I hope they heard.

My phone rings. I could let my voicemail answer, but on the third ring I pick it up. I'm a reporter. I'm supposed to take calls.

A voice that I recognize but can't quite place asks for Ted Lowe. I say he's got the right person and the voice identifies himself as Michael. I try to recall every Mike, Mick, Mikey and Mickey I've ever met. He must sense I'm having trouble because he quickly adds, "Michael from the coffeehouse."

"Of course," I say. "I remember you. How are you doing?"

Michael says he can hardly stand it now that the trial's begun. He was glued to the TV all day. So was everybody else. In fact his place was packed and during those *interminable* breaks people offered their theories on what had happened and who was doing best and whether Brad Devlin would be acquitted. It was a lot of fun. I say it sounds like a feature story. Maybe we can send a lifestyle reporter over there one day when court is in session. I figure he'll thank me for this and hang up. Michael says he appreciates the offer and of course he'd never turn down free publicity, but that's not why he called. He says he wants me to meet someone.

"No offense, Michael," I say, "but I think my sexual orientation is different from yours."

He laughs and says I'm being silly. That isn't what he means *at all*. It would never *occur* to him to try to fix me up. I'm such an *obvious* straight person.

"Whom do you want me to meet?" I ask.

Michael says a friend of his has some knowledge of the case. Firsthand knowledge. And he's extremely upset by what he's seen and heard the past few days.

"I kept looking for you on television," Michael says to me as we sit at a table catty-corner with a green cement wall. "What happened? Banished from the rarefied air of the courtroom?"

"Another reporter is covering the trial," I say.

"Maybe we should talk to him."

"Do you have something interesting?"

Michael nods.

"Then talk to me."

He leans forward and lowers his voice, which acquires a seriousness I have not heard before. He says his friend wants to make this seem like a chance encounter and also wants to be as far from the street as possible. He's a little bit paranoid about all this. I say I understand. These are paranoid times. Michael says all of this has to be off the record of course and I say, "Of course." He tells me the coffee of the day is Jamaican and I say it sounds fine.

In a few minutes he returns with my order and a tall and thin middle-aged man who's clutching a leather carrying case. The man extends a soft moist hand and says his name is Brendan. I don't know if I believe him.

"I've known Brendan for years," Michael says as he sets down our drinks. "He's absolutely reliable."

"I've been watching the case on TV," Brendan says. "I've been watching it for days. From start to finish. It's made me sick to my stomach."

"Why is that?" I ask.

"Because what's going on in the courtroom is not the truth. At least not the entire truth."

"How do you know?"

Brendan looks down at his hands. His nails are stubby, as if he's been gnawing them. His leather case is pressed hard under his arm. He says he's been a good citizen. He's always voted, paid his taxes, never had a blemish on his driving record. He served in the military and when he came out he used his experience in electronics to start his own company. It did all right—in fact it did quite well—but a few years ago he became HIV-positive, so he decided to sell it to Jeremiah

Devlin. It was a difficult time, but Mr. Devlin paid him a good price and allowed him to do some work as a consultant. He doesn't want it to sound as if he's complaining. A lot of people are worse off than he is.

I don't feel like listening to this guy's life story. I want to tell him to get to the point. But sometimes you have to let them talk.

Anyway because of his condition there were times he could do a lot of work but at other times he couldn't even get out of bed in the morning. That's why he appreciated everything Mr. Devlin did for him. He was quite understanding. In many ways Brendan thinks it's disloyal to talk this way but still there is a duty to the truth, isn't there?

Michael pats Brendan on the hand. He tells the older man it's all right, he should just tell me what happened, if he gets it out he'll feel better.

Brendan says he hired Megan's mother several years ago. For his company. He needed an administrative assistant and had put out feelers to a number of people but nobody qualified had turned up. So he placed a Help Wanted ad and of course he was *deluged* with responses and that was exactly what he'd hoped to avoid, but what are you going to do? He sifted through all of them and narrowed it down to a few and invited all of them in for interviews.

She stood out. Certainly an attractive woman, but more than that he sensed she had a drive to make herself better and it's always been his belief that people like that improve the companies they work for. With no prodding from him she talked about going to graduate school at night and learning about the electronics business and taking on additional responsibilities.

He asked if she had any children and she said no.

I look at him with something approaching amazement.

"That wasn't the last lie I caught her in," he says.

Her résumé claimed she had worked as an executive assistant at a law firm downtown. It turned out she'd temped there. She also claimed to have a bachelor's degree from Cal State, Northridge. But she'd dropped out more than fifty credits short.

"I found out all of this in dribs and drabs," Brendan says. "She was an excellent worker. Within six months she was indispensable. I was beginning to not feel well and she just started taking on more duties.

"I took her to lunch one day and told her what I'd discovered about her background. I like to think that I did it gently. She was quite upset. Over and over again she said she was sorry but she thought this was such a great opportunity she exaggerated her qualifications."

Mrs. Wright said she loved the job. It was a really good experience for her. She asked Brendan if her work was satisfactory and he told her it was excellent. Under normal circumstances he would have fired her—with some regret of course—but the circumstances under which he was living had become anything but normal. So he asked her if she had any more surprises and she assured him she didn't.

Shortly after that, Brendan sold his company to Jeremiah Devlin.

I ask how she felt about that.

"Well, everybody was quite apprehensive," Brendan says. After the sale Brendan stayed out of the office for a while because of his health, but when he returned he noticed pictures of a couple of children on Mrs. Wright's desk. He asked who they were and she said they were her son and daughter.

"I said, 'You told me you didn't have children,' and she said, 'Would you have hired me if I told you I did?' And I told her, 'Yes, if I thought you could do the job.' "

Brendan says he didn't know how to handle the situation. He considered raising the issue with Mr. Devlin, although he wasn't sure of the protocol for approaching him about a personnel matter. Anyway one day Mr. Devlin was in the office and they had a general type of discussion for a few minutes, and then he asked to be introduced around the room to all of his people. When they reached Mrs. Wright's desk, she stood up and shook Mr. Devlin's hand firmly and looked him right in the eye.

"I could have said something then," Brendan says, "but I didn't feel it was the appropriate time or place."

Mr. Devlin noticed the pictures on her desk and complimented her on having two fine-looking children. He seemed particularly taken with the photograph of her daughter. He said she was a striking girl.

I wonder if it was the same photograph Mrs. Wright handed to me.

Anyway they talked about their children for a few minutes and then he moved on to the other employees. Shortly after this Brendan got sick again. He never did have a chance to talk to Mr. Devlin about her. When he got back to work he noticed she was gone. At first he thought she'd quit or been dismissed but when he asked he was told oh, no, that wasn't it at all, she'd been transferred to Jeremiah Devlin's main office in the Valley and had received a raise and a promotion.

"There were the usual rumors," Brendan says. "She was sleeping her way to the top, that sort of thing. Perhaps they were true, but I also had no doubt she was doing good work."

The last time he saw her was at Jeremiah Devlin's companywide Christmas party. They were on opposite sides of the room and acknowledged each other by nodding. He noticed that she was wearing pearls and a Donna Karan dress that had been the big hit of the New York shows. She spent a lot of time talking to Jeremiah Devlin. Whenever they were together they stood quite close.

"Why have you been so upset by what's come out in court?" I ask.

"I think they're trying to minimize the relationship between Mr. Devlin and Mrs. Wright," Brendan says. "I don't know why. But I think something went on between them that they don't want anybody to know about.

"So I guess my bottom line is this: I think Mr. Alvarez is being deceitful when he says the defense doesn't know where she is."

An image flashes before me of a woman bound to a bed, drugged, a woman I might have helped if I had courage.

Brendan's face is chalk white except for a little color at the top of his cheeks that's so red it could have been made by rouge. He stares into a cup that has nothing remaining except a few muddy grounds of espresso.

There's only one call on my machine at home. Noreen says she and Kristen are at a motel on the outskirts of Vegas. She leaves a number. I call back and ask how she's doing. She says she's okay, all things considered. In the background I hear Kristen saying she doesn't like this place. Noreen tells her to be quiet. Mommy's talking. Kristen says she wants to talk too. She wants everyone to know she doesn't like this place.

I ask Noreen if she's certain nobody followed her. She says she is. I ask if there's anything I can do for her, and she says yes. They left in such a hurry that Kristen didn't get a chance to pack some of her favorite dresses. Noreen asks if I still have a key to her place and I say I believe I do. She says the dresses are all hanging up in Kristen's closet. Noreen tells me how to disable the house alarm and says Kristen particularly wants the one with the pink floral pattern.

As soon as I put the phone down it rings. I'm always suspicious when something like this happens, as if They're watching me and know exactly the moment I become available.

I pick up the phone and say, "Hello?"

"They found the mother," Frank Gruley says.

"When? Where?"

"Last night. Jeremiah Devlin's place in Sun Valley. You hear good rumors."

"And?"

"Some investigators from the DA's office tried to

serve a warrant. Devlin blocked them. Alvarez was there too. It was like they were expecting them."

"Is that what Monica wanted to tell the judge this morning?"

"No, Monica wanted to talk about the fucking weather. Christ, you ask stupid questions sometimes."

"Anything else happen in Sun Valley?"

"They had a bunch of doctors there. The doctors said the woman had suffered a nervous breakdown, what with the strain and everything."

"She didn't strike me as the type."

"Me either. But they have documents out the wazoo. The woman's incapacitated. She needs lots of bed rest. Can't be disturbed."

I think about what I'm going to say next. The words come out this way: "Can I talk to you? In person? Right now?"

"I was thinking about going to sleep. In case you've forgotten, I have to testify tomorrow."

"This shouldn't take long," I say, and suggest a mutually inconvenient location.

I hear waves lapping up, once in a while crashing. Overhead a sliver of moon is framed by clouds. I think of Rebecca on a blanket, her flesh waiting for mine.

Frank Gruley and I walk near the water. The sand is firm underfoot. A few boats are still in the bay.

"Why did you want to talk?" Gruley asks.

I put on a pair of latex gloves, reach into my pocket and take out a small manila envelope. I shake the contents onto my gloved hand. Even with only a trace of the moon, light glints off the gold and diamonds.

"I found it at the scene," I say. "Your guys missed it."

"You sonuvabitch," Gruley says. "You goddam sonuvabitch. How long have you had this?"

"A while."

"It can't be used at trial. There's no chain of evidence."

I tell him he should check it for prints anyway. Hairs and fibers too.

Gruley shakes his head. "If we find anything, Alvarez will say we planted it."

I put the necklace back in the envelope and hand it to the detective.

"You should have given this to me right away," he says.

"Why? So you could put me on the stand?"

"It's evidence, shithead. Evidence in a murder investigation. You're supposed to turn it over to the police. I could arrest you for withholding it."

"But you won't."

"If he discovered that we missed this"—Gruley waves the envelope with his right hand—"Alvarez would chew my ass up one side and down the other. Besides, we have the receipt. We proved Brad bought this for her the night she was killed. So we don't need it." He puts the envelope in his pocket. "Maybe I'll give it to my wife."

I reach into my shirt pocket and take out the envelope Noreen gave me.

"What is this?" Gruley asks. "A fucking magic show?"

He opens the envelope and reads the note. I tell him

about the messages Noreen's been receiving. He nods and says he's heard about this. In fact they asked Noreen if she thought I was sending these things. She said she doubted it. I was in another relationship.

"So let me ask the question," Gruley says. "Why are they doing this?"

"To get back at me. I think it's being done by Brad Devlin and his friends. They're pissed off about the stories I've been writing."

"That's an interesting theory. I don't know if I buy it."

I tell him that Noreen has gone to Vegas. I give him her phone number and address.

"Why did she leave? We were sending guys around."

"Did you hear about the latest Valley break-in?"

He shakes his head. I recount its details. "For some reason, you guys never saw fit to relay that information to the intended victim."

"We're like any large organization," Gruley says. "Nobody talks to anyone else."

"Can you call the cops in Vegas and ask them to keep an eye on her?"

He nods, then asks if there's anything else I want to tell him.

I say there is. "Somebody who's smart might want to check Brad Devlin's fingerprints against those from the Valley break-ins. The early ones. They're wearing gloves now."

"Do you really believe Brad Devlin is involved in those things?"

I don't reply. We walk up the stairs cut into the bluff. I

hear music and the sound of a carousel coming from the Santa Monica Pier.

"And how did you know the mother was in Sun Valley?"

"I hear stuff. It's my job."

"I hear stuff too. I never heard that."

As we trudge along Ocean a car slows. Teenage guys with ponytails lean out the windows.

"Fucking fags!" one of them yells.

"I hope you fucking die!" another one says.

"I feel like fucking killing you myself!" a third one shouts.

The car speeds off. We continue walking. Homeless people ask us for change and dollar bills.

"I have a theory," Gruley says at last.

"What is it?"

"We need the Communists back. We need the Cold War. A common enemy. Without one, we turn on each other."

I nod. This makes as much sense as anything. A random theory to explain our times.

We reach a crosswalk. My car is in a lot on the other side of the street. As I wait for the light to turn, Gruley punches me lightly on the shoulder.

"You knew where the mother was, and you had the necklace. You also have a belief, which I'm not discounting, that Brad Devlin is involved in the Valley break-ins. Maybe I'm a suspicious bastard. Maybe I've been in this business too long. But maybe, just maybe, you know a lot more about this case than you've even told your readers."

I stare straight ahead. I want the light to turn.

"I'm one of them, you know," Gruley says.

I want Rebecca. I want her arms and legs to engulf me.

"I have some advice for you. Off the record. Just between us."

The light turns. I step into the crosswalk.

"You better think about getting a lawyer."

When I started covering cops in a small but rapidly growing desert city, the public information officer often talked to me about the parade of trashy whites, blacks, Latinos, Asians and Native Americans being marched to the holding cells. One day a teenage African-American was led past us. He was five foot two and weighed barely one hundred pounds. I looked at his arrest sheet and saw he'd been charged with aggravated assault. I told my tutor that I was skeptical.

"Let me tell you something," he said. "And I want you to remember this.

"Everybody we bring in here deserves to be arrested. They may not have done what we say they did. But they deserve to be arrested."

seven

When Frank Gruley takes the stand again, Alvarez asks if he's located the receipt.

"NosirIhavenot."

"Did you ever find the necklace itself?"

Gruley fidgets and coughs before taking a long drink of water.

I see myself on the stand after all, telling the world everything I know, stripped of the shields my profession and personality have given me.

I certainly do have relevant information, Your Honor. I have seen the victim's mother bound against her will. She was drugged too. I also have insights into the character of the defendant. I believe they're pertinent. I'll begin by telling you how he swings a baseball bat.

Gruley says neither he nor his fellow officers have ever found the necklace.

Alvarez looks over his notes. I feel as if I'm suspended between my chair and the TV screen and the proper question from the defense attorney could suck me right in. I am neither inhaling nor exhaling.

"How secure was the scene where the body was found?" he asks.

"As secure as any other scene where a murder may have occurred."

"You allow newspaper reporters to walk all over crime scenes?"

I straighten involuntarily, as if a vise has begun squeezing the base of my spine. In the courtroom I hear a stirring as Alvarez takes some pieces of paper from a folder and approaches the bench.

"This is a deposition from an officer who was present at the scene," Alvarez says. "He tried to prevent a reporter from gaining access to the area, but the detective overruled him."

"We'd finished gathering evidence by that point," Gruley says.

"Did you observe him at all times?" Alvarez asks.

"He came in, took some notes and left. Couldn't have been there for more than two minutes."

"Answer my question, Detective."

"He was with me most of the time."

"But he was unsupervised for a while. He could have had a chance to plant or alter or—"

Monica is on her feet with the loudest objection I've ever heard in a courtroom.

"What's your point, Mr. Alvarez?" the judge asks.

"My point, Your Honor, is that an unscrupulous journalist in search of a story that would bring him great fame and monetary reward may very well have placed items to, shall we say, make his tale a little bit better."

"This is preposterous, Your Honor," Monica says. "The defense is engaging in wild speculation without a shred of proof." She asks that Alvarez's remarks be stricken from the record.

After hesitating a second, the judge agrees.

I climb three flights of stairs through air reeking of dry-cleaning fumes. His door is open a third of the way. I listen but hear nothing. I believe he's alone. As I'm about to knock, or at least push the door open, a voice tells me to come in. He says he knows who it is and he's been expecting me.

Maynard's feet are on his desk. He says he's surprised it's taken me this long.

I sit in a chair covered with torn vinyl.

"Maynard knows things about you."

"Such as?"

"For starters, he knows you ditched your old lady for that young sister. Not that he blames you."

"It's not like that. One was winding down and the other just sprang up."

"Maynard doesn't believe you. What did that dude Freud say? 'There are no coincidences'?"

"Freud also said that young boys want to sleep with their mothers and fear their fathers are going to castrate them."

"Is that what white people think? No wonder they're so fucked up."

Maynard puts his feet on the floor and leans toward me. His eyes narrow.

"Maynard also knows the young sister was expecting a delivery, but that she's had the problem, shall we say, terminated. You probably weren't planning on any of that, were you?"

"I didn't come here to talk about my personal life."

"Maynard finds your personal life fascinating, not having one of his own these days."

"What else do you know about me?"

"Maynard knows you went to Tahoe recently and you didn't go skiing. Maynard suspects you found something interesting up there. What's more, Maynard observed his esteemed colleague Richard Alvarez on TV this morning. As always, Maynard's admiration for Mr. Alvarez was unbounded. In Maynard's professional opinion, you are in deep shit."

"I need an attorney."

"You can use your newspaper's attorney. Why the fuck are you talking to Maynard?"

I cough. This is a question I was expecting. I've rehearsed my words.

"I think I need a personal attorney because of some issues that have arisen from this case. Because of the nature of these issues, I don't feel comfortable using my newspaper's counsel."

"There are a million attorneys in Los Angeles. Why Maynard?"

"When you're sober, you're the best lawyer I've ever seen."

Maynard paces. He still limps slightly from the injury he suffered after making the tackle that saved UCLA's victory in the Rose Bowl twenty years ago. I remember seeing highlights of that game on the news.

Maynard Reynolds was an all-American cornerback, a projected first-round draft pick.

"Maynard resents the implication about his current state of sobriety," he says quietly.

The room is so small he covers its length in three strides.

"Maynard has been through the twelve steps. Maynard has been through the twelve goddam steps twelve goddam times! He's more sober than a judge, which means he's certainly more sober than some goddam dipshit newspaper reporter!"

I reach into my wallet, take out a hundred-dollar bill and slap it on his desk. Maynard looks at the money as if a winning lottery ticket has materialized in front of him.

"Is that enough for a retainer?" I ask.

"It's enough."

Maynard puts the cash in his top desk drawer and takes out a pen and a legal pad.

I begin by clearing my throat and saying, "Let me tell you about Tahoe."

I listen to updates on the trial as I drive to the country club that my publisher's family founded. Rochelle, the clerk at the jewelry store, says she definitely saw Brad Devlin with a girl who looked like the victim. She remembers because she sold him the necklace and besides he seemed kinda cute. She giggles. The courtroom laughs. The judge admonishes her. This trial is a serious business. It's a search for the truth. Rochelle says she's sorry.

Richard Alvarez asks if she's absolutely certain the girl was the victim and Rochelle says actually the girl was quite a distance away but she resembled the pictures the police showed her. Alvarez asks if she's certain of the date and she says yes, she sold the necklace on September fifteenth. He asks how she's so certain of the date and she says it's because of the receipt. It was dated the fifteenth. At least that's what the detective told her. He asks if she has any independent recollection of what day it was and she says no but it was on the receipt. So that must be correct.

I park in the visitors' lot. The country club's main building is done in an Italianate style, with porticos and columns copied from classical design. I once heard that before he even began to draw up the plans, the club's architect spent a year on the Continent sketching Roman ruins.

A balding man in a pressed blue suit sits behind the main desk in the reception area. I am looked at with disdain so I smile and flash my press card. The balding man says the Open isn't for six months. I say I realize that but my paper wants to do a feature about the longtime caddies at this legendary club. I was wondering if he could point me in the right direction. He looks at me quizzically. I lean close and say the story isn't my idea. It came from the publisher. The balding man says he understands perfectly. Mr. Savage has been playing here since he was old enough to carry a club. It occurs to me that I shouldn't have laid on the bullshit so thick, but now it's too late to put it back in the sack.

I'm told where I can find the chief caddy. I head out-side and go around to a small dark room with an Astro-Turf carpet. The man I'm looking for is a sixty-something African-American with clumps of gray hair and a gut that jellies over a thin belt that looks like it's made of card-board. I give him the same story and then tell him that, as a matter of professional survival, I should probably begin by talking to the gentleman who regularly caddies for Mr. Savage. The chief caddy looks over the guys who work for him like a drill sergeant examining a platoon of mis-fits before shouting, "Manolo!"

A wiry Filipino, almost my height but a few years older, walks toward us.

"This fella wants to talk to you," the chief caddy says before going away.

I introduce myself and tell him I'm from the news-paper. I ask if he's Mr. Savage's regular caddy and he says he is. I ask if we can talk privately. He says he was hoping to attach himself to a foursome. I say I'll make it worth his while to talk to me.

We walk toward the parking lot. I don't want any-one to hear us. I want the ability to reach my car quickly in case something goes wrong.

"How often does Mr. Savage play golf?" I ask.

Manolo shrugs. "Three, four times a week. Always asks for me." Manolo smiles.

"Was he here last week?"

"Sure. Three, four times. Same as usual."

"And did he play in a foursome or was he with just one other man?"

"One other man."

"Was this the man?"

I extend a picture of Jeremiah Devlin. Manolo looks carefully. I can tell the answer from how gingerly he's holding the photo.

"Can't say. This is Mr. Devlin, right?"

I nod.

"Can't remember. Sorry."

I extend a ten-dollar bill toward him. "Remember, Manolo."

He folds the bill in thirds and puts it in his right pants pocket. He says the two men played together three times last week. They started early in the morning, which was unusual. Mr. Savage never gets here before lunch. He eats, has a few drinks, then plays a round. Then has more drinks.

"But Mr. Devlin usually plays early in the morning?"

Manolo nods.

"What did they talk about?"

Manolo says he doesn't remember. I take out another ten-dollar bill. Manolo glances over both his shoulders before taking it.

He says mostly they talked about the case that Mr. Devlin's son is involved in. Manolo shakes his head. It's a nasty business. There are so many bad things in the newspaper these days. Lately he reads only the sports section. But even that can be bad too.

"Did Mr. Devlin say anything specific about the case?" I ask.

"He said the newspaper was not treating his son fairly."

"And what did Mr. Savage say?"

"He said he agreed."

"Did Mr. Savage indicate he'd do something to help Mr. Devlin?"

"Mr. Devlin suggested something. I'm trying to remember what it was."

I extend another ten dollars.

"He suggested that another reporter be put on the story."

"And what did Mr. Savage say?"

"He said it seemed like a good idea. But they couldn't replace the current fellow just like that. They'd have to find a reason."

As I listen to another trial update on the news-and-talk station I tell myself I shouldn't be doing this; I should let the story go; this thing is no longer mine. But then her picture pops up full-blown in front of me, especially the corners of her lips curved upward.

I tell myself I am not obsessed.

Alexis, the girl who spoke at the funeral, is testifying. She says she was at Megan's the day she was killed. They used her pool and some boys came over and they used the pool too. Monica asks if one of the boys is present in the courtroom and the girl says yeah. She points to Brad Devlin.

This causes a murmur that Judge Baden-Howell quickly suppresses. Monica asks if, to her knowledge, there was any kind of a romance going on between Brad and Megan. Alvarez objects but is overruled. The girl says Brad and Megan were going out. Everybody talked about it. He was so much older.

Alvarez asks the girl what day today is. She hesitates a moment before saying, "Thursday?"

The courtroom titters. She's not even close.

"And what's today's date?" Alvarez asks.

The girl guesses again. She's off by double figures.

"How do you know you were at her house on September fifteenth?" Alvarez asks.

She says to be honest she wasn't sure at first, but after talking to the police and the people in the DA's office she became certain.

"So you've held conversations with the police and the district attorney?" Alvarez asks.

"Oh yeah," Alexis says. "We've talked a lot."

"Please go on," Alvarez says. "What did you talk about?"

Well, they wanted to clarify what day Alexis was at Megan's house. And they figured it must have been the day before Megan was reported missing. Alexis says she now remembers this clearly because when she was at school that day she kept asking where Megan was and nobody knew and she kept saying it was impossible, she'd just been swimming there the day before.

"So now you can recall that day?" Alvarez asks.

"Yes, Mr. Alvarez."

"Did you smoke marijuana that day?"

Monica objects. This is irrelevant. The witness is not on trial.

Alvarez says the witness has been cited on numerous occasions for possessing and smoking marijuana on school grounds. I hear the rustle of papers. The commentator says Alvarez has presented some documents to the judge. The defense attorney is allowed to continue.

"Well?" Alvarez asks the witness.

"Well what?"

"Will you answer my question?"

"What was it?"

"Did you smoke marijuana that day?"

"I don't remember."

"Where did you go after you left the victim's house?"

"Home."

"Did you see anybody there?"

Monica objects again. She says Mr. Alvarez keeps dragging in irrelevancies. Alvarez says, with the court's permission, he will show that this is indeed relevant. Judge Baden-Howell says she'll allow this line of questioning for now.

"When you got home that day," Alvarez asks, "whatever day it was, did you see anybody?"

She says some friends came over.

"And what did you do?" Alvarez asks.

"We got high," she says.

"I thought you said you didn't remember."

"I didn't before. I do now."

Alvarez reads some names to her and asks if these were the people who came to her house. Most of the names he reads are male. She says she can't be sure about all of them, but she knows everybody he just listed and many of them were probably there. Alvarez notes for the record that the young people he just named have all been arrested for various offenses, including drug possession and burglary. He asks the witness if she ever introduced Megan to any of these people and the witness says yeah.

"Did you ever introduce her to Grant Fisher?"

"Yeah. I think so."

Alvarez asks if Megan ever hung out with Grant Fisher and his friends. Alexis says yeah, sometimes. He asks how they liked her.

"Okay, I guess."

"Did she get high with them?"

"A couple of times."

"Did she know that some of them were committing burglaries?"

"Sure."

"Buying and selling drugs?"

"Sure."

"Did she ever say anything about that?"

"She said she thought it was stupid."

Alvarez introduces a dossier on Grant Fisher. Besides numerous arrests on drug charges, he's been suspended from school several times for assaulting fellow students.

"Did you and Grant Fisher ever talk to a newspaper reporter about this case?"

Monica objects. Irrelevant. Sustained.

"You hadn't known the victim very long, had you?" Alvarez asks.

"No. She'd just moved."

"Would you say she fit in with you and your friends?"

"No. She tried to, but she didn't."

"And did any of your friends—particularly Grant Fisher—feel threatened by her?"

Monica objects. She says these questions are pointless. The judge overrules.

"I don't remember," Alexis says.

When I get back to the office I ask Trish if we can talk. I open the heavy metal door to the stairwell and let her walk through. It closes with a banging thud behind us and for a moment I think of a rock being slid across the entrance to a tomb. Trish wears heels that sound like a hammer striking its target, driving the nail deeper into the wood. She sits on her accustomed step. I lean against the wall and fold my arms across my chest. I look down at the floor and recount my talk with Brendan at the coffeehouse.

"Why are you telling me this?" Trish asks.

"There's more," I say before describing my conversation with Manolo. At the end of it Trish pushes her glasses to the top of her head and rubs her eyes.

"Fuck," she says. "Fuck. Fuck. Fuck."

These words have the impact that can be achieved only when they're uttered by someone who never curses.

"Goddam backstabbing," she says softly. "Goddammit." All her life, she says, she's wanted to do honest and ethical work. And she thought she'd found a place where that was possible. For all its flaws—the pressure, the shallowness, the occasional sensationalism—she truly believed that journalism was a fundamentally honest profession, and this was a fundamentally honest publication.

"I only want to do the right thing," she says. "Why do they make it so difficult?"

"Because they can," I say.

She sits still, breathing hard. Her lips have vanished, as if she's trying to suck them through her teeth.

"I have to get back on the story," I say.

"They'll never let you," she says.

We share the silence. I know she's right.

After a moment I tell her I have an idea. She asks what it is.

"Put Rebecca on it."

"I can't do that. She's an intern."

"She did a great job covering cops. Everybody says so. And on this she'll just be doing backup."

Trish nods slowly. Subterfuge is not as natural to her as it is to me, but she grasps my point. She says she'll see what she can do. As we head up the stairs she asks if I've ever read Machiavelli.

On my way home I buy a padded manila envelope at an office supply store. When I'm alone in my bedroom, with the door closed and the blinds drawn and latex gloves on my hands, I address the thing to Monica by clipping out words and sometimes letters from the publications I subscribe to. After I paste them onto the envelope I affix five dollars' worth of postage and slide in Megan's videotape and the visitors' page I removed from the guest book at Jeremiah Devlin's place in Tahoe. I erase my questions from the audiotape of Megan's mother, leaving only her voice screaming murder. I put that too into the envelope, then seal the package and apply Scotch tape and staples. As I leave my apartment I hide the envelope under the light jacket I'm wearing. I drive several miles while the night falls and stop at a mailbox on a street with no traffic. I drop off the envelope and speed away.

Back at my apartment there's a message from Rebecca. She says there's something we have to talk about. I call her right back.

"What have you been up to?" Rebecca asks.

"What do you mean?"

Rebecca says Trish pulled her aside just as she was leaving the office. It seems that after a grand total of three days on the drought project, she's been reassigned to do the sidebars on the Brad Devlin case. She's supposed to check in with Van Arsdale at the courthouse tomorrow morning before nine.

"I see your fingerprints all over this one," Rebecca says.

"Would you rather stay on the drought project?"

"That's not the point. It's my career and I should have been consulted."

I think of the handcuffs still in her apartment and I know I could drive there quickly and force my way in; although Rebecca is strong I believe I could overpower her; drag push pull carry her; throw her onto the bed and lock the metal around her wrists and do what I want. I would not be punished. These things happen all the time and men get away with them.

But then I hear a belt striking flesh, tearing away at the thin layer of whatever it is that protects us. I hear a girl's voice saying things I know she does not mean while the gruff harsh voice of command makes her submit.

I sit heavily in a chair. My breath comes in staccato bursts.

"Are you all right?" Rebecca asks.

"No," I say. "I'm trying to be. But I'm not. Not yet."

"You are, without a doubt, the strangest motherfucker I have ever met in my life."

"Let's think about the story for a minute," I say. My breath is still weak. "We never found out what happened to Megan's father."

"He was going to Australia, right?"

I grunt something that could be construed as confirmation.

"Should be easy enough to find out if he ever got there. I'll track it down in the morning."

I tell her I'm tired. I'm going to try to sleep. But before I can hang up she asks, "Was there anything to what Alvarez said in court this morning?"

"About me? About what I did at the scene?"

"Uh-huh."

If I were a theatrical person I'd loudly proclaim my innocence and slam down the phone with a flourish.

Instead I say this: "Nothing I did at the scene could possibly have any bearing on the outcome of the case."

"Too bad," she says in the thrilling voice I still find seductive.

Richard Alvarez has created an aura of public danger around me. I'm sure Rebecca finds this alluring.

As I put my things on the checkout belt I skim the offerings of the Grocery Press. Brad Devlin has made it to the front of several tabs. "SHOCKING NEW EVIDENCE THAT PROVES HIS INNOCENCE" is on the cover of one publication. Another proclaims his "GUILT BEYOND ALL DOUBT." A third has a highschool girl talking about "MY WILD NIGHT WITH BRAD DEVLIN," while a fourth has a space alien discussing the case with Richard Alvarez.

The clerk rings up my order and tells me what I owe. It doesn't seem like much.

eight

I get to the office at eight. Rebecca is already there, her head attached to the phone. From my perspective it looks as if she's engaged in an involved discussion that's being hindered by a bad connection.

When she hangs up she walks toward me and says she spent more than an hour on the phone with Australian immigration. The people are quite friendly down there. They informed her that no American with a name even close to Megan's father's has applied for a work permit in the last three months. No American with a name like his has even entered the country.

"Maybe he's using a different name," I say. "Or a different nationality."

Rebecca says he probably wouldn't use a different nationality because his accent would mark him as an American. Perhaps he used a different name, but immigration told her only 268 Americans have received Australian work permits in the last three months and most of them are computer engineers and people like that. She asked if any of them were working as lifeguards or in surf shops, and she was told that Australia has plenty of people who can do those things.

"What do you think?" I ask.

"I think he's dead," she says.

Rebecca leaves the office but calls me shortly before ten. I ask how it went with Van Arsdale and she says she's going to search for the right word to describe his reaction.

Peeved. That's it.

Apparently no one had told him about the new arrangement. So when she introduced herself and described why she was there, he looked at her as if she were telling him that Princeton had just merged with Jersey City State College. He picked up his cell phone and called the office. She assumes he got Fussman because Van Arsdale started saying some *girl* was here claiming to be assigned to the story and he knew *nothing* about this and what *in blazes* was going on here? There was a response she couldn't hear and then he said it was all very well and good but he certainly wished he had been *consulted* on this. He snapped his contraption shut, looked at Rebecca and told her she was on the story. Rebecca said she already knew that. She asked if there was any element he hadn't had time to develop that perhaps he'd want her to cover. He said he wasn't sure. He hadn't even thought about this. He told her to work on something on her own. Watch the trial from the pressroom and get up to speed. Perhaps he'd think of something by lunch.

Rebecca pauses before saying, "I'm having a lot of

trouble liking men these days. Or even tolerating them."

I tell her I have a story idea.

"You think I should go to the beach and see if I can find out anything about Megan's father."

I tell her that's it.

"I'm way ahead of you. I'm calling from my car phone."

During the morning session in court, forensic and fiber experts from the police lab testify that various items found on the victim's body match hair and clothing taken from samples provided by the defendant, Brad Devlin.

"Assuming these materials are a match," Richard Alvarez asks, "does that necessarily mean the defendant had personal physical contact with the victim on the night she was killed?"

The experts concede it does not necessarily mean that.

I call the registrar's office at Pomona College. A woman's voice answers. I use the name of Noreen's supervisor and say I have a position to fill and I'm going through résumés. One that made a favorable impression belonged to Maryann Wright. She said she recently received an MBA after going to school part-time for several years. Obviously this is just a routine request but I'm trying to verify that all of this is accurate.

The woman asks me to hold. She says she'll look it up right away. In a minute she comes back on and says she searched the database but there are no records indicating that a Maryann Wright ever studied for an MBA. I tell her I'm puzzled. Mrs. Wright's résumé has checked out in all other respects. I ask if she'll do me a favor and she says she always tries to be obliging. I ask if she can check on whether the college has any records at all that Maryann Wright ever studied there. She asks if I can hold again and I say I certainly can. Once again she returns in a minute.

"Our records indicate that Maryann Wright took two extension courses in management last year, one in each semester. Our records indicate that she didn't complete either one."

"That's interesting," I say. "I'd like to follow up on this. I hope you don't mind. We're pretty far along in the hiring process and this throws us for a loop."

"I understand, sir."

"Could you give me the name of her professor or professors?"

It was the same man in both classes. I ask if she has a number where I can reach him. She says he has a voicemail number at the college that he checks periodically. After she gives it to me I tell her she's been most helpful.

"Sir?" she asks. "This job you're looking to fill—what does it entail?"

I describe something along the lines of what Noreen has done for the past few years. I say the salary and benefits are excellent, and the company doesn't intend to do any downsizing anytime soon.

"It sounds awfully good," the woman says. "If you

rescind this offer to Maryann Wright—and I can certainly sympathize if you do—I'd like to apply for the job. I don't have an MBA, but it doesn't sound like you need one to do the work."

"Not at first, but we envision this as a fast-track position."

She says it sounds like a great opportunity and she'd be willing to get an MBA and her pay is low and she has no benefits and her supervisors keep throwing more work at her without adding staff. Nobody appreciates what she does. In fact her bosses act as if she should be grateful to have a job.

Her voice has the desperation of a woman suddenly leaping at Chance after giving up all hope of ever improving her condition.

I tell her to mail or fax a résumé. I promise to give it as much consideration as possible.

Rebecca calls again from her car phone. She says she went to the apartment where Megan's father used to live and asked the landlady if she'd heard anything about him recently. The landlady said no. Rebecca said she knew the guy once worked at a surf shop, but she was curious about what his girlfriend did. The landlady laughed and said she didn't do much. Rebecca asked if she ever hung out anywhere and the landlady said she used to get her nails done a lot. It sounds silly, but sometimes you notice certain things about a person. So one day she asked her where she went for her manicures and the woman told her about this shop just a block from the beach. It was run by these Korean gals and they did a really nice job even though they didn't speak English too well. They gave pedicures too. She always asked for Susie.

"So what happened?" I ask.

"I went there," Rebecca says. "It was great."

When she entered the store she told them who she was and whom she was looking for. They asked if she wanted a manicure. Perhaps a pedicure too. They were having a special today—fifteen dollars for both. Usually it was twenty-five. Rebecca said it sounded tempting but she was looking for information and besides she didn't know if she had time. She was kind of playing hooky as it was. They said that maybe they could help her. Maybe not. It all depended. Rebecca said the special sounded like a good deal.

Susie came out from a room in back and bowed a bit. Rebecca sat in a chair that was raised off the floor. She put her feet in a bowl that had a soapy solution in it and asked Susie if she ever met the woman who'd been living with Megan Wright's father. Susie turned to the woman who seemed to be running the place and talked furiously in Korean for several minutes. As she took Rebecca's feet out of the bowl she said oh, yeah, she used to come in here all the time. A very good customer.

"Then came the best part," Rebecca says.

Susie rubbed Rebecca's feet with a pumice stone and used a razor blade to scrape the calluses on her soles. Dead skin flaked onto the floor as Susie asked Rebecca why she was looking for this woman. Rebecca told Susie that she worked for a newspaper and was trying to find her for a story. As Susie dried Rebecca's feet with a white cloth towel she shook her head and said she hadn't seen her. Rebecca asked how long it had been and Susie shook her head again. Long time.

Then she put polish on Rebecca's toenails. Purple passion.

As Rebecca soaked her hands she asked Susie how this woman seemed the last time she saw her. Susie said she was like real scared like. She used to be calm like normal people but now she kept looking around—

Here Susie demonstrated what she meant, constantly looking over her shoulders and checking her watch and glancing in the mirror, but not at herself, at reflections of other things.

So Susie asked what was wrong and the woman said oh, a lot of things were going on and she just had a lot of stuff on her mind. She and her boyfriend were thinking about moving. Susie asked where to and she said they were thinking about going far away. Susie said she was sorry. She liked her. A very good customer.

The woman looked at her watch again and Susie asked if she had to go somewhere. The woman shook her head but then she smiled and said she guessed it was obvious. She was just so goddam tense these days. She was going sailing with her boyfriend and some of his business associates. She didn't want to. She felt uneasy and besides she didn't like sailing anyway. But her boyfriend told her she had to be there. Susie said it sounded nice and her customer said she was afraid the men were going to spend all their time talking about business or football. As usual she was just along as a decoration. She was getting tired of it.

Susie said it still sounded like fun. A real good time.

• • •

I call the voicemail number that the woman in the registrar's office gave me, then swivel my chair and turn up the sound on the TV. Dr. Jack Karch begins his testimony by reciting the academic and professional credentials that led to his appointment as Los Angeles County medical examiner.

Karch is overweight and his jacket is frayed. He combs his few strands of hair over the top of his head in an effort to hide what's apparent to everyone. He sweats easily, so he constantly reaches into his jacket to take out a handkerchief. This calls attention to his fingertips, which are a deeper shade of green than when I saw him last.

It has been his practice to send one of his deputies to testify in criminal cases. But perhaps in this one he feels it's his duty. Or perhaps he can't resist the lure of one final dance in the spotlight.

Monica asks if he can pinpoint the time of death and he gives a range between nine P.M. and midnight on September fifteenth. She asks how he can be sure and he describes his observations, especially the onset of rigor mortis.

"And in your opinion what caused the victim's death?"

"Drowning."

"How do you know this?"

The medical examiner describes the presence of water in the victim's lungs.

"There were bruises on the victim's body, were there not?"

The medical examiner says there were.

"Could you describe them, please?"

He says there were numerous blunt injuries about the head, as if she'd been struck with an instrument of some kind. He now believes it was done by a baseball bat. Splinters and slivers of wood were removed from the victim's body. However, in his opinion she was struck by the bat *after* she'd been drowned.

My phone rings and I don't want to answer because Karch's testimony promises to be particularly gruesome. But I pick up the receiver and put on my headset. The voice at the other end says he's returning my call. It's a hesitant voice that sounds as if it belongs to an older man. I go blank for a second before he adds that he got this number by checking his voicemail at Pomona College.

"Thank you," I say. "Thanks very much." I tell him I'm preparing some background stories on the various people involved in the Brad Devlin case and I've been informed that he taught a couple of extension courses that were taken by Maryann Wright. I ask if my information is correct and if he remembers her at all.

"I do remember her," he says. "I don't know how much light I can shed on her personality, if that's what you're interested in."

"Why don't you tell me about the class? What was she studying?"

He says the first course was called Principles of Management and Organization and was designed to give an overview of modern business techniques. "It's a 'big picture' kind of a deal," he says. Mrs. Wright usually sat in the front of the room and asked lots of questions. Some were insipid and some were penetrating, but overall he was struck by her curiosity and eagerness to learn. Several weeks into the class something came up, and she was unable to complete the work. He asked her what it was and her reply was vague, but whatever it was seemed to be personal in nature. He gave her an incomplete instead of failing her because she said she wanted to finish the course someday. Actually she was thinking about getting an MBA. He told her to pursue it. The degree is a useful tool for anyone who wants to get ahead.

I find it interesting that a woman who never got a bachelor's degree was thinking about graduate work, but I keep this to myself. Instead I ask when all of this occurred and he says it was late last year. I open an almanac and check the calendar. If my chronology is correct, Megan's mother dropped the class around the time she began her relationship with Jeremiah Devlin.

"Tell me about the second class," I say.

It was earlier this year. He was surprised to see her because she still owed him work from the previous semester. He mentioned this to her, and she said she intended to complete that work as well as whatever he wanted in this one.

"I was delighted to hear that," he tells me. "I thought she had a lot of drive. So few people nowadays have any desire to improve themselves. It's a different ethic from when I was growing up."

I ask what the class was about and he says it was called Supervising Practices and Techniques. It was geared toward middle management, office managers in particular. It was designed to promote more efficient oversight and human-relations skills. The class is usually taken by people who want to move up the corporate ladder. It's also been an effective networking site for people looking to change companies or careers.

Anyway Mrs. Wright again sat near the front of the class and again asked lots of questions of the same caliber as before. Her work was quite good. She had even approached him about getting a reference for an MBA application and he was favorably inclined. But then she stopped coming. When she missed her third successive class, he called her. She said she was sorry but she'd suddenly become quite busy. She was buying a new house and her kids were changing schools. He asked about her career plans and she said she was confident everything would work out. In fact she was more than confident. She'd just received a big raise and promotion.

"Was that the last time you ever talked to her?" I ask.

"It was—but something else occurred a little while later. You may find this of use." He says he got a call about two months after she stopped attending class. He'd given her another incomplete because . . . well, maybe it was just because he liked her. In any event, one day a man called and asked about Mrs. Wright and the classes she took. The professor gave this caller his impression of her, which was favorable. He thought it might be a prospective employer. Then the caller asked if there was any way it would be possible to erase the incompletes from her record. With a chuckle the professor said yes—she could finish the work. The caller said that wasn't what he had in mind. He was wondering if perhaps he and the professor couldn't achieve an accommodation on this matter.

"I knew exactly what this man was suggesting," the professor tells me.

"So what did you do?" I ask.

"I hung up."

I thank him for his time.

"I've been following that case," he says. "The one about her daughter. A nasty affair."

"Yes," I say. "Yes, it is."

"It seems she had a breakdown?"

"That's what they tell us."

"But she'll pull through, won't she?"

"I doubt it," I say. "I think it's too late for her."

Monica finishes questioning Karch at four-thirty. The judge looks at her watch and says she'll dismiss court a little early today. They will not convene tomorrow because of the federal holiday, but trial will resume the next morning at nine with cross-examination if that's all right with Mr. Alvarez.

He says it certainly is.

Trish and I go into the stairwell and I wonder if people are beginning to talk or at least notice. I tell her what I found out about Megan's mother and offer to put it up as a sidebar. She shakes her head. She says I have to give it to Van Arsdale.

"He'll bury it," I say.

"I know," she says. "But that's the way it is right now."

On our way up the stairs she informs me that the paper is folding its San Diego and Santa Barbara editions.

"That's too bad," I say. "Some good people work there."

"Worked there," she says.

I call Gruley's office but I'm told he's not talking to the media. I say the call is of a personal nature. I'm not looking for comment. He gets back to me in about five minutes and I tell him I appreciate what he did in court yesterday. He says he actually did it for both of us. He sure as hell didn't want to tell Richard Alvarez that a newspaper reporter found the necklace and the answer he gave wasn't exactly a lie, was it?

I say Alvarez gave him a rough time and he says he expected it. Alvarez gives everybody a hard time except his murdering scumbag clients.

I tell Gruley that I've just found out something. It may be important or maybe it isn't, but I can't figure out what it means. He asks what it is, and I tell him what I discovered about Maryann Wright's educational experiences at Pomona College.

"Why did Devlin lie about that?" Gruley asks.

"That's what I don't understand," I say. "He runs the damn company. He can appoint whoever he wants, to whatever he feels like."

"Unless he felt she was so unqualified for the job that he had to make something up."

We remain silent on either end of the phone. Jeremiah Devlin's companies are privately held. There's no way to find out these things.

"I have a question for you," I say.

"Your message said this call was personal."

"I had a hidden agenda."

"You always do."

"Has anybody been trying to block the investigation? Or slow it down? Go easy on things because this is Jeremiah Devlin's son?"

"Not from my end," Gruley says.

"What about the other ends?"

Gruley says we have to go off the record. After I agree he says, "We haven't gotten squat out of the DA's investigators. Monica's a pro and she's doing the best she can, but those guys have been sitting on their asses. Everything she's used has come from us. Or from you, although I hate to admit it."

"Devlin and the DA go back a long way. They've been through thick and thicker."

"It's not doing the DA much good. You see the latest poll? He's only two points ahead."

I tell Gruley I have to go.

"The kid's gonna walk," he says. "He did it, but we don't have the horses. And they have Alvarez."

I wonder if he wants me to say something. I wonder if he knows what I know or at least suspects it, and for a moment I think about opening up. Perhaps I'd get immunity. I can ask Maynard to talk to the right people and then sit down in the witness stand and calmly tell the world everything I've seen. I tell myself the act would not be hard. Only reaching the decision is difficult.

By the end of my testimony, my career would be over. Then Alvarez would get a chance at cross-examination. By the time he was through, the shreds of my reputation would be lying in tiny pieces as small as confetti on the courtroom floor. I cannot say that such a fate is undeserved. But it is not one that I want. I envision heading back to my apartment and putting a gun in my mouth. I'd surround myself with newspapers to soak up the stains.

"I told Monica about our conversation," he says.

I feel as if a hairy paw has clamped my heart.

"I was hoping that would stay off the record."

"I couldn't do that. Your information is too good. It wouldn't surprise me if she tried to question you."

"I followed your advice," I say slowly. "I hired an attorney."

"Who is it?"

"Maynard Reynolds."

"Oh fuck. What the fuck did you do that for? Last fucking thing we need is to have Maynard fucking Reynolds back in the fucking limelight."

Rebecca calls me at home and asks me to come over. She waits outside her apartment and tells me as I pull up that she'd like to go for a walk on the beach. I say I read in on her sidebar while Trish was working on it and I thought it was a nice piece of work. Since she had received no guidance from anyone on putting together a story that could actually run in the paper, she went outside the courthouse and interviewed the teenage groupies who've been waiting for Brad. The tone of the article struck me as properly ironic.

She sticks her hands in her pockets. I notice that she's barefoot and her jeans are rolled up. She tells me that she filed from the courthouse and then went to the marina where Jeremiah Devlin keeps his yacht. She asked the harbormaster about him but he wouldn't say anything so she started throwing out all kinds of generic questions, like how many boats were there and what kind they were and how much a typical one cost and oh, yes, what about the docking fees? She kept saying things like, "Really?" and "Oh, my," and "That's interesting," and took page after page of notes. After she'd been there an hour, he asked if she wanted a drink. She said she'd like a Coke. He poured himself a gin and tonic that seemed to have a lot more gin than tonic. He asked if she minded and she said no. He downed it in a couple of gulps and made himself another. She leaned toward him and put her hand on his wrist and said just between them she'd heard that a lot of famous and powerful people keep their boats here. Movie stars. Politicians. Celebrities. Wealthy entrepreneurs. He said just between them—yes, it was true. But he didn't like to advertise that fact. They just come down and take their boats out and keep it quiet. He respects their privacy. He understands why they need it. Then he poured himself another drink and smiled at her and leaned so close he almost put his mouth in her ear. He asked if there was anybody in particular she was interested in. He asked if she was sure she didn't want a drink.

Rebecca said she'd like another Coke if it wasn't too much trouble. The harbormaster asked if she'd like something a little stronger and she said no, Coke

would be fine. As he poured her another she said she
wanted to ask him again about Jeremiah Devlin. She
heard he kept a boat here, and if it's true she'd be interested because she bets he has the most fabulous yacht
in the marina.

The harbormaster gave her the Coke. It even had
lemon in it. He said she wasn't far from the truth, but
he shouldn't say anything about Mr. Devlin. Now there
are a couple of movie stars who have really nice boats.
The stories he could tell.

Rebecca asked how big Jeremiah Devlin's boat was.
The harbormaster said it was close to ninety feet.
Rebecca whistled and the guy said yeah, it's a big one
all right. A full-time crew takes care of it. At least it
seems full-time. They're always around.

He burped. Rebecca smelled gin. She asked if he
kept any kind of log that kept track of when the boats
entered and left the marina.

Of course he did. It was an important part of his
job. Perhaps the most important.

Rebecca slid a little closer to him. She let her thigh
brush against his hip. And so, she said, if she wanted to
check whether Jeremiah Devlin took his boat out on
such and such a date, all she'd have to do is look at
the log.

That's right, he said.

She smiled at him and said she was going to pick a
random day. She chose September twenty-ninth. He
asked why and she said it was her birthday. He grinned
and said he was going to remember that day. He'd like
to give her a treat.

Actually Rebecca, by working backward, had figured that that was the most likely date for the boat ride that Megan's father took with his girlfriend.

The harbormaster patted her on the knee and said he'd be happy to look. He stood up, made himself another drink and walked over to the log. They still handwrote the information in this big book with a heavy leather cover. She figured stuff like this would be on computer by now. He opened the book, looked at it and nodded. He said she was in luck and motioned for her to join him. He pointed to the page and said he must have written this himself, although he didn't really remember it. But it's his handwriting. He noted that the boat, which was named *Sea Angel,* had departed the harbor with a crew of eight at about two in the afternoon.

Rebecca said that seemed a bit late to begin a day of sailing.

The harbormaster said that sometimes people like to stay out late and watch the sunset from the ocean. It's quite romantic.

He put his hand on her back. She stepped away.

He said the boat must have done just that because the book notes the *Sea Angel* returned about ten that night. The entry was written by somebody else, most likely the night watchman. Rebecca asked if someone's on duty twenty-four hours a day and the harbormaster said oh yes, most definitely, it's like 7-Eleven, the place never closes. In fact sometimes, when there's a full moon, people come down at midnight and take their boats out. You'd be amazed at what goes on. The stories he could tell. Wild. Bizarre. X-rated. He grinned again.

Rebecca grinned back and said she assumed everyone who had gone out on the boat had returned. The harbormaster laughed and said he guessed so. He was off-duty by then. But he lives around here. His place has a nice view. Maybe she'd like to check it out.

Rebecca pointed to a notation on the entry and asked if it meant anything. He looked at it as if for the first time and said it was a distress call that had been quickly withdrawn. Since nothing came of it he'd never been informed, but he was glad she'd brought it to his attention. The next time he sees Mr. Devlin he'll have to ask about it.

Rebecca said she was sorry she'd taken up so much of his time. He said it was his pleasure. He asked if she was interested in boats and she said to tell the truth she'd never really thought about it. He said he could take her out on the water sometime. The combination of sun and sea and spray was the most sensual feeling in the world.

He said he'd never had a black woman before. But he was certainly willing to try.

He held out a drink for her.

He was standing only inches away.

She said she had to go. She slipped past him and felt his hand grab her elbow but she shook him away and behind her she heard him stumble and fall. She heard glass breaking and shouts for help but she opened the door of the cabin and slammed it behind her. On the pier the sun was just a foot from her eyes and the gulls were louder than any jackhammer she'd ever heard and she was afraid she'd walk into the water but she just had to keep going along the pier, her shoes echoing on what sounded like hollow wood, until finally she reached a parking lot and sat on the bumper of a cool blue minivan. Her heart was jumping and sweat dribbled around her face. For a moment she thought she was going to vomit.

I was once at a party that Richard Alvarez attended. He was surrounded all evening by attractive women clutching long-stemmed glasses of white wine. They said his work must be exciting and he said it was, it thrilled him, he loved to argue in front of a judge and jury with the facts in doubt and a person's life at stake.

The women were charmed. Many gave him their business cards. Several paid him the highest compliment you can give someone in America: They said he should go on television.

nine

Maynard wants to tell you about his evening."

I lower the volume on my headset before telling him to go ahead. My attorney's voice tends to boom.

Maynard was out with some people from the DA's office last night. He rarely socializes but they saw him at the courthouse the other day and asked if he wanted to go out for old times' sake. When he agreed they seemed surprised. He noticed they put it off for a couple of days. Maybe they were hoping he'd forget about it, but Maynard does not have an extensive social calendar. He reminded them of their engagement so they probably decided to just get the goddam night over with.

Maynard doesn't drink. But those folks do. When you work for the DA, it's required. So Maynard wound up doing the designated driving as they traveled through the Valley. After a while they started talking about the case and they agreed Alvarez would get the kid off even though he was guilty as hell. Monica was so pissed she was even more miserable to be around than usual.

Why is that? Maynard asked.

She got something today, they said. It could convict Brad. The old man too, on unrelated charges. But she can't use it.

Why not? Maynard asked.

They wouldn't say.

What did she get? Maynard asked.

They wouldn't say that, either.

His former colleagues ordered another round of drinks, and as Maynard listened it became apparent that Monica had received a package that contained an audiotape of cryptic but disturbing comments, a piece of paper that shattered at least part of the story that Brad Devlin and his father have been telling, and a videotape that left her faint and sick after viewing it in her office. She kept wondering who had sent these things, how that person had obtained them, how he or she knew to send them to her. If she could find out the source, she could put that person on the stand and introduce the items. She'd have Alvarez begging for a plea bargain.

The package had a Los Angeles postmark. It had no return address and there were no fingerprints on the envelope or the tape or the paper. Practically anybody could have sent them.

"Why are you telling me this?" I ask.

"Maynard recalls that you told him you paid an unauthorized visit to Megan Wright's house, as well as a similar venture to Jeremiah Devlin's country retreat in Tahoe."

I told Maynard just about everything. There was a gap of several hours in my narrative that I did not share with counsel. It concerned events at a house in Glendale.

"Maynard theorizes that perhaps his client discovered something in one of those places that he is now attempting to share, in a clumsy fashion, with the prosecution."

"I appreciate what you've told me," I say. "But I have nothing to add. At least for now."

Maynard says he believes I'm making a mistake.

I tell myself of what I used to believe, that one choice is the same as the other.

Trish walks over shaking her head. She says that in the ten years she's been in the business, she has never heard a more ludicrous story idea than the one that's been cooked up by Fussman and Van Arsdale.

"I disagree," I say. "I'm sure I've heard of something more ludicrous."

She says they want Rebecca to do a sidebar about fashions at the Brad Devlin trial. An analysis of what Monica is wearing. A description of Richard Alvarez's suits. Are the defendant's clothes impressing the jury?

"It'll be easy to write about the judge," I say. "She's wearing basic black."

They want Rebecca to call designers and editors and consultants and Mr. Blackwell. They want her to ask some observers at the trial what they think. They want it all by five so they can run it on the metro front.

"What did you tell them?" I ask.

"That I didn't think she could have it by five. A story like that requires a lot of research. At least a full day and maybe two." She rolls her eyes. "They said they really wanted an off-day feature, since court's not in session. So I told them Rebecca was working on another angle. Now I have to figure out what it is."

"There is something," I say. My lips feel dry and cracked. I don't know if I should tell her, but from somewhere deep within me the words are forming.

Sometimes I believe I don't know why I do anything.

"What is it?" she asks.

"Monica received some information. From what I hear it could do some damage to the defense." Without telling Trish how I know, I give her the names of the prosecutors who spent a night in the Valley with Maynard Reynolds.

Kristen's father once gave me his number. I felt awkward but he said it was all right. He knew about the relationship between Kristen's mother and myself and it was okay by him. He just wanted me to have his number in case something happened to his daughter and her mother couldn't get to the phone. I said it sounded reasonable. You can never tell when things might go horribly wrong.

A woman answers and asks who this is. I identify myself by name but don't tell her my business. She asks what I want to discuss with him and I say it's a private matter. She says she's not sure she should let me through. She doesn't like it when people are secretive. It's unhealthy. I ask her to tell him that Ted Lowe is calling. He should recognize my name.

The phone is silent for a minute.

"What do you want?" he asks.

"There's something I have to ask you," I say.

"I should never have given you my number," he says. "I don't know why I did. Today's a holiday for me and I should be enjoying it. I've earned that right."

I'm about to say something but he goes on.

"If it's about Kristen or her mother, I don't want to hear it. I'm with someone else now. Someone who cares about me. Someone I can make a life with. I think. We're still testing things out. We've both been wounded, but that's why we're good for each other." He says this is a woman he could have children with, but he can concentrate on only one family at a time. It would be unfair to the new people in his life to be burdened by the old ones.

I haven't even asked my question yet.

"Do you understand any of this?" he says. "Are you even capable of understanding?"

"I doubt it," I say. "I wanted to ask you something anyway."

"I'm not sure I should let you. I haven't discussed it with my helpmate. We make all our decisions together. That's the only way you can create a relationship that works."

"Well, it's just that you're an air traffic controller and I was wondering if you knew where Jeremiah Devlin keeps his company planes."

He says nothing. I sense an opening.

"This is for a story I'm working on," I say. "It's just a piece of information. It's not very significant."

He says he's always been told to refer press inquiries to the public information office and he's not sure if this type of material is actually in the public domain and most of all he really resents the fact that I've intruded on his holiday. But before slamming down the phone he tells me that Jeremiah Devlin's company planes are kept in a hangar at Santa Monica Airport.

Gruley calls shortly before noon and immediately asks if we can go off the record.

He says he put in a request for the fingerprints from the Valley break-ins more than a day ago. At first the people in the records bureau said they'd get right on it. Then they called him back in the afternoon and said there had been some delays. He's been in the bureaucracy a long time, so he said he understood. They promised to look into it first thing in the morning.

Around ten A.M. Gruley got a call from the sergeant in the Van Nuys division who's handling the investigation. He asked what the fuck Gruley wanted to see those fucking fingerprints for. They were none of his fucking business. Gruley said he wanted to check those prints against the ones they took of Brad Devlin when they arraigned him.

You don't really think Brad Devlin is breaking into houses all over the Valley, the sergeant said.

Maybe I do and maybe I don't, Gruley replied.

We've figured it out, the sergeant said. Drug gangs are doing it. Same thing with that murder. You've got the wrong guy. It's gotta be a drug lowlife. That girl who testified is probably involved. And the guys she hangs out with, especially that Grant Fisher kid. The sergeant has run him in a couple of times. The kid's capable of anything. In fact he can't understand why the newspapers haven't looked into him.

Gruley asked the sergeant if he intended to get the fingerprints or if he was going to make him talk to his commander—who was, by the way, a personal friend. They'd gone through training together.

The sergeant said he'd get right on it.

Another hour passed. Gruley had made what he considered a routine request and all he'd gotten was a runaround and stonewalling. He was being treated like a civilian.

His phone rang again. It was the commander in Van Nuys.

You're not gonna fucking believe this, he said.

I'll believe anything, Gruley replied.

The fingerprints are missing, he said. All of them, he said.

I don't fucking believe it, Gruley said.

I ask Gruley what he makes of this. He says stuff gets misplaced all the time but they've never lost track of fingerprints for God's sake. Somebody must have gotten into the file and removed them.

"There's another interesting wrinkle," Gruley says. "Want to venture a guess as to the name of the sergeant who checked in the fingerprints at Evidence Storage?"

"Harris Benton?"

"The one and only."

"Where is he?"

"We have no idea. He put in his papers two weeks ago and cleared out. Sold his house for a loss and didn't say shit to his two ex-wives."

• • •

The electronic library contains a number of stories about Police Officer Harris Benton. Most of them ran several years before I was hired. Benton, an African-American, had spent most of his career slogging through the department's lower echelons. One day he sued his employer, alleging he'd been passed over for promotion because of his race. The department denied it of course. All promotions are based on merit, wink wink.

From reading the clips it's hard to escape the conclusion that Harris Benton was an unremarkable cop. But when I think of all the undistinguished white guys I know who've made sergeant or better, it's also hard to escape the conclusion that his suit had some basis in fact.

The local NAACP picked up Benton's legal fees, and there were marches and protests on his behalf. On the other side, the LAPD's honchos and rank and file complained about this uppity n-word.

The case was resolved just before it went to trial. Benton was promoted to sergeant, but the department admitted no wrongdoing. The department also paid for his lawyers (the NAACP insisted on this), but he received no back pay or punitive damages.

Some of the more cynical members of the Los Angeles law enforcement community suggested that the suit was not about redressing a blatant case of discrimination. They suggested it was about Harris Benton's desire to collect a sergeant's pension.

After the settlement, Harris Benton vanished from the media's radar. It's interesting he wound up in the evidence room. That's where the department sends its burnouts and fuckups. I imagine Benton sitting there day after day, logging in pieces of evidence, always presented with a side of the force of which he is no longer a part, his mind obsessing about his colleagues' resentment and those two failed marriages. Slowly the job became a contest between the blessed release of early retirement or total collapse under the accumulation of petty indignities.

What would happen, I think, *if someone with a lot of money were sympathetic to such a man?*

I get chicken salad from the cafeteria and bring it back to my desk. Rebecca calls shortly before two and tells me how she descended into the warren of offices used by the assistant district attorneys in the courthouse. When she got there the place was buzzing with the desperate energy that abounds in capital cities just before the rebels march in. The latest overnight poll had District Attorney Robinson Shields running three points behind the challenger Murray Cain. Analysts attributed the evaporation of Shields's once-healthy lead to a backlash against the way the Brad Devlin case has been handled. Thirty-five percent of the respondents believe the DA is engaged in a whitewash. An almost equal number feel the teenager is being prosecuted unfairly. The rest have no opinion or have never heard of the case.

Rebecca found the prosecutors she was looking for in a cubicle that couldn't have been bigger than the bathroom in her apartment. They were talking about updating their résumés and speculating about who would stay and who would go. Perhaps new opportunities would arise here. Perhaps it was time to enter private practice.

Rebecca stood in the entrance to their cubicle and coughed loudly. When they looked at her, she identified herself as an intern at the newspaper.

That's nice, they said.

She said she was doing some of the backup stories on the Brad Devlin trial.

Don't you remember what the judge said? they asked. There's a gag order.

She said she thought it applied only to the attorneys who were directly involved in the case. Besides, she wanted to ask them about something that hadn't come up in court yet.

What is it? they asked. She sensed they were lovers. They kept looking at each other and their bodies seemed drawn together.

She said she'd heard that Monica had received a package anonymously in the mail. Rebecca said she'd heard that it contained a cryptic audiotape, an incriminating piece of paper and a video that had upset Monica tremendously. Now she's trying to figure out a way to submit these as evidence.

Who told you that? they asked.

Rebecca said she couldn't reveal her sources.

The male prosecutor—his name was Wismer—walked to the edge of the cubicle and glanced around before telling Rebecca to step in.

The female prosecutor—her name was Gross—sat

behind a desk drumming her fingers on the fake wood top. She said she could really use a cigarette. She hated these goddam no-smoking ordinances. Goddam health Gestapo is driving everybody crazy.

Wismer told Rebecca they all had to talk in very low tones.

Rebecca said she understood.

Monica received the package a couple of days ago, Wismer said. I haven't seen it.

Rebecca asked if Monica had described what was on any of the things she had received.

Not in so many words, Wismer said.

Rebecca asked if she had somehow indicated what they showed.

Wismer nodded. He inferred that the audiotape contained comments from a potential witness and the piece of paper somehow refuted at least part of Brad Devlin's alibi. He also said that he'd never seen Monica more upset than when she talked about the video. They were prosecutors so they've viewed everything—bodies torn to shreds by knives, heads blown in half by shotgun shells, infants turned into blobs of purple and blue by parents who had stopped caring about anything except their own anger. After a while you get used to it.

Rebecca asked if the tape showed the murder. Wismer said he doubted it. Rebecca asked if it showed sexual relations between the defendant and the victim. Wismer told her it was a good guess but he was not one hundred percent sure. He had asked Monica the same question and she didn't confirm it. Of course she didn't deny it either.

Gross said it was her impression that something else was on the tape besides the teenagers' trysts. Rebecca asked what it was. Gross told her to use her imagination. She was old enough to figure it out.

Rebecca asked if the tape showed the victim having sex with someone other than Brad Devlin.

That's what I think, Gross said. Monica told them the tape could land some other people in jail. Not just Brad. People old enough to know better.

That's why it's so important to find out who sent the package, Gross said. Then Monica could put that person on the stand. The witness would describe how he or she came into possession of it and then the thing could be shown to the jury. But there's no chance the judge will allow blind items like these, with no chain of evidence to authenticate them, no matter how compelling they are.

"Good work, Rebecca," I say. My voice sounds hollow, as if I'm talking on a phone from the other side of the world. "I'm gonna transfer you to Trish."

"Who sent that package to Monica?" Rebecca asks.

I pause before saying, "Probably someone who knows Brad."

I finish my chicken salad and walk to the men's room. I take special care to wash my hands.

When I call the Van Nuys division I ask for the commander. The cop at the switchboard asks who's calling and I tell him it's Harris Benton.

The commander comes on the line immediately and says, "Where the fuck are those fingerprints, Benton?"

"Still haven't found them, huh?"

"Who the fuck is this?"

"Ted Lowe."

He swears at me for pulling a cheap goddam stunt so I tell him I know all about the missing fingerprints and Harris Benton's apparent involvement and I'm going to do a story about them one way or another, so he'd better talk to me if he wants his version to get into the newspaper.

"Christ," he says. "This is a fucking disaster. Am I on the record?"

"I'll do you a favor. I won't use the f-word."

"Christ. We've intensified our search for Harris Benton. I'll confirm that."

I ask why the fingerprints had been requested. He says a detective wanted to match them against the prints in another case. I ask which case that is.

"I can't tell you that," the commander says.

"Was it Brad Devlin?" I ask.

I hear the heavy breathing usually associated with obscene phone calls.

I rephrase the question, asking it fully and deliberately: "Did a detective in the Los Angeles Police Department want to see if Brad Devlin's fingerprints matched any of those taken from the Valley break-ins?"

"I can't answer that question."

"Because you don't know the answer, or you don't want to tell me?"

"The latter. But I do want to ask *you* something. Off the record."

I tell him to go ahead.

"Where the fuck are you getting your information?"

I file a story about the missing fingerprints shortly before five. Trish reads it and says I need a comment from the NAACP. We're pretty much crucifying Harris Benton and we should have somebody say something that might be remotely favorable. Just to be fair.

I call the NAACP and am put through immediately to one of the attorneys who represented the now-former sergeant. Civil rights law is a lonely profession these days. The attorney asks why I'm calling and I tell him about the trouble Harris Benton seems to be in. He says he hasn't talked to Mr. Benton in a couple of years. In fact the last time they spoke, he tried to persuade the officer to appear at an NAACP fundraiser. Benton declined and began denouncing the organization in what the attorney would characterize as extreme terms. He does not care to repeat the language, but it seemed that Harris Benton believed the NAACP was interested in him solely as a symbol, not as a man or a police officer.

I do not share with the attorney my own belief that Harris Benton had come uncomfortably close to the truth.

The attorney clears his throat and says he supposes he's on the record. I tell him I just need a comment.

His voice gathers speed and his cadence becomes rhythmic as he says he finds the police department's conduct outrageous, but then he always does. He supposes the LAPD has been after Harris Benton since the day he dared challenge it. This officer has done nothing wrong and now he's the target of a smear campaign. He stood up for his rights and the racists who run the department were determined to make him pay. It wouldn't surprise him if the officer just decided to move someplace more quiet and now that he's no longer around, the racists have decided to turn him into a scapegoat.

"This is such a racist action," he says. "It's not a prosecution—it's a persecution, typical of a department that has oppressed our community for years, discriminated against our people for generations, and subjugated us on a daily basis."

I ask if it bothers him that Benton may be responsible for letting Brad Devlin go free and for hindering the investigation into the Valley break-ins.

"No," he says. "Why should it? These crimes pale in significance to the historic injustices done to the African-American community. The white media only care about crimes when the victims are Caucasian. We've been victimized for centuries. Where are the stories about that? Why don't you print those in your newspaper? See if your readers can handle the truth."

I thank him for talking to me. He tells me to have a nice day.

I stay late at the office and read in on Rebecca's story, which was filed from the courthouse, about the mystery evidence Monica Rosen has received. Before heading out I look through the wires. A brief item from Tahoe catches my attention. The local tour guide Peter

Rourke has been reported missing and authorities fear the worst. One of his boats was found floating on the lake but nobody was in it. Police theorize he fell overboard although it's a strange time of year to be out on the water. Rescue teams are dredging but they're not hopeful. Sometimes people just fall in and disappear.

When the black of the sky locks with the edge of the Pacific, I leave the Volvo and head across the street with my hands thrust deep in my pockets, as if I'm expecting a chill wind off the water. A car alarm springs on while I walk through the parking lot, *whoop-whoop-whooping* for twenty or thirty seconds before fading. Nothing is done to stop it or investigate. By now we know these things usually go off for no reason at all.

There's a shack at the foot of the main pier. The keyhole door is closed, but a bare bulb dangling from a wire lights the interior. I press my ear against the door. I think I hear music but it's muffled.

I knock. No answer. I knock louder.

The door opens a bit but not all the way. I step back. I'm not sure if this is to show the occupant I mean him no harm, or to give myself a little extra room if I have to flee.

Before me is a gaunt man in his thirties with a beard and a ponytail. I make out the Grateful Dead on a portable tape player. The song is "Casey Jones," if I remember correctly. I expect to smell marijuana, but the only scent I detect is foggy salt in the mist drifting past us.

I identify myself and apologize for bothering him.

"That's okay. What's up?"

I ask if a boat named *Sea Angel* is moored here regularly.

"Sure is. That's it over there."

He points to the far end of the marina. The boat's dark silhouette stretches the full length of its dock, and the masts disappear into the night. I see a few lights flaring in the cabin windows belowdeck.

"Are they expecting you? I can bring you over."

"They're not expecting me."

"I can ring them up. It's no problem."

"That's okay. I have a few questions I want to ask you. Can we go inside?"

"Sure."

We enter the shack and I close the door behind us. The space is cramped. Tacked to the walls are drawings and photos of all sorts of sailing vessels. I try to imagine what it was like for Rebecca in here, what it felt like with that guy almost on top of her. . . .

I tell the watchman I understand the *Sea Angel* made a distress call to the Coast Guard on September twenty-ninth.

"I'll have to check the book."

He opens the big leather-bound thing that Rebecca described. He flips through a few pages before saying, "Here it is. It sure did."

I look over his shoulder. If I read the notes correctly, the call was made about six-thirty. That's right around sunset, maybe a little after.

"Were you here that night?" I ask.

"Yeah, man. Sure was."

"Do you remember that call?"

He folds his arms across his chest and lets his chin fall forward until it rests on his neck. His head starts bobbing up and down in time to the music.

"This is a good song, man," he says. And then, a few seconds later, his head nodding as if his brain cells are regenerating, he says, "I do remember it. The whole thing was weird."

"Random?" I ask.

"That too."

He says he heard a woman make the call. She sounded really upset. He thought it was serious but then the transmission stopped. When it resumed some guy was talking. He said everything was fine and they should ignore the signal. He spun it out like she was just being hysterical but something in her voice had sounded genuine. It sounded like terror.

When the boat came back it was after dark and the watchman went down to the dock to make sure everything was okay. He got within thirty yards or so and some guy on deck asked who the fuck was out there.

It's only me, man, the watchman said.

The guy on deck asked what the fuck he wanted. The watchman said he just wanted to make sure everybody was all right. He'd heard that call earlier and the lady sounded upset. The guy on deck told him to stop worrying. The lady was taken care of.

"Did you see her get off the boat?" I ask.

The watchman shakes his head and says he noticed another funny thing. He'd forgotten, but it's all coming back to him now that he's thinking about it. He could swear only six people got off the boat. The log noted that eight had gotten on it.

I tell him he's answered a lot of my questions and he says he was glad to do it. He enjoys helping people. That's what we're here for, isn't it? I say I guess it is and tell him I have another question. It's a bit off the wall, but maybe he knows something.

"Go ahead, man."

"Were you working here a few years ago, when Jeremiah Devlin's wife died in that accident?"

His eyes flicker for a moment, almost as if they see her. He says it's a day that's stuck with him for—well, it seems like forever. The radio traffic was intense and the Coast Guard rushed out some boats, but the problem wasn't that she'd fallen in the water. When the wind shifted, the boom had swung around and smacked her in the back of the head. So the boat got back to shore as quickly as it could and an ambulance was waiting for her, but apparently she'd died as soon as the thing hit her. It was too bad. He'd met her once and she seemed like a nice lady.

"How did Mr. Devlin react?"

"He was really cool. I would've gone to pieces, but he kept telling people what to do, ordering them around like he'd done stuff like this before. The Coast Guard had this idea of sending a helicopter out to try to pick her up. I guess they'd strap her into a stretcher and try to airlift her, something like that. He said they were ridiculous. It would never work. He said he'd have the boat in pretty fast. And he did. But he was battling head winds. It was during a Santa Ana. I guess that's why the wind shifted."

"I thought his wife liked the mountains better than the ocean."

The watchman shrugs. As he said, he met her only once.

I kill the Volvo's lights as I enter the grounds of Santa Monica Airport. One side of my brain tells me this is stupid, but the other side says my more significant problem is the lack of a plan.

I take Noreen's car to the edge of the tarmac and look up and down the runway. Nothing is approaching and the outline of the runway is unlit. I ease onto the concrete strip and cruise past the open hangars. Light planes and small jets fill the cavernous spaces, waiting for a summons from their masters so they can be whisked to another place where the country's business is done.

The last hangar, of course, is the one I want. I see the word "DEVLIN" etched in a small, neat sans serif on the tails of four small jets.

I stop the car. A couple of figures are moving around in the hangar. I'm not sure they know I'm here and I'm not even sure I can find what I want, but this is probably the only chance I'll get. So I shove some papers in the big brown envelope I keep for occasions like this one. Then I turn on the lights and speed right for the hangar. I screech to a halt and hop out of the car. I keep the lights on and the engine running. I want whoever is inside to believe the situation is urgent. As I stride toward the planes I boom out, "Who's in charge here? Who the fuck's in charge?"

A woman in her early forties, a bit on the heavy side, walks toward me. She wears pumps and slacks, and I'm willing to bet her hair isn't its natural color.

She says she's in charge and asks what's wrong. There's no reason to barge in like this at this hour and she has a mind to—

I wave my wallet around and hope nobody looks at my ID too closely.

"I'm Henderson from the FAA," I announce, using the last name of Noreen's ex-husband. "We've got a crisis on our hands. And it's all your fault!"

"We haven't done anything."

"That's just the problem!"

I hear stirrings within the hangar. I wonder how many of them there are.

"You guys haven't been filing your goddam flight plans! You just take off whenever you feel like it and you're fucking up the system! We've had four near misses in the last month because of you!"

"Bullshit," the woman says. She's more correct than she probably imagines. "We've sent you everything that's required. Why don't you come back in the morning? You can look over everything."

"I just got off the phone with Washington," I say. "They chewed my ass up one side and down the other. Said I should've been on top of this situation from the get-go. The deputy director told me himself to get my ass down here and check things out even though it's a goddam holiday. He said he didn't care if he had to pay me triple time, he wants a goddam answer and he's waiting for me to call him back and it's two in the fucking morning there."

She shakes her head slowly, as if she can't believe this night avenger from the bureaucracy has swooped into her lair. I think I've about ninety-five percent convinced her that this is legitimate.

"Let me look at some of your flight plans," I say. "If everything's okay, then the fault is at our end. But if you don't let me look at them right now, the deputy director might ground your jets for a few days because . . . well, because he's that kind of guy."

She tells me to follow her into the office and asks why I didn't call. I say I didn't want to lose the element of surprise. This is the first truthful thing I've told her.

She takes out her keys. The stirrings get louder. I hear the words "Some shithead from the FAA" followed by "That's impossible." I hope nobody gets on the phone to Washington to check out my story.

The office is small and has a fan overhead. The setup reminds me of an old Warner Brothers movie. She flips on the light, sits at the computer and boots it up. She asks if I'm looking for flight plans from any days in particular.

"September fourteenth and fifteenth," I say.

"That's a while ago," she says.

"That's when we think the trouble started."

She searches. I look out the window. The Volvo is still there. I believe I hear footsteps coming toward the room, so I discreetly push the door closed with my foot.

"It's right here," she says. "We filed the plans. See for yourself."

She pushes herself away from the tube. I peer at it and start taking notes. Two of Devlin's planes flew out on the fourteenth, one to San Francisco and one to Reno. The San Francisco flight had no passengers, so I assume it was picking up someone. The jet to Reno carried one passenger.

"I assume Mr. Devlin used the plane on the fourteenth?" I ask.

"That's correct," she says. Obviously she can decipher all the notations on the flight entries. "He spends a lot of time in Tahoe."

The computer notes that two more flights occurred from Santa Monica to Reno on the fifteenth. The first jet carried two passengers, the second only one.

I point to the two flights and ask, "Are you sure this is accurate?"

She shrugs. "As far as I know."

"Who took them?"

She squints and says, "Mr. Devlin's son was on the first one. I'm not sure who he was with." The plane left around six P.M. I find this disconcerting. It means Brad wasn't in Tahoe during the day—but he was there when Megan was killed. If this information is accurate.

"Who took the second flight?" I ask. "It looks like it left only an hour later. Shouldn't they have taken the same flight?"

She nods and says she knows what I mean. With all the cost cutting, you'd think the people at the top of the corporation would be more responsible.

I think I hear the doorknob turn. As she accesses another file I step away, lean my back against the wall and put my hand on the knob.

"That's funny," she says, more to herself than to me. I feel the knob turning. Someone is definitely trying to get in.

"Maryann Wright took that flight. I didn't know she was authorized to use the company planes."

The door bursts open and I'm swept across the room. I turn and look at the door. It's only a few feet away. Someone is shining a flashlight directly in my eyes.

"Who the fuck are you?"

I recognize the voice from Tahoe. I wonder if he saw me then.

"I'm Henderson, with the FAA. I've been talking to your boss."

"She's not my boss. Let me see your ID."

"Fuck you. I'm gonna report this."

I take a step toward him but I can't see anything because he's still pointing the light right at me. I wonder if he has a gun and if he's going to shoot but then I feel a rough palm hit me flat on the chest. The light is only inches away.

"It's all a misunderstanding," the woman is saying. "The FAA screwed up somehow. What else is new? But we cleared it up."

"Let me see your ID."

I reach into my back pocket and feel my wallet. As I begin to take it out I throw myself at the window. The breaking and shattering sounds are familiar to me as sharp-edged glass once again tears into my face, neck and hands. I feel blood come out and I know I deserve this.

The darkness beckons me. Once again it is my friend.

The Volvo is no more than ten yards away. I want to fling myself into it and speed away but as I jump into the driver's seat I feel a hand reach in. At the end of this hand is a gun. The barrel raps me in the left eye and my first instinct is animalistic but that is what we are, so in fury and pain I clamp down on the wrist and bite into hairy human flesh. Warm blood spurts into my mouth and someone cries out and the gun clatters onto the seat and then the floor and I press the accelerator hard and fast. The car lurches forward.

Behind me I hear shouts and screams and the *pop-pop-pop* of bullets being fired. I slouch and drive faster. Car engines start. I look in the rearview mirror and see bright headlights getting closer. I cut to the left and pray no planes are landing. The headlights follow. Then I cut to the right and head straight for the exit. I speed through it and onto the main road without stopping. Behind me I hear screeching and swerving and crashing.

I look into the rearview mirror again. The headlights emerge from the airport and follow me. Ahead a traffic signal turns red but I go through it, honking my horn as loudly as I can. Cars plow onto the sidewalk and spin into one another but I press on.

The headlights are closer.

I make a left without slowing. My head bumps into the roof as my tires climb the curb and then I'm on the street again going quickly . . . trying to get away . . . pursued by high-burning lights that blind me when they catch the mirror. Up ahead is an entrance to a freeway and my left eye is now shut and I feel it swelling and I still taste blood on my lips. I race up the ramp and have to twist my whole body around to make sure nothing is in the right lane and I get onto the freeway and behind me, now merely a couple of car lengths away, I again see the headlights of my pursuer.

I race over to the left lane and behind me cars squeal and spin and I hear honking horns and I even have a vague thought that one of these motorists might take out a gun of his own and try to use it against me. When I reach the left lane, my pursuer falls in right behind.

A gasoline tanker is directly on the right. My pursuer bumps hard into the rear of the Volvo. I'm doing eighty and I'm trapped and suddenly I cut over, directly in front of the tanker, and race for the exit ramp as vehicles brake and slide and screech, and behind me and to the left I hear a loud crash followed by a boom and a flaming light rises up; it's a supernova that fills the mirror and the car and the entire night sky, but I keep driving fast over the shoulder and the grassy strip that separates the freeway from the exit ramp, and when I hit the ramp I cut sharply to the left and speed down to the surface street. There's a yield sign but I go through it. A quarter-mile down the road I stop, finally, at a red light.

There are no cars on my rear. In fact there's nothing behind me except orange flames and a burning glow that threatens to overwhelm the night.

• • •

I cruise past Rebecca's apartment several times and finally park the Volvo about a block away. I observe the scene for about fifteen minutes, but I see no people or cars. Finally I start the Volvo again and take it around to the back of her building. Visitors are not supposed to park here, but there are usually a couple of empty spaces.

I climb the steps to her place as quickly as I can. My left eye is shut. I can only imagine what it looks like. I ring the bell and knock on the door and pray pray pray that she'll answer it soon so I can stumble into sanctuary.

I feel eyes looking at me. Bolts and locks come undone. She gasps when she sees me.

I have no place else to go, I tell her.

She holds out her hand. When I grab it she draws me in. Then she slams the door shut and throws all the safety devices back into place. She runs into the kitchen and makes an ice pack that she presses to my eye. She tells me to keep the ice right there. It'll make the swelling go down. She fills the tub, comes back to the living room and takes my hand again. She guides me to the bed and sits me on the edge and removes my shoes and socks, followed by my shirts and pants and underwear. I'm too tired to cooperate but I do not resist. I keep the ice pack pressed to my eye. She grabs my hand and leads me toward the water. She turns off the faucet and throws in an Egyptian bath product that she says is supposed to heal the skin.

She tells me to get in and holds me as I do. At first

the water and whatever is in it assault my wounds, sting them, remind me of the pain and death and suffering I have caused since the day Megan's body was found.

Rebecca puts lotion on a sponge and rubs it over the back of my neck. I expect it to hurt, but instead it soothes whatever has injured me.

"Tell me what happened," she says.

I do, as best I can.

She takes the sponge to my face and scrubs around my scalp and forehead before gently rubbing my cheeks and nose and chin. I tell her she doesn't have to do this but she says it's all right. This time.

A heat wave grips my hometown in the Midwest. Reports say it's the worst of its kind in decades. After a couple of days the municipal agencies start getting calls about overpowering odors in many of the older apartment buildings. Police go in. So do firefighters, paramedics, social workers. They find people dead. Almost all are elderly. They had shut their doors and windows years ago to keep away the raging terror of urban America.

When the heat struck, none of them tried to get out. They did not open their windows or use the telephone. Most were found in their beds, hands clasped over their chests, as if in prayer.

The death toll is in the hundreds. The morgue is out of room.

ten

i call Monica at home shortly after seven and apologize for bothering her so early in the morning.

"I don't sleep much these days," she says.

"Nobody does anymore," I say.

She tells me that I of all people should know she can't talk to the media. I say I'm not calling to pose questions. She says in that case she does want to talk to me, but asks if this can wait. She has to get the kids ready for school.

I tell her it can't wait, then ask if we can go off the record.

"That's what I'm supposed to say."

I ask if she's familiar with the architecture magazine I saw in Michael's coffeehouse. She asks if this is going to lead somewhere and I say I think it will. She says she's heard of it but never actually read it.

"Take a look at the most recent issue," I say. I describe the pink bicycle in the pool enclosure at Jeremiah Devlin's place in Tahoe.

In the background I hear children fighting with one another. It seems someone used all the Froot Loops.

"You think that's Megan's bicycle?" Monica asks.

"Who else would've used it?"

"But why would they lie about that?" she asks. Her tone is one of wondering aloud, not inquisition. "Why not admit that Megan made a couple of visits to Tahoe?"

"If she kept her bike at the house, it indicates she spent a lot of time there."

"But why don't they want to admit that?"

"Beats me. Unless there's something up there . . ."

My voice trails off. Monica completes the thought. "That establishes his guilt beyond a reasonable doubt."

I wouldn't have put it that way, but she is an attorney.

"There's something else you should check," I say. I tell her I have sources in the FAA and suggest she examine the flight plans for Jeremiah Devlin's airplanes out of Santa Monica Airport on the evening of September fifteenth.

"You better do it soon," I say. "Before somebody does something to them."

"What do they show?" she asks.

"A lot of activity. But I'm not sure what it means."

She says she appreciates what I've told her. She asks if we're still off the record. I assure her we are.

"I wish I had somebody like you investigating this for me," she says. "I want to find out things and I can't. People drag their feet. They sit around for hours telling me why they can't do something, but if they just went out and did it . . ."

I look around the kitchen counter for the coffee filters.

"Like that thing about the bicycle," she says. "You'd think somebody on our end would have discovered that article. Doing a Nexis search isn't that hard."

I find a filter and separate it from the pack. I line it into the basket on Rebecca's machine and open the refrigerator.

"I have a question for you," Monica says. "Just between us."

I grunt a noise that could be construed as assent.

"Would you testify?"

"Come on, Monica, I can't do that."

"Why not?"

I mumble something about conflict of interest as I fill the basket with Folgers.

"I don't see a conflict," Monica says.

"My career would be over," I say.

"Is that worth letting Brad Devlin get away with it?"

"From my standpoint, the answer could be yes."

I open the faucet and fill the carafe. This water comes from hundreds of miles away. It does not belong to the area.

"I read that story today," she says. "The one about the package."

I haven't seen it yet. I haven't even opened the door to look for the paper.

"Are we still off the record?" she asks.

I tell her we are.

"The story's accurate," she says. "I have an audio-tape that's so disturbing it makes my heart race. I have a piece of paper that blows Brad Devlin's story apart, and a video that will send him to jail for a long time. His father too. But they were sent to me anonymously. There's no chain of evidence. I can't use them."

I pour the water into the machine and flip the switch so it glows red. I hear the sounds of bubbling and brewing. The carafe catches black liquid.

"Do you know anything about that package?" she asks.

In the background I hear a male voice telling children to hurry up. I assume it's the father.

"I've been talking to Gruley," she says. "I could try to make you testify."

"Don't threaten me, Monica."

"I'm not threatening you. I'm just telling you what I could do."

"If you're even thinking about that, you better talk to my attorney. Did Gruley mention who it is?"

"No."

So I do. She whistles softly and mutters a few obscenities. I hope the children are out of earshot.

The carafe is full and the machine has grown silent. I open the cupboard and take out the largest mug I can find.

"Why is it—?" she asks in a voice that catches. She might be crying or trying not to. "Why am I the only person who seems interested in justice? You saw her body. You know what they did to her."

I cannot, will not, must not connect. Part of her head was smashed in. Police figured she'd been raped. She was just another victim of the violence we deplore but enjoy. The latest casualty. Part of the price we pay for being Americans.

I tell Monica I have to go. She says she does too. At this rate she'll be late for court.

I drain the contents of the carafe into the mug, then walk to the door and peer through the peephole and out the windows. There is nothing to see except the usual stirrings of a workday morning. I open the door and bring in the paper.

A thought occurs to me that I have not considered before. *If Brad was in Tahoe, did he tell his friends to take care of Megan?*

I put the paper on the kitchen counter and sip my coffee. The taste is both sour and bitter.

Rebecca sips orange-strawberry-banana juice as she looks over the front page. She says she's excited because she's never had a story out there before. It wasn't even rewritten that much.

I leaf through the sports section, hoping to distract myself by concentrating on a subject I care little about. But every major professional league is embroiled in a labor dispute, and my alma mater has been cited for recruiting violations.

Rebecca says I seem awfully quiet and I tell her I don't have much to say. She turns to the metro section and says my story isn't bad. I mumble something that could be interpreted as gratitude.

"What do you think about these break-ins?" she asks. "What are they about?"

This question could be the kind of idle brain-picking

that current and former lovers do with one another—or it could be a ferreting out, an elicitation, an attempt to further explore what she already knows or perhaps only suspects.

I could tell her. I could describe my trips to the dark side and my pleasant plunge to the depths, where the confident and strong brush away the weak and timid as if they're bugs crawling across glass.

"Don't you have any ideas?" Rebecca asks in a voice several decibels louder than normal. When I say nothing she puts the paper aside and leans toward me. Her eyes narrow as she realizes she's asked a better question than she originally believed.

"What are you keeping from me?" she asks.

"Brad Devlin is involved in them."

I say this quite slowly. I'm surprised I allow these words to escape.

Rebecca's eyes grow wide. I sense her backing away from me.

"You're kidding," she says.

I shake my head.

"Why?" she asks.

"If I were a shrink, I'd say he's acting out his hostility and aggression. But I'm not a shrink. I think he's evil. I think he enjoys it."

"That's not what I'm asking," Rebecca says. "Why do you think he's involved?"

I can tell her facts. But I can never tell her the truth. I can never tell that to anyone.

"Things I've heard," I say. "I'm trying to pin it down. I'm not sure I'll be able to."

"Is there something you're not telling me?" she asks.

I get up and walk into the bathroom and look in the mirror. The skin around my left eye is blue and purple. I can open the eye only a bit and everything it registers is blurry.

I wear sunglasses in the office and everyone asks if I think I'm a movie star. I gross out a few by pulling down my shades and showing them my injury. When they ask what happened I say it's my own fault. I'm too damn clumsy.

Just before court begins Sander Van Arsdale is on TV telling the anchor that sources close to the defense have said Richard Alvarez is supremely confident he'll be able to expose inconsistencies in the medical examiner's report and in his testimony.

"What kind of inconsistencies?" the anchor asks.

"My sources wouldn't elaborate, but they did say the defense has several surprises in store for the prosecution. There was great excitement among the defense lawyers this morning."

I wonder why Van Arsdale hasn't saved this material for the newspaper that employs him.

"Moreover," Van Arsdale says, "the defense also believes it has proof the authorities have ignored evidence that exonerates the defendant, and points toward the guilt of somebody else."

"Would that be Grant Fisher?" the anchor asks.

"I'm not at liberty to say."

"Thank you for your time. I know you have to get

into the courtroom, but there's one more thing I want to ask you."

Van Arsdale tells the anchor to go ahead. But he does have to run.

"I've heard you're writing a book about the case."

Van Arsdale flashes his teeth in what some people might consider a smile.

"I signed a contract last night, as a matter of fact," he says. He tells the viewing audience that Connie Battaglia suggested the idea. He expects to write the definitive account of the case.

As the camera shows Van Arsdale walking toward the courthouse, the anchor says he's a remarkable young reporter. I notice Rebecca approaching Van Arsdale at the courthouse entrance. I can see her saying something to him as he shakes his head, but she keeps talking and finally he throws up his hands and enters the building.

A Nexis search on Jeremiah and Eleanor Devlin reveals only a handful of stories. My newspaper's accounts of her death and funeral were brief and dry. But my search reveals that *People* magazine did an article on the funeral, so I ask one of the librarians to retrieve the issue. A two-page spread has a picture of an oceangoing yacht as well as gray and somber photos of a middle-aged man and a boy. The headline says "A FATHER'S ANGUISH, A SON'S GRIEF," and the text describes the funeral of Eleanor Devlin, who died in an accident aboard the family's boat, the *Sea Angel*. Adding to the tragedy, the story says, was the Devlins' recent reconciliation after a six-month separation.

On TV everyone stands as Judge Baden-Howell enters court and pours herself a glass of water. She says she has just received an important piece of information from the defense. She has instructed Mr. Alvarez to hand it over to the prosecution. The judge says the information raises a number of troubling questions that she will rule on later today, probably after lunch. In the meantime she asks the prosecutors to familiarize themselves with the material Mr. Alvarez has uncovered.

"What do you think that means?" the anchor asks in an urgent voice.

"It means Richard Alvarez has probably discovered some exculpatory evidence," one of the legal commentators says. The camera shows the judge shuffling some papers.

"Or there could be evidence of prosecutorial misconduct," another commentator says. "Perhaps something has been withheld from the defense."

"Is there a chance there could be a confession," the anchor asks, "or some kind of a plea agreement?"

The commentators agree this is unlikely.

Judge Baden-Howell says that for now she will allow the defense to proceed with its cross-examination of the medical examiner.

"There are some things in your report that I find puzzling," Alvarez says.

"I think the report is pretty clear, Mr. Alvarez," Karch says.

"Of course you do," Alvarez says. He settles behind the lectern. He seems to be reading from the autopsy report. "How did the girl drown?" he asks.

"I'm not sure."

"And where did she drown?"

"I'm not sure of that, either."

"Would you care to hazard a guess?"

Karch raises his head a bit and smiles at Alvarez.

"Well, Mr. Alvarez, there's a pretty big ocean nearby. And we have lots of swimming pools too."

"I believe both those scenarios are unlikely." Alvarez takes several pieces of paper from his folder and walks toward the medical examiner. "Have you read this report? I sent it to your office last week." He hands the papers to Karch and says, "We employed an outside consultant to review the results of your autopsy."

"I don't put much stock in those guys. They'll say anything to—"

"Have you heard of Dr. Franklin Yasukawa?"

Karch gulps and nods. Alvarez turns to the jury.

"Until last year, Dr. Yasukawa was the chief medical examiner for the city of San Francisco. He now heads the department of pathology at Yale Medical School."

Alvarez turns back to the witness.

"You know Dr. Yasukawa?"

Karch nods. Alert viewers can see a white flag being run up the side of the witness stand.

"I've met him professionally several times," the medical examiner says.

"You have not read his report?" Alvarez asks.

"I have not."

"Could you please read the paragraph I've marked in red?" Alvarez asks.

The medical examiner mumbles (deliberately, I think). His report had not bothered to specify what type of water was found in Megan's lungs. Yasukawa's analysis has determined that her lungs were filled with freshwater.

"Freshwater, Dr. Karch," Alvarez says. "Not salt water. Not chlorinated. And where is the closest body of freshwater to where the girl was found?"

Monica objects. Badgering the witness. The judge agrees.

"I'm sorry, Your Honor," Alvarez says. "I'm merely trying to point out that the autopsy report is riddled with errors and omissions. Dr. Yasukawa believes the girl may have been murdered many hours before the medical examiner says she was."

"Objection, Your Honor." Monica is still on her feet.

"I will prove my point, Your Honor," Alvarez says before the judge does anything. He turns to the witness stand, strides toward the medical examiner and rips Yasukawa's report out of his hands.

"How did you miss this?" Alvarez asks, flipping to another page and pointing angrily at the paper. He thrusts it back at the medical examiner and says, "The decedent was two months' pregnant."

There is a gasp and *whoosh* in the courtroom followed by some audible shouts from the spectators' benches as the judge pounds her gavel yelling for quiet while Monica is still on her feet shouting "Objection, objection, objection!"

The sound in the courtroom lessens but does not dissipate.

"This is totally irrelevant, Your Honor," Monica says. She is almost biting the words. "Whether the victim was pregnant has absolutely no bearing on this case."

"Your Honor," Alvarez says, "the errors and omissions in the medical examiner's report undermine everything the prosecution has said in this courtroom."

Judge Baden-Howell leans back in her chair. Her eyes are round with surprise, as if she's been hit hard by something she did not see or expect.

The camera pans to Brad Devlin. His face is expressionless and his hands are folded neatly on the defense table. Next the camera shows his father, who is making his first appearance at the trial. Jeremiah Devlin is looking up, his eyes fixed on an indeterminate site somewhere between the end of his nose and the ceiling.

"I will let the question stand, counselor," the judge

says. "And I will allow this line of questioning. It strikes me as pertinent."

"How did you miss this fact, Dr. Karch?" Alvarez says.

The medical examiner mumbles something about budget cuts and overwork. Sometimes important facts don't get noticed.

I've been doing this so long I've abandoned all hope in fair and reasonable outcomes. And I don't believe in justice. I have no idea what the word means, although in my darker moments I maintain it is merely the institutionalized form of revenge.

I wonder if a dead girl can betray you. Then I catch myself and I say this: Megan was a girl. She was living her life and she had never harmed anyone and she was murdered. In other times that would have been enough to make us care, but now we demand perfection from our victims.

eleven

the same instinct that makes you slow down to observe a train wreck inspires me to turn on the television shortly after one. Sander Van Arsdale's face fills the screen.

"We fully expect the judge to issue some kind of definitive ruling as soon as court reconvenes," Van Arsdale tells whoever is listening. "This place is abuzz with rumors."

"What kind of rumors?" the anchor asks offscreen. It's like being questioned by the voice of God.

"Some people believe the judge will issue sanctions against the prosecution for withholding evidence. There are even some stories going around that claim the judge will dismiss the charges."

"Thank you, Sander," the anchor says. "Incisive as usual."

My phone flashes. I pick it up before it rings.

"He's gonna walk."

It's Rebecca's voice, flatter than the prairie.

"Someone in the DA's office told me. They heard it from one of the judge's clerks. Seems that receipt showed up. It's dated September fourteenth."

"I saw that receipt myself. It was dated the fifteenth. I have it in my notes."

"Apparently Alvarez got it from the credit card company. That impeaches the credibility of that salesgirl in the mall. Now nobody can place Brad and Megan together on the day of the murder. Alvarez is implying that the prosecution had the receipt all along and wouldn't turn it over because it proved Brad was innocent."

"Could you look up something for me?"

"Sure."

I ask her to find out anything she can about the separation proceedings between Jeremiah Devlin and his late wife, Eleanor.

"Is this significant?" Rebecca asks.

"It could be," I reply.

Judge Baden-Howell enters the courtroom. All rise. She pours herself a glass of water and asks Alvarez to address the court about an important piece of information.

"When the state informed the court that it had misplaced the receipt for the necklace that my client purchased for the decedent, I contacted American Express and asked for a copy. The police said they too had taken this action—but the representatives I spoke with said they had no record of such a conversation. At any rate, Your Honor, I received a copy of the receipt late yesterday afternoon via Federal Express. I have shown it to you, and I now submit it in evidence to the court. The receipt clearly shows that the item in question was purchased on September fourteenth—the day before Megan Wright died."

Murmurs, whispers and conversations in the background are silenced by the judge's gavel.

"In view of this, Your Honor, the defense is moving for an immediate mistrial, and a dismissal of all charges."

"Your Honor," Monica says with hints of pleading and desperation that are beneath her, "The People would like to address the court."

"I'm going to rule you out of order, Ms. Rosen," the judge says. "And I'm going to issue my decision right now." She says she was greatly disturbed to receive word from Mr. Alvarez that he had located a copy of the receipt. It was her understanding that the police were looking for this and, by all rights, this type of search properly belonged to the state. The prosecution has offered excuses for its failures, but she accepts none of them. In any event this evidence is exculpatory in the extreme. Moreover, the state's inability to locate this evidence can be construed as bad faith. She has never seen misconduct so egregious.

"Ladies and gentlemen of the jury," she says, "I am about to issue an order I customarily refrain from making. In fact I am loath to make it. I believe it should be up to you to examine the evidence and make a decision based on the facts. But they are clear in this case, and to allow it to continue would be unfair to you, and to the defendant, and to the cause of justice.

"Therefore, I am granting the motion for the mistrial. Moreover, I am also ordering that all charges against Bradley Devlin be dismissed forthwith."

Shouts, cheers and yelps of congratulation fill the courtroom. In voiceover the announcer says the outcome is no surprise—nobody ever expects Richard Alvarez to lose—but the timing is certainly unexpected. This may be the first time he's beaten the prosecution before a case even got to the jury.

I walk over to the metro desk and ask Trish if there's anything she wants me to handle. She says Van Arsdale will write the main but I should try for a sidebar on how the police are reacting to the decision. "I'd like to avoid the obvious," she says. "You know, 'LAPD screws up another big one.' "

"We can't avoid it, but I'll play it down."

I go to the bathroom and return to my desk. There's a message on my voicemail. It's from Noreen. She asks if I've ever taken care of Kristen's dresses. She tells me to call and leaves a new number.

I phone Frank Gruley.

"I'm gonna get drunk," he says. It sounds as if he's well on his way. "I'm gonna get so drunk my wife'll have to come down here to drive me home. Then I'll throw up all over the backseat. Just like when we were dating." He pauses, then announces, "He's guilty! You know it. I know it. So's his old man. And that bitch of a mother. The brother's probably in on it too."

"He's nine years old."

"Doesn't matter. They're all guilty. Every goddam one."

"Can you give me something I can print?"

His voice thins and grows clearer. He says he's disappointed with the judge's ruling. He believes the department conducted its investigation with absolute professionalism.

It pains him when slurs are made against the Los Angeles police. The force is full of dedicated people doing a difficult job under extreme circumstances.

"What about the receipt?" I ask. "You said you'd talked to the company."

"They gave me a fucking runaround. Alvarez paid somebody off."

"I can't print that."

"You always print facts. You never print the truth."

I'm not sure how to respond to this.

"Let's go off the record," I finally say. "How are you doing?"

"You've asked some pretty dumb fucking questions over the years, but that's about the dumbest. How the fuck does it sound like I'm doing?"

"What are you gonna do now?"

"After I get over my hangover, I'm gonna hand in my papers. We've got a place picked out in Wyoming. Beautiful country, clean air, and nobody for miles. I don't wanna deal with people. I'm fed up with them."

He asks what I'm going to do. It's a question I've never even thought about.

"What I've always done, I guess."

"A fucking vulture?"

"Vultures do well in America."

"You're a cynical sonuvabitch. You believe in nothing. So you're in step with the times. I'm sure you'll do well." He stops. I think I hear him taking a few swigs. "I don't fucking believe it," he says. "Richard fucking Alvarez on fucking CNN. I think I'll puke right now. Might as well get it over with."

I wheel around and look at the TV. The courtroom has been converted into a media pen with cameras, photographers and reporters crowding around a long wooden table. Alvarez sits in the middle, flanked by Jeremiah Devlin and his son.

"I think I speak for everyone when I say I'm glad this ordeal is over," Alvarez says.

Questions are shouted. It's impossible to hear any of them distinctly. A cameraman knocks over a still photographer's tripod.

"At this time," Alvarez says, "I'd like to extend my heartfelt sympathy to the family of this poor girl."

Megan, I feel like shouting. *Her name was Megan Wright.*

Jeremiah Devlin holds up his hand as if asking for quiet, but the questions only come in an ever-quickening din. Brad examines his fingernails.

"I'd like to say something," Devlin says. Something approaching silence ensues. "Both Brad and myself have been greatly touched by this young girl's death. And to show our concern, I am offering a reward of fifty thousand dollars to anyone who comes forward with information that leads us to a solution as to how she died. It's the least I can do."

"Can you tell us anything about her mother?" a female reporter shouts quickly.

"She's still in seclusion," Devlin says. "We're taking care of her as best we can."

"How do you feel, Brad?" It sounds like Van Arsdale.

"Great."

"Do you have any idea who was responsible for her death?" The female reporter again.

"I do have some thoughts on that," Alvarez says.

He pulls a piece of paper from his briefcase and holds it aloft. His action reminds me of the way a matador both enrages and entrances a bull.

"I have a statement," he says. "It's been signed by Alexis Collins, the young girl who testified the other day." He puts on his reading glasses and holds the paper at arm's length. "Miss Collins says she had a conversation with Grant Fisher the day after she completed her testimony. During the course of this conversation, she told Mr. Fisher that she wasn't sure anymore who had killed her classmate. And now let me quote from her statement directly:

" ' "I know," Grant said.

" ' "Who did it?" I asked.

" ' "I did," he said.' "

The noise level picks up. I hear Van Arsdale asking if copies of the statement will be made available.

"Moreover," Alvarez says, his voice trying to surmount the din, "Miss Collins says she tried to relay this information to the district attorney's office, but she was rebuffed."

"Did you say anything about this to the judge?" somebody asks.

"It was one of the items I conveyed this morning, yes. There is something I would like to add," Alvarez says, his voice again adding decibels. "We have located the victim's diary."

Shouts, yelps, screams, hysteria. The media baying like a pack of wild dogs.

"We have turned the contents over to the authorities. But I will summarize some interesting items for you. First, Grant Fisher's name appears several times. She wrote of how much she was afraid of him. In fact, she called him—and this is a direct quote—'creepy.' Second, there is mention on several occasions of an older man. This man is unnamed, but he is described as tall and thin, with hair turning to gray. She wrote that she was terrified of this man."

"Do you have any idea who that man is?" Van Arsdale again, helpful as ever.

"I have some thoughts," Alvarez replies. "There is a reporter—I do not want to dignify these proceedings by using his name—who more than anyone else was responsible for bringing this case about. His stories were filled with distortion, innuendo and inaccuracies. And yet, let us consider: Why did he know so much about this case? Why did he obtain information that the police and prosecutors could not? What does he know that he isn't telling the rest of us? Why was he so interested in casting suspicion on an innocent party, and smearing a young man who was not involved in this crime?"

There is a great silence in the courtroom and around me. The description Alvarez cited in Megan's diary certainly matches mine.

"I do not mean to suggest this reporter was in league with the police, or the prosecution, or Mr. Fisher. That is for others to discover. But it seems to me that these questions must be raised. I've had them since the beginning."

"But why would he do something like that?" A female reporter. I wonder if I know her.

"I learned long ago never to ascribe motive to any-one. But let us consider a few things: This story has dominated the news for weeks. It's a great story if Mr. Devlin and his son are involved—and not a great story if they're not." Alvarez smiles, and a few reporters chuckle at this acknowledgment of the realities of our profession. "Moreover, I know this reporter has been negotiating a book contract that would, I am sure, make him a wealthy individual. What is the truth when there is so much to gain? And why shouldn't he protect the guilty, and let the innocent suffer? Why not even orchestrate events?"

An explosion of questions. Alvarez holds the paper aloft again. Representatives of the media claw one another, straining to get close to what he claims to have.

I put on my headset and call the number Noreen left on my voicemail.

"I've been watching TV," she says. "It's not true, is it? What he's saying? Tell me it isn't true."

"I don't know what's true anymore."

"Brad did it, didn't he? He killed that girl. And he's getting away with it because his father's rich. Isn't that what's happening?"

I tell her I'm sorry I haven't sent Kristen's dresses, but I've been extremely busy and to be honest it slipped my mind. I promise to stop at her house tonight and find them and ship them out first thing in the morning. She gives me her address, which I jot on a piece of paper that I put in my shirt pocket.

She sighs. It's the sound of a woman who hasn't

wanted much, but has wanted it desperately, and now realizes she's never going to get it.

Maynard calls. He says he thinks I need some legal advice.

"I'm gonna keep my fucking mouth shut. How's that?"

"Good! It's a simple goddam idea, but you'd be amazed how many people screw it up. They talk to the police, and the next thing they know they're strapped into a gurney in San Quentin wondering how this shit happened."

I say nothing. I am in the middle of a newsroom with two hundred people and I have never felt more isolated. Ever since Alvarez's press conference, nobody has come within thirty feet of me.

"As your attorney of record, Maynard is wondering if you have any response to what Mr. Richard Alvarez said a short time ago."

"I'm keeping my fucking mouth shut, Maynard. Especially on the phone."

"Maynard understands. In the meantime, he wants to relay to you the contents of a conversation he just had with Monica Rosen."

I tell him I'm listening.

"Monica told Maynard that if the trial had continued much longer, she was going to subpoena your butt, shield law or no shield law. She thinks you know something. She thinks you know *a lot*. To be perfectly candid about it, Maynard thinks she's right. Maynard may not believe everything Mr. Richard Alvarez just said, but as your attorney, he would have advised you to take the Fifth."

Rebecca stops at my desk. She's slung a knapsack over her shoulder and Ray-Bans over her eyes. I sense everyone looking at us as if they can't believe we are somehow, impossibly, a current or former couple.

She dumps her unopened knapsack on my desk.

"Tell me it isn't true," she says.

She takes off her shades. Her brown eyes are rimmed with red, as if she's been crying over the worst form of betrayal she could imagine. I want to say something but the words refuse to work, so I just shake my head and mouth, "It's not true," although she could just as easily read them as "I love you."

"I'm disgusted," she says. "Disgusted with the lawyers, disgusted with the judge, disgusted with the newspaper—and I'm especially disgusted with you. I used to think that things made sense, but now I realize they don't. So now I feel everything is . . . meaningless."

The words come back to me. I feel them rush in and tell her: "It's not meaningless. Not after you've thought it through. I understand why you'd feel that way, but at some point you begin to realize just how wrong it is that people like Brad Devlin get away with things just because they can buy their way out of trouble."

These are thoughts I didn't even know I had. But I hear them coming out of my mouth.

"Today nobody asks the question, 'Is it right?' Instead they say, 'Can I get away with it?' Somewhere along the line the ideas of right and wrong, and good and evil, fell out of favor. I was one of the people who went along with it. I thought they were just arbitrary concepts. But they're not. They're real, and they mean something. Everything isn't relative. There are absolutes."

She says she looked into that matter I asked about. According to court records, Eleanor Devlin sought a separation from her husband some months before her death. She wanted custody of Brad and filed some preliminary papers that indicated she intended to seek a divorce in the state of California.

"This is significant because—"

And here I chime in.

"—California is a community property state."

One week before the fatal accident, Eleanor Devlin dropped the motion and moved back in with her husband.

"What were the grounds for separation?" I ask.

"She said he was having an affair with a nineteen-year-old office assistant."

"And why did they reconcile?"

"I guess she got over it."

Across the room Van Arsdale is at his terminal surrounded by a gaggle of editors. He's writing the story in his personal queue, so I can't read in on it.

"Would you please stop badgering me?" Van Arsdale announces to the crowd around him. I try to hover at the edge. People move away from me. "I can't stay here much longer."

He's been invited to a victory celebration that Jeremiah Devlin is hosting at a Westside nightspot. Van Arsdale will be the only journalist in attendance. He says it will be great material for his book.

"We certainly want to accommodate you, Sander," Fussman says. "We'll try to wrap this up quickly."

Van Arsdale says he's been exploring the Grant Fisher angle himself for the past few days. Sources in the defense have been giving him excellent and troubling information. He looks at me directly as he says this. It's the first time he's looked at me since he took over the story.

Back at my desk I put on my headset and call Monica's home number. I expect a busy signal but instead it rings. When the machine kicks on there's a long beep and then I begin:

"Hi Monica it's me; I'm just calling to see if you have any reaction to—"

"I knew you'd call. I've been waiting for it. You know what's on that video, don't you? You sent that package to me. You know everything."

"Are you formally questioning me? Because if you are, I'll go to your office tomorrow morning with my attorney and we'll do it properly."

"Fuck no, I'm not formally questioning you. I've just finished a bottle of chardonnay, for Christ's sake. I'm thinking about having another one."

"Watch it, Monica. Wine hangovers are the worst."

"I should've put you on the stand. It would've been worth it just to see you squirm. What would you have done?"

"On the advice of counsel, I would have taken the Fifth."

"Fuck! I knew it. Fuck. You know, don't you? You fucking know."

"You should get together with Alvarez. You two can figure out what I know and what I don't."

"He's closer to the truth than he suspects, isn't he?"

"Come on, Monica, I'm calling only because we're looking for a comment on the judge's decision."

"I'm not gonna give you a goddam comment. You can go fuck yourself. Print that. Because of you Brad Devlin has gone free. Are you happy about that? Do you think he's gonna stop now? He's a borderline psychotic protected by walls of money."

"Because of me, Brad Devlin got indicted in the first place. So cut the shit and give me a fucking comment."

I expect to hear a dial tone. She'd certainly be justified in hanging up. Instead I hear the sound of a cork popping and wine being poured into a glass.

"For the record," Monica says, "I'm disappointed in Judge Baden-Howell's decision. I believe we had a strong case, and that the action she took was disproportionate to the concerns she had. Moreover, we were continuing to develop information about the murder of Megan Wright, and I believe we had several leads that would have proved fruitful. For the record, I'd also have to say that I don't believe the cause of justice has been served."

"Is it ever?"

I hear a few gulps. It sounds as if she's drinking the entire glass. "The system guarantees process, not result. That's the great flaw in the system."

I ask what she's going to do now. She says she hasn't thought that far ahead, but she wants to get out of prosecuting homicide cases. The crimes are too gruesome. She keeps seeing the victims in her sleep, blood-drenched bodies asking why their killers have gone free.

"Have you seen Megan?" I ask.

"All the time."

"What does she say?"

" 'Do something.' "

I hear Monica pour some more wine into a glass.

"We followed up on your suggestion, by the way. About the FAA. Interesting activity out at the airport the night of September fifteenth."

"Two of Jeremiah Devlin's planes flew to Reno."

"And one came back."

"Really?"

"Is this something you didn't know?" She sounds surprised.

"Who was on it?"

"I have no idea."

Several people whose contributions to the story are no longer required have congregated around the metro desk, where they're watching "CONTINUING LIVE COVERAGE" on the local newscast. I tell the clerk I'm looking for Trish and he says she's in Fussman's office. I take a few steps toward it but then I stop. As Fussman speaks, Trish stares as if he's just told her that someone she loves has died.

On TV a bubblehead stands outside The Serpent Club, which Jeremiah Devlin has rented for the evening. Police have roped off the area to keep the crowd under control. Dozens of teenage girls strain at the barricade.

During one of those beery late-night pseudo-intellectual discussions that college students like to have, my roommate and I once debated the question of whether the ends justify the means.

"If the ends don't justify the means," I said, "what does?"

He accused me of sophistry. We once used words like that.

twelve

trish walks directly from Fussman's office to her desk, opens the drawers and empties them as if she's getting ready to leave for the last time. I slide up to her to ask what's going on but before I can utter a word she says, "He wants to see you."

I walk over to his office and knock on the door even though it's open.

"Hi howareyou."

"Trish said you wanted to see me."

"Yes. There are things we need to discuss."

I close the door and sit down. He opens the top drawer of his desk and takes out a hefty envelope that he pushes toward me.

It's a piece of internal correspondence. My name and employee identification number appear in the plastic window.

As I open the envelope I tell him, "All that stuff Alvarez said is groundless. My stories were legitimate and I can go into my notes to verify—"

I stop.

There is a letter addressed to me from the new chief

executive officer. It says that due to increased newsprint costs as well as declining revenue and circulation, the newspaper has found it necessary to institute a serious round of cost cutting that includes reducing the workforce by ten percent. These steps are painful but they have to be taken to ensure the future profitability of the company. The fact that I have been selected for termination is in no way a reflection on my work. It's just that, in the opinion of senior management, the job I've been doing can also be handled by others.

"There's six months of severance," Fussman is saying. "And we'll continue your health benefits for a year."

I think about tearing everything off his walls and smashing the pictures of his wife and children that occupy a large portion of his desk. I could grind his skin into the glass and watch his blood flow and dip my hands in it and scrawl obscenities in red.

"I'm sorry it had to end this way," he says with the perfunctory tone of a man who has gotten his way.

"You're not sorry at all," I say.

"I never liked the story. I told you that from the beginning. And you had it wrong."

"Do you believe what Alvarez said?"

"There might be some truth to it. You're a dangerous man. If I'd been the city editor at the time you were hired, I would never have approved it. You have a calm facade, but you should see what the psychological reports say about you."

He looks out his glass cage. Three security guards in drab olive uniforms stand a few feet away.

• • •

It takes a few minutes to empty my desk. I throw most of my stuff in the garbage but keep the notes from the Brad Devlin case. I put them in a plastic bag and head for the elevator. Trish is already there. She carries a cardboard box that's overflowing, as if she wants to take all of her memories with her.

The elevator pings. She gets in first. I follow and hit the button for the lobby.

"I'm sorry I took you down with me," I say after the doors close.

"What Alvarez said," she replies, "is there anything to it? Are there things you didn't tell me?"

I wait a few seconds, watching the light slowly approaching the lobby.

"They're trying to ruin me," I say. "They'd rather destroy me than kill me."

"My parents were interned during World War II," she says. I'm startled. She's never told me anything about her family. "They never talked about it and I never felt comfortable raising the subject. But one day we studied it in high school, so I asked them. And they told me there was no point in being angry. They also said this was a fundamentally fair country that believed in rectifying its mistakes."

The door opens and we step out.

"They're dead now," Trish says. "I know this sounds cruel, but in a way I'm glad they are. I'm glad they never saw what's happened to us."

The news comes on as I drive to my apartment. The district attorney's office has issued a terse statement saying it respects Judge Baden-Howell's decision but by no means is this matter closed. Prosecutors believe crimes have been committed. The authorities intend to pursue these issues to the full extent of the law.

At home I turn on the TV. The same bubblehead is still in front of The Serpent Club. He says the sense of excitement is palpable as the crowd awaits the arrival of Richard Alvarez and Jeremiah Devlin and of course his son, Brad. At the mention of Brad's name the girls behind the camera squeal. The bubblehead turns to his right and brings a teenager into the spotlight. She's chewing gum and smiling and rolling her eyes. He asks her name and where she's from. She says she's Mindy from Brentwood. He asks why she's here and she says it's, like, because she wants to, like, see Brad Devlin because he's, like, totally adorable and she'd, like, *rilly* enjoy the chance to, like, meet him so she could, like, tell him that she was, like, always sure he wasn't guilty and stuff. The crowd cheers. The bubblehead says it's time to go back to the studio.

The anchor thanks him for his report and lowers his voice an octave. "From the beginning," he intones, "this case has stirred deep emotion."

He stops and says, "Wait," putting his hand to his ear. "This just in—Jeremiah Devlin has arrived for the party." The TV shows him emerging from a black Jaguar and handing his keys to the valet. His face is taut and smooth, as if the trial has not been a burden.

"From the beginning," the anchor says, "the case has stirred deep emotion." The station shows a clip of Megan's funeral. I see myself again—taller than I imagine, thin, hair beginning to turn to gray—coming down the steps of the church. As I reach the bottom of the stairs, the casket emerges from the dark interior. Megan's mother, shrouded in black, comes out. She is not dabbing at her eyes with a handkerchief or blinking back tears or biting her lower lip or doing any of the things one normally associates with a grieving mother. Jeremiah Devlin is beside her. He puts on his shades as he enters the light. His face looked different then. It had lines and marks that seem to have vanished.

Behind him are Brad and Jeffrey. Brad looks grim. Jeffrey is blank.

The anchor says the subsequent investigation into the girl's death grabbed the imagination of Southern California if not the nation, spurred in no small part by a series of newspaper articles written by—

"I'm a goddam idiot," I say to myself as I stare at the TV.

I drive to The Serpent Club, park on the street and watch the lot. I keep the engine running in case I have to leave quickly.

On the radio Farley O'Neill holds forth in a special nighttime edition. He says it was *ridiculous* for these charges to have even been brought and it shows what the *jackals* of the press can accomplish when they set out to *devour* an innocent young man. As for himself he can't *believe* so much fuss was created over a girl whom the facts have revealed to be—let's be candid about this—of loose morals. Oh, he knows some of those *bleeding hearts* and *feminists* and of course *liber-*

als will accuse him of *blaming the victim,* but let's be honest, ladies and gentlemen—does this country really need one more unwed teenage mother? And couldn't she have avoided putting herself in harm's way if she'd behaved a little better? He knows he sounds hopelessly old-fashioned, but *shouldn't people be held responsible for their own actions?* A woman calls in to disagree and he cuts her off by playing a tape of a firing squad.

I lean over and check the glove compartment. The gun that clattered into my lap at the airport now rests atop my maps and service station receipts. When I resume my position in the driver's seat—back straight, mirrors adjusted, two hands on the wheel—I see Jeremiah Devlin coming out of the club, and the valet running toward a black Jaguar.

The car swings up to the club's entrance. Devlin hands the valet a bill and takes off. I follow, keeping a couple of cars between us as we drive toward the freeway. When we merge onto it, he gets in the fast lane and heads toward the ocean, then turns north on PCH. We drive through Santa Monica and Pacific Palisades and up into Malibu. At one of the canyon roads, the Jaguar signals for a right. I do the same.

I press the accelerator to the floor. Tires squeal as I navigate unfamiliar hairpin turns. Up ahead I see the Jaguar cruising easily, its driver familiar with the road. He slows as I get closer, no doubt concerned about this rampaging Volvo swerving all over the road but always creeping nearer. Finally he pulls over to the shoulder and slows, as if inviting me to pass. I speed by him, then jerk the wheel to the right and stop suddenly. The

Jaguar brakes, but it still glances into the Volvo's front passenger door as dirt and gravel fly upward.

I open the glove compartment and grab the gun. Devlin is already out of his car, standing on the side of the road.

"What the hell are you doing?" he shouts. "You hit my car!"

He doesn't realize it's me until I'm almost upon him. I'm holding the gun at my side and clutching it by the barrel and when I get within a foot of him I swing my arm toward his face. The barrel of the gun smashes his cheekbone and sends him back with a *thunk* into the side of his car. I march to his windshield and bring my arm down repeatedly, filling the darkness with the sound I love so much.

When I see him reaching for his car phone I point the gun at him.

"I know everything," I say.

"You know nothing," he says. Blood covers the lower half of his face. I must have struck his nose too.

"Monica has the videotape. The one of you and Megan. She wants to put you in jail."

"She'll never be able to. It doesn't matter who the district attorney is. In fact, in our conversations Mr. Cain has proven to be a quite reasonable man."

"You were never interested in the mother, were you? It was Megan you wanted, from that time you saw her picture in the office."

I imagine the conversations that took place: Jeremiah Devlin initiating a discussion about a deal; Mrs. Wright being receptive, of course she's interested in improving her standing . . . Devlin carefully laying out what he wanted, revealing his desire only in increments . . . Mrs. Wright recoiling when she realized his terms, issuing a rejection, asking how he could even suggest such a thing . . . Devlin persistently pursuing his goal . . . *This is a great opportunity, I want to help, think of what you can buy and do* . . . Mrs. Wright threatening to leave his company and enrolling in college extension classes . . . Realizing what a horrible slog it is to claw one's way up in the business world, the virtual impossibility of it . . . Devlin still there, tempting her, a patient man when he has a goal . . . The mother wavering . . . Finally introducing her daughter to Devlin, asking how she liked him after he left . . . Mrs. Wright sitting down with Megan in her small room in a cramped house in a run-down neighborhood and telling her it was all right, this arrangement wouldn't last forever and besides she'd always been there for her daughter, but in the meantime it gave them a chance to . . .

"Richard Alvarez says differently. He has a statement from that girl. She's quite striking, don't you think?"

I smash the barrel of the gun against the window on the passenger side. He makes a motion toward me, but I point the gun at his chest.

"Why did you kill your wife?" I ask.

"You're deluded."

"Was it because she wanted Brad? She might've been able to help him. He's sick. He needs help."

"He's not sick. He takes what he wants. That's what all the great men of history have done."

He stares straight at me. This is the voice of American business, blunt and calculating and unsentimental. It doesn't matter if you're closing a plant or building a strip mall or killing someone.

"I assume Megan's father is dead?"

"If that's what you want to believe."

"You gave him the money to get the drug ring going. Because he was blackmailing you. Because he knew about Megan and why you bought his ex-wife that nice new house."

"He believed he could make a lot of money. Everyone believes they can make money. But only a few really know how to do it."

In the distance I hear a siren.

Devlin tells me that he called the police when he noticed he was being followed. "If you stay here," he says, "we'll have to tell them the truth. If you leave, I'll tell them a story they'll like."

I pull into Noreen's driveway, put the gun in the glove compartment and walk around to the back. I use the key for the back door and disengage the alarm.

Kristen's room is down the hall. To my knowledge I never entered it during my relationship with her mother. When I turn on the light I see soft pink blankets and covers and pillows, as well as stuffed pandas and bears and lions. I walk across the room and open the closet. I'm confronted by clothes—slacks, jeans, sweatpants, shirts, pullovers, sweaters, skirts. The floor is covered with shoes.

Two pink dresses with floral patterns hang in prominent positions. Noreen did not specify which one

Kristen wanted so badly. I decide to take both, as well as a few skirts, and sling the hangers over my shoulder. When I reach the hall, I kill the light and turn for the kitchen.

That's when I see them—just inside the door, the foot soldiers of the night with their ski masks and dark jackets and gloves. I could scream for help but no one would respond. I could try to reason with them but it would be useless. I could plead for mercy but they have none.

"We've been waiting for you," Brad says. "We've been waiting for days. We knew you'd come here."

A heavy wood object strikes the back of my head but the pain, which feels like a million needles piercing my skin, shoots through me only after I have pitched face first to the floor.

And then they're upon me.

I once read about a study of psychopaths. When told they were about to be punished for a behavior they were engaging in, they had no reaction at all— no increases in heartbeat or perspiration or blood pressure or any of the other signs of nervousness that were recorded by the respondents in a control group.

The scientists who conducted the study said they were puzzled by these results. Further research was needed.

thirteen

dawn.

I'm surprised to see it. I drag my right leg and then my left behind me as I crawl toward the kitchen table. Kristen's dresses have been torn to tatters; as I look around through puffed-up eyes, I see that the house has been sacked.

I put my hands on the edge of the table and pull myself up, then stumble through the debris and enter the bathroom. The mirror has been smashed but in the broken pieces that remain I see my swollen face caked with dried blood. I try to wash it off with soap and water. As I dry off I wonder what I should do now.

I feel my shirt pocket and suddenly I realize that the paper on which I'd written Noreen and Kristen's new address is missing.

I lunge from the bathroom and head for the phone but the jack has been ripped out. I stagger out the back door and into the Volvo and open the glove compartment. The gun is still there. I back down the driveway.

The only people around are garbage collectors far down the street.

I stop at a pay phone and call the number in Las Vegas that Noreen gave me. A woman answers with the name of the motel. I ask for Noreen and give the room number.

"Oh dear."

She says nothing more and I hear a man gruffly asking "What is it?" and a hand being placed over the mouthpiece and muffled words being exchanged.

The woman comes back on the line and asks, "Are you a friend of hers?"

"Yes. Yes, you could say that."

"It's terrible. A tragedy. I've never seen anything so awful."

"What happened?"

"Are you a God-fearing man?" she asks.

"No. I suppose I should be."

"We all should be. We can't make it on our own anymore. She's going to need your prayers, and the girl . . . the poor girl."

"Please. Tell me what happened."

"They broke in. Sometime during the night." Her voice breaks. "That poor girl . . . they did such unspeakable things to her. She's probably better off where she is. I'm sure she's with the Lord."

"And her mother?"

"She's in the hospital. They beat her. Oh mercy did they beat her. The police say they made her watch. Oh it was the most horrible thing."

I can picture what happened. I see all the details— the masks, the ropes, the bats and most of all the fear. I sink until I'm on all fours on the dirty asphalt. My stomach heaves but nothing comes out.

I call Rebecca. She asks where I am and how I've been. She says she heard about what they did to me at work and then she didn't hear from me and I wasn't at my place and she was worried all night.

"Can you get out of town for a few days?" I ask.

"*What?*"

"You're not safe. None of us is safe."

"Should I leave right now?"

"This minute. Go to Barstow and stay with your parents. Take a bus. Keep people around you."

I get on the freeway and drive, although there's no place I can go. As rush hour begins I find myself crammed among thousands of other cars all occupied by solitary drivers, our windows rolled up and radios turned on as we crawl past boxlike houses in communities none of us have ever set foot in. Most of the homes have metal bars over their windows.

The news-and-talk station leads with the attempted carjacking of Jeremiah Devlin's Jaguar last night. Mr. Devlin told CHP officers that a black male in his late twenties or early thirties cut off his car on a deserted stretch of road in Malibu Canyon. The assailant damaged the car and tried to drag him out of it, but Jeremiah Devlin resisted. Police praised his courage but noted that he suffered some injuries, including a broken nose and cheekbone. He said he did not get a good look at his attacker. He also said he dislikes media attention and would prefer to withdraw from the public eye.

I snap off the radio as I pull into a service station. I don't want to get out of the car but the needle hovers near "E" and I have to spend the rest of the day on the road.

It hurts to move but I unscrew the gas cap and put the nozzle in the tank. After I've filled it I limp toward the bulletproof cage to complete the transaction.

Raul sits there, looking at me with the curiosity we reserve for people who've endured terrible accidents and emerged alive but scarred.

"I thought it was you," he says. "I was unsure at first."

"Hello Raul. How are you?"

"Much better," he says.

"You're working days now."

He makes a motion with his arm, as if sweeping in the entire station. "Soon I will have a franchise," he says. "It's a good business."

I nod. He leans close to the glass and says softly into the microphone, "If you will pardon me for saying so, you do not look well."

"I've been through a lot, Raul."

"The trial," he says. "All those events. They took a lot out of you?"

I nod again.

"The conclusion," he says. "It was unsatisfactory. Many people feel justice was not done."

Now it's my turn to lean close to the glass and speak softly into whatever amplification device is planted nearby.

"It never is, Raul," I say.

He asks about Noreen and I try to say something, anything, but my voice catches and breaks into a sob and I lower my head onto my sleeve and let warm salty tears run out.

"She was attacked, Raul. Attacked. She's in the hospital. And Kristen . . . It's all my fault . . . What they did to her . . . Kristen is dead."

"*Ay Dios mio.*"

He makes the sign of the cross and I do too. I was raised Catholic myself.

Shortly before two I stop on a street about a block from the Hilliard School. The forecast says a storm is coming in from the Pacific. It's likely to be followed by several others that are forming over the ocean. They could break the back of the drought.

I take the gun from the glove compartment and thrust it into my jacket. High gray clouds cover the sky. I enter the parking lot and walk among the rows of Porsches and BMWs and Infinitis and Ferraris.

When I find Brad's Lexus I sit on the curb. To wait. I want no one to see me.

A bell rings. I raise my head so I can see through the car's windows. Brad approaches, wearing a baseball cap backward and smoking a cigarette. His left hand is thrust deep in the pockets of his baggy pants. He carries no books.

I crouch down and hear the door open and the

stereo cranking before he even engages the engine. I take out the gun and stand. A few kids are walking through the lot, so I use my body to shield the weapon from their view. I rap on the passenger window with the barrel. Brad turns to look.

"Better let me in, Brad."

"What do you want?"

"I'm doing a fucking story."

He unlocks the door and I slide in next to him. He backs up and pulls out of the lot. I use the gun to point to the radio.

"I can't stand that shit."

He turns it off. We drive past well-tended homes fringed by palm trees.

"How does it feel to be a free man, Brad?"

"Okay, I guess."

"Your classmates say anything to you?"

"They all said they knew I'd win. I knew it too."

"You must be awfully tired after driving to Vegas and back in one night."

"I took some pills. I'm fine."

"Why did you let me live?"

"I dunno."

"I don't believe you."

He looks at me for the first time since I got in the car. "We want you to suffer," he says. "We like watching people suffer."

"You want to destroy me."

"Exactly," he says. "When we're done with you, you'll kill yourself."

"You're just as sick as your old man."

"I'm just doing what everybody else would if they could get away with it."

A few drops of water appear on the windshield. Overhead the sky is the color of steel.

"Actually, Brad, I owe you an apology of sorts. I know you didn't kill Megan. Actually, as far as I can tell, you kind of liked her, didn't you?"

Brad's eyes fixate on the bumper of the car in front of us.

"I know your father killed her."

He reaches for the radio but I rap his knuckles with the barrel of the gun.

"Talk to me."

"We'd sit around for hours," Brad says. "We talked. I'd never talked that much to anybody."

"What did you talk about?"

"Stuff."

"What stuff? Did you talk about school? About the weather? About how your dad killed your mom?"

I hear rain drumming against the top of the car.

"I told her everything. She said it must be awful to know all the things that I know. She said she didn't understand how I could go on living."

"Was the baby yours or your father's?"

"His, I think."

"Do you know how I got involved in this story, Brad? I was doing my job. Just doing my fucking job. My editor asked me to re-create Megan's last night— and do you know what? I think I finally have. I can't print this, but I want to tell somebody. So I'm gonna tell you."

I begin.

Brad and some of his friends went over to Megan's on the afternoon of September fifteenth. After everybody else left, Brad and Megan had sex. They then drove to the Beverly Center and got something to eat before Brad bought her the necklace.

"You were trying to bribe her, weren't you?"

"No. It wasn't like that. I just wanted to get something for her. I liked buying things for her."

Brad then told Megan they should fly up to Tahoe. Just the two of them. They'd never gone away together and they could use the company plane. She agreed.

"But your dad was already there. He'd flown up the day before. To wait for her."

Brad nods.

"You betrayed her."

Brad nods again, quite slowly this time.

This is what happened on the night of September fifteenth at Jeremiah Devlin's country retreat on the banks of Lake Tahoe:

Immediately after Brad and Megan arrived, Jeremiah Devlin confronted them. He demanded to have sex with her. She said she didn't want to, but he told her to shut up and do what she was told. She resisted and scratched his face. He slapped her and tied her down on his bed and tore off her clothes. She screamed. It didn't matter.

When he was done, he took her out on the lake and demanded that she get an abortion that night. Everything was set. The doctor was ready and the clinic was expecting her. She had nothing to fear. Megan refused. She wouldn't do it without talking to her mother. She needed her permission anyway. Jeremiah Devlin told her she was going to have an abortion whether she wanted one or not. Megan began hitting him. She scratched him again. Jeremiah Devlin grabbed her by the shoulders and smacked her face a few times and thrust her head under the water.

It is not clear whether he meant to kill her. Brad stood on the dock yelling at his father to stop. But by the time he pulled her up, she was perfectly still.

That's when Megan's mother arrived. She knew Devlin was in Tahoe because he'd left word at the office. Jeffrey told her that Brad had come over earlier, and after Megan missed dinner, Mrs. Wright became afraid that the Devlins had taken Megan away. So she phoned Santa Monica Airport and asked if Brad Devlin had flown out on one of the company planes. When she found out he had, and was accompanied by a girl, she went to the airport and demanded to be flown to Reno or else she was going to raise all kinds of hell.

When she saw her daughter's body, she broke down sobbing, but then she began beating on Jeremiah Devlin with her fists. He pushed her away and, to show how angry he was, started hitting the girl's body with a heavy wooden oar. Mrs. Wright sank to her knees crying "Murder! Murder! They killed her!" at the top of her voice. A full moon was overhead and she sounded like a banshee lamenting the dead.

Some of Jeremiah Devlin's people shot her full of drugs to calm her down.

• • •

"Why did you bring her back?" I ask. "If you'd just dumped her body in the lake, no one would have known."

"That's what my dad wanted to do. But it didn't seem right. I couldn't leave her up there."

"So why did you leave her in Sepulveda Pass?"

"She liked it there. She liked the view."

Brad says he flew back that night in a company plane with Megan's body. Megan's mother, heavily sedated, was also on board. Brad took Mrs. Wright to her house and then drove to the top of Sepulveda Pass.

He asks how I figured it out.

"When it came out in court that she was pregnant, you and your father were the only ones who weren't surprised. Then last night I saw some footage of your father at Megan's funeral. I noticed that his face was scratched. And I remembered something. When the prosecution asked for a sample to match your DNA to the skin found under Megan's fingernails, you didn't object."

The rain drums louder on the roof of the car. It sounds like cannon fire.

"That night in Tahoe—did Megan say anything at all to you after you got there?"

"She said I was a liar. She said I was the only one in the whole group she trusted, but I was just like the rest of them. I wasn't fit to live."

"How did you feel about that, Brad?"

"I dunno."

I jam the gun into his ribs. He winces. I like seeing him in pain.

"Angry," he says. "I was angry at her. Angry at my dad. I wanted to hurt them. I wanted to hurt everyone."

"As much as you've been hurt?"

He says nothing.

"Why did your father kill your mother?"

He turns to me and grabs for the gun but I pull it up quickly and smash it against his temple. He cries out. Blood spurts from the break in his skin. I grab the wheel and straighten it.

"Be careful, Brad. The roads are slick."

We drive in silence for a minute.

"Those records in the courthouse are phony, aren't they? Your mother never dropped her divorce action."

"My father said she was weak. He said weak people don't deserve to live."

"Do you believe that?"

"I do now. Nobody's ever stopped him."

"And so you and your friends are proving a point? You're showing that you can get away with anything you want? Is that what this is?"

He raises his hand to his temple. The blood is beginning to scab.

"It pissed you off when your father killed Megan, didn't it? So you decided to take his lessons one step further. Stretch them to their logical conclusion. You were always on the edge anyway and this pushed you over. That's what you told me once. You like things that are on the edge."

"It's the only time I ever feel anything."

I lean back in my seat.

"Let's go, Brad," I say. "You know where."

It's close to dusk. The rain pelts the roads and the cars and the hills starved for water.

"We went up there after they found the body and the cops were gone," Brad tells me. I assume he's talking about his friends. "And we were talking about it and stuff. And I said anybody can get away with anything. You just have to make up your mind to do it. I said we should just pick a house and bust in and do whatever we felt like. And that's when it started. We liked doing it. We all did."

He looks at me. His eyes have the vacant and glassy look I associate with sharks. When I see him, I see what I could become.

"You did too," he says. "You liked watching."

"At first. Not anymore."

We park at the top of Sepulveda Pass. Below us a carpet of lights unrolls in the Valley.

"You've thought about killing yourself, haven't you, Brad?"

"None of this shit matters. Sometimes I get so fucking tired of it."

"But other times you like it. When you're in those people's houses, and they're terrified, and you have control over them—you're thrilled. You like the power."

He stares at the lights below. This is the future head of a great business empire and I can't escape the feeling he might be quite good at it.

I look at the gun in my hand, this object that has

given me the temporary illusion of power, and for a second I consider using it, but instead I take out a handkerchief and wipe the gun clean and leave it on the dashboard. Brad looks at me as if I'm the one who has lost his mental faculties, but I continue to proceed methodically, wiping off the windshield and the steering wheel and the window next to me and anything else I might have touched. I even clean the stereo that Brad likes so much. As I open the door I turn to him.

"You know what to do," I say.

I lock the door and close it, stepping into the rain. I wipe off the handle although I can't imagine any fingerprints surviving the downpour. I back away from the car one step at a time, trying to cover my footprints with dirt and grass and mud and sand.

After a few feet I hear the sound of thunder bass, screech guitar, megadrums. Brad's head nods up and down in time to the noise. When I'm about fifty feet away I see him reach for the gun. I cannot be sure of what he does next because the gun seems to disappear and for an instant I imagine him leaping from the car and coming after me in a final assault on his tormentor. I wonder if I'll run.

The shot, when it comes, is muffled, as if someone had wrapped a blanket around the gun. I believe he put it in his mouth. Blood and brain matter splash against the car's rear windshield, which shatters, most likely from the force of the bullet.

I feel as if a part of me has died. But the effect of this death is liberating. I can feel my heart beating again, and for the first time in months the act of breathing seems natural and unlabored. By the time I reach the road I'm soaked through, but the water feels good; I even like the way it mats my hair and runs into my eyes. Soon there will be reports of floods and mudslides, but that's all right. We need the rain.

Dr. Jack Karch ruled Brad Devlin's death a suicide. Many journalists and armchair psychologists interpreted his action as a sign of complicity in the murder of Megan Wright. But every so often a story comes out challenging the official findings. The stories cite some of Brad's classmates, who saw a mysterious older man riding with him in his car as he left school that day. The stories also cite hairs and fibers in the vehicle that can't be matched to the victim, as well as tracks near the scene. Farley O'Neill often makes a big deal of the bruise on Brad's temple. He says the bruise could not have been self-inflicted.

Alexis's statement and the excerpts from Megan's diary were discounted by police, who said they were inconsistent with the evidence as well as inconclusive. Grant Fisher denied everything, sued both Alexis and Alvarez, and received an out-of-court settlement.

I was never charged with withholding evidence or being an accessory or anything else. I took my severance pay and moved up the coast to a small beach town, where I opened a coffeehouse. Sometimes, when business is slow, I like to sit on the terrace and watch the sun glide down toward the ocean and smell the salt air mingling with the aroma from my store.

Rebecca came up one day. She is no longer interested in journalism; in fact her attention is shifting to poetry.

I suspect this is my fault. While she was here, I persuaded some locals to do a reading. I asked her to stay the night but she said she really had to return to L.A.

I drove the Volvo to Vegas to see Noreen in the hospital. She was wrapped in bandages and her doctors said they'd like to get her out because her HMO was complaining about the bills but she needed a lot of help. I told Noreen I was sorry about everything and through her wounds and the gauze around her she said it was all right, God has a plan for everything and now that she has accepted Him into her life, she can handle anything with serenity and peace. As I left her room I met the woman who ran the motel where she and Kristen were attacked. We talked briefly and the woman gave me some copies of The Watchtower. I drove my own car back to the coast.

While I was in Vegas I handwrote a document setting down what I know about the murder of Megan Wright. I put the document in a safe-deposit box and mailed the key to Maynard Reynolds with instructions that he open the box if anything ever happened to me. From the middle of the desert I sent a brief letter to Jeremiah Devlin informing him of the existence of this document, although of course I did not specify where it was or who had access to it. I assured him the document would remain sealed as long as I was alive.

Sander Van Arsdale's book made the best-seller list and was turned into a movie of the week that got good ratings. He theorized that Megan's father actually committed the crime, then tried to set up Brad to get revenge on Jeremiah Devlin for refusing to bankroll his drug ring. My old paper granted Van Arsdale a leave of absence to complete this piece of fiction, but instead of returning to his job he took a position with CNN.

Megan's mother died in Sun Valley. The local medical examiner said she had an aneurysm. Her burial was private.

The Valley break-ins ended abruptly. No one was ever charged.

The newly reassigned Monica Rosen and about-to-retire Frank Gruley walked into my coffeehouse unannounced one day. I made sure they sat at the best table and joined them for a cup of Colombian.

They said I was a hard guy to find. I said I liked it that way. They asked how I was doing and whether I enjoyed it and did I miss journalism and L.A.?

"Look," I told them, "you guys didn't drive up here to admire the view and ask about my health. What's up?"

Gruley said the Las Vegas police had been asking some questions about the attack on Noreen and Kristen. They wanted to know about the threats Noreen had received—threats that made her flee hundreds of miles in a futile quest for safety.

"I've told you what I know," I said. "In fact I thought the Vegas police were supposed to keep an eye on her."

"She moved without telling them," Gruley said. "She thought she was all right. She wanted an efficiency."

"What are they curious about in Vegas?" I asked.

"They're wondering how those guys knew where Noreen was," Gruley said.

"*Do you think I know the answer to that?*" I asked.

"*I'm not saying you do and I'm not saying you don't,*" Gruley said. "*They're just wondering. And we are too. The MO fits in with the Valley break-ins.*"

I thought of telling them the truth about everything. But this knowledge is my solitary burden. I have to carry it by myself forever.

"*I don't think I can shed any light on this,*" I told them.

"*Maybe you can shed some light on something else,*" Gruley said. "*A Volvo was parked in Noreen's driveway that night. The description of that car matches the description of Noreen's car, but Noreen was in Vegas at the time. To make it more complicated, a similar car was also reported parked near Brad Devlin's high school the day he died.*"

I saw a vision of myself strapped to a gurney surrounded by scrubbed gray prison walls. I remembered the advice I got from Maynard Reynolds.

Monica said the gun found in Brad Devlin's car was traced to a maintenance worker on the company planes at Santa Monica Airport. The guy had no idea how Brad obtained his gun. He said he must have lost it one day at work.

"*I don't have any comment about any of that,*" I said. "*It's all in the past.*"

We must have spent ten minutes in silence, looking at the seals sunning themselves and playing with each other and their pups, then diving into the foaming surf and emerging with fish in their mouths. Sometimes they just floated on their backs.

"I guess it is," Monica said at last.

I asked about their families and Gruley said his daughters were getting used to the idea of moving to Wyoming. He told them he'd buy them horses although he didn't have a clue about how to do it. I smiled at this and then Monica said she and her husband had split. I told her I was sorry and she said it was the result of a lot of little things, but the strain of the trial certainly hadn't helped. Now they were arguing about custody of the kids.

They got up to leave. I told them I was glad to see them. At that moment I believe I meant it.

"Jeremiah Devlin is an angry man these days," Monica said to me. The words burst out as if they'd been corked inside her for days.

"He blames a lot of people for what happened to Brad," Gruley said.

"But not himself," I said.

"No," Monica said. "He's never blamed himself for anything."

Gruley asked if anyone else knew where I was.

"Only Rebecca," I said.

"Keep it that way," Gruley said. He didn't think I was in danger, but it's always best to be careful.

"I'm always careful," I said. "I know exactly what Jeremiah Devlin is capable of. I think we all do."

I looked at Monica as I said this. But I didn't tell her about my last communication with him.

"There's one more thing," Gruley said.

His voice had a portentous tone I found alarming.

I looked at him and then at Monica, but neither one of them even wanted to glance at me.

"Jeremiah Devlin is Jeffrey's legal guardian," Monica said. "Megan's brother. The boy's father has dropped out of sight."

"The papers made a big deal of it," Gruley said. "I don't know if you pay attention to them anymore."

"No," I said. "I don't believe them."

"He's getting fantastic press," Monica said. "He's altruistic. A 'humanitarian.' "

"He has a son again," I said, the words echoing in my ears as if my fate had been determined at the final judgment.

"I'm afraid so," Monica said.

acknowledgments

I want to thank Melody Lawrence, Tim Wendel, Thea Caplan and Bob Shayne for their careful reading, advice and suggestions. Jimmy Vines embraced this project with enthusiasm, and Mitchell Ivers and Amanda Ayers helped shepherd it to completion.

A special note of gratitude goes to Brian Morton and the Advanced Novel Writing Workshop at The New School.

Most of all, I want to thank my wife, Jill. Without her support, this book would never have been finished.

Tom Coffey
New York City
February 1999

Visit
❖ **Pocket Books** ❖
online at

---

www.SimonSays.com

Keep up on the latest new
releases of your favorite authors,
as well as author appearances,
news, chats, special offers
and more.

SIMON & SCHUSTER
A VIACOM COMPANY
www.SimonSays.com

POCKET BOOKS

2381

**Visit the
Simon & Schuster Web site:**

www.SimonSays.com

**and sign up for our
mystery e-mail updates!**

Keep up on the latest new releases,
author appearances, news, chats,
special offers, and more!
We'll deliver the information
right to your inbox—
if it's new, you'll know about it.

2345